## THE DEATH PIT

'More than lives up to its creepy name... The pace is excellent, the characters are well and sympathetically drawn and the ending chills'
*Sunday Times*

'Gruesome, highly intelligent and agreeably over the top and far away'
*The Times*

'Strong offers rich scene-setting descriptions and sharp dialogue, and submerses readers in the fates of numerous distinct characters... His plot is innovative, charged with erotic energy and rife with tight forensic detail. And it cleverly incorporates the vast Scottish countryside all the way to its harrowing conclusion'
*Publishers Weekly*

## THE POISON TREE

'A début to die for... *The Poison Tree* is several notches more intelligent than most of its genre... So assured is the writing that I found it hard at times to believe that *The Poison Tree* is the author's first novel. Débuts don't come much better'
*The Times*

'A detective novel for the nineties. *The Poison Tree* is intelligent, erotic and violent... A brilliantly written thriller that is as chilling and claustrophobic as a deathbed'
Tony Parsons

*Also by Tony Strong*
*and published by Bantam Books*

THE POISON TREE

# THE DEATH PIT

## TONY STRONG

**BANTAM BOOKS**
London • New York • Toronto • Sydney • Auckland

**THE DEATH PIT**
**A BANTAM BOOK: 0553 50543 2**

Originally published in Great Britain by Doubleday,
a division of Transworld Publishers

PRINTING HISTORY
Doubleday edition published 1999
Bantam Books edition published 2000

3 5 7 9 10 8 6 4 2

Set in 11/12pt Sabon by Falcon Oast Graphic Art

Bantam Books are published by Transworld Publishers,
61–63 Uxbridge Road, London W5 5SA,
a division of The Random House Group Ltd,
in Australia by Random House Australia (Pty) Ltd,
20 Alfred Street, Milsons Point, Sydney, NSW 2061, Australia,
in New Zealand by Random House New Zealand Ltd,
18 Poland Road, Glenfield, Auckland 10, New Zealand
and in South Africa by Random House (Pty) Ltd,
Endulini, 5a Jubilee Road, Parktown 2193, South Africa.

Reproduced, printed and bound in Great Britain by
Cox & Wyman Ltd, Reading, Berks.

*For the farmer:*
*one day, a golden harvest.*

# ACKNOWLEDGEMENTS

In writing this book I have used three books in particular as source material. The first is *Studies in Crime: An Introduction to Forensic Archaeology*, by John Hunter, Charlotte Roberts and Anthony Martin (Batsford, 1996), a brilliant guide to the little-known work done by archaeologists in criminal investigations. *The Cassell Dictionary of Witchcraft*, edited by David Pickering (1996), guided me through the seventeenth-century Scottish witchcraft trials, as well as providing the quotations on page 80. And *A Witch's Bible*, by Janet and Stewart Farrar (Phoenix, 1996), introduced me to the liturgy of Wiccan rituals, as well as much useful background. I hope that they, and all other Wiccans, will forgive the many distortions and cuts that my fictional coven has made to the tradition. Finally, I wish to thank Sara Strong for correcting errors about pig farming, and my friends Ian Wylie and Siân Griffiths for telling me that much of the first draft was rubbish.

*He that diggeth a pit shall fall in it.*
Ecclesiastes 10:8

# PROLOGUE

He had already cut his headlights: now, as the Land Rover came over the crest of the hill, he reached out to the dash and cut his sidelights too. Above him the clouds were thin and patchy, cobwebbed with phosphorescence where the moon illuminated them from above. In any case, his eyes were redundant: the mud track down the mountainside was deeply rutted, and the ruts held the Land Rover's wheels like tramlines, twisting the steering wheel from side to side as if on some kind of ghostly autopilot.

He reached the flat ground and killed the engine, letting the car come to a bumpy halt in silence. There was a rifle lying on the seat next to him. Picking it up, he slid a round into the breech – his military training had conditioned him never to load a weapon until his vehicle had stopped moving – rested it on the window ledge, and looked through the night sight. For a moment he could see nothing, like peering through a microscope at a wriggling red haze of blood cells. Then, as he adjusted the focus, shapes became visible through the blood-coloured drizzle. The field in front of him was dotted with small, arced buildings, each one like a miniature

Nissen hut, surrounded by low electric fences. Sounds of grunting and the movement of bodies came from the nearer ones: somewhere a piglet screamed as it struggled to squeeze out from under the enormous, suffocating weight of its mother. The reek of animal shit caught on the night breeze, making his nostrils flare.

He swung the weapon through a hundred and eighty degrees, checking the area. A couple of sows, teetering absurdly on the high heels of their trotters, waddled up and down the electric fences. Somewhere a distant truck, on its way to the dawn fish markets at Aberdeen or Inverness, blared its klaxon at a late-night motorist, careering drunkenly home.

John Hobbes leaned the rifle against the window, reached for the hip flask filled with whisky that had also lain ready on the seat beside him, and prepared to wait. The whisky was cask strength – 100 per cent proof, not diluted down to the 70 per cent or even less demanded by commercial bottlers – and he had to rest each mouthful in his throat, numbing it, before he could swallow without choking. To pass the time he rolled himself a cigarette, running his tongue sensuously down the edge of the paper, but the action was purely habitual. He couldn't smoke it: the scent might have alerted his prey. With a sigh he placed the finished cigarette carefully on the dashboard and prepared to roll another.

There were seven cigarettes on the Land Rover's dash and the flask was three-quarters empty when he heard a sound, halfway between a cough and a bark, coming from the field to his right. Instantly alert, he swung the rifle round and sighted through the night scope.

Through the red landscape moved a small red shape, slinking up the line of one of the electric fences. For a moment it stopped, turning its face towards the man in the vehicle and sniffing the air suspiciously, its eyes pale discs through the night sight. Then it was gone again. Hobbes swore under his breath – he hadn't had time to take a proper shot – and waited, his finger curled around the trigger, for the fox to reappear.

A few minutes later it was back in his field of vision. This time it was moving more slowly, its progress impeded by something small and white which it was carrying in its jaws. A piglet, Hobbes guessed. They were meant to be shut into the farrowing huts at night, but occasionally some were born after the farmer had done her rounds: easy prey for a fox, or even for a crow or a large rat.

*Hold breath, close left eye, squeeze trigger.* The recoil jerked his shoulder and he saw the fox drop soundlessly. *Excellent.* With a sudden adrenalin rush of exhilaration he swung the door open and ran over to where the animal lay.

He scanned the ground with his Maglite until he found it. As he had thought, it had been a good shot, just above the forelegs. With a grunt of satisfaction he took his military knife out of the sheath he always wore at his belt and started to hack at the fox's brush. The animal's warm blood gushed over his hands, cooling and coagulating. A good feeling. The brush would join the eleven others hanging outside his croft.

He rolled the body over to get at the brush better – there was an awkward joint he couldn't quite get the knife into – and the torch was on the ground now, because he was using both hands. The grass threw long shadows, so that for a moment he thought the white thing underneath the fox, the thing it had been carrying, really was a piglet, before he saw that it was too small. He had picked it up for a better look before he knew that something was wrong – not because the severed thing in his hand was unfamiliar: on the contrary, what was wrong was precisely that it was too familiar – but his brain was slower than his eyes and even with the beam of the Maglite it was a moment before he realized, before he could put a name to what it was. A hand, he thought dumbly, a girl's hand; the chipped scarlet nail varnish catching the torch beam in the few seconds before the whisky in his stomach rebelled and came snorting out through his nose and throat, hot now and acrid too, emptying in a steaming torrent onto the grass and the half-dismembered body of the fox.

16A Greencroft Gardens
West Hampstead
London NW6 4RJ

Mr Magnus McCulloch,
Babcock Castle,
Babcock,
Nr Inverness

Dear Mr McCulloch,

I have been given your name by Professor
Jennifer Atlee of London University, to whom I
believe you expressed an interest in making
available for academic research certain family
papers relating to your ancestor, Catherine
McCulloch. She has suggested to me that they
might make a suitable subject for a doctoral
dissertation. Would this still be acceptable to
you? I understand from Jennifer that you
would like to see Catherine McCulloch's letters
and other material from her trial published in
some way. Obviously I cannot guarantee this
but I believe there is a good chance that my
thesis might find a publisher – I enclose a
note to this effect from an editor at
MoonWaves, a respected academic publisher
which specializes in books on feminist and
lesbian topics.

If you are still interested in this project, do you
know of anywhere nearby where I could stay
whilst I examine the documents? I expect this
part of my research to take at least a month, so
it would need to be somewhere fairly cheap – a

boarding house, rather than a hotel, would be ideal.

Yours sincerely,
Therese Williams MA (Oxon) MLitt.


Babcock,
April 24.

Dear Therese,

Sounds good to me. And no need for a boarding house – I rent out rooms myself, and since we're out of season, you can take your pick. We can discuss terms when you get here.
Give me a ring when you're coming, and I'll collect you from Inverness. There's a good sleeper service from Euston – leaves around midnight.

Regards,
Magnus McCulloch

# PART ONE

# ONE

The woman who stepped shivering off the train onto Platform Two of Inverness station was in her late twenties. Her hair – a mop of black ringlets, dishevelled by sleep – had been pulled back roughly and stuffed through an elastic tie. The suitcases and backpack she was manoeuvring onto the platform were evidently heavy: her arms shook as she picked them up and staggered towards the ticket barrier. A small knot of people had gathered there, some holding cards on which were scribbled the names of those they were meeting, and she scanned them slowly.

'Therese Williams?'

She turned. The question had come from a man of about forty-five or so, wearing jeans and a waxed jacket.

'Yes. You must be Mr McCulloch.'

'Magnus, please.' He offered his hand and she put down the cases to shake it.

'And most people call me Terry.' She spoke politely enough; but her handshake, he noticed, was listless and brief, as if she did not care to touch him for longer than was absolutely necessary.

'Pleased to meet you, Terry. Here, let me.' He took one of the cases and swore jovially in a soft Scottish accent. 'Jesus! Feels like you've packed an entire wardrobe in here.'

'They're books,' she said flatly. 'For my research.'

'Oh, of course. Anyway, the car's out here.'

Slightly taken aback by the coolness of her manner, he led her to an old Land Rover, parked on a double-yellow just outside the station. Rain pattered softly on the canvas roof. She shivered again.

'Hop in, won't you?' he said, noticing. 'I'll see to these.' He started to hump her luggage into the back.

'My coat's in one of the suitcases. I wasn't expecting – it wasn't raining in London.'

'Oh, this isn't rain, lassie,' he said cheerfully. 'This is Highland mist.'

She said nothing, picking up the second suitcase herself and hoisting it with some difficulty next to the first. He grabbed the backpack and was about to swing it in when she stopped him. 'Careful. That's got my laptop in it.'

'Rightio,' he said. She winced as it landed with only slightly less force than the suitcases on the wet floor of the Land Rover.

As they put their seat belts on he took the opportunity to take a closer look at her. A pretty enough little thing, but painfully thin. Only the faint curve of her breasts, defined by the strap of the seatbelt, gave a hint of sensuousness to the angular body. And, if first impressions were anything to go by, as quiet as a mouse. A shame: he'd been looking forward to some adult company, and this ice maiden didn't look as if she was going to be much fun.

18

He turned the key and pulled out into the traffic. 'Good journey?' he asked conversationally.

'It was fine.' In fact she had found being in a sleeping compartment with so many other bodies only feet away, privy to their dream-murmurs and their snores, their mutterings and – in the case of one young couple – their muffled lovemaking, strange and slightly unsettling. It brought back memories of school dormitories, and something more as well; some atavistic recollection of pre-civilized cave-dwelling. Or perhaps it was just that sleeper trains reminded her of wartime films. She'd even woken in the middle of the night and found that they were at Crewe, a name somehow deeply redolent of old black-and-white movies. She had not in any case been sleeping well since her illness – she still couldn't bring herself to give it the blunt and somewhat melodramatic term her doctor used – and at Crewe someone had got on with a baby, which had cried intermittently for the rest of the journey. For the rest of the night Terry had lain awake, as she so often did these days, not angry or restless, but simply numb, her eyes open but staring sightlessly at the ceiling.

'I've got some news on the publication side,' she said. 'A magazine called *Slant* is definitely interested in a series of pieces on Catherine.'

'*Slant. Slant* . . . Don't think I've come across that.'

'It's an academic magazine specializing in lesbian studies. It's got quite a small circulation.'

'Really?' She felt him take his eyes off the road to glance at her. Was it her imagination, or was he suppressing a smile? But all he said was, 'Babcock's a small place, Terry, but you'll find us a pretty broad-minded lot. We take people pretty much as we find them.'

'What if they don't want to be found?' she murmured, half to herself.

'I'm sorry?'

'Nothing.'

A sudden downpour pelted the Land Rover with raindrops the size of gobstoppers. The stubby little windscreen wipers were soon rendered completely useless, and visibility shrank to a few yards. They were beyond the outskirts of Inverness now, the granite houses giving way to open countryside. Magnus didn't slow down. Terry – who knew perfectly well that to criticize a man's driving was tantamount to criticizing his performance in bed – decided she might as well be hung for a sheep as a lamb. 'Could we slow down a bit until the storm's over?' she asked.

He glanced at the sky. 'Oh, this isn't a storm, lassie. It's a shower.'

'Slow *down*,' she snapped.

'I'm only doing forty,' he muttered. But he reduced the Land Rover's speed a little.

'Thank you.'

They drove in silence for a few minutes.

'I don't mean to be rude,' she said carefully, 'but I would also prefer it if you didn't call me lassie.'

He said nothing, though the Land Rover's speed increased again.

'This has nothing to do with feminism,' Terry went on. 'It's simply that to me, Lassie is the name of a small and rather repellent sheepdog.'

'You know, you're not the first English visitor we've had up here,' he said conversationally. 'Have you ever heard of the Iron Lords, Ms Williams?'

She shrugged. 'No.'

'They were Englishmen who came up to smelt iron in the nineteenth century. They weren't allowed to chop down the oak forests in England for their furnaces, so they came and used ours. We had mountains of oak – literally: the mountains were covered with the stuff – but of course no-one in London was going to worry about preserving *them*.'

Some response seemed to be required of her. 'I thought Scottish hills were covered in heather.'

'They are now, Ms Williams. They are now. But three hundred years ago they were covered in forests. Beautiful oak forests that had been there since the beginning of time. There weren't any forests in the valleys, of course, because that was where the farmers had their crofts.' He paused expectantly.

'And what happened to the crofts?' she asked dutifully.

'The English landlords cleared them for sheep,' Magnus said. 'These were the same Englishmen who invented the kilt, incidentally. Not a lot of people know this, but that famous article of our national dress was actually provided by our oppressors, because they were too fucking mean to sew trousers for their workers.'

Terry was rapidly getting a very bad feeling about this conversation.

'Oh, and then there was Queen Victoria. Another polite English visitor. She fell in love with the whole mist-and-mountain bullshit that Walter Scott dreamed up. You have heard of Walter Scott, I take it?'

'Of course. A hugely popular nineteenth-century Romantic novelist. *Ivanhoe, Rob Roy* . . .'

21

'The fact that it was fiction didn't seem to matter to her,' Magnus went on, ignoring her. 'She decided to buy a castle and live the fantasy for herself. Only when she got here, she found the place a little more civilized than she'd been led to expect. So she built a castle, the way she thought the Scots ought to have built them if they'd read the old stories, and decreed that everyone on her estate should wear clan tartans, just like the savages in her favourite books. And where the Queen led, all the other English landlords followed. Imagine: it's like an American president building a wooden fort in Mayfair and deciding that from now on all Londoners have to wear woad. This isn't a country, Ms Williams, it's a theme park. Scott Land, with two ts, as in Walter fucking Scott. So just remember that we've had a lot of practice at being condescended to, eh? About five hundred years' worth.'

There was a brief silence.

'What makes you think I'm being condescending?' she said puzzled.

'Well . . . let's just say you seem less than delighted to be here,' he said dryly.

'I see.' She rubbed her hand over her face. 'I'm sorry. I didn't mean to appear rude. It's just that . . .' She struggled to explain, but couldn't find the words. How could you describe a feeling of complete indifference to every human being, whatever their sex or nationality? 'I didn't sleep very well on the train,' she offered at last.

There was another long silence.

'Tell me,' she said, 'why did you invite me if you hate the English so much?'

He shrugged. 'History's important to me.'

'Evidently,' she muttered.

22

'None of the Scottish universities were interested, and I want Catherine to get the attention she deserves.' He glanced across at her. 'What about you?' he said aggressively. 'Why are you so interested in my ancestor?'

She saw no reason to be polite. 'I'm not, especially. My previous thesis didn't work out, and I needed to find another one in a hurry, or I'll lose my grant. It's not that easy to find subjects for a doctoral dissertation – the idea is that you have to cover something that hasn't ever been done before. So a bunch of unpublished papers is ideal. Besides, there's a lot of interest in witchcraft trials at the moment – particularly hers.'

'The gay angle?'

'Possibly,' she conceded.

A month ago, all Terry had known about Catherine McCulloch was that she had been burnt as a witch some time towards the end of the seventeenth century, and that it had been suggested – by no less a person than Jennifer Atlee, Professor of Women's Studies at London University, in her groundbreaking book *Sisters of the Sabbat* – that her real crime was not witchcraft at all but lesbianism. Jennifer had found one of Catherine's prison letters in an obscure book published in the 1950s by a local historian, and had drawn attention in her introduction to two key sentences – *My only crime is not to have loved who or how as I should have been more wise*, and *I neither need nor desire the attentions of any man alive: my desires are other*. The reviews had followed Jennifer's lead and focused on Catherine more than any of her other examples; partly, Terry suspected, because the eminent professor's prose style, whilst undoubtedly erudite, was also so dense as to be almost unreadable, and Catherine's story had the advantage of being at the very beginning of the volume.

Since then Catherine had become something of a folk hero to a certain sort of feminist academic. Naomi Wolf had mentioned her in an article, and Camille Paglia had included a brief biography in a television series. Like Mary Shelley or Sylvia Plath, hers was a name that could be annexed to many different shades of feminist opinion, if only because so little was really known about her.

'Anyway,' Terry said, 'I'm not convinced yet that Catherine was really what today we'd call gay.'

She had his full attention now. 'Why's that? The stuff in the letters seems clear enough to me.'

'You've read them?'

He shook his head. 'Only the odd snippet – I find her handwriting almost illegible. But what's been published already seems pretty conclusive.'

'I'll need to look at all the material before I come to any conclusions, obviously. But you have to remember that even if she hadn't been extremely beautiful, as I understand she was, a single woman in control of a large estate would have had a lot of suitors vying for her hand. Perhaps she just got fed up with being courted. A bit like that film star – "I just want to be alone."' She stopped, wondering if it was still Catherine she was talking about, or herself.

'What about the other lassie? Catherine's companion?'

She shrugged. 'Rich single women had paid companions in those days. It doesn't necessarily mean anything. One thing I will check, obviously, is whether there was any allegation of sexual impropriety at the trial.'

Her attention was distracted by the scenery. Outside Inverness had been a valley like any other – flat fields of yellow rape and green pasture, pleasant but no different from the valleys she had left behind in England. Now, as the rain cleared, she saw they had left that landscape behind and were climbing alongside a mountain, its peak dark as charcoal. Rastafarian cattle and impossibly shaggy sheep dotted the lower slopes, and a shimmer of rainbows chased the dark rain clouds.

'There must be material like this closer to home, though,' Magnus was saying.

'I would have thought a man with an interest in history would know the answer to that one.'

'What do you mean?'

'In England we didn't have witchcraft trials. Well, one or two, but there were no outbreaks of mass hysteria like those you had in Scotland. In England torture was illegal and any charges had to be proven in the courts, in the usual way.' She spoke evenly, but there was a note in her voice that hadn't been there before. 'In Scotland a woman, once accused, would be tortured until she named the other members of her so-called coven, who would then be tortured in turn. And then they would all be burnt alive. They used green wood, you know, so that the fires would burn more slowly. They even burnt pregnant women – there's one record of a girl who actually gave birth as she was burned, from the shock and the pain; they scooped up the baby and thew it back onto the flames to die with her. Until the Act of Union finally brought Scottish procedures in line with England's, over four thousand women died at the stake or in burning pitch barrels – and those are just the ones there are records of.' She paused. 'Still, I'm sure it was a great satisfaction to them to know that they died in the noble cause of national self-determination.'

'Well, of course that was a long time ago,' Magnus said defensively.

'So were – what were they called? – the Iron Lords.'

'Touché,' he admitted. She really wasn't so bad once you got her going, he decided. There was plenty of fire underneath the ice.

'Stop the car, please,' Terry said suddenly.

'Sorry?'

'Stop the car,' she hissed.

'Look, I didn't mean—'

'Let me out,' she shouted at him. Turning to look at her, he saw that her face was covered in sweat. Puzzled, he pulled over to the side of the road.

'If you're feeling sick, the best thing's to—' he began. But she was already outside, bent double, sucking great mouthfuls of air into her lungs.

He waited patiently in the car until she got back in. 'Better?'

She nodded, too exhausted to speak.

'Car sickness, was it?'

'No. Not exactly.'

'What, then? Are you pregnant?'

'God, no.' She sighed deeply. 'It was a panic attack. I thought I was over them. Evidently not.'

'What triggered it?'

She shrugged. 'I don't know. They just happen out of the blue.' She managed a feeble smile, and he was amazed by the way it transformed her face. 'Perhaps I'm just not used to all this countryside.'

He didn't ask her to explain further, for which she was grateful. 'Come on, then. If we hurry we can get to Babcock before the storm.'

'What storm?' she wondered. For the first time since they left Inverness, the skies in front of them were clear.

He pointed out of the driver's side window, and she ducked her head to see what he was indicating. For a moment she saw only mountains. Then she realized that one of the dark peaks was itself moving: not a mountain at all, but a black crag of cloud, sweeping inexorably along the valley.

'Now *that's* a storm,' he said, as he put the Land Rover in gear.

They reached Babcock just as the heavens opened, so that Terry's impressions of the little village were glimpsed through a sheet of water. Raindrops as big as rocks hit the road and shattered into fragments. Under the metal roof of the Land Rover the din made conversation impossible. She would not in any case have wanted to distract Magnus from driving. It was suddenly so dark that Terry could see steam coming off the Land Rover's headlights, and flash floods had appeared at every dip and drain. She half-saw a street of granite-grey houses, a couple of shops and a pub, before he swung the car onto an unmade track between two sagging gateposts.

'Welcome to Babcock Castle,' he said. 'Home of the McCulloch family for five hundred years.'

She saw the house in front of them, and almost laughed out loud. She'd been expecting – she didn't know what, exactly, but ever since she'd announced that she was off to stay in a castle her friend Mo had been teasing her about being served tea on the lawn by the butler and getting the chauffeur round with the Bentley for a spot of shopping. Terry hadn't gone quite that far – the upper classes weren't all stinking rich these days – but she'd certainly had a kind of platonic understanding of the word *castle*; something old, certainly, with a moat, and possibly a drawbridge: something big, too, with arrowslits in the walls and plenty of draughty rooms where one could whisper behind the arras and search for the ghost of Hamlet's father.

The building in front of her was a Victorian fantasy, quite small, but with a profusion of nineteenth-century turrets and decorative crenellations. The façade was dotted unevenly with sash windows, and the whole thing had been rendered in some kind of white plaster. It looked like a cross between a school sanatorium and something you'd put in a goldfish tank.

'It's very nice,' Terry said doubtfully.

'It's hideous,' Magnus said curtly. 'Since you're wondering, it used to be quite a good-looking house before the English arrived.'

Not that again. 'You just said it had been in your family for centuries. How do the English come into it?'

'More of Queen Victoria's poisonous influence. We're just up the road from Balmoral here. Once Victoria had built her own hideous pastiche of what she imagined an old Scottish castle should look like, she encouraged everyone else to do the same. So all the local lairds took their perfectly authentic castles and slapped these disgusting façades on them in a pathetic attempt to be fashionable. The style is called neo-baronial, in case you were wondering.'

'Why don't you take it all off again?'

'I'd love to, but it would cost a fortune. There's

no money in the estate now – we've gradually sold off everything except the fishing.'

'Hence the need to take paying guests?'

'Exactly.' He pulled up in front of an imposing porch. 'Come on, let's get your cases in and you can come and meet the children.'

Remembering the baby that had kept her awake half the night on the train, Terry said cautiously, 'How many do you have?'

'Two. Flora's fifteen, Alex is seventeen.' Oblivious to the rain, Magnus jumped out of the car, shouting. 'Alex? Come and give us a hand, please.'

'It's OK, I can manage.' The shouting seemed to have had no effect anyway, other than to rouse a rather stooped and balding deerhound, which tottered lethargically to the front door to see what was going on.

'That's Dougal.'

'Very neo-baronial.'

'Named after the dog in *The Magic Roundabout*, actually. The kids used to love it when they were younger.' Soaked, Terry picked up the backpack with her laptop in – she certainly wasn't leaving that to the tender mercies of the McCullochs – and followed Magnus into the entrance hall.

'I take it they weren't so keen on *Bambi*,' she muttered under her breath, looking around her.

The room was entirely lined with row upon row of severed deer heads. Most were stuffed, with huge glassy eyes and leathery black noses; but some were bleached down to their white skulls.

'And these are Boyle, Galileo and Archimedes,' he said, indicating the cats asleep on a chaise longue that had been roughly covered with a tartan rug. A fourth cat rushed in from the room beyond. 'That's Newton.'

'Why did you name them after scientists?' Terry asked.

'Because they're a law unto themselves.'

'Ho ho,' she muttered under her breath.

But though she preferred the bad jokes to the hostility she'd initially provoked in the car, Terry couldn't help feeling that both were, to some extent, play-acting; a deliberate attempt on the part of her host to impose his own authority, and perhaps even his own agenda, on her work. Despite what he said about the importance of history, Magnus McCulloch clearly had his own reasons for getting Catherine McCulloch's papers edited. She wondered what on earth they were.

# TWO

'Thanks,' Iain Pullen told the WPC who had driven him out from Inverness. 'I'll walk from here.'

The WPC smiled. 'No problem.'

He pulled his knapsack and a portable CD player out of the back of the car and, squinting against the driving rain, hurried along the rutted track towards the taped-off area he could see at the end of the field.

A casual passer-by might be forgiven for mistaking the scene ahead of him for an abandoned campsite or a rained-out fête. White tapes delineated a muddy car-parking area, and a path that led towards a collection of white canvas tents, a generator truck and some portable toilets. The field had recently had pigs on it: mounds of soggy ordure still littered the grubbed-up earth, and in the distance dozens of animals could be seen patrolling pens made out of two or three strands of electric fencing.

A uniformed constable stopped him as he approached the first of the tapes. 'No admittance, I'm afraid, sir.'

'Iain Pullen. The archaeologist. Detective Superintendent Talbot's expecting me.'

He waited, getting steadily wetter, while the constable went off to find the senior investigating officer he would be working for over the next few weeks. After a few minutes he returned with a man of about fifty.

'Adrian Talbot,' the older man said. 'Thanks for coming.'

They shook hands, Talbot regarding the newcomer curiously. He'd never worked with a forensic archaeologist before. Iain Pullen was young, about twenty-five or so, and his ponytail unnerved the policeman a little, but he came highly recommended by one of the pathologists who'd examined the body. Apparently Pullen had done good work on some skeletons that had been found during building work in Edinburgh.

'And this is Detective Sergeant Nicky Heron,' Talbot said, indicating a young woman who was coming briskly towards them with an umbrella. 'Acting crime scene manager.'

Together the three of them walked towards the largest of the canvas shelters.

'I don't know how much you've been told,' Talbot said, 'but I'll tell you again anyway. The body – or rather part of it – was discovered last Tuesday by a local gamekeeper, man by the name of Hobbes, who was out shooting foxes for the farmer. He shot one carrying off what turned out to be a human hand. Uniform came and searched at first light, and found the half-eaten body of a young IC1 female in a pit full of dead pigs.'

'How did she die?'

'Cause of death was a broken neck. But the pattern of decomposition indicates pre-mortem lacerations around the back of the torso, the wrists, and, to a lesser extent, the genital area. The implication is that she was tied up and mutilated in some way before she died.'

'Couldn't that have been the result of dragging the body across stony ground?' Iain asked. He looked around. 'Not that it's stony here.'

'I asked about that. The pathologist reckons post-mortem wounds, which wouldn't have bled as much, wouldn't have decomposed to the extent these have.'

Iain nodded thoughtfully. 'Was the hand gnawed off or severed?'

'Gnawed, presumably by the fox.'

'And the pigs? How did *they* die?'

'Natural causes, mostly.' Talbot grunted. 'When I said a pit full of dead pigs, I mean just that. It's the farmer's death pit – where she chucks all the spare carcasses. There must be dozens of the bloody things in there.'

'She? The farmer's a woman?'

'Yes. She's only a tenant, though – she rents a cottage and a few fields from the landowner.'

'Why does she throw the dead pigs away? I thought the whole point was to turn them into bacon.'

'I asked about that. Apparently animals that die of natural causes on the farm – diseases and so on – the slaughterhouses aren't allowed to accept these days. And of course there's all the stillbirths and piglets that get sat on by their mothers. So rather than have a mound of decomposing pork leaking into the water-table, the Environment Agency requires all stock farmers to have a death pit, dug into non-porous soil and sealed with a lid. In this case she's covered it with a few sheets of corrugated

33

iron, held down with breeze-blocks. Not quite as per guidelines but', he shrugged, 'we're a long way from any Environment Agency inspectors here.'

'I gather the corpse isn't *in situ* any more?'

'No. We took it to St Benedict's for a PM. At the time there didn't seem any reason not to.'

Pullen nodded. The removal of the body, though understandable in the circumstances, would make his job much harder.

'There was a rucksack buried alongside her with some clothes and personal effects in it – we assumed at first she might be a hitch-hiker or a MisPer, a missing person, but she was identified easily enough from a tattoo on her shoulder – luckily the fox hadn't got round to that bit. Donna Fairhead, twenty-two years old; used to live locally, in a sort of hippie commune on the other side of Babcock. She hadn't been seen for about six months – she'd packed her bags and left for India, according to the people she lived with. Our biggest problem is that we can't establish a date of death. But you probably know more about that part of it than I do.'

Pullen nodded. 'Decomposition happens at a different rate in a body once it's buried. Unless you can establish whether the body was buried straight away, it's very hard to estimate when it died.'

'So,' Talbot said. 'Do you think you can help us?'

Iain scratched his head. Despite the rain, the midges were biting already. 'It's unlikely I'll be able to give you a specific time of death myself. We tend to talk in terms of bracketing a *terminus post quem* and a *terminus ante quem* – that's archaeology-speak for establishing a time when we can prove the body wasn't there, and a time when we can prove it was. But if the brackets are tight enough, the pathologist should be able to compare it with the forensic evidence to come up with something more accurate.' A thought occurred to him. 'The pigs – do they wear ear tags?'

Talbot peered around him at the fields. 'Looks like it. Why?'

'If there are any records of when a particular pig died, and that pig is under the body, we'll establish a *terminus ante quem*. The *terminus post quem* will be a bit more tricky.'

Talbot nodded. 'Fair enough. I'll check with the farmer. But as well as establishing when Donna died, there's another reason for wanting the pit properly excavated. For all we know, she wasn't the only victim of this particular killer. We need to be absolutely sure there aren't any more human corpses lurking under the pigs. It's pretty hellish, I'm afraid – God knows what diseases are floating around in that lot. But we've got you an excavator.' He gestured to a JCB that stood a little way off, its digger curled over the cab like the tail of a giant mechanical scorpion. 'Can you operate one of those things? We can supply a driver if you need one.'

'I can operate a JCB,' Iain assured him. 'But I doubt very much whether I'll need to.'

Talbot looked anxious. 'Are you sure? Apart from anything else, time is of the essence.'

Pullen opened his rucksack and pulled out a stainless-steel bricklayer's trowel and a toothbrush. 'I've got my tools here, thanks.'

He caught the doubtful expression on Talbot's face and laughed. 'There's a certain methodology to forensic excavation, Superintendent. Anything that disturbs the soil strata before we can record it, for example, is virtually unusable in court, so your JCB's out of the question.'

'Some of these pigs weigh half a ton,' the policeman warned him.

'I'll just have to get a few Scene-of-Crime officers to help me, then. We'll probably want to lift them out one by one with ropes.'

Talbot sighed. 'How long will it take you?'

'Depends. I should think you're looking at a couple of weeks for the excavation itself.'

Talbot swore under his breath.

'But even before we start on that, I'll need to make an archaeological plan of the site – watercourses, soil types, acidity, that kind of stuff. That could take a day or so.' He gestured at the tent. 'Is this the inner scene?'

Talbot nodded.

'I'd like to take a quick look while you're still here.'

'Of course. The changing tent's over there.'

Talbot and Heron waited while Pullen went to change into the sterile white overalls and overshoes that ensured the burial site, or inner crime scene as it was now designated, would remain uncontaminated by fibres from his clothing. 'Two bloody weeks,' Talbot said despairingly. 'There goes my budget.'

'Why are we using this bloke, anyway, sir?'

'Him in particular, or why are we using an archaeologist?'

'Both.'

'Forensic archaeology started after the Dennis Nilsen investigation. There were some photos in the press of coppers digging up his garden—'

'I remember that. Melrose Avenue, wasn't it?'

'That's right. Anyway, a couple of archaeologists

wrote to the papers pointing out that they weren't doing it properly. Luckily Nilsen confessed, so CID never had the humiliation of having their work rubbished in court by an expert witness, but ever since there's been a standing order to bring in a forensic archaeologist when there's any excavating to be done. Hamilton's worked with our man before, seems to think he's all right.'

Pullen returned, covered from head to toe in whites and with a breathing filter looped round his neck. His ponytail was tucked into the neck of his overalls, and he carried a spotlight in one hand.

'You'll be watching on the video?'

Talbot nodded. As an investigating officer he wasn't himself allowed into the inner scene, since he might find himself interviewing suspects who could claim cross-contamination if forensic evidence linked them to the site. A video monitor had been set up just outside the scene shelter, a long canvas hood protecting it from the rain. Heron wiped some drops off the screen with her sleeve, fiddled with the buttons, and the image came to life. 'Not the most pleasant dig I've worked on,' Pullen said, looking at the monitor. Dead pigs lay curled up against each other in various states of decay. In some cases their intestines spilt messily onto their neighbours.

Access to the death pit was down a narrow path, taped off to limit disturbance to the site. Either side of the path was a mass of violets. Pullen paused and knelt down to examine them. Then he picked one and sniffed it appreciatively.

'Hello flowers, hello sky,' Nicky Heron muttered in Talbot's ear. 'What's he up to?'

'Interesting,' Pullen said, standing up and

brushing earth off his knees. He put the flower carefully into one of his pockets.

He pushed aside the tent flaps and climbed down inside the scene shelter, stepping on something soft. Immediately, despite the mask, he almost gagged on the foul air. Shit: it was even worse than he'd anticipated. He might need an aqualung if he was going to be working down here for any length of time. He picked up the spotlight and played it over his surroundings.

The space he was in was perhaps twelve feet square, its sides sloping gently towards the bottom of the pit. It had been dug with a mechanical excavator: he could see the tooth marks left by the JCB's bucket in the walls. One wall had recently been partially destroyed, and a six-foot-deep trench dug to allow access. That would be where the police had themselves used a digger to get to the body.

Having come down this access trench himself, he was effectively underground now, looking up at what had once been the roof of the death pit. All around him were strewn the corpses of pigs, floppy in death, their long jaws stretched open. Most seemed to be adults, but dotted amongst them were tiny piglet corpses, filling in the spaces between the sows so that it resembled one perfectly assembled jigsaw puzzle. He moved his feet slightly, and felt the corpse beneath him spring and shift as he did so.

Donna's body had been to one side, its position marked by a further series of tapes. He sighed. He had hoped to establish exactly where the fox had gained entrance, but it could only have been where the trench was now.

Going back out to the trench, he walked along it, examining it closely. As well as the clean cuts made by the JCB, he could just make out a rougher-edged piece of digging bisecting it. There was a root sticking out of the soil, which he examined carefully. As he'd thought, it had been bitten rather than cut. He rummaged around until he found some spoor. Bagging it carefully, he took it back to where Talbot and Heron were watching curiously.

'We need to get this analysed,' he said.

Talbot raised an eyebrow.

'*If* it's fox shit, and *if* the lab can date it, and *if* it contains traces of digested human flesh, it's a possible *terminus post quem*,' he said mildly.

Talbot nodded slowly. 'Good,' he said.

'The other thing I need to know', Pullen said, 'is exactly where the fox was shot.'

'Over here,' Heron said. She led them up the hill and into the pig fields proper. 'Mind the electric fences,' she warned. 'She uses truck batteries. They carry one hell of a crack.'

Pullen crouched down to examine the point Heron indicated, then looked up at the layout of the field. 'Hmmm,' he said thoughtfully. 'Interesting.'

'What is?'

He straightened up. 'There's a whole science associated with what's called scatter patterning. Broadly speaking, once scavengers have access to a body they start by feasting on it where it lies. They eat the eyes, the intestines, and then the exposed surface tissue. Even foxes don't gnaw off bones before they need to – but once they do, they carry them away. The longer the exposure to scavengers, the wider the radius in which remains are dispersed. For a fox to bring a hand this far, you're looking at – well, I'd have to check the literature, but I think it's of the order of two months. What we don't know in this case, because your JCB has destroyed the evidence, is whether or not the foxhole was an old one, in which case it had access to the corpse as soon as it was hidden, or whether it dug the hole after the body was put there. The other complicating factor is that any scattered remains inside these electric fences could have been eaten by the pigs themselves. We'll need to have a task force do a fingertip search of the whole area.'

'Now hang on a minute,' Heron said, flushing. 'You're the expert witness, I'm the crime scene manager, and Superintendent Talbot is the man in charge. We'll be the ones to decide if and when a full-scale search is called for.'

'Is it really necessary?' Talbot said placatingly. 'My budget . . .'

Pullen shrugged. 'It's necessary now you've dug that trench.'

Talbot thought for a moment. 'OK,' he said, 'I'll organize it. But not today – the overtime would be stupid at a weekend. Anything else?'

'I'll want to talk to the farmer. I take it she's not a suspect?'

'Not so far as we know. She knew the victim by sight, but there doesn't seem to have been any cause for friction between them. That's it?'

'A soil map of the area. Available from any big map shop, or from the National Farmers' Union.' He went to his knapsack and pulled out two hazel twigs. 'I've got plenty to keep me occupied in the meantime.'

Talbot nodded at the sticks. 'Are those what I think they are?'

'Water-divining rods. It's the quickest way of working out where the underground watercourses are.'

Behind him, Talbot distinctly heard Heron mutter an expletive.

'Oh, and I'll need some accommodation in Babcock. I can't waste three hours going back to Inverness every night.'

'I'll organize it,' Talbot promised. An idea struck him. 'Tell you what, I'll see if you can billet with the farmer. Her cottage is the nearest house to here, and she might be glad of the company now a body's been found on her farm.'

He left Pullen to it and walked back to the car park with Heron. 'Christ,' he muttered as they passed a field in which a boar was energetically humping a disinterested sow. 'Look at the balls on that.'

'You mean the pig, or our expert witness, sir?' the woman beside him enquired icily.

'Oh, come on, Nicky. I know he's an arrogant young bastard but he clearly knows what he's talking about.'

'Isn't this all a bit of a waste of time, though? Attractive young bit of skirt gets herself killed. Ten to one it's either the bloke who found her or a boyfriend. What about that commune she was living in? Anything going on there?'

Talbot snorted. 'Virtually everything. Toilets flushing all over the house as soon as we turned up. But they're all adamant that she left them six months ago, of her own accord. Their stories match up, so there's not much we can do for the moment.'

'Perhaps they're all lying.'

'Perhaps. Me, I think you might be closer with your other suggestion. The man who found her. By all accounts he's a bit of a nutter. One of these survivalist freaks. Subscribes to about three different gun magazines.'

'We'll be having him in again, then?' Heron asked eagerly. Being a crime scene manager was a shit job at the best of times, but when you were stuck out here in a field it was unadulterated boredom. And the opportunities for glory were absolutely nil. You didn't get on as a woman in the police service unless you pushed a bit.

'Later, Nicky. For this afternoon, you just concentrate on looking after the SOCOs and Mr Pullen, eh?'

All the same, when Talbot left the scene a few minutes later in his car and he looked back to see the young man pacing slowly up and down in the rain, holding the water-divining rods in his upturned palms like some perambulating Buddha, he muttered 'Christ Almighty!' to himself. If Nicky was right and Pullen was wasting their time, he didn't need a lab analysis to tell him that what he'd be up to his eyes in would be pure, grade-A horseshit.

# THREE

From a window at the top of the house, Flora watched her father showing Terry round the outside of the house. 'She's here,' she called over her shoulder.

Alex didn't look up. A dead hare, its fur encrusted here and there with blood from the shotgun pellets that had killed it, lay stretched on its side on the table in front of him. He eased the blade of his scalpel into the scruff, just behind the shoulder, and pushed.

'Do you think she's pretty?' Flora asked.

'How would I know, doughbrain? I haven't seen her.'

'Come and look, then.'

He had the skin off the shoulders now, the strangely white dermis peeling away from the animal's limbs with a slight sucking noise, like shrink-wrap. Without it, the hare's bulk was revealed to be an illusion, its muscles scrawny as a greyhound's. He could see the holes made by the shotgun pellets more clearly now, each one mashing the fibres where it had penetrated the meat.

'She *is* quite pretty,' Flora said, when he didn't

move. 'Quite thin. Not very nice clothes, though.' She glanced back at her brother. 'Do you have to do that in here? It stinks. There is a kitchen downstairs.'

'It's a post-mortem, stupid, not a recipe.' He glanced at her. 'Why are you dressed like that, anyway?' His younger sister was wearing a T-shirt, stretched tight across her tiny breasts and exposing her midriff, and a pair of minuscule shorts. Clothes that might have been suitable for a sweaty club at two in the morning were wildly inappropriate for a chilly spring day in Babcock: her arms and legs were blue with cold. 'Hoping she'll fancy you?' he said witheringly.

'What do you mean?'

'Didn't you know? She's a dyke. I heard Dad telling Tom.' He turned his attention back to the hare. Just behind the stomach cavity, from which he'd earlier removed the guts, was an unfamiliar pouch. He cut it open. 'Cool!' he breathed. The little sac was full of tiny foetuses, each one as unformed and curled in on itself as the tip of a fern-frond. Delicately he fished one out with the end of his scalpel and laid it on the table.

'*He* could still fancy *her*,' she muttered.

'Who could?'

'Dad.'

He shook his head, his attention still fixed on the tiny shape in front of him. Experimentally he drew the blade across it. He'd been hoping to see all the organs in miniature, like opening up a Russian doll, but either they hadn't formed yet or he needed a microscope: all he could make out were tiny swirls of different-coloured flesh. 'What are you on about?' he muttered.

'Dad. Men like dykes, don't they?'

'What would you know about it?'

'I know there are lesbians in *Knave*,' she said. He looked up quickly at that, and she smiled triumphantly. 'I found it under your bed. Original hiding place, doughbrain.'

He returned to the animal in front of him, his face impassive.

'I read it, actually,' his sister said. 'I thought it was pretty neat.'

Alex said nothing.

'God, I'm so bored. Why don't you invite some friends over? Jack Leach is all right.'

'He doesn't fancy you,' Alex muttered.

'I'll tell Dad about the magazine.'

'No you won't,' he said, getting up and pushing her towards the door.

'I will.'

'You won't, because if you do I'll tell him about you going out at night.'

Flora looked at him guiltily. 'What do you mean?'

'I've seen you. Slipping out when you think we're both asleep. Where do you go to, anyway? Meeting a secret lover?'

'Fuck off,' she said. She tried to slip out of the door but he caught her wrist and held it. The scalpel was still in his other hand, and he rested the point against the blue-veined flesh of her forearm. A tiny ball-bearing of blood welled from the very tip.

'Where do you go?' he whispered. 'Tell me.'

'Nowhere,' she said, twisting herself free and running out of the room. He smiled. After a moment he sat down again, placed the scalpel delicately on the hare's cloudy eye, and slid it gently under the cornea.

*   *   *

'I've put you in Catherine's room,' Magnus said. 'I thought it might help with the research.'

'Thanks.'

'It's the nicest room, as well,' he said grudgingly. They were in the kitchen, a dark and comfortable room strewn with clothes, fishing rods, wellington boots and cats, all drying in front of the old Rayburn.

A man of about forty came in through the kitchen door, shaking the rain off himself like a dog. He was dressed from head to toe in tweed, from his deer-stalker hat to the trousers he wore tucked into his socks. As he took the hat off Terry saw that he had a crab-apple complexion and a shock of ginger hair, badly in need of a barber's attentions.

'This is Tom Teare. He looks after the fishing and what little estate we have left.'

Terry extended her hand. 'Pleased to meet you.' Tom pressed it and muttered something in an accent so broad she could barely make out a word.

Magnus looked at his watch. 'The children will have eaten already. Do you want anything?'

'Not right now. I'd just like to unpack and wash. The train was a bit primitive.'

'Righto. Follow me and I'll give you the quick guided tour.'

The house was larger, and older, than it had appeared on the outside. Magnus led her through a family sitting room next to the kitchen and into the main hall. A beautiful white stone staircase spiralled up through the house, flanked by ancestral portraits, ancient weaponry and yet more deer heads.

'Mmm. Tartan wallpaper,' Terry murmured. 'Queen Victoria *would* have approved.'

46

'Don't. I'd rip it down if I could, but it's actually quite valuable. Incidentally, this is how you can tell it's a real castle,' Magnus said over his shoulder as he bounded up the stairs.

'Why's that?'

'In Scottish castles staircases always spiral to the right, so that a right-handed swordsman defending it has the advantage. Here, this is Catherine's bedroom.'

He opened a door off the first landing and waited for her to enter. She whistled. It was quite a room – huge, and dominated by an old four-poster bed hung with drapes of yet more tartan. But it was the portraits on the walls which drew her attention.

'Is that Catherine?' she asked.

'That's her. Painted the year before she was killed.'

The picture showed a young, striking-looking woman dressed in black, her hair pushed up under a bonnet and a blue shawl draped over her shoulders. It was hard to put an exact age to her, because the clothes she wore were so unfamiliar, but Terry knew that she must have been in her late twenties. She had been pictured seated on a garden bench, feeding a dove, but the conventional pose was belied by a cool, almost imperious gaze directed at the viewer.

'One of my American guests pointed out that the eyes seem to follow you around the room,' Magnus said.

'Oh, come on. All portraits do that. You'll be telling me she haunts the place next.'

'Actually . . . in some of the rooms associated with her there *are* sudden unexplained changes in temperature.'

'Magnus,' Terry said, 'save it for the tourists, eh? So you've got draughts. Big deal.'

He did at least have the grace to look a little embarrassed. 'Yes, well, the Americans do seem to like that sort of thing.'

'And who's this?' Terry pointed to another, smaller portrait, hanging opposite Catherine's. It too was of a girl, younger and prettier than Catherine, her hair piled on her head in a profusion of ringlets.

'That's Anne de Courcy, Catherine's companion and presumed lover. Here, these'll interest you.' Above a little desk were two framed documents. Magnus took them down and handed the first one to her.

'Ah,' Terry said. 'The famous letter.'

She scanned it quickly. *My dearest Anne* . . .

'You can read her writing, then?'

'We're taught basic palaeography as part of our postgraduate course. It's not too difficult when you get the hang of it.'

'I'm afraid her writing gets progressively worse as the letters go on.'

'Really? I wonder why that is.'

'Thumbscrews, probably,' Magnus said with relish. 'She was being tortured pretty regularly at the time the letters were being written. I should imagine it's quite hard to hold a pen in those circumstances.'

'Oh. Of course.'

The letter continued over the page. 'You realize I'll have to take this out of its frame at some point?'

'No problem. It unscrews at the back. Here, take a look at this.' He handed her the second framed document. It appeared to be some kind of list. Puzzled, she started to read. *For twenty loads of peat: 40 shillings. For 6 bushels of coal: 24 shillings.*

*For four tar barrels: 26 shillings, 8 pence. For fir and iron barrels: 16 shillings, 8 pence. For a stake and the dressing of it: 16 shillings. For 4 fathoms of rope: 4 shillings. For carrying the peat, coals and barrels to the hill: 8 shillings, 4 pence. To one Justice for the execution: 13 shillings, 4 pence. The whole, £7 9s. Yr. obedient servant, Thos. Varney, executioner.*

'Jesus,' she breathed. 'It's a bill for burning her.'

Magnus nodded. 'It was sent to Duncan McCulloch, the cousin who inherited Babcock. My grandfather found it with some old papers in the library.'

Terry put the bill down and glanced up at the portrait of Catherine. For the first time she began to realize that this was not just some abstract academic exercise she was engaged in. Catherine had stood where she stood now, had breathed the same musty smells, had climbed the same stone staircase and slept in the same bed. Perhaps she had slept there with another woman, perhaps not. But she had suffered horribly for weeks, maybe months, before she was finally burnt on a dressed wooden stake, surrounded by tar barrels that had been heaped with coal and peat. She shivered.

Not wanting Magnus to see how spooked she was, she walked to the window. 'Nice view,' she said.

They were at the back of the house, looking out over farmland towards a dramatic peak which reared out of the valley a mile or so away. 'Ben Dubh,' Magnus said, pronouncing it *duth*. 'The dark mountain. The peat contains phosphates that keep the grass that wonderful rich green.'

'It's beautiful,' Terry said truthfully.

Magnus pointed. 'See that building just beyond the farm? That's Catherine's Tower.'

In the distance Terry could just make out a round turret, standing on its own in a field of grass. 'Why's it called that?'

'According to legend, it's where Catherine used to hold her witches' sabbats. Myself, I wondered if it was where she went to be alone with her lover. Away from gossiping servants.'

'If Anne *was* her lover. What is it, anyway? Some kind of hunting lodge?'

'No, it's a doocot. Dovecot in English. Doves and venison were just about the only fresh meat they would have eaten up here in the winter.' He hung the framed documents carefully back on the wall and went to the door. 'I'd better let you unpack. When you've settled in I'll show you the library, where the other letters are.'

'Thanks,' she called after him. They seemed to have reached an uneasy truce, and so long as it continued she wasn't going to be the one to reopen hostilities.

She had started going off the rails three or four months before. Nothing had precipitated it – indeed, it came at a time when she would have said that she was at last getting over the various traumas that had attended the break-up of her marriage and her flight from the postgraduate degree she had been studying for at Oxford. To begin with she had simply felt lethargic, to the point where she became unable to get up in the mornings: once up, activities that had once interested her no longer seemed worth the effort. After a week or so she went to a doctor who in the absence of any definable illness had diagnosed ME, suggesting she investigate various homeopathic remedies. Terry realized he was just trying to get her out of his surgery but, unusually for her, she couldn't be bothered to have a fight about it.

The first panic attack came a few days later, in the supermarket. Suddenly, the simple act of choosing pasta overwhelmed her with its infinite, chaotic complexity. How to decide between hollow tubes of penne, plump cushions of ravioli and others whose names she didn't even know, pasta in the shapes of shells and bow ties and one which the packet informed her was inspired by the belly buttons of Renaissance beauties? Egg pasta and wholemeal pasta, pasta made from durum wheat and pasta made from corn, pasta died black with the ink of squids; fresh pasta, dried pasta, pasta that could be cooked in only five minutes . . . looking up, she saw the shelves stretching away from her, each one requiring a thousand choices, a thousand decisions. Waves of anxiety sluiced through her bowels. For a moment she thought she had food poisoning, then the anxiety turned to terror. Sheer terror. She had heard of panic attacks, of course. Panic: such a cosy little word. 'I'm in a bit of a panic today.' It was what you said when you'd lost your car keys or were running late for a seminar. It certainly didn't describe this numbing, screaming fear, this certainty that you were going to suffocate; here, now, this minute, choked by fear itself and unable to even breathe, much less cry out.

Somehow she had made it out of the shop and had got herself home. More than four hours later, Mo had found her in the kitchen, still sobbing and shaking.

'Christ, Mo, I think I'm having a breakdown,' she had wailed, clutching her friend for comfort.

'Of course you aren't,' Mo had said reasonably. 'You're just ill.'

But the doctor, when he saw her again, had also used the b-word – albeit hedged around with plenty of maybes and medical caveats. He had referred her to a psychiatrist, who in turn had prescribed Prozac. Terry had read about Prozac: it was an all-purpose wonder drug for treating depression. Yet so far as she could tell, she wasn't in the least bit depressed. Numb, yes: disinterested, detached, listless; but no more depressed, she told him, than any sane person would be on discovering that they no longer cared about anything at all.

'Sane . . . *hmm*,' the psychiatrist had said, polishing his glasses with the end of his tie. 'That's not a word we use much, clinically. After all, one person in four experiences mental illness at some point in their lives.'

'Good God,' Terry said, horrified. 'Do you mean I might be going mad?'

'Whatever gave you that idea?' the psychiatrist said. Really, patients were so paranoid.

So she had ditched the doctors and instead went to an old friend, a research psychologist at Oxford. Ann had substituted therapy sessions for the Prozac, and while the panic attacks did not disappear, their appearance no longer caused her to question her own sanity.

She had abandoned her thesis, of course: or rather, it had abandoned her. Whatever mysterious quality of her brain had enabled her to pursue and grasp abstract concepts, to make connections between apparently unrelated intellectual ideas, had left her as suddenly and decisively as the muse was said to abandon a poet. She spent long hours crouched in front of her laptop, staring at the meaningless rows of words, only to switch to a computer game instead, and waste the day in shooting silly alien monsters. Now, as she slowly regained the ability to work, her friends looked around for something for her to do. Putting her doctorate on hold, even for a while, was unfortunately impossible. The rules stated categorically that a postgraduate had only four years in which to finish a thesis; after that, the grant was withdrawn. The prospect of finding a new career filled Terry with dread; yet, if she didn't complete a new thesis within twelve months, that was exactly what she'd have to do.

After talking to some colleagues, Ann came up with a solution. Jennifer Atlee, Professor of Women's Studies at Birkbeck and the good friend of a good friend, knew of some letters that needed editing. The work would be dull, but unchallenging. All Terry would have to do was some basic historical research, followed by a scholarly edition with footnotes, cross-referencing and an index, and the faculty would be virtually obliged to give her a doctorate. Even so, it was another month before Terry wrote to Magnus, enquiring whether his ancestor's letters were still available.

In the meantime, her friend Mo had decided it was time for Terry to start dating again. She found her what she described as the perfect woman: gentle, kind, intelligent and beautiful. And it was true: Terry did like Janet. It was just unfortunate that none of those were qualities that Terry found in the least erotic. Somewhere along the way, Terry's sexual circuits seemed to have been rewired in a way that Terry wasn't even sure she approved of. If she was honest, one of the reasons she had finally agreed to come to Scotland was that she didn't yet feel ready to confront the truth of all that.

Magnus found Tom brewing up some tea in the kitchen. 'Well? What do you think?'

The farmer took his time before replying. 'She's a jumpy wee thing,' he grunted.

'Aye. I'd say she's tougher than she appears, though. And somewhat, ah, independent for our purposes.'

Tom looked at him from under bushy eyebrows. 'Will ye have any trouble?'

Magnus shook his head. 'She'll do what we want,' he said calmly. 'We'll just have to be careful, that's all.'

# FOUR

Rested and dressed in clothes that were clean, if a little crumpled from her suitcase, Terry took her laptop and went in search of the library. When she found it, however, it was occupied. A youth of about seventeen was sitting at the long table which ran down the centre of the room, his attention fixed on something held in a miniature vice, which he was manipulating with the aid of tweezers and an ancient magnifying glass.

'Hello. You must be Alex,' she said brightly.

The youth glanced at her for the briefest moment before turning his attention back to the magnifying glass. 'Yeah.'

'I'm Terry.'

He didn't answer. Terry went and stood behind him. From this angle the tiny object he was working on became a brightly coloured fishing fly, the sharp gleam of a hook protruding from its belly like a lethal, disproportionate penis.

'That looks tricky,' she offered. 'What is it?'

'It's a gold-ribbed hare's ear.'

'A what?'

'A trout fly. It's meant to look like a nymph.'

'Where do you get the hairs from?'

'From a hare's ear,' he said succinctly. She waited, but that was apparently all she was going to get. Shrugging, she opened her laptop and looked round for a power socket to plug it into. Instantly the teenager sat up and watched her.

'That got Windows 98?'

'Er – I think so.'

'Got any games?'

'A few, actually. *Myst, Tetris, Tomb Raider 3* . . .'

Alex grunted dismissively. 'I've got *Street Fighter* on that,' he said, jerking his head at an old grey PC at the other end of the room. 'It's really violent.'

'I don't think I've played that one,' Terry said. She indicated the laptop. 'Want to take a look?'

When Flora walked in five minutes later she found Alex sitting at the long table in front of Terry's laptop while Terry crouched down next to him.

'The mouse is a bit tricky if you've never used a laptop before,' she was saying. 'You have to kind of stroke it in the direction you want to go. Like this.' She put her hand on his and showed him. 'That's it.'

Flora coughed theatrically.

'Hey, Flo,' Alex said. 'Take a look at this.'

'No thanks,' Flora said icily.

Terry got to her feet and held out her hand. 'Hello, I'm Terry.'

'Delighted to meet you,' Flora said. 'Alex, are you coming upstairs? There's something I want to talk to you about.'

'No thanks. I'm going to play this.'

'Oh well, since you're both so busy,' Flora said, tossing her head irritably.

What a little madam, thought Terry, although outwardly she tried to be friendly. 'I like your piercing,' she said. 'I'm always meaning to have my navel done, only I'm too much of a wimp. Did it hurt a lot?'

But Flora wasn't to be coaxed into a conversation so easily. 'No,' she said coldly.

'I see you've all met.' This was Magnus, coming in unnoticed.

Flora turned to him, a big smile lighting up her face. 'Dad, I need a lift into Stour. I'm going out with Jacquie tonight.'

'I thought she lived in Aviemore.'

'We're meeting at a pub.'

'I was sort of thinking that we might all have dinner together. Since it's Terry's first night.'

Flora groaned. 'Dad, it's Saturday. And I've arranged it now.'

'OK, OK. You want me to pick you up as well?'

'Maybe. I'll phone you.'

'Right. No later than eleven, though.'

Flora tutted and raised her eyes to the ceiling.

'Elevenish, then.'

'Maybe,' Flora said casually. She left the room, shooting Terry a triumphant look as she did so.

Terry said nothing. If Magnus wanted to let his daughter twist him round her little finger, it was none of her business.

'Settling in all right?' he asked her.

'Fine. I was just wondering where the other Catherine papers were.'

'Over here,' he said, showing her to a display case. 'Though I can't vouch for what order they're in.' He pulled open the drawers to show her the jumble of manuscripts.

'Don't you lock them away? They're probably worth a fortune.'

'Are they? Really?'

'Well, maybe not a fortune, but certainly more than you'd get from a paying guest.'

'I'll lock them in future,' he promised.

'By the way,' she added. 'I was wondering who the other portrait in Catherine's room was.' There had been a third painting on the far side of the bed that Magnus hadn't identified.

'Oh, that.' He seemed a little embarrassed. 'That's Hamish McCulloch. A distant cousin of Catherine's. It's just a family story, really.'

'Go on.'

'According to my grandfather, Catherine was taken to some sort of preliminary hearing made up of local gentry, one of the members of which was Hamish. Anyway, the family legend runs that Hamish pointed out that people would confess to anything if they were tortured. The chief torturer – the witchfinder – denied this, so Hamish proved his point by having *him* arrested and tortured. Sure enough, the witchfinder soon confessed to being in the service of the devil.'

'Very neat. Then what happened?'

'Unfortunately, the Church authorities kicked up a fuss, the witchfinder was released without charge to continue his work on Catherine, and Hamish was briefly thrown into jail himself.'

'He must have been very brave.'

'I like to think he did it because he was in love with Catherine. So I put his portrait in her room, opposite Anne's. It makes a nice story for my visitors, anyway. A seventeenth-century love triangle.'

'Complete with kinky sex, barbaric torture and violent death. For a man who professes to hate it when people romanticize Scotland's history, Magnus, you're not doing so badly yourself.'

'As I said, it's only a story,' he muttered.

Iain Pullen looked up from pacing the field and saw a woman watching him. She was standing in one of the pig corrals, an empty paper sack in her hand. At her feet the sows shuffled and snatched greedily at a pile of brown food pellets, each the size and shape of a shotgun cartridge. 'Afternoon,' he called.

'Afternoon.' She indicated the divining rods. 'Does that really work?'

'Of course.' Dropping his knapsack to mark where he'd got to, he strolled over to the electric fence. 'Want to try?'

She laughed. 'A spring wouldn't be much good to me, I'm afraid. I use about five hundred gallons a day through these.' She nodded at a water trough, which was connected by plastic pipes to the troughs in adjacent corrals.

'How many animals have you got up here?'

'There are five hundred sows. If you include boars and babies, we've generally got about eight hundred at any one time.'

'Quite a big operation.'

'Wouldn't be viable if it wasn't,' she said cheerfully. 'In fact, it's barely viable as it is. You lot aren't helping much. Sometimes it feels like I've got more pigs of the police variety up here than the animal kind.'

Now that he was up close, he could see that she was in her early twenties. She was wearing a shapeless pair of overalls caked with dirt, wellingtons and a grimy baseball cap, out of the back of which protruded a blond ponytail.

'Sorry about that. We'll be as quick as we can. And actually, I'm not quite a policeman. I'm a forensic archaeologist.'

'Are you the one who wants somewhere to stay?'

'I am indeed. Would that be all right? We'll pay, of course.'

She snorted. 'Wait till you see it first. It's not exactly pristine, I'm afraid. And I'm told there's a lingering smell of pigshit, though I can't smell it myself.'

'After a day out here, I don't suppose I'll be able to either,' he assured her.

'All right. I'll collect you when I finish, shall I? I can give you a lift back in the tractor.'

'What time will that be?'

'Late. I've got half a ton of pellets to feed round before I go, and the bloke who works for me has had to go into Casualty. The silly bugger accidentally injected himself with two cc of erysipelas vaccine. He'll be feeling a bit poorly for the next couple of days.'

'Let me give you a hand, then,' Iain suggested. 'If you don't mind, I wanted to ask you some questions about the soil make-up.'

'Sure. We can talk while we do it. I'm Laura Macpherson, by the way.'

'Iain Pullen. Pleased to meet you.'

Terry surveyed the pile of papers in front of her and sighed. Catherine's legacy consisted of a strange assortment of manuscripts, only some of which were letters to her companion Anne. Most seemed to be notes to her factor and other estate officials, relating to the accounts of the farms and their tenancies. She picked one up at random. *And the fifty acre field may be sown with barley and not wheat, for I have had it on good account that wheat shall not be sold well at Stour mkt. this yr . . .* She tried another. *I wish to advise yr. gd self that I shall be willing to sell the tenancie of Lower Fm, inasmuch as I have need to pay for my confinement here and other privileges, for the sum of £90, and 7 shillings for the stock . . .* Evidently Catherine had been a hands-on laird, even trying to run her affairs from prison: remarkable in the circumstances, but hardly riveting stuff.

For a few minutes she sat there, daunted by the sheer scale of the project ahead of her. Transcribing the letters was only part of it: there would have to be cross-referencing, checking for historical details, an index, footnotes . . . Still, the first thing was simply to make an inventory of all the material. She created a file in her laptop and went through the papers one by one, not attempting to read them, but simply grouping them by recipient.

Towards the bottom of the pile she found a letter typed on a twentieth-century typewriter, from a firm of lawyers.

Cartwright and Gayle,
10 Bolton St,
Edinburgh
5th June '57

John Mcteer, Esq.,
1 Belham Avenue
Stour

Dear Mr Mcteer,

Further to our meeting, I can confirm that we
do indeed retain in our archives certain
correspondence relating to Catherine
McCulloch. You will appreciate that normally
such letters between a lawyer and a client
would be subject to the strictest confidence, but
in view of their very great antiquity, and the
possible historical importance you spoke of, I
am fraternally minded to give you sight of
them. Please bear in mind that these papers may
be of some value and should be returned to us
as soon as you have had the opportunity of
transcribing them.

Yrs,
Edward Cartwright Jnr.

In the margin of the letter someone had written
the single word: *Idiot!* Terry peered at it. Written
with a fountain pen, but not the same hand as the
signature. Presumably this was Mcteer's writing.
She looked under the letter. The next manuscript
was a note from Catherine to her lawyer, one Joshua
O'Neill. Hmm, she thought. So Mcteer hadn't

bothered to return the letters after all. And what was that about being 'fraternally minded'? Had Mcteer been playing on some kind of Masonic connection?

It was eerie, and slightly disturbing, to know that she wasn't the first on this particular trail. Mcteer, she recalled, was the local historian in whose book Jennifer Atlee had found Catherine's letter. She went and got the copy of *Sisters of the Sabbat* she'd brought with her and checked the bibliography. *Mcteer, John, The Scottish Witch Trials, pub. the Shadowcourt Press, 1959.* She'd tried to track down a copy herself in London, without success.

It occurred to her that if the McCulloch family had helped Mcteer with his book by giving him access to these same papers, he might well have thanked them by sending them an inscribed copy. She searched the shelves that ran round the length of the library. Were the 'Mc's and 'Mac's under M in the normal way or did they precede it? Ah, here they were. 'Macmillan, MacPhee, Macstannon, McTorby,' she read out loud. Damn: no Mcteer. Though oddly enough, there was a gap on the otherwise tightly packed shelves where several volumes had been removed, just where Mcteer ought to be. Perhaps Magnus had taken them. He was driving his spoilt daughter to her date at the moment. She made a mental note to ask him when he came back.

# FIVE

By the time he got to Laura's cottage Iain was shattered. Every muscle in his body ached, as much from wading through the relentless mud as from hefting the sacks of food, each one the size and weight of a bag of coal. To his chagrin, Laura, despite being half his body weight, seemed to lift them with hardly any effort.

He had also been attacked by a mothering sow, much to her amusement.

'Kick the bitch,' she shouted helpfully as Iain had cowered back from the snapping jaws. 'Not like that. On the nose!' He had tried, rather timidly, and she'd come over to rescue him, landing a kick on the pig's snout of which a rugby player would have been proud. Apparently unhurt, the animal had backed away.

'They're Durocs,' she explained in the tractor as they made their way home. Iain was crammed onto the side seat with Sam, the collie, who was even wetter and muddier than he was. 'Bred for their high reproduction rate, rather than their temperament, I'm afraid.'

'Do they ever get really nasty?'

'Oh, sure. If you get into one of the huts to clip a litter – we cut their teeth after birth so they don't damage the sow's teats – and she catches you at it, you'd probably need stitches. I've had to go to Casualty two or three times this year.'

'What on earth made you want to become a pig farmer?' he asked, curious.

'Not through any particular love of pigs, that's for sure. I just wanted to farm. But I don't come from a farming family, so I wasn't about to inherit three thousand acres of arable. Land's expensive, even up here: pig farming doesn't use much. It's one of the few agricultural enterprises you can set up from scratch without being a millionaire. Even so, I owe the bank a quarter of a million.'

He whistled. 'That's a lot of money.'

She nodded. 'The stock's expensive, and of course you have to feed them for quite a long time before you've got any piglets to sell. The cash flow is an accountant's nightmare.'

'How about you? Does it give you nightmares?'

'I work too hard to sleep badly,' she said matter-of-factly. 'But it's not an easy life, that's for sure. Quite apart from the cash flow, modern pig herds are vulnerable to all sorts of diseases. Meningitis, porcine pneumonia, Blue Ear – that's a particularly nasty one: it makes the pregnant sows abort – mastitis, which is an inflammation of the tit: no joke when you've got twelve tits, I can tell you; strepto-coccus, swine fever . . . any one of those could wipe me out tomorrow. And then there's the minor irritants, like having stock nicked, electric fence equipment going missing. People will even steal the ballcocks from the drinking troughs.'

'Even out here?'

'Even here. I've had quite a problem recently with fences being vandalized, stock getting onto the roads – for which I'm not insured if they cause a pile-up. What else? Foxes, crows, hot-air balloons . . .'

'What's the problem with those?'

'Pigs can't look upwards,' she explained. 'Their ears come down too low over their eyes. So if they hear the burner of a hot-air balloon above them, they panic. Last summer I had to have three shot because they'd got entangled in the electric fences and broken their legs.'

'You must like it, though,' he said, 'to go on doing it.'

'I love it,' she confirmed. 'Here we are. Home sweet home.'

She jumped out of the tractor and led the way to the back door of an idyllic little cottage. There were roses over the windows and a rusting yellow sports car in the driveway.

'I couldn't work in an office or sit in a traffic jam every day,' she continued, pushing the door open – it had been left unlocked, Iain noticed – and sitting down to lever off her mud-encrusted boots.

'Me neither.'

She stopped him. 'Rules of the house,' she explained. 'You take off your work clothes outside, shake off the straw and pigshit, and dump them in here.' The door led into a narrow back porch containing two washing machines. She indicated the first one. 'This is for farm clothes, and this is for ordinary washing.'

'Why two?'

'When it gets really wet and muddy out there, all the biological in the world wouldn't clean my whites. The farm clothes stay grimy, but at least my other stuff gets clean.' She unzipped her overalls: underneath she was wearing a faded T-shirt with 'New Zealand' emblazoned on it, and a pair of shorts. 'The bathroom's in there. A rigorous shower-cleaning policy is strictly enforced.'

Having washed, unpacked and changed, he emerged from the spartan spare bedroom to find Laura in the kitchen. Out of her bulky overalls, she was surprisingly slender – he still couldn't work out how she'd managed to hoist those bags with so little effort – though when he looked more closely, he saw that her lean frame was sinewy with muscle. She had washed her hair, which now hung, blond and wet, down to her shoulders.

'Since you're the archaeologist, you'd better be the one to take a look in the fridge. I warn you, though: Tutankhamun's tomb is nothing compared to what you'll find in there.'

'This is . . . interesting,' he agreed, looking at a desiccated and rather sorry piece of chicken. 'Late neolithic, I'd say.'

'We're a long way from the nearest supermarket. I was going to go last weekend, but I had a sow with a prolapsed uterus and I had to stay with her.'

'Do you have any pasta?'

'Dried, lots of it. Why?'

'You've got plenty of bacon, an onion and some tomatoes. Why don't I see what I can make of it?'

'I could get used to this,' she said a few minutes later, watching him cook. She had opened a bottle of wine, some of which he added to the sauce.

'Don't you ever get lonely, living out here on your own?' he asked conversationally.

She considered the question. 'Not really. Besides, I'm only on my own during the week. My fiancé comes most weekends.'

He glanced at her hands. There was a plain silver band on her engagement finger. 'Unusual ring,' he commented.

She shrugged. 'These hands spend half their time up pigs' vaginas. A ring with a protruding diamond could lacerate their birth canal – and believe me, a sow that can't produce piglets is not a sow I want. I've told Gareth to try and find me a ring with a stone set back into the metal, but this is fine for now.'

'Is he a farmer too?'

She shook her head. 'A stockbroker.'

'Rich?'

'What do you mean?' she said warily.

'Sorry. I only wondered – in view of what you were saying earlier – whether he'd be able to buy you those three thousand acres of arable land.'

'Oh, that. No, he's a very junior trainee in a very large firm. I'm afraid I'm never going to live in a nice Georgian farmhouse with an Aga, a few chickens and a Range Rover.'

'Was that your dream?'

'Maybe once.' She swallowed the last of her wine, then changed the subject. 'What about you? How did you get into archaeology?'

'I was fascinated by dinosaurs as a small boy – my father had taken me to the Natural History Museum to see the fossils – and it just sort of went on from there. And then at school one of the masters gave us the chance to go to Egypt with him on a dig. I loved it. So I read archaeology at university, stayed on to do a doctorate – the usual stuff.'

'Not all archaeologists work for the police, though.'

He shrugged. 'Dad's in the army. Maybe I just got used to people in uniform. I do other stuff as well – until a few weeks ago I was running a dig near Glasgow, excavating the tomb of a Celtic princess. But the forensic stuff is interesting. At least you know that what you're doing is useful, which is more than you can say about picking over some medieval rubbish tip.' He left the sauce to simmer and came and sat within reach of the wine.

'If your father's in the army, how does he feel about that ponytail?'

He smiled. 'You're right. It was my first act of rebellion. He used to cut my hair with electric trimmers when I was a kid – the regulation short back and sides. As soon as I got to university, I let it grow. I even had a rather unwise beard at one time.'

'Oh I don't know. A beard would suit your face,' she said idly.

There was a short silence. Although both of them knew that she had meant it as a statement of fact, and not to flirt, both were also aware of the need to keep their distance.

Following her train of thought, she asked, 'You married?'

He shook his head. 'Though I did have a relationship with someone on my last job.'

'What was her name?'

'I never found out. She'd been dead for over two thousand years.' He sighed. 'Generally, I find my girlfriends easier to cope with when they're putrefied.'

'That's disgusting!' Laura protested.

'So is sticking your hand up a pig's vagina.' He

got to his feet. 'And so will our supper be, if I don't go and stir it.'

Flora sat in the pub, a warm glow of contentment in her stomach. There were eight or so of them squeezed round the dark old table, its surface littered with empty glasses and pouches of rolling tobacco. Just to be here, in the public bar, was thrilling in itself – whenever she went out with her father and his friends they always went into the lounge bar, where the drinkers kept their voices low. The raucous, smoky atmosphere of the public made her feel rebellious and adult at the same time.

As did the hand on her leg. She was sitting on Andy's left, and the hand that wasn't wrapped meatily round a glass or dextrously rolling a cigarette rested casually on her upper thigh: not groping her, just lying there, the pressure of its weight reminding her of the reality of his presence. Sometimes it was all she could do not to wriggle against him, to feel that hand grip her harder . . . She must have squirmed slightly, since he broke off from listening to his mates and glanced at her over the top of his roll-up.

'All right, darlin'?'

'Sure,' she said with what she hoped was a sexy look. To be honest she didn't understand half of what they were talking about. Andy worked in the distillery, as did most of his mates, and most of their jokes seemed to consist of sly references to people she didn't know. There were two other girls at the table, and both of them sat there without talking, so she did the same.

'I'll get you another drink, doll,' he said, getting unsteadily to his feet.

'I'll pay for these,' she said quickly, 'if you'll go to the bar for me.' She cast an anxious look at the table. She'd brought what she thought would be plenty of cash, though she hadn't reckoned on buying a round for all these people. But Andy was waving her down. 'My treat, love. Stones and vodka, wasn't it?'

He eased past her and went to the bar. 'Don't worry, you can pay me back later,' he muttered under his breath. He grinned to himself. It had been three weeks now since he'd met Flora at her father's posh old house. He'd been helping his mate Craig with some work on the roof, the two of them stripped to the waist in the spring sunshine, betting with each other on who'd manage to pull the daughter with her upper-class voice and her tight clothes. Not that he *had* pulled her, yet. Not quite. So far she'd touched it and not much else. But he was getting there. He leaned on the bar as the barman pulled the pints, tenner in hand, watching her. She looked up suddenly, caught his eye and smiled hesitantly. Christ, he thought, I'm going to have that soon. 'And a ginger wine and vodka,' he said. 'Make that a triple vodka, OK?'

John Hobbes was losing his temper.

He could put up with the casual jokes – 'Hey, John! Want a hand with those?' was the most frequent, whenever he went to pick up a round of drinks from the bar, along with other variations on the same theme: 'John, can you lend me a hand?', 'Got to hand it to you, John', each accompanied by gales of raucous laughter. What he couldn't stand was the implication from some of the locals that, just because he'd found part of the body, he must

71

somehow be more deeply involved.

There was a group of them sitting over by the fire, workers at the distillery, laughing whenever they looked in his direction. Once he strained his ears to hear, and heard them talking about combat knives that left a distinctive pattern on the body. He picked up his drink and moved away.

He was standing in the Gents when one of them came in. Andy Wringe: Hobbes had done business with him in the past. They urinated in silence, then Hobbes said, 'I'll take some more of that malt when you've got it. Couple of bottles, like.'

The lad looked around nervously. 'Well, Christ, John, I don't know if we'll be getting any out now.'

'What's wrong,' Hobbes growled sourly. 'Afraid I might kill someone?'

Andy moved quickly over to the washbasins. 'It's not that,' he muttered. 'It's just – what if the police come round? I could lose my job.'

Hobbes grunted. 'Why should they?'

'Look, maybe in a few weeks, hey? When all the fuss has died down.' He scuttled away before Hobbes could disagree.

Back in the bar, Hobbes drowned his fury in another few pints, chased down with scotch. When he left the pub in his battered Land Rover, he was weaving erratically, easy prey for the police car that had been assigned to patrol the area ever since the body had been found. Whilst they were breathalysing him the young constable spotted a rifle behind the seat, its barrel protruding from the canvas in which it had been loosely wrapped.

'Would you step away from the vehicle, sir, please,' he said politely, then called his colleague over to keep an eye on Hobbes while he examined it.

'Oh for Chrissake,' Hobbes growled. 'It's a fuckin' gun, all right? I've a proper licence and everything.'

'We'll have to take it back to the station, though, sir,' the policeman said, unwrapping the canvas. 'You're in no state to drive home, and the weapon can't be left unsecured in the vehicle all night.'

'It's not even fucking loaded,' Hobbes grumbled.

The policeman wasn't listening. His attention was on the other objects that had fallen out of the canvas wrapping, where they had been placed along with the gun. 'I think you'd better come with us,' he said at last, reaching for his radio.

Terry worked on, undisturbed, in the gathering dusk. Gradually she was bringing some order to the mass of manuscripts in front of her, sorting them by date, and finally narrowing down those which related directly to her quarry.

'Are ye settling in all right?'

A woman had come into the room and flicked on a switch, flooding it with light. Terry blinked: she hadn't realized how late it was.

'You must be Miss Williams,' she said in the musical, lilting intonation Terry was already coming to recognize as the accent of the Highlands. She was wearing jeans and a cheap sweatshirt, and her hair was drawn back in a bun.

'Yes.' Terry got to her feet and extended her hand. Now that she was standing, she realized that she towered over the other woman. 'And you must be Mrs McCulloch.'

'Och, no. I'm Gail Teare. There's no Mrs McCulloch now. Magnus and Clare were divorced, many years ago.'

'Oh, I hadn't realized.'

'Aye. It was a very great shame.' Gail Teare pursed her lips. 'I'm no' saying I disapprove, mind, but when there's bairns to be cared for . . . well, let's just say a woman has her duty.'

'Mmm,' Terry, whose views on divorce were rather different, murmured vaguely.

'Anyway,' the little woman said, 'I help Magnus now with the paying guests. I hope your room's to your satisfaction.'

Terry mumbled something appreciative about how wonderful it was to be sleeping in the same room as her subject. But by the time she had finished Mrs Teare's lips were drawn even more thinly.

'Aye. Magnus told me why you're here. I cannae say I agree with it, but there you are.'

'You don't approve of research?' Terry said incredulously.

'That depends what it's for. I've no doubt they're doing some wonderful things nowadays. Looking for cures for cancer and such. But I cannae say I hold with raking up a witch-burning. There are some things in any family about which the less said, the better.'

'I'm not looking for anything which will embarrass the McCullochs, honestly. I just want to establish what Catherine was really like.'

'And you're getting a grant for all this? From the government?'

'Aye,' Terry found herself saying – Christ, the accent must be catching. 'Yes. So long as I finish it within the next year. It's a very small grant,' she added quickly. 'Not really enough to live on.'

Gail shook her head incredulously. Clearly, she regarded Terry's sponging off the state as an affront to all normal hardworking folk. 'Well, I'll not be disturbing ye any longer. If you want some supper, there's cold meats in the larder.'

'I can't,' Flora said desperately. 'I'm sorry, Andy, I just can't.'

'Oh, come on doll,' he breathed, his mouth against her ear. 'Don't you want me?' They were in the car park behind a vet's surgery now, completely deserted. She hadn't protested when he brought her here – she'd wanted to go with him, in fact, though part of her had already been anxious about how much he'd demand; how little she could safely get away with. And he had wasted no time, reaching under her T-shirt for her breasts even as he kissed her, finding them aroused, sliding a hand down the small of her back into the cleft of her jeans. It was when he'd started to take them off that she'd stopped him.

With a sigh she reached down and felt the hard tube of his erection under the front pocket of his Levi's. 'I'll do this,' she said in a small voice, reaching into his fly and popping a button. 'OK? I'll make it really good, I promise.'

'Eleven twenty-three, Superintendent Talbot enters room,' Heron said for the benefit of the tape recorder.

Talbot nodded at the man sitting at the interview table and pulled up a chair. 'Thank you for coming in, Mr Hobbes,' he said sardonically. 'Appreciate it.'

Hobbes grunted. 'Thought you'd be having a night off.'

'Oh, we don't keep regular hours on a murder investigation, sir,' Talbot said genially. 'Bit like yourself, I understand.'

Hobbes reached for his cigarette papers and started a roll-up. 'What d'you mean?'

'The night you found the body. Was that usual for you, to be out so late?'

Hobbes stared at him, his face impassive. 'It's in my statement. I was shooting foxes.'

'Of course.' Talbot flicked through his papers. 'For the farmer, Miss Macpherson. Does she pay you to shoot foxes for her, then? Or is it something you do for free?'

Hobbes shrugged. 'I don't charge her,' he said at last.

'Why not? It's hard work, isn't it, being out all night? In the cold and the rain?'

'Weather doesn't bother me.'

Talbot waited.

'I like shooting foxes, anyway. Vermin. Get my chicks if I let them.'

Talbot leaned forward. 'You like shooting foxes? Or you just like shooting?'

'What do you mean?' Hobbes growled.

'It's a simple enough question, isn't it? You collect guns. You've got a shotgun, a two-two rifle, a forty-five – that's a real enthusiast's weapon, I understand – not to mention a collection of knives that wouldn't look out of place in a butcher's shop. I'm just curious as to what you do with them all.'

'I'm a gamekeeper. I use them in my work.'

Talbot paused. 'Weren't always a gamekeeper though, were you?'

'I used to be in the forces. Is that a crime?'

'No, but getting hold of a man's head and slashing it with a broken beer glass is. GBH, in fact. For which you received, as I understand it, six months suspended and a dishonourable discharge.'

Hobbes nodded sullenly. 'Long time ago, now.'

'And now you go out and murder small animals instead. Did you know Donna Fairhead, John?'

He shook his head. 'Never met her.'

'She lived not far from you.'

'One of those nutters, wasn't she? New age types. They don't come into Babcock.'

'Got a girlfriend, John?'

He twisted his hands. 'Not at the moment.'

Talbot glanced at Heron and nodded. Time for the good cop. 'Must be hard meeting girls, stuck out there all year,' she suggested.

'I'm not complaining,' Hobbes muttered.

'What about the farmer?' Talbot interjected. 'Laura. She's quite tasty, isn't she?'

'What is this?' Hobbes said, flushing.

'Ah. So you do fancy her then?'

'She's all right. Got more balls than some of them up there. Hard worker, too.'

'That's why you don't charge her for the shooting, John? Because you're sweet on her?'

'She's engaged,' he muttered, his eyes darting from one to the other.

'So the girl you fancy's unavailable. That must be frustrating for you. Must make you angry. So when you found some other nice bit of skirt wandering around, you thought you'd have your evil way with her. Course, she put up a bit of a fight – a girl like that, a hippie type, she wouldn't have gone for a bit of rough like you, ex-army, gone a bit mad and smelly out here in the wilds on your own. But that wasn't a problem for a man with your background. You just shagged her and killed her. Then you dumped her body in the death pit, which you knew all about from your previous night-time

77

shooting expeditions round the pig farm.'

'You're daft as a fucking brush, you are. If I killed her, why would I find her again?'

'Remorse. You didn't like to think of her decomposing in that stinking pit without a proper burial. Maybe you even wanted to show off to the pretty farmer – be the local big man for a while, the one who found the body.'

'Bullshit.'

'Recognize these, John?'

'Superintendent Talbot is showing Mr Hobbes a pair of handcuffs,' Nicky Heron said for the tape.

Hobbes sat back, his face impassive.

'My men found them in your Land Rover this evening,' Talbot said.

'I suppose they're mine, then.'

'Now, I'm just wondering why a gamekeeper would need a pair of handcuffs. Bit big for restraining pheasant, aren't they?'

Hobbes stared at him for a long time.

'I'm waiting,' Talbot said quietly.

Hobbes reached for his tin of tobacco and began to make himself another roll-up. 'What you've got to understand', he said at last, 'is that there aren't any busies out in Babcock. Nearest police station's here in Stour, fifteen miles away, right? We don't see a copper from one year's end to the next.' He grunted. 'Not till someone dies, any road.'

'Go on,' Talbot prompted.

'Well, I'm a gamekeeper, aren't I? What I'm saying is, if there's any trouble, I'll sort it.'

'What do you mean, trouble?'

'Laura had a bit of bother with kids. Electric fences broken, condoms left in the pig huts. Me, I reckon they were just looking for somewhere to do it out of the rain. But they disturbed the animals, see? I promised to keep an eye on the place.'

'Let me get this straight,' Talbot said incredulously. 'You were going to catch a couple of kids shagging, restrain them with handcuffs and – then what? Shoot them?'

Hobbes shook his head. 'Citizen's arrest,' he said flatly. 'I'd have brought them straight to the police.'

'And given them a bit of a fright along the way, no doubt,' Talbot said dryly. 'Mebbe waved a shotgun in their faces?'

The other man shrugged.

'Look,' Talbot said. 'Let's get one thing straight. We don't need people like you acting as an unofficial police force. Particularly when you're waving guns and handcuffs around. You've a criminal record, Mr Hobbes, and frankly I'm very surprised you've been able to get a gun licence at all, let alone build up an armoury of high-calibre weapons. If you want to hang on to them, you're going to have to tread very carefully indeed from now on. That means that if you see anyone hanging round the pig farm, you call us, you hear? No citizen's arrests, no instant justice, no trying to scare them or warn them off. We'll want to talk to them ourselves.'

'What do you reckon, sir?' Nicky asked when Hobbes had gone.

'Me? I reckon he's hiding something, or telling us as little of the truth as he thinks he can get away with.' Talbot sighed. 'Check with the farmer tomorrow, would you, to make sure that she really did ask Hobbes to keep an eye on the place. If she did, I guess we'll have to pretend to believe him. For the moment. We'll charge him with the drink-driving and let him go in the morning.'

'You don't think there's something a bit creepy about him doing all this shooting for Miss Macpherson? Reminds me of a cat I had once. Used to show his affection by bringing me little bits of dead mouse.'

'I'll tell you what,' Talbot said grimly. 'If our friend Pullen does find any more bodies in that death pit, we'll certainly want to have another chat with Mr Hobbes.'

# SIX

Terry woke early, disturbed by a nightmare. She had been lying, spreadeagled and bound, while a faceless figure dressed in black dripped hot liquid onto her skin. The pain had been excruciating, but in the dream the pain had become strangely mixed with pleasure. When she woke it took her a moment to remember where she was.

She took a deep breath as the dream-feelings receded. Damn, she thought, entertaining a moment's self-loathing. Why can't I have erotic dreams about nice normal things, like everyone else? It was tempting to ascribe the dream to her research, but the truth was that while the details might have been influenced by her work, she had been having similar dreams for months now, long before she had heard of Catherine McCulloch.

She climbed out of the big four-poster and stood in front of the window. Although it was no longer raining, the view across to Ben Dubh was water-logged with mist: a luminous expanse of tracing paper, through which she could just make out the wet coal-silver slate roofs of the castle outbuildings below her and the neat corduroy stripes of the lawn, dotted with dewy cobwebs. She decided to go for a walk.

In the kitchen she found some wellingtons and a greasy old Barbour that smelt of guns and peat. Dougal, sleeping in front of the Rayburn, lifted his head unenthusiastically, so she left him. After the kitchen's warmth the outside air was bitingly cold. Her boots scrunching on the gravel, she made her way past Magnus's Land Rover – beaded with dew like a wine bottle straight from the fridge – and across the lawn. There was a childish pleasure in being the first to pattern the pristine, glossy expanse of grass: deliberately she circled and weaved, double-stitching a crazy pattern of spirals into the lush wet vegetation underfoot.

She decided to walk to the tower. Though she couldn't see it in the mist, she knew that it was uphill, just behind the farm, and she was soon puffing with exertion. It seemed unlikely, she thought to herself, that Catherine would have walked all this way to meet a lover, when there must have been a hundred places in and around the castle itself she could have gone for privacy.

She was wading through longer meadow grass now, her jeans wet to the thigh. Her attention fastened on the ground, it was with a sudden shock that she saw she was no longer alone.

The stag was about thirty yards away, its head frozen at the sapling it had been grazing, regarding her warily with slug-black eyes. Muscular, the size of a small pony, its head was crowned with a vicious-looking candelabra of pointed antlers. Breath steamed from between its black lips.

Terry held her breath. After a few moments, though, she realized this wasn't the timid creature of school poetry anthologies. The deer had no intention of fleeing. Instead, it lowered its head and began to dance towards her – absurd prancing steps, bucking a foot into the air each time, but with its head down, so that the sharp points of the antlers were always facing in her direction.

She had just begun to consider the possibility that it might actually intend to do her some harm when it charged, feet drumming as it hurtled across the field towards her. There was no point in trying to outrun it. She opened her mouth and roared at it as loud as she could. The deer swept its head up, pausing momentarily. Then it lowered its head to charge her again.

A gun went off to her right. Terry and the deer jumped simultaneously. The deer swerved away from her, plunging off into the woods.

She looked over to where the shot had come from. Alex McCulloch was walking calmly towards her. Three or four rabbits, tied together like some bizarre necklace, dangle round his chest. In his hand was a small shotgun, pointing in the air.

'Are you all right?' he asked.

'I think so,' she said, trying to keep her voice as calm as his. 'Thank you.'

'He's a bugger, that one,' the teenager said matter-of-factly. 'He should have been culled last year, but we missed him.'

'Why did he do that? Are they always so aggressive?' she asked.

Alex glanced at her – an appraising, strangely adult look. 'Are you wearing perfume?'

'A little. Why?'

'Perfumes sometimes contain musk.'

'So?'

'It's a pheromone produced by hinds – female deer – in the mating season. It makes the stags wild. I suppose that's why they put it in perfume.'

'Good Lord. I never knew that.'

'The stag probably thought you were a slightly odd-looking doe,' Alex said. 'It's pretty late in the season, so he's desperate.'

'Thanks,' Terry said dryly. 'Why can't he find a mate?'

'They're herd animals. One stag per herd. The top stag fights off the others, and any that aren't culled just wander around making trouble.'

'Typical males, then.' But the joke was wasted on the youth.

'Shame I've only got my two-ten. If I'd had my rifle with me, I could've shot him.'

'Since I was standing right beside him,' Terry said, 'I'm rather glad you didn't try.' She pointed to the animals strung around his neck, one of which was dribbling bloody mucus down his coat. 'You look like you've had a productive enough morning already, anyway. Are those rabbits or hares?'

'Hares. I get a fiver each for them in Babcock.' He broke open his gun and ejected the cartridge. 'Are you going back?'

She shook her head. 'I was going to the tower.'

He nodded. 'You want to go that way, then. I'll see you later.'

After the deer, the dovecot was an anticlimax. It was simply a crumbling, circular stone building lined with what, to Terry, looked absurdly like pigeon-holes in a giant filing system – until she remembered that they really were pigeon-holes, this presumably being where the metaphor came from. Definitely not a good place to meet a lover, she thought, looking at the earth floor: when the dove-cot was in use, it would have been strewn with bird shit, and the noise must have been indescribable. A good place to leave a note for someone, though: those compartments would have made an excellent dead-letter box. She pulled the door to and hurried back towards the house. She wanted to ask Magnus if he'd take her to church.

Iain had been woken at six by the sounds of Laura getting up. Pulling on a pair of jeans and a T-shirt, he went into the kitchen and found her filling a thermos with tea.

'You're up early,' he grunted, fetching himself a cup.

'The pigs have got to be fed.'

He yawned and stretched. 'What about the farmer?'

'I'll have something when I come back. But there's cereal in the cupboard if you want it.'

He shook his head. 'If you can wait a couple of minutes, could you give me a lift to the fields? I might as well get started.'

'You don't want breakfast either?'

He made a face. 'Not today. Today is going to be a bit unpleasant, and, quite apart from anything else, if I start throwing up it'll contaminate the crime scene.'

'I was going to ask you,' he said as the tractor bumped over the rutted tracks towards the pig fields. 'The death pit – is it always surrounded by violets?'

'I think so. Why?'

'It's nothing much. Just that violets like a very

rich soil, so they're probably growing in the seepage from the pit. The extent of the violets gives some indication of how porous the ground is. I'm just a bit surprised the ring of violets is so contained – that there's very little seepage, in other words.'

They arrived at the encampment of police tents, deserted except for a solitary squad car in which Nicky Heron and a uniformed WPC were sound asleep, their seats tilted back as far as they would go. 'At least my piglets should be safe,' Laura said dryly.

Iain clambered down from the cab. The women sat up, bleary-eyed, woken by the sound of the engine. Iain waved to them. Then he pulled a breathing mask and some rubber gloves out of his knapsack and prepared to get to work.

'Christ,' the WPC said, peering through the half steamed-up windscreen. 'He could bring me a cup of tea any morning.'

Nicky grunted monosyllabically. Stuck up cow, the WPC thought. Joins CID and all of a sudden she pretends she doesn't fancy it. She yawned and picked a packet of cigarettes off the dash.


'My text today is taken from the gospel according to St Matthew, chapter eighteen, verse twenty-one: "Lord, how oft shall my brother sin against me, and I forgive him? Until seven times? And Jesus sayeth, I say not unto thee, until seven times, but until seventy times seven." '

Gavin Fyfe paused and surveyed his congregation nervously. 'Of all the Christian virtues, charity is the one which was most central to our Lord's teachings. Not charity in the modern sense of giving, of course, but in its true sense of *for*giving. "Though I bestow all my goods to feed the poor, and though I give my body to be burned, and have not charity, it profiteth me nothing." '

Terry sat high above the minister in the laird's loft, a kind of medieval tree house built against one wall of the church to give the gentry a better view. It felt, she reflected, a bit like having a box at the theatre: you were both more private and more on view, and before the service started she had noticed several of those in the stalls below craning their necks to get a good look at the newcomer sitting next to Magnus. Or perhaps they were simply scandalized by what Flora was wearing. Much to Terry's surprise, when she had announced she'd like to attend that morning's service, the teenager had elected to accompany them, and had come as she was, wearing a midriff-revealing mohair pullover in shocking pink and a pair of skintight leggings which emphasized her adolescent slimness. She still hadn't deigned to address more than two words to Terry. Perhaps, Terry thought, she was only there to make sure Terry didn't get too pally with her dad. She smiled to herself, mindful of what the minister had just said: the thought was hardly a charitable one.

Her attention was suddenly dragged back to the service.

'Donna Fairhead was, albeit briefly, part of our community here at Babcock,' the minister was saying earnestly. 'Her beliefs and values were not ours, but I believe we should recognize that Donna, and those like her, are searching for the same things we are all searching for. In this world there are a multitude of faiths, denominations and beliefs, but they are all paths to the same place.'

'Oh dear,' Magnus muttered under his breath.

Beneath them a huge, dour-faced man in a vast three-piece tweed suit was getting slowly to his feet. From the look Flora gave her father Terry gathered this wasn't a usual part of the service.

Waving a small black hymn book at the young minister like an angry referee giving an errant footballer the red card, the huge man bellowed, 'THERE IS ONE FAITH, AND ONE FAITH ONLY. AND THAT IS THE FAITH OF THE PEOPLE OF ISRAEL. TO WHOM GOD HAS REVEALED HIS HOLY WORD. TO WHOM GOD SAYETH, "THOU SHALT HAVE NO OTHER GOD BEFORE ME. THOU SHALT NOT MAKE UNTO THEE ANY GRAVEN IMAGE. THOU SHALT NOT BOW DOWN THYSELF BEFORE THEM. NOR SHALL YOU SERVE THEM. FOR I THE LORD THY GOD AM A JEALOUS GOD, VISITING THE INIQUITY OF THE FATHERS UPON THE CHILDREN, UNTO THE THIRD AND FOURTH GENERATION OF THEM THAT HATE ME." '

'Bloody hell!' Magnus muttered.

'Er – "Any man's death diminishes me, because I am involved in mankind," as the poet John Donne put it.' The minister had raised his voice slightly, to combat the growing murmurs around him. 'I would ask you all to join with me in prayer for this unfortunate young woman, whose terrible death does not just diminish us as individuals, but also diminishes the whole community of Babcock.' He lowered his head. 'We pray, O Lord, for Donna Fairhead—'

'THEY HAVE DEFILED GOD'S HOUSE. THEY HAVE BROUGHT SATAN AMONGST US. WE

SHALL NOT PRAY FOR IDOLATERS AND HEATHENS!' The giant turned on his heel and gestured to a small, mouse-like woman beside him, who scuttled obediently out of the church in front of him. On the other side of the congregation two elderly ladies were gathering their umbrellas with much clattering and banging of prayer books. Giving the minister a last aggrieved look, they too stalked towards the exit. After a moment, and a buzz of conversation, several other listeners also rose to their feet and made for the doors. Amongst them Terry recognized Tom and Gail Teare.

'What's going on?' she whispered to Magnus. 'I haven't seen so many people walk out since the last time I gave a lecture.'

'I'll tell you later,' he muttered, his eyes bright with interest. 'I don't want to miss a moment of this.'

After the service, while they waited in the loft for the rest of the congregation to leave, he explained: 'We've got a community of Wiccans who live at a farm called Nineveh, just outside the village. You can imagine what the locals make of that – particularly the churchgoers. As far as this lot are concerned, Gavin should be taking a lead against the idolaters, not extending the hand of friendship. His predecessor, old Cameron Ewart, would have damned them with hellfire in a jiffy, but Gavin's from a more liberal school. Something like this was bound to happen sooner or later, but I must say I wasn't expecting a walkout.'

'So who was the human ox?'

'Hector Morrison, the church warden. Otherwise known as the Ayatollah of Babcock. He's not very keen on the Wiccans, as you probably noticed.

Good speaker, though. He preaches mad hellfire sermons occasionally: unfortunately for poor old Gavin, they're always rather well-attended.'

'When you say Wiccans, I take it you mean modern-day witches?'

'Yes.' He shot her an amused glance. 'I thought you'd know all about that.'

'There's no connection between the New-Age version and the stuff people got worked up about in the seventeeenth century,' she responded tartly. 'So this Donna Fairhead was a white witch, but why the prayers?'

'Her body was found on Laura Macpherson's pig farm a week or so ago. Been there for some time, they say. Of course this lot', he indicated the congregation below, 'weren't at all surprised. To them it just proves what they always suspected: heathenism and nasty things like murder go hand in hand.'

'Have the police arrested anyone?'

'Not that I've heard.'

'Perhaps it wasn't the Wiccans, then. I mean, they'd be the obvious suspects. The police must have investigated them fairly carefully.'

Magnus shrugged, getting up and leading the way down the loft steps to the church below. 'It was a sex attack, I gather. Could have been anyone.'

'Any man, you mean.'

'Personally, I've always found the Wiccans a pretty harmless bunch,' he continued as they joined the small knot of people edging towards the doors at the back of the church. 'They ask to be shown round the house occasionally – they're another lot who are interested in Catherine, for obvious reasons. They keep muttering about the Old Religion and chanting their mantras or whatever

90

they're called, but they're no odder than half the people who choose to live up here.'

'I hope you don't include me in that assessment,' a genial voice said behind them. They turned. Terry saw a short, thickset man, Middle-Eastern in appearance, the thinness of his closely cropped grey hair revealing the mahogany tan underneath.

'Hello, David,' Magnus said with more politeness than warmth. 'David Nicolaides, Terry Williams. I hadn't realized you were in residence.'

'All the snow has melted in Switzerland, so I thought I would come and spend a little time amongst your rather smaller mountains,' the other man said. To Terry he made an odd, formal bow, a mischievous lift of his eyes suggesting that the gesture was at least partly ironic.

'You've come here to ski?' she said, making conversation.

He laughed, showing off two rows of expensive-looking teeth. 'Good Lord, no. When I want to ski, I go to my chalet in Gstaad. I come here for the wildlife.' He lowered his voice. 'And I don't mean Mr Morrison.'

'David owns most of the moor behind Ben Dubh,' Magnus explained. 'As well as a rather fine salmon river. We usually see more of him after the Glorious Twelfth.'

David made a slight shrug, as if to say that this state of affairs was regrettable but only natural.

'But the company here is always so pleasant,' he said. 'And the lasses, of course, are always so bonny.' This time his smile was directed at Terry, and his eyes flickered lazily over her body. 'It's always good to meet a friend of Magnus's.'

'I'm not actually a friend. I'm doing some

research into Magnus's family history,' she said sharply, irked by the assumption that she was some kind of trophy girlfriend.

Unfazed, David raised an eyebrow. 'Plenty of skeletons in that cupboard, I should think, eh Magnus?'

Magnus had switched his attention to Flora, who was flirting outrageously with the minister. 'Perhaps,' he said vaguely.

'Why don't you all come over? We were thinking of having a small party next Sunday. The whole village is invited.'

Magnus looked at Terry unenthusiastically. 'Terry?'

She shrugged. 'Great.'

'Excellent. See you next Sunday, then.' He nodded at them both.

'And who was that?' Terry asked in an undertone as they made their way out of the church.

'David Nicolaides. Ex-playboy and oil tycoon. He used just to be known as Nico, in his wilder youth.'

'Oh, of course.' She remembered the name now. 'Didn't he used to play polo with Prince Charles?'

Magnus nodded. 'He stopped calling himself Nico when his father died and he had to take over the family business. As you probably gathered, he's about as Scottish as a McDonald's milkshake, but they ship a lot of oil out of Aberdeen, which is why he's always had a base in Scotland. It was his father who bought the moor off my father. David's always wanted to buy the title off me as well. It may be sentimental, but I don't really think things like that should be bought and sold. I can hardly despise him for wanting it – after all, if I didn't want it myself I might as well fleece him for it – but I do resent the fact that he thinks I'll sell it to him.'

The minister was standing by the door, shaking hands. He looked, Terry thought, far too young to have to deal with Babcock's sectarian problems. 'Interesting sermon, Gavin,' Magnus said mischievously.

'Some of it fell on rather stony ground, I fear,' the minister said anxiously.

'Let them that have ears to hear, eh?' Magnus said genially. He introduced Terry, who explained what she was doing in Babcock.

'Actually, I'm here today under false pretences,' she added. 'I'm not really much of a churchgoer. I wanted to ask if I could have access to the parish records.'

'Certainly. They're here in the chancel, though I'm afraid they're in a terrible state. We had a break-in a few years ago.' He smiled faintly. 'You probably heard Mr Morrison mention the defilement of the house of God. Anything you could do to sort them out would be most welcome. Which period were you after?'

'The seventeenth century.'

'Oh, of course. The witch-burnings. A terrible blot on our church's history.' He lowered his voice. 'Though quite frankly, looking round our congregation today, you can see how such things happened. The fear of the outsider is just as strong as it ever was.' He looked pointedly over to where Hector Morrison was still declaiming to a small knot of people in one corner of the graveyard.

'Speaking as an outsider,' Terry said, 'I find that rather alarming.'

'Hang on, Gavin,' Magnus interjected. 'You're

not suggesting the poor lassie might have been killed by someone from Babcock?'

'Not necessarily. Just that evil and intolerance are always with us.'

'Oh, come on, Magnus,' Terry said. 'It's hardly going to be a passing stranger – you're fifteen miles from the nearest town. If it isn't one of the other Wiccans, then it stands to reason it's got to be someone from the village. After all, it wouldn't be the first time in Babcock's history that fear of the unknown has led to the killing of a young woman, would it?'

In an effort to win brownie points with Gail Teare, Terry offered to help prepare lunch. She was soon set to work peeling and slicing potatoes, Mrs Teare clearly being of the opinion that no-one born south of Hadrian's Wall could be trusted with anything more demanding than a root vegetable.

'What sort of woman was Magnus's wife?' Terry asked conversationally when they were alone. She had Gail down as a gossip and wanted to see if she was right.

The other woman regarded Terry through pursed lips, as if debating how much to tell her. 'Clare was not robust,' she said at last.

Terry nodded, hoping there was more to come. Sure enough, after a few seconds Gail added, 'She was highly strung. A good-looking woman, of course. Very much admired, I believe.' Gail's expression made it plain that she, at least, had not been counted among Clare McCulloch's admirers.

'Was that why Magnus got custody of the children? Because she was highly strung, I mean?'

Gail shot her a sideways glance. 'I believe it was

something to do with the house. Being in trust and so on.'

'Oh, I see. If the house is in trust, there wouldn't have been any assets to divide, so unless Magnus got custody the children wouldn't have a home.'

Clearly baffled, but equally clearly unwilling to admit it, Gail nodded. 'It was something like that, I believe.' A look of sudden suspicion flitted across her stern features. 'Not that I've any interest in speculating about Magnus's financial position,' she said firmly.

Oh, shit, Terry thought: now she thinks I'm after Magnus myself. Gail could hardly be expected to know that Terry coveted being chatelaine of this goldfish-bowl castle about as much as she coveted a bad attack of thrush. Meekly, Terry tried to change the subject to Flora – she was sure Mrs Teare would have plenty to say on that subject – but the other woman had clammed up, shooting Terry little hostile looks from time to time over the *gratin dauphinoise*. She even refused to be drawn on the subject of the exodus from church that morning, though she was clearly still bristling with in-dignation about the minister's sermon.

'We're going to have a party,' David Nicolaides said.

'What for?' Madelaine barely looked up from her Sunday newspapers.

'What for? For the usual things. Drinking, danc-ing, fun.'

'*Who* for, then?'

He smiled delicately. 'Ah. Now that is a very different question. Are you going to get dressed before lunch, my dear?'

'More parties, Nico? More bloody parties?' Madelaine got to her feet and tossed the papers onto a chair. 'When are you going to understand that all the parties in the world won't make any difference?'

# SEVEN

By mid-afternoon Terry was hard at work in the library, copying Catherine's letters onto her laptop. She had arranged them into three categories: letters relating to the running of the estate, letters to the lawyer and personal correspondence to Anne de Courcy. Of the three categories, the latter seemed to have the most potential.

It was painfully slow work – each individual word took anything between a few seconds to half an hour to transcribe. In some cases she had to play a sort of algebraic game: if that's an r and that's a t, then the word doesn't make sense, but if that's an s and that's a b, it might be . . . Gradually, though, as the hours wore on, she found that the work became quicker as she got used to the idiosyncrasies of Catherine's hand.

She took a short break for tea, acknowledging Magnus's polite enquiry as to how it was going with a curt 'OK', then got straight back to work. Gradually, like the image on a photograph slowly emerging from the red-tinged liquid in a developing bath, the manuscripts in front of her were turning into the story of a living human being, with her own particular inflections and grammatical quirks, her own voice. Like many seventeenth-century writers Catherine's spelling was inconsistent: 'colde' or 'cald' for cold, 'courte' or 'cort' for court. Where she could, Terry modernized these obvious anachronisms. There were also occasional Latin phrases dotted through the text, which she translated roughly with the help of a primer she'd had the foresight to bring with her – there would be plenty of time later to go back and check the details. With a start she realized that it was evening, and that her eyes and head were aching from prolonged concentration. She had transcribed two letters now.

My dearest Anne,

I am now brought to the Assize, where I am to be judged if there is truth in these charges, & if I must answer to the court for them. Let us hope and pray by God's good grace that it does not come to that, for I am much afraid, and have heard that even the innocent must endure greatly, before they are proved to be so. Last year at Aberdeen, my jailers say, twenty-one gentlewomen stood accused by a child, who said that they had given her bad dreams, and all of them were burnt. And in Fyfe also there was a woman, not sound in her mind, who confessed to the killing of an infant, and defiling his body with the devil's signs: but the judge was not sure, and gave orders that the grave be opened, and the body examined, and it was found to be unmarked, so her confession was false.

I have been told that my accuser is one Joseph Turner, a farmer. I know the man well & never thought him uncivil, or done him harm, but he has said that I have cursed his cows, so that they will only give sour milk. I have prayed for him. Also there is a girl, one Mary Tyler, who says she has seen me at a sabbat, or gathering of witches, tho' I know her not.

I am treated as a gentlewoman and indeed my jailers seem solicitous & confident that I will not remain here long. *Dominus illuminati mea, et salus mea, quem timebo?* The Lord is the source of my light and my safety, so whom shall I fear? Master Balwhinnie is to have the running of the farms: he will know what is to be done.

Your loving mistress,
Catherine


My dearest Anne,

Most terrible are the ways of the courts, for they have determined that I must be prick'd, gentlewoman or no. One Andrew Mann, witchfinder for the court, has given evidence, and sayeth that a witch might be known by the Devil's mark or Witch's spot, that all such persons have about their body, which spot may be invisible to the eye, but feels no pain and when prick'd does not bleed. So I am to be stripp'd, allowing no modesty, and prick'd in the presence of the court, and any persons who care to attend. And I am told that these prickings are a great entertainment for the populace, and that often a woman is shaved of her hair before such a pricking, because a devil or spirit can hide about her body. I had never imagined before now that they could shame me in this way, who have never been seen naked by any man, or any woman saving yourself and my maids. But I remember the trial of Our Lord, and think what He endured, so much greater a suffering. Pray for me.

Your loving mistress,
Catherine

*Notes*: No evidence of any relationship between the two women other than close friendship. Calls her 'My Anne'; signs herself 'Your loving mistress'. A usual salutation at this time? Catherine has 'never been seen naked by any man, or any woman saving yourself and my maids.' But presumably perfectly usual for a companion to see her mistress naked? Context suggests being dressed or bathing rather than sexual intimacy. Check: names of accusers. Any biographical traces? Possible motives? For example, could Joseph Turner – 'I know the man well, and never thought him uncivil,' – have been a rejected suitor?

*Overall*: tone suggests a woman who entirely believes in her own innocence and has nothing to hide or fear.

She hit the Save button, rubbed her eyes and went in search of a cup of coffee.

By late afternoon Iain had excavated thirteen pig carcasses from the death pit. Their rotting remains had all been photographed *in situ*, and then again when they were removed, together with a close-up of their ear tags. Occasionally the tags, which were plastic and didn't degrade, had become detached from the rotting flesh. Where the position of the carcasses didn't make it obvious which tag referred to which pig, he photographed both from every angle and made a separate pile. The carcasses couldn't be left in the open air for scavengers to get at, so he used the JCB to dig a second death pit alongside the first, into which he unceremoniously bulldozed the stinking heap.

It was without a doubt the most unpleasant dig he had ever been involved with. Each fresh trip into the pit was like a descent into hell – all the more so as the pigs' skin was uncomfortably like a human's, and every time he shifted a carcass he was never quite sure at first if what he was uncovering was another pig, or the corpse of a second young woman, distorted by death. As the day wore on the heat under the canvas shelter had risen, and with it rose the sickly stench of rotting flesh, even penetrating his mask. He had to take regular breaks outside, tearing the mask off and gulping down huge lungfuls of clean Highland air. He would have liked to have smoked in these breaks, but his rubber gloves were so covered in foul-looking residues that he didn't dare put his hands anywhere near his mouth.

He had been exaggerating when he told Talbot that he would only use a trowel and a toothbrush. Although these were his normal tools when excavating a skeleton, that was in a situation where the position of every single bone was a potential clue. Here, the important thing was to get the sequence of burial absolutely right. There was no need to take any particular care of the carcasses once they had been identified and logged; they simply needed to be hauled out of the way so that the next layer could be uncovered, and for that he used the JCB and a length of rope, tying their trotters together and then hauling them up and out like, he thought, some ghastly ship of death being unloaded at a quayside. He was, however, dreading the lower layers of the pit, where the flesh would be progressively more rotten and the individual carcasses would start to meld into one another in an amorphous stinking sludge of body parts.

Laura came to collect him just as he was digging the second death pit, waiting patiently while he manoeuvred the huge claw of the JCB into the ground.

# EIGHT

All the time she had been working, the house had been as silent as a broken clock. Terry went out into the stone-flagged hallway and called, 'Magnus?' up at the serried ranks of deer heads. There was no answer. Damn: she wanted to show him what she'd got so far.

The kitchen was deserted too, but the door to the stable yard behind, now used as garages, had been left open. She wandered outside. Dusk had brought with it more rain, a light drizzle that itched in her hair like the ever-present midges. The Land Rover was nowhere to be seen. Had they all gone out? As much to get out of the rain as anything else she pulled open one of the big double doors and stepped inside.

She was in a windowless room about fifteen-feet square. The walls were only half plastered, as if the room was in the middle of being renovated, and the floor was littered with workmen's tools, bits of timber, a saw and what looked like a half-made table. But it was what was hung on the walls that made Terry gasp.

She was in what could only be described as a

shrine to torture. On her left was a series of gruesome old prints, depicting women – mostly naked –
being subjected to floggings and other forms of
punishment. One woman was having her eyes
gouged out with hot pincers: another was sitting
with her feet in a kind of metal bath filled with
water, underneath which a fire had been lit. Yet
another was being pulled along by a rope attached
to her breasts. It wasn't only pictures, either.
Magnus had evidently gone to great trouble to find
original instruments of torture for his collection. On
a shelf to her right was a pair of ancient iron boots,
each boot divided into two halves joined by a screw
like a workman's vice, so that they could be crushed
together. Hanging next to it was a kind of iron
collar, its inner surface studded with spikes. A whole
display cabinet was given over to various kinds of
thumbscrews.

There was also a bookcase full of books and files.
Terry picked a file at random and opened it. Inside
was a single sheet of photocopied paper:

There is a frequent phrase that is used by
judges, that the accused has confessed without
torture and is thus undeniably guilty. I
wondered at this and made enquiry, and
learned that in reality they were tortured, but
only in an iron vice with sharp-edged bars over
the shins, in which they are pressed like a cake,
bringing blood and causing intolerable pain,
and this is technically called without torture,
deceiving those who do not understand the
phrases of the Inquisition.

Terry shuddered and put the file back where she'd

found it. Turning her head sideways, she ran her finger along the spines of the books. *The A-Z of Torture . . . Crime and Punishment in Germany . . .* She opened one at random and read:

First-degree tortures, designed to obtain confessions, included stripping suspects, binding them tightly with ropes and flogging them. Prisoners might be fed salty foods and denied any liquid, so that they suffered raging thirst; they might actually be placed on the Ladder (or 'rack') and stretched by ropes until their muscles tore; or their limbs might be crushed in vices. Other tests employed in this 'preparatory torture' – the *question préparatoire* – included giving the prisoner a guided tour of the torture chamber, so that he or she might see what horrors they risked by not admitting at once the full measure of their guilt. If the accused was an attractive woman or girl she risked being raped by the torturer's assistants. Those who confessed at this stage would frequently be reported to have made their statements without being tortured, as these measures were considered relatively mild by many courts.

If a confession was still unforthcoming, the accused person was then subjected to tortures of the second degree, the 'final torture' or the *question définitive*. The first stage of this was 'ordinary torture', which included the procedure known as strappado, variously augmented by the application of the thumbscrews or other supplementary torments . . .

The most uncommunicative prisoners moved from the second degree to the third degree – the 'extraordinary torture' or *question extraordinaire*. Strappado was now succeeded by the even more savage procedure known as squassation, which might be repeated many times and which all too easily culminated in the suspect's death.

Various other measures used included forced drinking of holy water on an empty stomach, breaking on the wheel and, in Scotland, 'thrawing', which involved the prisoner being jerked violently about by means of ropes fastened around the neck (these were sometimes attached to a spiked collar that tore the victim's flesh as he or she was thrown about). Other extreme tortures included cutting off hands and ears, immersion in scalding baths laced with lime and the tearing of flesh with red-hot pincers (a punishment usually reserved for those who had been found guilty of desecrating the host). Some prisoners were forced to wear large leather or metal boots into which boiling water or molten lead was poured.

Recantations of confessions made in the torture chamber only led to the prisoner being returned there directly . . .

Terry replaced the book and moved on. As well as the historical accounts of torture, there was a whole shelf dedicated to books on sado-masochism. The Marquis de Sade's *Justine* and *120 Days of Sodom* were both there, along with a collection of pseudo-Victorian pornography with titles like *A Girl in Training* and *Mistress of the Birch*. She shuddered. Should she go to the police? To say what?

Magnus might be a pervert, but getting your kicks out of reading about torture wasn't actually illegal.

On the other hand, Magnus's wife had left him – and for rather more sinister reasons than his sense of humour, she now guessed – leaving him with two teenage children. Alex – did his sullenness result from sexual abuse? Flora – wasn't there something rather odd about her over-developed sexuality? Not to mention the fact that a murder had recently taken place in the area.

She suddenly looked at the object in the middle of the room, seeing it with fresh eyes. It wasn't a half-constructed table at all – there were ropes attached to each end, and a thick sliding platform in the middle. It was a torture rack.

A torture rack awaiting a victim.

A sudden spasm of anxiety knotted her guts. Shit, she thought: not here, not now. She breathed deeply, struggling to control the waves of panic.

Dear God, she thought, I've got to get out of this place.

Without transport, two hours' drive from the train station, that wasn't going to be easy. Perhaps there was a taxi service in Babcock or – what was the nearest town called? – Stour.

But a taxi from Stour might take hours to arrive, by which time Magnus would be back.

She made a sudden decision. She'd go into the village, find a pub and phone from there. She ran to the library, wrenched her laptop's power unit from the wall and hurried upstairs to her bedroom. She'd barely unpacked: it took only a few seconds to throw her overnight things and the computer into her back-pack. At the door she turned and looked at the room. There was nothing here she couldn't live without.

Her books. They were only paperbacks – volumes on Scottish history and a couple of reference books. They weren't worth more than twenty or thirty pounds. But they were books. It was completely irrational, but she couldn't leave books behind.

Upending a suitcase full of bras and knickers onto the bed, she put as many volumes into it as she could carry, and lugged it down the curving staircase. The suitcase banged on the steps, gathering momentum. It was all she could do to keep hold of it.

'Are ye leaving us, Terry?'

She jumped. It was the ghillie, Tom, standing in the shadows of the hall. Terry gabbled something about going for a walk and fled into the night.

Halfway down the drive it started to rain more heavily. Her arms ached and she had no coat, so she sheltered for a few moments in the shadow of a rhododendron bush. The big, dark leaves tipped water down her neck.

Someone with a torch was walking slowly down the drive from the direction of the house, rain flickering through its beam. It must be Tom, following her.

'Shit,' she said out loud. She thought: don't run. Lugging the case beside her – she couldn't in any case have run without abandoning it altogether – she set off again.

Headlights turned the corner from the road, trapping her in their beams. Defeated, she stopped and stood there, drenched, waiting for it.

Seeing her standing in the middle of the track, Magnus brought the Land Rover to a stop and got out. 'What in God's name are you doing?' he asked.

The torch beam caught up with her. 'I thought ye might need an umbrella,' Tom said mildly.

'I don't need an umbrella,' she said defiantly. 'I need a fucking taxi.'

'Why? Where are you going?' Magnus said, puzzled.

'I've found your little torture shrine,' she said. 'I'm leaving.'

The two men exchanged glances.

'Damn,' said Magnus. 'You'd better come back to the house.'

They sat in the castle kitchen drinking Lagavulin, while Terry's clothes dried on the Rayburn. A couple of stag's antlers on the wall had been pressed into service as makeshift clothes racks.

'All that bullshit in the car,' Terry said bitterly. 'You wanted me to think your motive for getting me up here was that you're passionate about Scottish history. And it was bollocks, wasn't it? All you're interested in is making some money out of tourism. Welcome to the Babcock Museum of Witchcraft, home of the famous Catherine McCulloch exhibition.'

'It's not quite as tacky as that,' Magnus muttered. Terry's tongue-lashing had already lasted several minutes, and he had absolutely no desire to set her off again.

'But you do want to open the castle to the public. Well, of course. After all, everyone else is doing it. Only thanks to Queen Victoria and her dreadful taste in architecture, Babcock is too small and ugly to merit a visit without some kind of extra draw. Which you might just happen to have, in the shape of your almost-famous ancestor.'

'She's sharp,' Tom said admiringly. 'The lassie's verra sharp.'

'We started building the collection about a year ago,' Magnus said. 'People love all that torture stuff – once the idea had occurred to us we were amazed that no-one else had done it yet. We're right in the middle of what the Scottish Tourist Board like to call the Whisky Trail—'

'I know,' she interrupted. 'Glenlivet's less than half an hour away, Ardberg's even closer, Tamnavoulin and Knockandhu are in the next valley, and Glenorc is just up the road.'

He nodded. 'You obviously like whisky.'

'Depends on who I'm drinking it with,' she said dryly.

'Anyway, my point is that this area is teeming with tourists, all getting pissed out of their skulls on distillery tours and looking for something to do with themselves in the mornings. What better hangover cure than an introduction to Scotland's gruesome witch-burning past? You see, Terry, whether we like it or not, heritage is this country's USP – that's short for—'

'Unique Selling Proposition,' she said. 'I know.'

'All we're doing is exploiting our asset. We've got backing from NatWest – we'll want to put a little shop in, maybe in one of the old farm buildings, and we'll probably build a playground for the kiddies.'

'Thumbscrews and roundabouts,' she said sarcastically. 'A fun day out for all the family.'

'If it pays for us to renovate Babcock – maybe even strip off some of that hideous façade – I'm all for it.'

She nodded. 'Except you had one little problem, didn't you? You had all of Catherine's letters – the one thing that makes you unique – but you couldn't read her handwriting. So you had to find someone to transcribe them for you. Someone cheap. And if you could get them properly authenticated and published at the same time – well, it would make a nice little memento to sell in the castle gift shop.'

'Exactly.'

'I ought to get straight on the next train to London.'

'Look,' Magnus said apologetically, 'I can see that you're not completely happy about this. All right, all right,' he held up a hand as she opened her mouth. 'I can see you're bloody pissed off. But does it really matter why we wanted you here? You've got the papers now.'

And I've also got a deadline, she thought to herself. If she walked out now, she'd never finish her doctorate – any doctorate. But it was more than that, she realized. ' "April is the cruellest month," ' she murmured, half to herself. ' "Stirring dull roots with spring rain." ' Deep down, the papers she had handled in the library had reignited something in her, some itch of curiosity that she had thought gone for ever. Like a child listening to a story, she needed to know what happened next.

'If I stay, you won't pressurize me to sensationalize my research?'

He held up his hands, the picture of innocence. 'Of course not.'

'There's no of course about it,' she said acidly. 'I understand now why you got so worried in the car when I suggested Catherine might not have been gay after all – the last thing you want to discover is that she was actually a seventeenth-century hausfrau who sat in prison writing grocery lists. If I am going

# NINE

As the days passed her life fell into a new rhythm. She would get up early, having slept more soundly than she had for months, and walk towards the mountain or alongside the quick-flowing little river that meandered across the moor, watching the tiny mountain trout nosing the cold morning air for flies. Sometimes she would meet Alex, returning from a hunting trip with his coat pockets bulging with hare or fish; or sometimes he would be standing on the lawn when she returned, practising his casting – a surreal image, the line whipping through the air, impossibly long, as if he hoped to hook a cloud. Then, after a breakfast that grew daily more hearty, she took herself off to the library and worked at the letters until lunch, saving the afternoon for a lazy trawl round the local villages in what she told herself was background research but which was really sightseeing. Mostly the family seemed to ignore her, though not in an unfriendly way. To them she was just another guest. Even Gail, the housekeeper, no longer looked askance at her. Flora, however, was a harder nut to crack, shooting her poisonous glances or turning away ostentatiously. Fortunately their paths rarely crossed.

By Wednesday she had transcribed four more letters.


My dearest Anne,

I thank you for the gift of eggs and cake. My situation here remains as it was. I have learnt that my cousin has paid eight pounds for me to reside in these apartments and not within the common jail. And he has ordered that the ordinary people be henceforth excluded from my trial – for so I think of it, tho' the true trial is yet to come.

I cannot write of the pricking. Pray to our Lady, who alone knows what a woman may endure. I have prayed much, and felt the sin of Despair.

Yr. loving Catherine


My dearest Anne,

I am much recovered, and have been assisted by Dr Harris. As you will know, I have been found to have a Devil's mark, what they call stigmato diaboli. And yet the wounds of the pricking are more like the stigmata of Our Lord, tho' His were made with nails and not a bodkin as mine were, & He had only four, upon his hands and feet, while I am prick'd all over. *De profundis clamavi ad te, Domine; Domine, exaudi vocum meum.* Up from the depths I have cried to thee; Lord, Lord, hear my voice. This pricking is a terrible thing, my Anne, for tho' I was not made to suffer the jeering of the people, I was taken to the Assize and roughly stripp't in a cell by Mr Mann and his assts, of whom there are two, both rough fellows. And I was in a great fear, and did faint several times, which they said was pretence, but indeed was only modesty. And then they held me still while I was shaved, but again most fiercely, and with a little cold water only, so that on many occasions the blade cut my skin. At which my Lords entered, my cousin amongst them. And he asked if I might not be dressed in a thin shift, and pricked through the cloth, but Mr Mann inform'd them that it was always so, and must be done properly or not at all. With bodkins then they pricked my neck, and after that my back and arms, at which time I tried to pray, but cried out many times. Each prick must draw blood, for that is the point of it, as a Devil's mark cannot bleed. And even my belly and breasts and legs were pricked, and I know not where else, for I was in a kind of fainting fit. I think my cousin would have left the room, but he was prevented by the others, who said it must be witnessed. I do not recall where the Spot was found. But after, I was very cold, and ran a fever all the night, so that the woman who tends to me feared for my life, and summoned Dr Harris. And tho' by God's grace I am recovered from the fever, I sometimes wonder if it were best so. Continue to pray for me, and in my name: you will know what I mean.

Yr. loving Catherine

My dearest Anne,

Know that I am to be brought before an ecclesiastical court to answer that the mistress of Babcock is a witch. For the jury of the Assize were told that the devil's mark having been found, to acquit me would render themselves accessories to my crime. My jailer tells me that these witchfinders often have two bodkins for the pricking: one true, and one false, with a blade that slides into the handle. Thus can they find a devil's mark that may not be apparent by the true one, and secure a conviction and their pay. For my pricking I am charged four pounds and three shillings.

I have engaged a lawyer, one Joshua O'Neill. Give him the money he will require of you.

Yr. loving Catherine

My dearest Anne,

I do not know how I shall be able to write to you, for my trial has begun, and I am to be removed from my chambers in the barracks to a gaol in Castle Street. The witchfinder Mr Mann spoke before the court, and told how he found the mark, and also cited scripture, namely, Exodus Ch. 22 vs. 18, 'Thou shall not suffer a witch to live', and divers authorities, to wit, Thomas Aquinas, the blessed St Augustine and our own King James VI of Scotland, who wrote a Daemonologie setting out how these trials may be conducted. And the long and the short of it is that I am to be put to the torture chamber, and the further attentions of Mr Mann, whether I confess or no; for as he has said, they must know the names of my accomplices, and whether I have consorted with the devil.

I will suffer anything, but I cannot admit that I am a witch, tho' I am very afraid. I take what comfort I can from our Faith, which I know to be the true one. Say prayers for me as I have previously directed. I am to be questioned tomorrow.

Yr. loving Catherine

*Notes:* Absolutely no indication of what M. would call 'juicy bits'. Explicitly accused of 'consorting with the devil' and not perversion. Also many indications of piety, biblical quotations etc. – hardly an indication of lesbianism, which was presumably a mortal sin.

Some secretive references: 'Continue to pray for me, and in my name: you will know what I mean.'

Reference to 'My cousin' presumably means Hamish McCulloch. Ask M. for family tree.

Clean at last, Iain came out of the shower to find Laura, still in her work clothes, slumped fast asleep on the sofa. Bits of straw stuck to her socks and hair.

He felt a sudden, unexpected tug of lust. It seemed somehow wrong, to be watching her like this, when she was at her most vulnerable, but also strangely exciting. Perhaps, he acknowledged, that joke he'd made about preferring his girlfriends decomposed had been truer than he'd realized. Seeing her asleep, half-buried by the pillows she'd pulled around herself, he felt the same sense of excitement he felt when, trowel in hand, he'd first approached his princess.

For a few moments he stayed like that, watching her. Then she moved slightly, and the illusion was broken. Quietly, so as not to disturb her further, he slipped out of the room to go and get his clothes.

When Laura woke it was dark. Iain was reading by the light of an anglepoise in the other chair. Stirring, she felt herself enveloped in something soft. Her duvet.

'Oh, shit,' she murmured, swinging herself upright. 'You shouldn't have.'

'You were dead to the world. I thought you might as well be comfortable.'

'I'll be stiff as a board now. Argh.' She stretched, painfully. 'What's that you're reading?'

He showed her. 'Poetry. It's a collection by Seamus Heaney. *North*. It was inspired by some preserved Iron Age bodies in Ireland.'

'Any good?'

Instead of answering, he read out loud:

> As if he had been poured
> in tar, he lies
> on a pillow of turf
> and seems to weep
>
> the black river of himself.
> The grain of his wrists
> is like bog oak,
> the ball of his heel
>
> like a basalt egg.
> His instep has shrunk
> cold as a swan's foot
> or a wet swamp root.

'It's beautiful,' she said. 'Gruesome, but beautiful.'

He nodded slowly. 'I take it everywhere.'

'Read me some more?'

He leafed through the pages. 'This one's my favourite. It's called "Punishment".'

> I can feel the tug
> of the halter at the nape
> of her neck, the wind
> on her chilly front.

*It blows her nipples*
*to amber beads,*
*it shakes the frail rigging*
*of her ribs.*

*I can see her drowned*
*body in the bog,*
*the weighing stone,*
*the floating rods and boughs.*

*Under which at first*
*she was a barked sapling*
*that is dug up*
*oak-bone, brain-firkin:*

*her shaved head*
*like a stubble of black corn,*
*her blindfold a bandage,*
*her noose a ring*

*to store*
*the memories of love.*
*Little adulteress,*
*before they punished you*

*you were flaxen-haired,*
*undernourished, and your*
*tar-black face was beautiful.*
*My poor scapegoat,*

*I almost love you*
*but would have cast, I know,*
*the stones of silence . . .*

He paused. 'You know', she said, 'if someone had

told me a week ago that tonight I'd be lying on my sofa while a policeman read me poetry, I'd have told them not to be daft.' He started to protest, and she held up a hand. 'All right, all right. You're not exactly a policeman. And I suppose I shouldn't joke about it, given that a girl was murdered.' She thought for a moment. 'I wonder if she was a scapegoat, too. Like the girl in the poem.'

'There's more,' he said. 'I hadn't finished. Listen:'

> I am the artful voyeur
>
> of your brain's exposed
> and darkened combs,
> your muscles' webbing
> and all your numbered bones:
>
> I who have stood dumb
> when your betraying sisters,
> cauled in tar,
> wept by the railings,
>
> who would connive
> in civilised outrage
> yet understand the exact
> and tribal, intimate revenge.

'That's you, then, isn't it?' she said. 'The artful voyeur, turned on by corpses. Numbering your bones, but not quite sure whose side you're on.'

He could not reply, aghast that she had understood him so clearly.

'Only joking,' she said, getting to her feet. 'I suppose it's my turn to cook, isn't it? So it'll have to be frozen pizza.'

# TEN

The next day Terry took herself into Babcock to check the parish records. The church was locked – a consequence of the vandalism the minister had told her about, she supposed – so she stopped by his house to collect a rather beautiful old key, the size of a soup spoon and twice as heavy.

The records of Babcock's births, deaths and marriages had been bound into large leather-covered volumes, each one spanning fifty years or so, kept on a high shelf in the little room where the minister changed into his robes before the service. There were just eight of them in all – any records prior to 1600, the minister had told her, were in the Public Records Archive in Inverness for safe keeping. It seemed remarkable, somehow, that her quarry could be connected to the present day by such a simple, continuous thread. But after all, she reminded herself, the end of the seventeenth century was only three hundred years away. Six books back.

All her protagonists were here: Catherine, her birth recorded but not her death; Hamish, who had married a girl called Elizabeth Hawthorne in 1703 and who had died himself sixteen years later; Anne de Courcy, whose father had been Robert de Courcy and whose mother had been one Liza Hedderwick, of Nineveh Farm. Nineveh Farm: where had she heard that name before? Of course – the place where the dead girl had stayed. She made some notes on a foolscap pad, browsing happily through the old parchment pages in search of familiar names.

Heavy footsteps approached from the church. The door swung open, and the massive figure of Hector Morrison stepped through it, regarding her suspiciously. Up close he was even bigger than she remembered from the service, his barrel-shaped body topped by a neck the size of a telegraph pole and a great slab of a head, the flesh running off it into a cascade of double chins below. He was younger, though, than she had thought him, perhaps only in his thirties, his bulk giving him the profile of a much older man. Somewhat incongruously, his meaty hands were clasping a tiny posy of spring flowers.

'Good afternoon,' she said nervously.

'How d'ye do.' Breathing noisily, he stood in the doorway, regarding her balefully. For a second she was reminded of the way the stag had looked at her just before it charged.

'I'm doing some work on the records,' she found herself gabbling. 'The minister said it would be all right if—'

'Aye. Catherine McCulloch,' he interrupted. 'I ken why you're here. The female sodomite of Babcock Castle.'

'Er – right,' Terry agreed, wondering if Hector Morrison's history was as vague as his biology. 'Though I have to say I've not actually found any evidence of that so far.'

122

'D'ye believe in witchcraft, Miss Williams?'

Surprised that he knew her name, she said, 'No. No, I think most of the confessions of the witches were suggested to them by their torturers. Who were mostly clerics, and therefore celibate, and who were therefore unhealthily obsessed with sex, sin and religion. I think they basically hated women, and projected onto them their own quasi-religious sexual fantasies.'

A deep rumbling emanated from the man-mountain's quivering chins. With a start Terry realized he was chuckling.

'Aye, well. At least ye aren't one of these happy-clappy types who think a spell's as valid as the Lord's Prayer. But what would ye say if I told you that I've seen evidence with my own eyes that the devil has worshippers on this earth?'

Terry felt out of her depth. 'That's . . . interesting,' she said lamely.

Hector Morrison leant closer. 'In this very church. The signs of a black mass. Blood and semen mixed together on the floor. The devil's symbols painted on the walls. The very crucifix on the altar inverted. Chicken feathers plastered to the altar cloth with filth.' He wheezed heavily. 'The devil doesn't walk the earth, Miss Williams. He struts it. For he is proud of his works. He sees all Israel scattered upon the hills, as sheep that have not a shepherd.'

'Gavin mentioned there were some vandals . . .'

'Vandals!' Morrison snorted. 'He barely believes in God, that one, so it's hardly surprising he disnae believe in the devil.' He levered his bulk off the edge of the table where he had been resting it and wagged a large finger at her. 'Just remember to lock the door when you leave, eh?'

Still feeling spooked – as much from the over-whelming physical presence of the man as from the nonsense he'd been spouting – Terry locked up and set off through the graveyard. There were fresh flowers on one of the graves, the little posy carefully placed against an equally diminutive headstone. Terry recognized them as the bunch Hector Morrison had been holding. Intrigued, she walked over and read the inscription: 'Samuel James Morrison. Born 24 November 1992. Taken to God 25 November 1992. Thy rod and thy staff comfort me still.' So the poor child had only lived a day – less, if it had been born near midnight. No wonder his father had gone off the rails.

David Nicolaides sat next to his wife on an un-comfortable chair in an ugly room in the Department of Social Services building in Aberdeen. In front of him, behind a table, sat three women and two men.

The woman in the middle – she called herself the chair – was speaking. 'Tell me, David. If you are successful, what sort of home environment would you be hoping to provide?'

'Obviously, a stable and loving one. One with the right blend of support and encouragement. Somewhere where the child feels happy and secure.' He saw the woman make a note on her pad and thought, Christ, these people. How many answers can there be to a question like that? He was still wondering what on earth the woman could have written about such a bland response when the next question came, so that he answered almost without thinking.

'And education? Have you thought ahead as far as that?'

'The best that money can buy, obviously,' he said promptly. 'Somewhere that is supportive and friendly, somewhere that doesn't push the child too fast . . .' His voice tailed off as he saw that all the other members of the panel had lifted their heads from their notes and were staring at him. The man on the extreme right got there first.

'When you say the best that money can buy, I take it you mean a fee-paying school?'

Nico shrugged. 'I suppose so. We live in a very remote area, the schools are not so good, and not very close.'

'A boarding school?' This from the chair again.

'Not necessarily. And certainly not at first. I myself was thirteen when I went to Gordonstoun.' Dammit, this was not what these people wanted to hear. 'What I mean is, we'll see what's best for the boy when the time comes.'

Again the heads went up. 'Boy?' the chair enquired icily.

'For the child, I meant. Really, we don't care which sex we get.'

There was a short pause. Perhaps he had got away with it.

'As you know, this council has a policy of placing adoptive children with families of a similar ethnic background. Are you aware how few children of Greek origin come up for adoption?'

He smiled. Surely they had misunderstood. 'No, no, we don't want a Greek child. We want an ordinary baby. I mean', he swallowed, conscious that he might be putting it badly, 'any baby. We don't think of ourselves as Greek. My wife is English. We are', he struggled to find the right word, 'cosmopolitan.'

Now the silence was longer. 'Do you mean you have more than one residence, David?'

He started to answer but she cut across him. 'And how many of these residences – exactly – are going to be the secure, stable home environment you talked about earlier?'

Terry wandered down Babcock High Street, investigating the shops. Bond Street it wasn't. There was a tiny newsagents, where she bought a copy of the *Independent* and a bag of sweets. A hairdressers, its window adorned with unlikely looking photographs. A shop crammed with Barbours, Drizabones, Huskies and various kinds of welly. An antiquarian bookshop. From its window display she guessed it mostly sold old hunting prints to tourists, but it was worth a second look. She went inside.

'Hi,' she smiled at the young man behind the counter. 'I'm after anything by a local historian, John Mcteer?'

'I'll have a look.' The young man went and checked the shelves. It was odd, Terry thought, how you could tell some men were gay just by looking at them: by the cut of their T-shirt, or the way they wore it. There was nothing particularly camp about the assistant, but equally there was absolutely no doubt that he was queer. Why had gay women never evolved a similar set of mannerisms to identify each other by?

'There's nothing here. I'll just ask, shall I?' She nodded, and she heard him repeat her question in a little room at the back of the shop.

'John Mcteer? Darling, we virtually *are* John Mcteer. Who wants to know?' A plump little man trotted out of the back room, bringing with him a distinct odour of Givenchy. Lucky for the stag it hadn't come across this character, Terry thought: that would really have confused it. The older man was so queenie he might as well have worn a tiara. He extended a pudgy hand.

'Russell Kane. You're interested in John Mcteer?' She nodded. 'Well, there's a blast from the past. We published him, you see.'

'You're the Shadowcourt Press?'

Russell Kane clasped his hands together and rolled his eyes like a Botticelli Venus. 'In my wild youth. Dreams of glory, dear, dreams of glory.'

'Right,' Terry said doubtfully. 'So do you have any of his books for sale?'

'Well, that's the tragedy. Not a thing. John insisted on keeping all the unsold stock himself.' He pursed his lips. 'Of which, I might say, there was rather a lot.'

'Do you have his address? I'd like to contact him.'

Russell Kane looked surprised. 'But he's dead. Didn't I say?'

Disappointed, Terry said, 'When was this?'

'Ooh, years ago. He was in his seventies, you know, when he went. They gave him a lovely funeral – not that they call it a funeral, of course, but it was lovely all the same.'

'Did he have any family?'

Russell shrugged expressively. 'He certainly wasn't married. Wait . . . there might have been a sister, but I'm afraid I wouldn't know how to get in touch with her.'

Oh, well. It had been worth a shot. 'Thanks,' she

said. Since she was there she bought a couple of postcards before nodding goodbye and leaving.

'Nice lady,' the young assistant said as Terry retraced her footsteps down the High Street.

Russell Kane stood beside him, watching her go. 'Liked her, did we?' he said coquettishly. He ran his hand down the young man's arm. 'That's a girl cub, Mowgli, and they ain't nothing but trouble.'

For a long time in the car they were silent.

'That didn't go very well,' Nico said eventually.

'No.' Madelaine agreed quietly. She pointed. 'Pull over, will you? I want to go in there.'

He parked the Range Rover, then followed her into the little shop. The assistant was getting something out of the window for her. A tiny green romper suit, its front decorated with embroidered animals.

'Look,' Madelaine said, her face bright with delight, 'isn't it perfect?'

'Yes,' he said gently, 'it's lovely. But we mustn't tempt fate, you know.'

'Nonsense,' she said happily. 'I know it'll be all right.'

He watched helplessly, silently, as Madelaine produced a credit card and the assistant found a bag. 'If only the girl . . .' he muttered.

'What's that, Nico?'

But he waited until they were back in the car, the shop assistant safely out of earshot, before he allowed himself to complete the thought, even under his breath: 'If only the girl hadn't died.'

Alex crept through the scrubby gorse, his body bent

double so that he would show no profile above the horizon. In his hand the deer rifle with the telescopic sights was nearly as long as he was.

He had been hunting the rogue stag for days now, ever since it had attacked Terry. Officially, the season was over, but an exception could always be made for those that had slipped through the cull.

A movement caught his eye over to his right, in a hollow of grass by the edge of the woods. It was too low to be the stag, but it might be a partridge or even a snipe. He found an old sheep track that took him in the right direction, and crept closer.

A man's head, moving. The man's shoulders – all that Alex could see of him – were bare. And there was the girl, suddenly, sitting up, also naked.

He swung the rifle round and rested it on a gorse branch. Through the telescopic sights the couple leapt into focus.

His sister, with a man he hadn't seen before. Her head dipping between his legs, working. The man's hands twisting in her hair.

She swung round to get on top of him. His head buried in her crotch. Her head buried in his. Alex shifted the sights slightly. The delicate crucifix of the cross-hairs swung down the girl's back, then aligned themselves with the cleft between her legs.

'Bang,' he murmured: but very softly, so as not to alert his quarry.

# ELEVEN

My dearest Anne,

I never dreamed that by means of torture a person could be brought to the point of saying such things as I have said. I beseech you, for God's sake, to ask my cousin if he cannot help me. I will pay any price, even if it costs me Babcock itself, for I can see no end but a burning.

Their manner of questioning was, first, to tire their captive out by walking me, under duress of violence, for many hours, and this they call 'walking a witch'. Then they removed me to the torture chamber, and showed me what horrors awaited me. At this I fainted, but was revived roughly, for they said that it was a trick of the devil to escape further questions. And then they placed me on a bench, with iron weights on my legs: this they call the most safe and gentle torture, or no torture at all, so that if I had confessed immediately it would have been called without torture. And then Mr Mann used me roughly about my person, and said that since I had not responded to merciful treatment, I must be brought to the chamber. God save me, but I cannot describe the agonies I was put to there, except to say that I was reminded all the while that this was as nothing compared to what was to come. And in my alarm I said I would tell them what they wanted to know, for my flesh was too feeble and I cared not what I said. And so I was removed to the court, and asked if I confessed freely, whereupon I said that it had not been the truth I spoke, but only what I thought would save my pain; whereupon I was ordered back to the torture chamber on the morrow.

There is someone here who will bring you this letter. Give them threepence.

Catherine

My dearest Anne,

My cousin Hamish has had the proceedings halted, and the witchfinder himself arrested. I am to wait here while their business is concluded. I do not know how long this will be. Let us pray that the intervention you sought was successful.

I am very tired, and may not write much more.

Catherine

My dearest Anne,

Mr Mann is released, and I am bidden to him tomorrow. May God have mercy on my soul.

C

My dearest Anne,

I have tasted the torments of hellfire, and my body burns in them still, tho' it is many days since. O my Anne, what have we done? You must flee, lest I name you – I accede to every name they give me, and they are still not satisfied, and I have had to tell them of my intimate congress with the devil, a thing I could not even have dreamt of saying before I came to this terrible place. Truly I have seen Satan now, and he has the face of Andrew Mann.

My legs are no longer serviceable, from a device they call the boots.

Catherine

My dearest Anne,

I think that this will be the last letter I can write you, and in any case I no longer have a wish to write. For I have confessed all that they need me to confess, and very nearly perished in the telling.

I neither needed nor desired the attentions of any man alive: my desires are other. Yet if I had been married, Babcock might have been saved, and I would willingly have made that choice. My only crime is not to have loved who or how as I should have been more wise, and for that I must be burnt.

I cannot retract my confession without being returned to the chamber, and, in any case, those who die penitent are, by the court's grace, strangled before the fire consumes them, so I shall be penitent. *Esurientes implevit bonis, et divites dimisit inanes.* He hath given good things to the hungry, but the rich He has sent empty away.

Yr. loving Catherine

My dearest Anne,

My trials are now over, and judgement made. My lawyer made a fist of examining the witnesses, but it made no odds, my confession being already known to the court. The girl Mary Tyler is a simple thing, who says she saw me in the doocot surrounded by spirits, having congress with a devil, and that this devil wore a black cape and his head was crowned with horns. She witnessed that my body was laid out like an altar for the devil to cover, and that she saw him do so, and his body was ten feet tall. And on seeing this she ran away, but I caused a storm to rise up that did pursue her all the way home; and many other such fancies, which must have been put into her head by some other person, or perhaps by a pamphlet, such as are sold at the markets.

Mister Turner says I treated him most coldly, and that he found himself unable to speak once in my presence, for which he believed I had used a spell on him: it was after this that his cows went sour.

The court, being a church assembly, may not sentence me, but must hand me over to the Assize. I am told they will ask for mercy, but that I should not be hopeful, for this they do in all cases and without expectation that the Assize may take notice. Indeed, if the Assize judges were to be clement, they would themselves be condemned for their leniency. For only by shewing the utmost vigilance and severity, we are told, will this scourge of witchcraft be exterminated.

They will wait until the signs of the torture are healed, which may be many months. *Non pave carissimus: dies saturnal transit.* Do not fear, my dearest: the days of madness will soon be over, & Scotland shall return to the old ways once more.

Yr. loving Catherine

My dearest Anne,

I have heard your news, and hardly know how to respond. At first I was surprised – I had thought you would flee to France, or better still to England – but on reflection I see the sense of it. Your Mister Hughes is a good man, and I have no doubt will make an excellent husband. I need hardly say that none could be a sweeter wife than yourself. Do not reproach yourself: I could not have borne to see you join me in this place. Tho' I do not deny your presence would have been a comfort, your freedom and future happiness is a greater comfort to me by far.

As it is, I have all the company I need. There are a dozen of us here convicted of the same crime, and in the same manner, tho' some have come to believe that they are guilty of what they have been accused of, because of the tortures they have been put to, which have broken their minds. These unfortunates pray to the devil to save them, saying that since our Lord has not helped them, perhaps his Adversary can.

Today I made a kind of waking vision of you, and it was as wondrous to me as if you were really here. I clasped you to me, and embrac'd you, and felt you solid in my arms. My Anne, do not reproach yourself. You have shewn me that which otherwise would have been hidden from me, so that I should not have known my own true self, and led me down that path where once all was dark. Perhaps only women can know such things, for our natures are open to ecstasy as men's are not. Enough of this. I am writing foolish things.

O sweet and terrible were the cries of thy passion, yet I cried with thee, for my passion was as thine.

Yr. loving Catherine

Terry lifted her eyes from the manuscript and exhaled thoughtfully. There it was: the nearest she was likely to get to concrete proof of Catherine's sexual orientation. *You have shewn me that which otherwise would have been hidden from me, so that I should not have known my own true self.* It was clearly Anne, not Catherine, who had initiated the love affair. *For our natures are open to ecstasy as men's are not.* Not just a platonic friendship, either: this was a full-blooded sexual relationship. *O sweet and terrible were the cries of thy passion, yet I cried with thee, for my passion was as thine.*

For a few minutes she remained like that, staring at the letter in her hand. The book, she saw now, could be much more than just an edition of the papers. It was a love story as well as a tragedy. She could shape it as a sort of double biography, with a section on Anne's early life as well as on Catherine's. Indeed, Anne might well become the more interesting figure. What had happened to her afterwards? Did she ever have children? Was there any evidence of relationships with other women?

Quickly she made some notes, then turned to a letter written in a different hand:

> To my most esteemed cousin Duncan McCulloch. Sir, I have the honour to report to you that I was present at the execution of our cousin Cath. McCulloch, late of Babcock, and witnessed the melancholy manner in which she met her end.
>
> On the morning a crowd was summoned to the sheep market by the sound of bells, which had been wrapped in wet cloth, as is the custom. These muffled bells make a mournful sound, so

that the populace immediately know when a burning is imminent, rather than some other occasion. A holiday having been declared, a great number were already gathered, which included many children with their mothers, while jugglers and men with food went amongst them, so that it was more like a fair or a feast day than any solemn event, which did not please me; but I was informed that it is always so.

A huge fire had been kindled in front of the church, to which after an hour or more of waiting came the cart in which our cousin was held. Its progress was much impeded by the throng, who shouted at her and shook the sides of the cart; not in anger as I saw, but as a kind of joke, for I witnessed many people laughing. And then a priest called for silence, and an indictment was made, which I being too far off could not at first hear; but making my way towards him, understood him to say that a witch is burnt for two reasons: namely, that the evil that is in them be destroyed, and also that it signifies the eternal agonies which are prepared for them in Hell. At this our cousin did cross herself, and seemed to speak a prayer, which drew some shouting from the crowd.

Her confession then was read aloud, which took some time. For she had confessed not only to being a witch, and making magic spells amongst her coven, but also to a pact with the devil, wherein she did renounce her baptism, and all the merits of Jesus Christ and his saints, and that she trampled underfoot the sacraments of the church. And that she honoured her new master with an obscene kiss upon his arse, and had intercourse with him on many occasions, and many other offences too numerous to recount here. And several times the lady did seem to shake her head, or protest that it was not so; but when the charge was complete, and she was asked if it was a true confession, and if she truly did repent her sins, she answered, 'Truly, that is the confession that I made, and truly I do renounce my sins, as any person should.' Which answer satisfying the priest, he said that she died penitent. A hymn was then struck up, which together with the tolling of the muffled bells did make a melancholy accompaniment to the events which now took place. While the crowd sang piously, the executioner got up behind her on a ladder, and strangled her with a length of cord; at which a kind of low groan went up among the crowd, as if it were they, and not she, that were expiring. And then her body was put to the fire, and a flame fetched from the candles on the altar of the church, so that there was soon a merry blaze. The crowd did not stay to see her body consumed, as I did, witnessing that the flesh burned with a green flame. And so she died, a terrible burning, and the ashes from the fire were later swept into the drains.

I have the honour to be, sir,
Ham. McCulloch

So Hamish, at any rate, had survived, though not as master of Babcock as he had hoped to be. *A terrible burning.* What a title! *A Terrible Burning:*

# TWELVE

'Don't you ever knock?' she said curtly.

'It's my house,' he said, puzzled. Terry sighed, realizing that he probably had a point.

'Getting anywhere?' he asked.

She hated sharing what she'd found, but he had a right to know. 'Yes. From what I've read, they were lovers. It was Anne who seduced Catherine, not the other way round. Then, when Catherine was being tortured, Anne accepted an offer of marriage in order to keep herself safe. It doesn't say so in the letters, but I'll be willing to bet that the man she married was rich and influential enough to make sure that she didn't get pulled into the net.' A thought struck her. 'In fact, this whole story may really be about Anne, not Catherine. I thought that Catherine might have been accused by this man Turner because he was a failed suitor for her hand in marriage, but of course that couldn't have been the case – a peasant farmer would never have aspired to marry the mistress of Babcock. I bet Anne rejected him: beautiful Anne, the humble servant who became a great lady's inseparable companion. He probably thought he could get Catherine out of the way with this witchcraft thing, and then move in on Anne. Or perhaps he was just so hurt at the rejection he wanted revenge.' She had got up from the table now and was pacing up and down the room, snapping her fingers excitedly as she talked. 'I know – he blamed Catherine for giving Anne airs above her station. He may even have genuinely thought she'd become enthralled by her, and called it witchcraft.'

'Hmm,' Magnus said. 'Got any proof?'

'No,' she admitted. 'Why? Is there something wrong?'

'It's just that if you haven't already made up your mind, I thought you might be interested in an alternative interpretation of the Catherine McCulloch story.'

'What do you mean?'

He showed her a book. 'You know you asked me to dig out anything we had by John Mcteer? I found this in one of the bookcases upstairs.'

It was a thin, hardbound edition, the typeface identifying it immediately as a product of the early part of the century. '*The Black Arts in Scotland*,' she read. 'Published by the Shadowcourt Press.'

'Chapter seven. I've marked the page.'

Frowning, she sat down and began to read.

What modern man scathingly refers to as 'black' magic or sorcery would once have been familiar to this island's inhabitants as no more than the ordinary worship of the pantheistic deities of Nature. For, prior to the Roman occupation, Great Britain (or Albion, the White Island, as it was then known) was the headquarters of an organized fertility religion whose influence extended throughout Western Europe; its practitioners being called 'Wicca' (a wise woman, or witch) and 'Wiglaer' (wizard).

There are many relics of this mysterious fraternity in the British Isles, particularly amongst those parts not conquered by the Latin. Nor should we imagine these traces to be only architectural – stone circles, folk carvings and the like – for the Old Religion was itself able to coexist, albeit covertly, with the Judaeo-Egyptian rites of the invader. Of this proposition, we have several proofs. For many centuries after the Saxon population's enforced conversion, bishops were obliged to commission books of penances condemning those who practised paganism. In the eighth century Archbishop Ecbert of York condemned the making of offerings to devils, i.e. the Old Gods, as well as swearing vows at trees, wells and stones, and the gathering of herbs using non-Christian invocations. And as late as the eleventh century King Canute was obliged to issue a law against those who 'worship heathen gods, and the sun and the moon, or forest trees of any sort, or who love witchcraft'.

With the rise of Islam in the East and growing intellectual scepticism in the West, by the thirteenth century the Christian Church believed itself to be under threat and – for the first time – formally declared witchcraft to be a heresy; in other words, a creation of the devil and practised by his followers, as distinct from mere superstition. Over the next four centuries over 200,000 people in Europe were executed for this crime. Many of these were undoubtedly guilty of nothing more than a lack of piety and an inability to conform to social norms; perhaps a few were genuinely worshippers of the Antichrist (for it was a time when the Christian Church spawned many strange sects); but it is only reasonable to suppose that a good proportion were followers of the Old Religion, the same earth-worshipping cult that had certainly survived in England from the Roman occupation until the twelfth century, and which might therefore be supposed to have lasted from the twelfth to the seventeenth in the same manner.

If we seek further evidence that many so-called witches were in fact adherents of an ancient mystery cult, we can do no better than examine more closely the witchcraft trials of seventeenth-century Scotland, for northern Scotia was never part of the Roman occupation; and indeed north of Aberdeen was unconquered even by the English until Cromwell's brief interregnum. In particular, there are the confessions of Isobel Gowdie in 1662, Mary Fell in 1671 and Catherine McCulloch in 1698.

To take the latter first, Catherine McCulloch was accused by one Joseph Turner, a local farmer, and despite being of noble birth, was taken to trial and submitted to the usual grisly inducements: squassation, strappado, thumb-screws and the rest. That she confessed is therefore hardly remarkable; but what is perhaps more interesting are the details of her confession, which, if invented, show a remarkable similarity to other accounts of the Craft. She claimed to have been part of a coven consisting of thirteen members, whose rites took place in a magic circle some nine feet in diameter, and in front of an altar consecrated to the spirits of air, earth, wind and fire. In this circle there appeared two demon figures: a Horned God, whom she called the devil but whom modern readers will readily identify as the Saxon deity Cerrunos, or Cerne; and a beautiful young demoness, his bride, who was introduced to the company as Lilith or Aradia. In Christian daemonology Lilith was the first mate of Adam, who rejected him in order to consort with demons. She was believed to steal upon mortal couples having intercourse, in order to steal a few drops of semen with which to inseminate herself and bring forth more of her kind. Catherine herself admitted to having intercourse with these spirits: the *membrum virile* of the devil, she claimed, was much larger than that of a human man, but his seed was as cold as ice. As the union of god and human took place the coven would chant the following rune:

As is the moon, so is the sun;
That which is above is like that which is below,
And that which is below is like that which is
above,
Blessed in union to achieve the wonders of the
One.

This wording, of course, is virtually identical to that found in the *Corpus Hermeticum* of Hermes Trismegistus, the ancient cabbalistic manuscript which was brought back from Constantinople by the Knights Templar, and which the occultist and scholar Cosimo de Medici purchased for his library in Florence. The fact that Catherine herself confessed to intercourse with the Horned God suggests that this was a dramatic or shamanistic religion, in which coven members took the place of the deities themselves, perhaps whilst under the influence of certain burning herbs, orgiastic dancing and the liberal use of the scourge.

It seems likely that one member of the coven was Catherine's companion, Anne de Courcy, who mysteriously escaped arrest herself. Indeed it may have been Anne de Courcy who initiated Catherine into the mysteries of the Craft, for on one occasion the latter wrote to Anne:

> You have shewn me that which would otherwise have been hidden from me, so that I should not have known my own true self.

Despite the occasional pious references to Christian doctrine – no doubt inserted lest the letters be read by any other than their intended recipient – they contain quotations from what seems to be a fully worked out and elaborate pagan ritology. One letter contains this haunting Charge, or invocation:

> O lovely and gracious Goddess of the night,
> Mistress of the moon, mother of all light,
> I stand in awe and worship thee.
> Come to me now, that I may blessed be.

This is followed by a version of the famous Wiccan Five-Fold Kiss:

> Blessed be thy feet, which have trodden in the ways of beauty.
> Blessed be thy womb, without which we would not be.
> Blessed be thy breasts, that suckle in sweetness.
> Blessed be thy lips, that shall speak the sacred names.
> Blessed be thy eyes, that shall adore and be adored.

Indeed, a close reading of Catherine McCulloch's letters, pocket book and other writings would enable a patient scholar, if he so wished, to reconstruct many of the rituals and observances of the Old Religion that have since been lost.

The confession of Isobel Gowdie is more well-known, but bears repeating here . . .

'Well?' Magnus demanded.

'If you ignore the bombastic style,' she said slowly, 'it's actually a perfectly respectable thesis. In fact, it isn't even particularly original. Robert Graves advanced much the same argument in a book called *The White Goddess*, as did an anthropologist called Margaret Murray in the 1920s.'

Magnus snorted. 'He's claiming that witches really do exist – that Catherine McCulloch was one – and you're calling that *respectable*?'

'Well, he's not saying she was a witch in the traditional sense,' Terry pointed out. 'What he's saying is that she might have been a member of a pagan religion that somehow survived in the Highlands for over a thousand years. Your local Wiccans would say much the same thing, if you asked them.'

'Just another nutter, then,' Magnus began to close the book but she stopped him.

'That's what's so interesting. Graves and Murray never claimed to be doing anything other than constructing a workable hypothesis – they *believed* that seventeenth-century witches were part of an unbroken tradition of paganism, but they never found any proof. Mcteer seems to be suggesting that he's got first-hand evidence, but, if that's the case, where is it? Most of those quotations don't come from anything I've transcribed, and I'd lay odds I haven't missed something. And what on earth was that reference to Catherine's "pocket-book and other writings"?' She drummed her fingers on the table impatiently. 'Either he's making it all up. Or else he did find some evidence that Catherine really was a witch, and he stole it.'

'The former, most probably. The man's clearly off his rocker.'

'Yes,' she said doubtfully.

'What's bothering you?'

'It's just that . . . there are one or two references in the letters I can't explain. Like this for example.' She found the penultimate letter and read from the end of it. ' "*Non pave carissimus: dies saturnalis transit.*" I've translated that roughly as, "Do not fear my dearest: the days of madness will soon be over." And she goes on to say "Scotland will return to the old ways once more." '

'So?'

'It can be read two ways. Either, Scotland will return to the way it was before the witch trials, *or*,

146

Scotland will return to the Old Ways, the religion it had before Christianity. Do you see?'

'Now you're starting to sound like Mcteer.'

'The thing is, why put that particular phrase into Latin? Most of the Latin tags are quotations from the Bible. So far as I can tell, that one isn't. Did Catherine feel she needed to conceal it from the eyes of whoever was acting as a go-between? And there's all this stuff about "seeking intervention" and "you will know what I mean". It's almost as if there's a subtext – some kind of secret she barely needs to refer to, because she knows Anne will understand the allusions.'

Magnus picked up Mcteer's book and thumbed to the very end. 'There's more, I'm afraid. Take a look at this.'

She glanced at the page he showed her.

### ADVERTISEMENT

The author wishes to advise all interested parties that he intends to instigate a discussion group of not more than twelve serious students, to investigate all aspects of esoteric lore and practice. This group shall hold its meetings in Scotland, and shall include a close study of the Cabbala, the *Corpus Hermeticum*, the occult writings of Catherine McCulloch and other important texts. All those wishing to submit themselves for consideration should contact the author care of the publishers.

'Good Lord. He's recruiting a coven.'

Magnus nodded. 'Twelve students, plus himself. Thirteen in all. That's the magic number, isn't it?'

She thought hard. 'So if there really are any occult writings by Catherine, and he pinched them, the coven might still have them.'

'If they're still going.'

'Well,' she said slowly, 'I reckon they might be. Your Wiccan community up the road – I think that's the direct descendant of the coven Mcteer set up. That would be why they bought – what's it called? – Nineveh Farm. Because of its link with Anne de Courcy.' What had the camp bookseller said? 'They don't call it a funeral, but you know what I mean.' 'They' could only be the Wiccans. 'Magnus – could I borrow the Land Rover? I think I need to pay a visit to this Nineveh place.'

Iain moved through the gloom of the death pit as if wading underwater, his breath noisy through the mouthpiece of the mask. Day by day, as his excavation continued, the level of the pig corpses was sinking, foot by foot, as if the whole rotting mass was slowly being drained out of some sink-hole at the bottom of the pit.

A gesture above him caught his eye. Talbot, his handkerchief clasped to his face against the stench, was waving at him from the top of the pit. Iain acknowledged the gesture, and waded cumbersomely to the ladder which led back to the surface.

When he was at the top he pulled the mask off and sucked clean air deep into his lungs before answering the SIO's question.

'It's going fine. Slowly, as you can see, but at least if we do find anything it will definitely be admissible.'

'Getting pretty revolting down there, I should think?'

Iain frowned. 'That's the odd thing. You'd expect

the pig corpses to be more decomposed the lower we go, but if anything the reverse is true. I don't know why. Something to do with the soil type of the surrounding walls, maybe.'

Talbot produced a transparent folder. 'I've been meaning to show you this. See if you can help us identify it.'

He peeled off his gloves before taking it. Inside the folder, protected by the clear plastic, was a single page of manuscript. 'Where's it from?'

'Donna Fairhead's rucksack. I was hoping you could tell us a bit more about it.'

Iain examined it curiously. 'Well, my speciality is bones, not books. But it's obviously old. Let's have a look – it was written with a quill pen: you can see where the nib was bending on the upstrokes. So earlier than the nineteenth century. But it's paper rather than vellum, so you're talking, oh, later than 1600. Other than that, you'd have to consult a specialist.'

'Is it valuable?'

'Depends what's on it.' He squinted through the plastic. '*My dearest Anne*. Something something something. *How can I ever repay your love and kindness? You are truly the most devoted* something. *I must warn you* . . . Sorry, can't read this next bit. *I shall write when it is time – it could be any day now – be ready.*' He shrugged. 'At a guess, it's probably worth a couple of hundred quid. But I can probably put you in touch with someone who knows a bit more.'

'Thanks. I'd appreciate that.'

'You think it might have something to do with the murder?'

'Probably not. She had all sorts of bits and pieces

in there. But we ought to check it out.' He nodded at the death pit. 'Better let you get back to work, then.'

'Sure. Any progress on that fingertip search?'

'I was rather hoping you were going to say you didn't need it now.'

Iain shook his head. 'No such luck, I'm afraid.'

'I'll organize it for Monday,' Talbot promised, as Iain started to climb back down the ladder.

# THIRTEEN

The lane to Nineveh Farm took Terry round the other side of the mountain, past fields bordered by ancient herringbone stone walls where lambs bucked and pranced like aspiring rodeo stars, and a new-born colt, its legs as long and unsteady as a dragonfly's, lowered itself gingerly to its mother's teat. Eventually the farmhouse itself came into view, a solid building three storeys high. The gravel that led to the door was thick with weeds. Over the lintel someone had painted the words: *Eight simple words the Wiccan rede fulfil: an ye harm none, do what ye will.* She pulled on the rusty doorchain. Somewhere deep inside the house a bell rang.

After an age she rang it again. Evidently there was no-one home. Then she heard footsteps striding impatiently to the door. It opened, and a young man about her own age stood there.

'Yes?' he demanded.

'I'd like to speak to someone who knew John Mcteer,' she said politely.

'Why?' The young man looked her up and down. 'Were you a friend of his?'

'No, I'm doing some research—'

'Piss off, then.' He started to close the door but she reached out a hand to stop him. 'I only want—' He pulled the door open again so that her hand fell inside, against the door jamb, and immediately slammed it. She got her wrist out of the way just as the solid oak crashed shut.

'Jesus!' She kicked the wood. 'You fucking moron! You could have broken my arm.'

'Piss off. We don't talk to journalists,' she heard his retreating voice shout back.

'I'm not a fucking journalist.' There was no answer. The inscription above the door caught her eye again. 'And what's all this bullshit about not harming anyone? I thought you people were meant to practise what you preach.'

A window above her opened. His head stuck out, along with an arm that was holding something small and white: a bowl or a dish of some sort. 'I'm the resident heretic,' he said, and tipped the bowl. Small black things tumbled and fluttered towards her. An ashtray. The bastard was emptying his stubbed-out fags on her. She leapt out of the way, cursing him, and he laughed. Then the window slammed shut again.

Back at Babcock, to add to her annoyance, some guests had arrived. Three Hooray Henrys in their early twenties, in the Highlands for the fishing and shooting, as one of them – either Johnny or Harry: they were all three pretty much interchangeable – insisted on telling her at great length. Bored out of her mind, she was nodding politely when she saw his eyes drift away and fix on something over her shoulder. She turned. Flora was walking past in a tiny yellow bikini. Well, there's a coincidence, Terry thought. She cleared her throat, and Johnny/Harry swung his startled gaze back to her.

'Hoping to bag any birds while you're here?' she said sweetly.

The library, from having been a quiet place to work, was now full of fishing rods and nets and strange industrial-looking knives, and people discussing the relative merits of Hairy Marys and Stripey Shaggers, which she took to be different kinds of flies. She unplugged her laptop and took it, and the remaining letters, upstairs to her bedroom.

The truth was, there was little for her to do now. The last letters were mundane business missives to the estate workers: ultimately they would have to be transcribed, but they were clearly of no use in solving the mystery of Catherine's relationship with Anne. She had to find some other way of finding out what Mcteer had stolen.

The sister. Russell Kane had mentioned a sister, though he didn't know the address. But *she* had an address – Mcteer had put one on the letter he'd written to the lawyer. Here it was: 1 Belham Avenue, Stour. If the sister had inherited the house ... At any rate, it was worth a try.

Magnus was busy playing the country host to his chortling gang of groupies in the library. She paused by the door to listen. 'I was trying to do a Macnab – which means taking a stag, a salmon and a brace of grouse on the same day. No easy feat, I can tell you.' She smiled and passed on. The keys were in the Land Rover, so she took it.

One Belham Avenue was a tiny terraced house built of blackened stone on the outskirts of the little market town. Terry knocked, and identified herself and her mission to a tiny white-haired lady, so stooped with arthritis she could only look up at Terry over the top of her glasses. Terry sat patiently in the sitting room while Sheila Mcteer made a pot of tea, whiling away the time by looking at the photographs which dotted the little room. Many were of a tall, thin man with an aggressively jutting goatee beard. She had picked one up to examine it more closely when Sheila returned with a tray.

'Yes, that's John. He preferred the ones where he was wearing his robes and things, but I don't, I'm afraid. I made most of them, you know, and I couldn't help seeing my old curtains.'

'You're a Wiccan too?'

The old lady tutted. 'Oh no. I never got into all that. John wouldn't have wanted me to. It was a bit, well, scandalous in those days. Nowadays, of course, nobody thinks twice about anything, do they, but then—' She suddenly stopped and peered at Terry doubtfully. 'It wasn't you who came before, was it?'

'No. Before when?'

'Somebody came to see me last year. A nice young girl. I just thought for a moment I might be repeating myself.'

Terry suddenly had a moment's panic about her thesis. If someone else was covering the same material, and registered their work first, hers would be null and void. 'An academic?'

'I don't think so. Well, she didn't say. I assumed she was one of his lot. She had a tattoo thing here.' Sheila Mcteer pointed at her shoulder. 'I must say, she was very polite.'

'What did she want?' Terry asked casually.

'She wanted to see if there were any papers John

154

had left that might help her. She was writing a history of the coven, I think. I told her I thought if there were any they would already be at Nineveh, but she had a quick look anyway. I made her give me a receipt.'

'A receipt? So she did find something?'

Sheila looked flustered. 'No, I – well, I can't remember. Perhaps she must have done.'

'Could I see this receipt?'

Terry got to her feet impatiently while the old lady pottered around looking in drawers and inside books. Eventually she found something in a drawer underneath the telephone. 'Here it is.' She held it up to her face, and tugged at her glasses to bring it into focus.

'May I?' Terry held out her hand. ' "Received from the study of John Mcteer. Three letters. D. Fairhead." ' Donna Fairhead: the dead girl. Now here was a puzzle. 'Can I take a look at his study?'

'Yes, of course.' Sheila took the receipt from her and carefully put it back exactly where she had been unable to locate it before. 'It's through here, at the back.'

Terry followed her into a tiny room, barely big enough for the Forties desk and revolving chair that were crammed into it. A cheap bookcase was perched on the windowsill. Terry scanned the titles. *Religion And The Decline of Magic. The Witch-Cult in Western Europe. The White Goddess. A History of the Jacobite Movement in Scotland.* No surprises there, but many were first editions. If Donna Fairhead had just been scavenging, she'd have tried to take some of these as well. She must have been after something specific.

As was she. 'I was wondering', she said, looking around her, 'whether you'd come across any old papers your brother might have had. I'm doing some work for the McCulloch family, in Babcock. John archived some of their old documents, and we think he may have borrowed some.'

Sheila looked worried. 'No. Well, there *was* some old stuff, but he took it all to Nineveh. After he died, some of it was buried with him – he asked for that, I think.'

'Buried with him? That's a bit unusual isn't it?'

'Most of what John did was unusual, dear.'

Well, that was one avenue closed. Terry gestured at the drawers of the desk. 'May I take a look? I won't disturb anything.'

'If you like.' Sheila was looking increasingly anxious. She probably thinks I'm going to pinch something, Terry thought: talk about bolting the stable door. It irked her that Donna Fairhead had clearly done a much better job of charming the old biddy than she was managing.

Under Sheila's watchful eye, Terry rifled through the contents of the desk. There was a drawer of fat old Parker pens, their caps clotted with dried ink. Blotting paper. Reporter's notepads. A portable typewriter, its semicircle of letters like an old man's toothless grin. An ancient stapler and a device for punching holes in foolscap paper. Keys, mostly unlabelled. A stubby glass bottle of Quink. The journal of the Scottish Philological Society, 1947–54. A few blue folders full of press cuttings and black-and-white photographs. She pulled out a sheet at random. John Mcteer, wearing a rather silly hat decorated with astrological symbols. Some spools from a portable reel-to-reel tape recorder. A yellow box of Kodak slides. Page proofs from one of his books, annotated with old typographer's marks.

Nothing of any interest. Damn. She slid the drawer shut and prepared to take her leave.

Lying on the lawn with a copy of *Mizz*, Flora heard a low whistle. She looked up. Andy was standing by the big oak at the end of the lawn. She jumped up and went over. 'What are you doing here?' she hissed.

'Charming. I thought you'd be pleased.'

'I am. But Dad'll see you.' She glanced across at the open French windows of the library. 'We've got guests at the moment.'

'Oh yeah?' Andy tucked his finger under the edge of the bikini top and ran it down her breast. 'This for their benefit, is it?'

She squirmed. 'No!' she pouted. He took his hand away and she said, 'I meant no it's not for them. Not, no stop.'

'I wasn't going to,' he said, taking a step closer. She smelt the beer on his breath. His rough hands slid down her back and pulled her towards him, out of sight of the house. 'What's this, then?' His hands had found the magazine. He grabbed it from her and flipped it open. ' "Ten top tips for oral sex"? Hey. Smutty.'

Flora giggled. 'Give it back!' But he held it above her head, just out of her reach. She jumped for it and he caught her wrist with his other hand, holding her still. 'Better see what you've learned, then, hadn't we?'

'We can't. Not here.'

'Can. And I'm warning you. I won't be satisfied with that much longer.' He caught hold of her other wrist too. Her arms were so tiny he could pin them both behind her back with just one of his own hands, trapping her, feeling the way she wriggled powerlessly against him. 'I want the real thing.'

'Not now,' she said. 'Tomorrow. I promise we'll do it tomorrow.'

# FOURTEEN

The room had been warmed beforehand with a portable heater: there was more warmth coming from the twenty-seven candles that marked out the Great Circle on the floor, and from the dozen or so robed figures who stood just outside it. Alone in the centre of the circle, Isobel let her robe fall to the floor. Underneath she was naked. Closing her eyes, she took a deep breath – not because she was shy about being sky-clad: on the contrary, Gerard had made it clear that one of the reasons he had chosen her, rather than his handfasted partner, Brigid, as the priestess tonight was that Isobel, at twenty-four, more nearly approximated to the perfect comeliness of the Goddess than his sixty-year-old wife – but because it was her first full rite as Priestess, and it was important to control all her psychic energies before she started.

After a few moments she heard the sound of rustling cloth as the other members followed her example and disrobed. She opened her eyes, and found herself looking straight into the eyes of Gerard. She lowered her gaze, then rather wished she hadn't. It was all very well for him, seeing her as the Goddess, but trying to accept that his ancient, sagging flesh was the incarnation of Cerrunos, the young and virile Horned God, required a rather greater leap of the imagination.

On the altar at her back were all the tools of the ritual – the chalice, a scourge of silken cords, her athame with its black handle and silver blade, a bowl of water, a bowl of salt and the pentacle. She picked up the knife and felt its tip with her thumb. Time to begin. In a low, clear voice, still heavily inflected with the accent of her native Massachusetts, she called:

> Cast the Circle thrice about,
> To keep malicious spirits out.

As she spoke she walked three times around the circle, invoking a wall in the air.

> Cast the Circle three times round,
> To consecrate this magic ground.

Approaching Gerard, she welcomed him into the circle with a kiss. His beard scratched her cheek, and rather to her surprise she caught a faint whiff of aftershave. Her nose wrinkled. The real Cerrunos, she felt sure, did not wear aftershave.

Gerard had turned to the woman behind him, and welcomed her into the circle with a kiss: she did the same to the man behind her, and he in turn to the next woman, until all of them were inside the circle, alternating male and female, facing her. Because they were a woman short, Jamie and Alan had to stand next to each other. Both looked a touch sullen – like two boys, Isobel thought, made to partner at a dance. She wondered if Alan had noticed that Jamie was better hung.

For a moment the contrast between the solemn faces around her and the dangling genitalia below seemed so absurd she almost giggled. *Concentrate*, she told herself severely. She wished she could be like Brigid, who carried out all her rituals with a serene half-smile on her face, completely unselfconscious.

Turning to face each quarter of the circle in turn, Isobel chanted:

> *I turn to the East and summon the air.*
> *I turn to the South and summon the fire.*
> *I turn to the West and summon the water.*
> *I turn to the North and summon the earth.*

There. She'd done the Quarters rather well, she thought: just the right mixture of dramatic excitement and easy familiarity. Taking up his cue, Gerard added sonorously:

> *Ye Lords of the watchtowers, immortal spirits, we do summon, stir and call you up, to witness our rites and to guard the Circle.*

As he spoke he invoked the sign of the pentagram in the air. Then he knelt before her.

> *Blessed be thy feet, which have trodden in the*
> *    ways of beauty.*
> *Blessed be thy womb, without which we would*
> *    not be.*
> *Blessed be thy breasts, that suckle in sweetness.*
> *Blessed be thy lips, that shall speak the sacred*
> *    names.*
> *Blessed be thy eyes, that shall adore and be*
> *    adored.*

Was it Isobel's imagination, or did he linger fractionally longer when he kissed her womb and breasts than when he kissed her feet?

She caught sight of Judith, who looked anxious. Isobel smiled at her encouragingly, but the other woman seemed not to notice. Her forehead was shiny with sweat, and she was rocking slightly from side to side. Isobel's smile turned into a frown. She hoped Judith wasn't going to spoil everything by going into a trance or anything attention-seeking like that.

> *I invoke thee and call upon thee, mysterious mother of us all, bringer of all fruitfulness: by seed and root, by bud and stem, by leaf and flower I invoke thee. Voluptuous virgin, bride of the world, descend upon the body of this thy servant,*

Gerard was saying, touching his right forefinger to each of her breasts in turn.

It was happening for Isobel now. The self-consciousness and the urge to giggle were gone. She was part of the ceremony, caught up in its rhythms. Quietly she said:

> *O lovely and gracious goddess of the night,*
> *Mistress of the moon, mother of all light,*
> *We stand in awe and worship thee.*
> *Come to us now, that we may blessed be.*

'Blessed be,' she heard the others mumble in response.

Isobel was herself, but she was not herself, for now she was Aradia, the White Goddess, whose beauty and terror men had worshipped since the beginning of time. She inhaled deeply, feeling the goddess's energy flow into her. She informed them:

> I am the mysterious mother of all,
> Virgin bride, fair and tall.
> All who adore
> Let them do so in awe.

The Goddess having been drawn down, the God was next to be summoned. When he was safely ensconced in Gerard's form, Isobel-Aradia turned to the assembled coven:

> Whenever ye have need of any thing, once in the month, and better it be when the moon is full, then ye shall assemble in some secret place and adore the spirit of me, who am Queen of all witches. There ye shall assemble, ye who are fain to learn all sorcery, yet have not won its deepest secrets; to these will I teach things that are yet unknown. And ye shall be free from slavery; and as a sign that ye be really free, ye shall be naked in your rites; and ye shall dance, sing, make music and love, all in my praise. I am the gracious Goddess, who gives the gift of joy unto the heart of man. Upon earth, I give knowledge of the spirit eternal; and beyond death, I give peace. Nor do I demand aught in sacrifice; for behold, I am the mother of all living, and my love is poured out upon the earth.

Raising his arms high above his head, Gerard said:

*Bagahai laca bachahe*
*Lamac cahi achabahe*
*Karrelyos*
*Lamac lamec bachalyos*
*Harrahya!*

'Harrahya!' repeated the coven. Taking each other's hands, they danced in a circle, and as they danced they chanted:

*Eko, Eko, Azerak,*
*Eko, Eko, Zomelak,*
*Eko, Eko Cerrunos,*
*Eko, Eko Aradia.*

Over and over again they chanted it, while Isobel let go of the hand in front of her and led the dancers into the Spiral Dance, weaving the coven in and out of itself like a snake. At last, when their bodies were pink with exertion and glistening with sweat – when Brigid led the dance it was performed at a rather more stately pace, but Isobel saw no reason why they shouldn't be a bit more energetic now she was in charge: dancing was a good way of unlocking etheric power – she shouted: '*Down!*'

The coven dropped to the ground and sat in a ring, facing her.

Isobel herself lay down in the centre of the circle, her arms and legs outstretched to form the pentagram. Gerard stood beside her, scourge in one hand and knife in the other.

'*How do we come to this mysterious altar?*' he demanded.

'*In perfect love and perfect trust,*' came the answer.

164

'*If there be any here who are not so,*' he said, '*let them speak, so we shall know.*'

Isobel felt it first as a psychic disturbance, a change in the pure silver light she envisioned flowing out from her. It seemed to darken momentarily – almost, she told the others later, like a faulty connection. Then she felt something snap, and the goddess energy seemed to wither. She opened her eyes. Someone was shrieking, and since she couldn't see very much with her head on the floor, she sat up.

It was Judith. She seemed to be having some kind of sobbing fit. Brigid had rushed to support her – literally as well as emotionally: Judith's knees were sagging and she would have fallen had it not been for the older woman's arm.

'What's wrong with her?' someone asked.

'Come and sit down,' Brigid said, trying to lead Judith away.

Judith struggled free. 'I'm not perfect,' she shrieked.

The coven was nonplussed. 'We're none of us literally perfect,' Gerard began, before he too was silenced by a look from Brigid.

'You don't understand,' Judith said, sobbing. 'I killed her. I'm the one who killed her.'

'Come with me,' Brigid said decisively. She led the hysterical woman away.

'Don't break the circle!' Isobel called.

Brigid shot her an angry glance. 'You silly, foolish girl,' she snapped. 'You're the priestess, you deal with it.' Isobel bit her lip.

When they had gone there was silence. Now that she was no longer clothed in the aura of the Goddess, Isobel suddenly felt very naked. She went and found her robe and put it on. One by one the others did the same.

'We should go on with the ritual,' Alan said nervously.

'We can't. The circle has been broken,' Gerard said. He turned to Isobel. 'Brigid's right. You have to heal the circle.'

Isobel was wondering whether Brigid had really meant it when she called her a silly foolish girl. 'How do I do that?'

'Open it and close it again.'

Isobel did as she was told, miming the cutting of a doorway in the circle and then closing it again.

'Now the blessing.'

Isobel said,

> Witches all, our night is ended,
> The spirits are departed into their strange lands.
> To all who have this rite attended,
> I place this blessing in your hands.
> In turn my rune keep in your heart:
> Merry meet and merry part.

'Yeah, *merry meet and merry part*,' muttered Jamie. He was the only one who spoke. The others filed silently out, leaving Isobel to banish the circle, blow out the candles, and contemplate the ruin of her first Great Rite.

# FIFTEEN

Magnus parked his Land Rover between a gleaming black Mercedes and a TVR and got out, slamming the door savagely. His mood on the way up the mountain had become increasingly taciturn. Terry guessed that parties at the homes of wealthy incomers were not high on his list of favourite occupations. She herself hadn't helped by her reaction to the mauve-and-yellow kilt in which he had, somewhat alarmingly, appeared just before they set off.

'There's no need to smirk,' he said crossly. 'This is the tartan of the McCullochs. It's an honour to wear it.'

'Where I come from it would be a bloody embarrassment, but then I'm just a simple Sassenach,' she assured him. 'Anyway, didn't you tell me the other day that kilts were an invention of the Victorian tourist industry?'

He shrugged non-committally.

'Oh, I get it. You're just wearing it to wind up David Nicolaides, aren't you? A visible reminder that you're the laird and he isn't.'

'Would I be that petty?'

'Do I even need to answer that?'

She herself was rather regretting the severity with which she'd thinned out her travelling wardrobe. She hadn't thought to bring any of her party clothes up from London, and the trouser suit she'd included, just in case Mo was right and Babcock Castle turned out to be the kind of place where you had to dress for dinner, was way too middle-aged for drinks at a millionaire's. In the end she settled for interesting rather than sophisticated: a cotton jacket with no shirt under it, a short skirt and Timberlands. Magnus's eyes narrowed when he saw her – he'd only seen her in jeans until now – though all he said was: 'The Highland air seems to be doing you good.' Flora, who was also coming to the party, was in her usual midriff-exposing club gear.

David Nicolaides might not be the laird of Babcock, but he'd certainly got the better house. Long and low, framed against a stunning backdrop of moorland and mountains, it was built of stones so dark and old they appeared almost black in the evening twilight. A small helicopter was parked ostentatiously at one end of the row of cars.

The door was opened by a woman, evidently one of the local hired help, who greeted Magnus warmly. Terry took a few steps inside, looked around her and whistled.

Brutal girders of polished steel soared upwards, supporting three levels of walkways and rooms. The staircase was made of concrete, with fine threads of tensioned steel as rails. Here and there bits of medieval wall stood in the middle of the white-carpeted space, made more dramatic by their structural redundancy. No attempt had been made to soften the collision of ancient and modern, but somehow the whole worked perfectly. It was, Terry thought, a very unBritish piece of design.

'Hideous, isn't it?' Magnus murmured in her ear. 'It was a ruin when his father bought it. Somehow they bribed the conservation people into letting them perpetrate this nonsense instead of restoring it properly.'

'I think it's beautiful,' Terry said honestly.

Magnus shrugged. 'Each to his own. But just look at that carpet. Whoever heard of a white carpet in the Highlands? You can tell the Nicolaides don't have kids. A pair of muddy wellies would make mincemeat of that.'

'And not a stag's head in sight,' Terry murmured.

Flora immediately wandered off towards a group of equally moody-looking teenagers, while Magnus was surrounded by a gang of his own cronies. After a while, under the guise of getting another drink, she took the opportunity to wander off and inspect the house. It had been designed as a series of spaces which flowed into each other seamlessly, not quite open-plan but neither quite a series of rooms. The whole of the ground floor was full of people, their needs attended to by a dozen or so waiters who were circulating with trays of champagne and whisky. Terry accepted a glass of whisky – not to play up to the dyke stereotype: she really did prefer scotch to champagne – topped it up with a little still water, and found that it was one of the soft, peaty Islay malts, a distant tang of sea-mist mellowed by age. Nicolaides treated his guests well.

The walls were covered in original works of art, many of them as colossal in scale as the house itself. She recognized a Paolozzi abstract and a huge Cinalli drawing of a hand, only its vast size revealing that it was a modern work and not a fragment of some Renaissance life study. There were photographs, too, tucked away in the smaller spaces. She stopped in front of a platinum print of a naked male torso and studied it thoughtfully, sipping her drink.

'Careful,' a voice said behind her. 'If you stare at it too long people might suspect your motives.'

She turned. David Nicolaides was standing behind her, a bowl of olives in his hand.

'Is it the subject or the photograph you were interested in, Miss Williams?' he continued.

'It is rather good,' she said, not answering him directly. 'Is it a Weston?'

He inclined his head gracefully. 'Well done. Most people think it's a Mapplethorpe, of course. Similar style, though Weston was the trailblazer. You know about photography?'

'Not really. I have a good friend who's a professional. Weston's one of her heroes.'

'And of mine, though I have never had the time or the talent to pursue photography myself. Luckily I do have some talent for making money, which means I can at least indulge my passions at second hand.' When he smiled his eyes half closed, reminding Terry of a sleepy lizard sunning itself on a rock. 'I have some more Westons upstairs. May I show them to you? They're in my library, along with some other things I think you might appreciate.'

Come up and see my etchings, thought Terry. But although Nicolaides' manner was lightly flirtatious, it was the flirtatiousness of a man who believed that flirting was simply a civilized way for men and women to discourse with each other. 'Thanks, I'd love to,' she said.

170

Placing a hand on her shoulder, he steered her up the concrete staircase to the first floor. Magnus, down in the throng below, noticed them and scowled. Terry smiled innocently back.

This floor was more conventional in layout, with rooms leading off a central corridor. The white carpet up here, untrodden by party-goers, was so pristine that their shoes left pale footprints in the pile, as if they were walking through hoar frost. Terry imagined an army of maids patrolling daily with hoovers, removing every speck of dirt.

'In here,' he said, ushering her into a small, book-lined room.

There were four nudes on the wall behind the desk, two male and two female, framed in black and lit with tiny ceiling-mounted spotlights. Nico leant against the desk and waved his arms expansively. 'Have a good look, please. Take your time.'

Feeling somewhat uncomfortable examining the photographs while being examined herself – was he about to make a pass after all? – she dutifully scrutinized them.

'Which do you prefer,' he asked casually from behind her, 'the female or the male?'

Was this some kind of test? she wondered. And if so, what was she being tested for?

'Technically or aesthetically?' she stalled.

'Either.'

'I'm not sure.'

She had meant only to avoid answering the question, but he seemed to take her answer more seriously than she had intended it.

'Well, you still have plenty of time.'

She turned round. Nicolaides was standing by the shelves of ground glass which lined one of the walls.

In his hands was a small, leather-bound volume.

'Here. I think this might also interest you.'

'My God,' she said, taking it and turning to the frontispiece. '*Malleus Malificarum.*'

He nodded. 'Otherwise known as *The Hammer of Witches*. It was reprinted over thirty times between 1486 and 1670. At one time it was the second most popular book in the Western world – after the Bible, of course. This is the 1548 edition. Arguably the one responsible for the whole witch-trial hysteria.'

'I've read extracts in facsimile. But I've never seen the real thing before.'

'And this?' He pulled out a second volume. 'Jean Bodin. *De la Demonomanie des Sorciers*. He was a judge, of course, so he felt he had first-hand understanding of the tricks witches would use to escape justice. And here: the *Disquisitionum Magicarum* of Martin Antoine Del Rio. Not a first edition, I'm afraid, but no less interesting for that. This one is dated 1747 – only a few years before Boswell's *Life of Johnson*, Adam Smith's *Wealth of Nations*, or any of the other landmarks of the so-called Age of Reason.' His dark eyes glinting, he lifted the *Malificarum* to his nose and sniffed it, inhaling appreciatively, as a man might sniff an unlit cigar. 'How many witch-trial judges have pored over these pages in their chambers? How many torturers have sought inspiration from its illustrations? How many inquisitors have blocked out the screams of their victims by concentrating on the words written here?' He held the little volume to her nose. Gingerly, she inhaled. 'You can almost smell the dungeons,' he breathed.

'Are you interested in witchcraft, Mr Nicolaides?'

'Nico, please. Not witchcraft: witchcraft books. Collectors are like gamblers, Terry: promiscuous in our attentions. Just as the true gambler will even bet on the passage of a raindrop down a window, so the true collector is more concerned with the rarity of a collection than the objects themselves.' He replaced the books on the shelves. 'What do you think of the room?' he asked casually.

She looked around. Like all the other rooms she had seen it was furnished in impeccable taste, a few pieces of antique furniture set off by the dramatic modernism of the house itself. 'It's wonderful,' she said.

'Would you like to borrow it? To study, I mean. I never use it.'

'That's very kind,' she began.

'There's a computer, internet access, everything you might need. There are no children to disturb you. The maids could bring you coffee. Really, I should like to feel that I had been of some use to a proper scholar.' He glanced at the photographs. 'And you could enjoy the Westons when you're not working.'

She muttered something non-committal, and he nodded.

'Just come whenever you feel like it. I'll give instructions to the staff to let you in.'

As they walked back down the corridor he threw open doors and gave a running description of each room's contents. 'That bed – it's a Charles Rennie Mackintosh. From Hill House in Glasgow. The bureau is Bauhaus. This is by Ron Arad. This is a Starck, of course. Philippe is a personal friend – he oversaw the conversion here. The dot painting is by Damien Hirst.' From anyone else's mouth it would have seemed like bragging, but the famous names were dropped with an almost sing-song weariness, as if to say that all these fabulous possessions were really of little account.

They heard someone talking in a side room and Nicolaides paused. 'Excuse me. I think some of the guests may have strayed. I had better move them on. This is my wife's room, and she'll be distressed if anyone disturbs it.' He opened the door. Terry caught a glimpse of a thin, elegantly dressed woman sitting on the immaculate white floor, playing with a child's toy doll. She looked up guiltily.

'Madelaine, what is this?' he said curtly.

'Oh, Nico, I – hello,' she said breathlessly, getting to her feet. Her hand shot out towards Terry's. 'I'm Madelaine Nicolaides.'

'Terry Williams. Pleased to meet you.' Thinking she should explain her presence upstairs with Madelaine's husband, she added, 'I was just looking at some of your wonderful art.'

But Madelaine was speaking to her husband. 'I was looking for you, Nico. Someone has trodden food into the carpet and I didn't know what to do.'

'The maids will take care of it.'

'Yes, of course, but I couldn't find the maids.' To Terry she said, 'The house takes such a lot of looking after, really.'

'We should go down, Madelaine. Are you coming?' Nicolaides asked gently.

'Yes, of course. Excuse me.' Mrs Nicolaides picked up the doll, opened a cupboard and placed it carefully on a shelf. The shelves were lined with more dolls, row upon row. 'I caught the bug from David,' she said to Terry with a breathless laugh. 'He collects precious things, I just collect these.'

'Hers is the more expensive hobby, of course,' Nicolaides said. It was evidently a joke he had made many times before. Neither of them smiled.

In their absence the party had filled up, a seething throng of noisy humanity. Fighting her way out of the crush she saw Magnus, red-faced and sweaty, with a bottle of malt in his hand.

'What were you two getting up to?' he roared into her ear.

He was already at that stage of drunkenness at which rational conversation would have been a waste of time. 'He wanted to show me some photographs of naked people,' she yelled back. Magnus nodded sagely. Mischievously she added, 'And he wanted me to leave Babcock and do my work here.' It was only as she said it that she realized that of course that was exactly what Nicolaides had been doing – trying to take her away from Magnus's collection and add her to his own.

'I hope you told him to piss off?' Magnus yelled.

'More or less.'

'Good girl.'

She left him to his bottle and wandered off again. Trying to converse with drunks was hard work even at normal decibel levels.

At the back of the house she discovered a huge room in which forty or so party-goers of all ages were exuberantly dancing reels to the music of a Celtic band. The fiddler was both lead instrumentalist and caller, shouting instructions to the dancers as his bow hand sawed energetically to and fro on the strings. Some of the older men were clearly experts, weaving intricate patterns with their feet, but most of the younger set were just hurling each other about good-naturedly. She watched as a middle-aged woman – mutton undressed as lamb, Terry thought bitchily – momentarily lost control of her dress, shrieking with laughter as her partner whirled her round and round. Then they were gone again, into the mass of dancers.

Across the room someone was watching her. Propped against a wall with one leg casually tucked under him, emphasizing the whippet-thin angularity of his body, a bottle of beer dangling from one hand, he was wearing nondescript black jeans, a white T-shirt and a waistcoat. Long sideburns trailed down almost to his jaw. Her first thought was, *my, you're a pretty boy*. Her second thought was, *I know you from somewhere*. Then she realized why he seemed familiar. In her teenage years she'd had a Doors album, the cover of which was a portrait of a bare-chested Jim Morrison, staring arrogantly at the camera. Pretty Boy's sulky lower lip and chiselled cheekbones were a dead ringer for Jim as he had been then, except that Pretty Boy had more facial hair. As she returned his gaze he lifted his beer bottle and drank, still looking at her.

She was used to being looked at, of course. Ever since she could remember, male stares had followed her across rooms and down streets. She was accustomed to the fact that if she shifted her gaze on the tube, her eyes would meet those of a man who had been gazing at her surreptitiously. Usually his gaze would slide guiltily away, but sometimes there were those who held her look, their own eyes filled with resentment and hunger. But luckily such looks were few and far between, and by and large men's glances were literally that: something which bounced off her.

Pretty Boy's stare was neither hostile nor begging. Insolent, yes, but also strangely matter of fact. She would have stared back, but just then one of Magnus's paying guests appeared from nowhere and grabbed her hand.

'You'll do,' he chortled happily. 'Come on.'

'I don't know how to do this,' Terry protested.

'Oh, you'll soon learn,' he said as the music started again. 'If in doubt, just jump up and down.'

Terry allowed herself to be dragged into a huge circle of girls, all holding hands, facing outwards at another circle of men. As the two circles began to spin, then stop, then clap their hands before spinning again, she realized that it was, in fact, remarkably easy and rather enjoyable. By the time it was over she realized that she was definitely going to stay for another one.

# SIXTEEN

Half an hour later, damp with sweat, she managed to extricate herself from the reel and staggered, exhausted, towards the open French windows. The feel of the cold night air on her overheated body was a blessed relief.

She was on a terrace at the back of the house, an artificially flat surface built onto the hillside. There was a railing, and she leant against it gratefully, catching her breath. A cigarette tip glowed red nearby.

It was Pretty Boy, bottle of beer still dangling from his fingers.

'I'd love some of that beer,' she said.

Silently, he held the bottle out to her. The beer was warm from being cradled in his hand, but at least it was liquid for her parched throat. The bottle was nearly full, but she kept drinking until she'd drained it, then handed it back to him. 'Thanks,' she said, with an insolence to match his own.

Looking at the empty bottle in his hand, he shrugged, and tossed it over the side of the terrace.

'Didn't your mother ever tell you not to drop litter?' she said.

'My mother didn't have a dozen gardeners to clear up the mess.' He was English, she realized, his public-school drawl slightly overlaid with a hint of Ladbroke Grove. 'This'll cool you down more than beer, anyway.' He pulled the cigarette from his mouth and offered it to her.

Only now did she catch the sweet scent of dope. 'Thanks,' she said, accepting it and taking a deep drag.

He laughed. 'You don't recognize me, do you?'

So she *did* know him from somewhere. 'Should I?' she said coolly.

'Depends on how many people you've slept with.' Seeing the look of incomprehension in her eyes, he laughed again. 'Oh dear. How very unflattering. I can see you're not going to remember. Jamie Shearn.'

'Christ, no!'

''Fraid so.'

'Shit! But you've – you're,' she was struggling. Jamie Shearn had been one of her first boyfriends at Oxford. A cricket player. She had coveted his Blues sweater more than anything else in the world, and used to take all her clothes off during sex simply so that afterwards she could dive into the pullover before he did – and subsequently savour the delicious feeling of walking into the college library with it still wrapped around her. But she could barely connect the soft-limbed public schoolboy he'd been then with this long-haired beachcomber.

'Changed?' he said. 'You too.'

'What happened? I thought you went to work in a bank.'

'Oh, I did. Flemings, in Hong Kong. Or Honkers, as my colleagues used to call it. Wore the ties, went to the dinners, played in the right matches, shagged the right girls. Then I realized I was bored out of my tiny mind. Decided it was time to start expanding it.' He took another drag of dope and handed it back to her. 'So I did a bit of travelling. Took a look at China, did the hippie trail round India, lost some weight on the Delhi diet. How about you?'

'My dieting tips?'

'Your life story. Still going out with that bastard?'

'Nope. Married him and divorced him, all within two years. I'm a student again now – I'm trying to finish a doctorate.'

'How long have you been up here?'

'About a week.'

'The novelty soon wears off, believe me. The rain, the sheep, the appalling food, the insane belief that Sean Connery is a great actor – though he tries very hard not to show it, your true Scotsman gets a deep spiritual satisfaction from these things. After a month you'll be more miserable than you've ever been in your entire life.'

'So why do you stay?'

He shrugged. 'I'm doing a sort of course, as well.'

'A university course?'

'Not exactly.' His eyes, more deep-set now than she remembered them, twinkled ironically. 'A sort of spiritual quest.'

'Jesus Christ. Don't tell me you've become a Wiccan?'

'That's right. What's so surprising?'

'That's what I'm doing my research on, indirectly.' She explained about Catherine McCulloch, and her abortive attempt to get into Nineveh Farm.

He laughed. 'That'll be Alan. He's a little abrupt

180

sometimes. If it had been one of the others, you wouldn't have been able to get away.'

'So you think they'll talk to me?'

'Of course. Gerard – that's the High Priest – likes nothing better than an audience. Particularly a pretty female one. You'll have no problem.'

'Can I mention your name?'

'Better than that. You can come back with me now, shag like a rabbit for old time's sake and I'll introduce you in the morning. Did I mention that you're really rather pretty?'

'You were never very good at chat-up lines, were you?'

'It must have worked last time.'

A waiter came by with a tray of whisky. Jamie took two glasses and handed one to her.

'Last time it was at the college disco, and you said something like, "Get your coat, you've pulled."'

'That bad, eh?'

'In any case,' she said, 'just so's we're absolutely clear . . . I ought to tell you that I bat for the other side now. As you public schoolboys probably used to put it.'

He raised his eyebrows. 'Oh. I see.'

'All that other stuff – at Oxford – was a mistake.'

'I see.'

Dammit, there was no reason why she should justify her sexual choices to an ex-boyfriend she couldn't even remember. She bit her lip.

'Actually,' he said, 'the thing about cricket teams – and public schools too, come to that – is that once you've had a turn at batting, you get a go at bowling as well.'

She giggled. 'Leave it out.'

'If you like.' He turned and leant on the railing, gazing out at the blackness.

'So what made you want to become a witch?' she asked.

He shrugged. 'You've got to believe in something, haven't you?'

'Hmm,' said Terry. 'I'm with E.M. Forster on that one. He wrote an essay called "What I believe": the opening line is "I do not believe in belief."'

'I'm the exact opposite, I'm afraid. I believe in belief, I'm just not quite sure what I believe in yet.'

She shook her head incredulously. 'But you of all people. You were always so straight.'

Jamie laughed. 'Come to that, so were you.'

'Sexual preference is different.'

'Is it?' He pulled out a packet of Marlboro: inside, ready rolled, were half a dozen joints, their ends twisted to stop the mixture from falling out. He took one and lit it, then passed it to her. 'I kept all your phone numbers,' he said reflectively. 'Copied them from one address book to the next as each one fell apart. Your parent's house, that place you shared in the Cowley Road. Odd, really, because of course you wouldn't have been at any of those places any more. I just didn't want to throw you away.'

'Relationships are like poems,' she agreed. 'Never finished, only abandoned.' She stared at the end of the reefer in disbelief. 'Christ. Is this dope extra-strong or have I just turned into an Athena greeting card? I can't believe I said that.'

He smiled. 'It *is* quite strong actually. Home-grown. One of the advantages of a remote Scottish location.' He took it from her and sucked smoke deep into his lungs. 'Do you ever wish', he said slowly, 'that you could go back to all your old girl-friends – boyfriends, whatever – and just shag them once, to show them that you're not shit at it any more?'

'You weren't shit then.'

'So you do remember some things.' He blew smoke out slowly. 'I don't mean technique. I suppose I mean – show them that you're not *a* shit any more. That you did get there eventually.'

'I've got a confession to make, Jamie. I think I only shagged you so I could wear your sweater in the library. It made me feel grown up and successful.'

'And I only shagged you because you were a gorgeous nineteen-year-old with a body to die for. And because I've always had a thing about lesbians.'

Terry levered herself off the railing and stood upright. Whether it was the dope, the whisky, or the certainty that in a week or so's time she'd be away from here, going back to her real life, she felt impulsive. 'Come on, then.'

'Where to? If you think I'm joining that lot . . .' he pointed at the dancers.

'Back to your place.'

'Really?'

'The shagging like rabbits part may or may not be on the cards. I'm not sure yet. Is that OK?'

'Of course.'

'And if it is,' she murmured, putting her arm through his as they weaved through the dancers, 'it won't just be for old time's sake.'

As she followed him through the crowd to the door she spotted Flora, part of a small group sitting on the floor. 'Oh, hell – I'd better let my friends know I'm going. Any ideas?'

Jamie shrugged. 'Tell them we're going to the pub for a drink.'

Flora received this information in a hostile silence.

'You'll tell Magnus?'

'Sure,' Flora said in a bored voice, 'I'll tell him. He's pissed, anyway.'

They set off down the narrow road, their shoulders bumping together as they walked.

'Tell me about Wicca,' she said to break the silence. 'What's it all about?'

'You don't want to know. It's really very dull.'

'Tell me anyway,' she insisted.

He sighed. 'Basically, it's about harnessing the divine polarity of male and female, so that we can cross the normal barriers between this world and the magical one. We create a kind of group mind, which we release through rituals, and then that mind is capable of various etheric powers that ordinary people aren't.'

'You're right,' she said. 'It's very dull.'

He shook his head. 'I can't stop now, I'm afraid . . . So the Earth Mother, or the White Goddess, or Aradia, is both the goddess we worship and a kind of life-force we can tap into to help us walk the Spiral Path. It's not a life-force we can use on our own: you need the collective power of the group mind, and the group mind is created by ritual. When we do magick we're both recharging the power of the group mind, and recharging the power of the Goddess, because without worship the Goddess's own energy is dimmed. So the contraries of the ritual are actually positive, not negative—'

She pulled his head to hers, fastened her lips against his and kissed him deeply, exploring his mouth with her tongue. When they eventually came up for air he said softly, 'Ah, the old White Goddess chat-up line. It never fails, you see.'

'I just wanted to see if I could shut you up.'

'That's why it never fails.'

'One other thing. Condoms. Do we need to make a detour via the pub?'

'Well, we could do. There's just a couple of problems with that.'

'What?'

'First, the pub doesn't sell condoms. They're still pretty Calvinist up here.'

'And the second?'

'They're so Calvinist that the pub's closed on Sundays.'

'Oh.' And then, as the implications sank in, 'Oh. You *bastard*. You let me tell Flora . . .'

He grinned wolfishly. 'Despicable, aren't I?'

Outraged, she slapped his face. He laughed, which hadn't been the reaction she was intending, so she hit him again.

'Bitch!' he hissed.

He grabbed her, trying to twist her arms behind her back, but she slipped free easily and ran from him. She could hear him coming after her. Knowing he'd be faster, she ducked off the road and into the trees where she could dodge and weave. Brambles and ferns dragged at her legs. She couldn't hear him so well on this soft ground, but the occasional crash told her that he wasn't far behind. She came to a low stone wall and tried to climb it, but she was still balanced precariously on top when she felt a hand on her neck, yanking her backwards.

She fell, and then he was on top of her, pinning her arms above her head with one hand. With a huge effort she managed to get a hand free and rammed it into his groin, grabbing his cock through his trousers. He froze, suddenly vulnerable.

Without letting go of the lever in her hand, she pushed him over onto his back and straddled his stomach, pinning him down. They were both panting.

'Bastard.'

'Bitch.'

With her free hand she started to work at the buckle of his belt. 'If you come inside me, I'll kill you,' she said.

Afterwards she lay nestled against the hard pillow of his shoulder, looking up at the shadows the moon made on the trees. There was come on her fingers. She wiped them on his chest, prompting a groan.

'What's the matter, Pretty Boy,' she whispered. 'Want another fight?'

'Don't tempt me.'

She touched his limp cock. 'Not so tough now though, are we?'

He raised himself onto one arm and looked down at her. 'You never give up, do you?'

She shook her head. 'Never.'

'Still prefer women?'

She laughed. 'Don't flatter yourself. You weren't that good.'

'Neither were you.'

'Bollocks. I was brilliant and you know it.' But they were just going through the motions now, the edge of their sparring blunted. She ran her fingers over his body, feeling the unfamiliar maleness of him, the hardness where her female lovers were yielding and soft, the sandpaper roughness of his cheeks. There was a twig in her hair and she pulled it out, frowning as it caught on a tangle. 'Ouch. Not the most comfortable sex I've ever had. Though at least neither of us can say "Shall I call you a taxi?"'

'Want to come back? We're nearly there now.'

'Talk me into it.'

'A bed, a duvet, something to eat, warmth . . .'

'Mmm. Any condoms?'

'Millions.'

'You silver-tongued charmer.'

'That too.'

# SEVENTEEN

She woke late, roused by the clang and gurgle of an unfamiliar plumbing system. Light streamed in through the thin curtains – which were, she now saw, not actually curtains at all but a thin Indian bedspread, draped across the window.

The contrast with her room at the castle couldn't have been greater. Instead of Catherine McCulloch's giant four-poster, she and Jamie were sharing a dilapidated double bed which sagged in the middle and which had swayed alarmingly, like a hammock, when they made love. Above them was the sloping roof of the eaves. Apart from the bed, the only furniture was an ancient chest of drawers. Clothes and boots were strewn all over the floor: a black plastic bin-bag, evidently doing service as a makeshift laundry basket, overflowed with boxer shorts and T-shirts. Instead of the oil paintings of Catherine and Anne de Courcy, there were a couple of posters advertising music festivals with names like Tribal Gathering and Ibiza Sleaze.

Terry clambered out of bed and went to the window, the morning air cold on her naked skin. The view was stunning, if less majestic than the one from the castle: Nineveh, being a farm, had been built in the lee of a hill for shelter. She was looking down onto a small terrace. Beyond that, a couple of fields dotted with goats led down to a small lake, its waters black with peat.

Behind her Jamie had sat up, watching her. She turned and smiled at him. 'Just enjoying the view.'

'Me too,' he said impishly. He took his watch off the bedside table and groaned. 'You realize we've only been asleep for four hours?'

'Correction. You've been asleep. I've been listening to you snore.'

'Don't tell me. Your female lovers never do?'

She smiled. 'Something like that.' She clambered back onto the bed and knelt above him, her breasts swaying over his chest. 'Ready for some more?'

He groaned again.

'Only joking. I'm sore too. Any chance of a coffee?'

'There'll be breakfast downstairs.'

'Is that a good idea? I can always come back later.'

'It's no big deal. The others won't mind.'

'Used to it, are they?' He smirked. She'd been teasing, but she obviously hadn't been wide of the mark. 'Come on then. You'd better lend me a shirt.'

Five minutes later, clean and reasonably attired in inside-out knickers, her skirt and one of Jamie's shirts, she went down with Jamie to the kitchen. Half a dozen people were gathered round a large table. Seeing Terry, they fell silent.

'Hi, everyone. This is Terry,' Jamie mumbled vaguely.

'Good morning,' Terry said brightly, thinking: why the hell am I doing this?

A woman in her sixties was the first to speak. Rather incongruously, her grey hair was a mass of matted dreadlocks. 'May the sun bless you, Terry. Would you like some toast and honey? Come and sit here, next to me.'

Terry did as she was bidden. Across the table a rather plump young woman with a baby on her lap and a ring through one side of her nose blushed furiously and then looked away. Next to her sat the young man who had tipped his ashtray over her. Terry nodded defiantly. 'Hello again.'

'Hello,' he said, amused. 'We meet again.'

'This is Judith,' the grey-haired woman said, indicating the girl with the toddler. 'I'm Brigid; Stephan and Anna—' the two people she indicated bobbed their heads and said 'Hello' in Dutch-accented English. 'That's Zoe at the stove.' Zoe raised one hand in greeting as she placed a large plate of toast in front of them. Like Anna, Judith and even Brigid, she sported an elaborate henna tattoo.

There were pots of sweet-smelling honey in front of them, still containing pieces of honeycomb. Terry had spread her toast and taken a bite before she realized that the others had bowed their heads, their food untouched. 'Whoops,' Terry muttered. She froze awkwardly in mid-chew.

Brigid cleared her throat. 'O Queen most secret, bless this food into our bodies, bestowing health, wealth, strength, joy and peace, and that fulfilment of love which is perfect happiness.'

The grace over, they ate. 'Do you live locally, Terry?' Brigid asked conversationally.

Shit, Terry thought: this was like being sixteen again, meeting your boyfriend's parents.

'No, I'm only here for a couple of weeks,' she said.

A tall, slender girl of startling good looks came in just as Terry was speaking. She was wearing a track-suit and jogging shoes: her blond hair was pulled back in a ponytail, and her face was glowing from exercise. 'My God, Jamie, you're such a pussy magnet,' she said. Her voice was American. 'Don't you ever believe in, like, *dating*?' She waved at Terry. 'Hi. I'm Isobel. Merry meet in the name of the Goddess.'

Terry mumbled her own name in response.

'So, is everyone's etheric energy low this morning or what?' Isobel continued, looking round the table. She plucked a piece of toast out of Jamie's hand and took a bite before handing it back. 'Mmm. This honey is sooo good. Don't you think so, Terry?'

Terry guessed that the proprietorial gesture was for her benefit. 'Wonderful,' she agreed.

'We make it ourselves,' Alan explained. 'Honey from the heather of the Highlands, the best in the world.'

'Is that your new slogan?' Isobel said sarcastically. Turning to Terry she said, 'Alan's our resident marketing man. And don't be fooled by that "we". Gregor makes the honey, Alan just takes the money.'

'You're very chirpy this morning, Isobel,' Brigid said calmly. 'Have you seen Gerard?'

'He's fine. He's outside.'

There were a lot of subtexts to these conversations, Terry thought. Aloud she said, 'I'd like to talk to Gerard, if that's all right.'

'Why?' Both Brigid and Isobel had asked the question simultaneously.

'I want to ask him about Catherine McCulloch. I'm editing her papers.'

There was a brief silence as this information was digested. Deadpan, she added, 'I'm actually an academic, as well as Jamie's pussy.'

Alan broke the silence by laughing out loud. 'From now on, Isobel, perhaps you'd be safer referring to Jamie as an academic magnet.'

Isobel flashed a brittle smile. 'Hey, no offence, Terry. We tend to forget how uptight non-Wiccans are about sexual matters.'

'I'll take you to see Gerard later, Terry,' Brigid said. 'Isobel, why don't you sit down. Before Terry and Jamie came, we were discussing whether or not it would be appropriate to hold an astral mass for poor Donna. What do you think?'

'Sure. Why not?'

'Jamie?'

Jamie shrugged. 'I suppose it would be nice.'

Alan said, 'The question is, is she entitled to one? She wasn't actually a member of the coven when she died, after all.'

'We don't know when she died,' Zoe said.

'True, but it was certainly after she'd left us.'

'Entitled to one. . . I think it is the wrong way of looking at this, Alan,' Anna said seriously in her accented English. 'We are not a trade union, with membership cards. I think as her friends we would like to say goodbye.'

'What's an astral mass?' Terry asked.

It was Brigid who answered her. 'Like the requiem in Christian tradition, we have special ceremonies to commemorate those who have passed on from the physical plane. Donna was a member of our community here, now sadly dead.'

'Yes, I heard,' Terry said. 'It must have been very difficult for you.'

'More difficult for some than others,' Alan said. 'Still, you're over it now, Jamie, aren't you?'

'Fuck off,' Jamie said irritably.

So Jamie had been involved with the dead girl. Terry wondered why he hadn't told her.

'Yeah, leave him alone,' Isobel said. 'He only slept with her. What's the big deal?'

'Excuse me.' It was Judith, the plump girl opposite, getting to her feet. 'Holly needs changing.' She hurried from the room with the baby. Looking up, Terry caught Alan looking at her across the table.

'Welcome to the house of peace and love, Terry,' he said. 'There's never a dull moment with these wacky Wiccan folk.' But though he spoke lightly, there was no laughter in his eyes at all.

After breakfast she was led outside by Brigid to the terrace where an elderly man, his hair as white as his goatee beard, was sitting cross-legged, facing the sun.

'Gerard, we have a visitor,' Brigid said.

He opened his eyes. 'May you walk with the Goddess,' he said in a surprisingly deep, firm voice.

'Terry, you'd better tell Gerard what you're after.'

Terry explained about her research, and the suggestion by John Mcteer that Catherine had been a pagan.

Gerard nodded. 'That much is certainly true. Catherine's rituals – which Old John rewrote as the *Book of Shadows* – form the basis of all our beliefs: our bible, if you like. Her writings were somewhat sketchy, of course, and there were many gaps to be filled in. But essentially we believe that she was initiated by her friend Anne de Courcy into a pagan congregation – what outsiders called a coven – that had existed here in secret for hundreds of years. The *Book of Shadows* is our link to that tradition.'

'Could I see this *Book of Shadows*?'

He shook his head. 'It's out of the question, I'm afraid. The *Book* is quite specific on this point: "Keep a book in your own hand of write. Let brothers and sisters copy what they will, but never let the book out of your hands and never keep the writings of another, for if found in their hand they may be taken and tortured."'

'But doesn't that mean it's all right to make copies?'

' "Let *brothers and sisters* copy what they will." In other words, members of the coven.'

'But from what you quoted me just now, the author intended that as a precaution against torture,' she pleaded. 'Now that circumstances have changed, can't the ban on outsiders relax a little too?'

He smiled at her. 'I wish I could be more helpful, young lady. I am sure your intentions are entirely honourable, but I'm afraid the word of the *Book* is final.'

Terry chatted to the old man for a few minutes, but it was clear that he wasn't going to budge. Eventually Brigid took her back to the kitchen, where she found Jamie. 'No luck, I'm afraid,' she said bitterly. 'I'd better be off.' To Brigid she added, 'And thank you for breakfast.'

'No problem. I expect we'll be seeing you again, will we?'

'I'll walk you to the road,' Jamie said.

'Pretty weird set-up here, I suppose,' Jamie said as they made their way along the farm track. 'I mean, to an outsider.'

'Oh, I don't know. Sexual rivalries. social competitiveness, bitchiness, rigid hierarchies. It's just like my college.'

'Sexual rivalries?'

She laughed. 'Well, I can tell exactly who *you've* slept with, anyway.'

'Oh yes, Miss Cleverdick? Who?'

She counted them off on her fingers. 'Isobel, but just the once.'

'How did you know?'

'She's too pretty for you not to have been curious about her, and too bossy for you to come back for more. Brigid I think we can rule out. Judith too, though not because the poor girl isn't interested.'

'Who else?'

'Zoe. I think you both agreed to keep it a secret. She doesn't want to have to fight Judith and Isobel.'

'Anyone else, smart-arse?'

'Donna,' she said carefully.

'Donna,' he muttered. 'Yes, there was Donna.'

'What was she like?' she asked curiously.

He shrugged. 'Lively.'

She waited, but that was apparently all she was going to get. She thought about asking him why Donna should have been trying to steal Catherine McCulloch's papers, then thought better of it. At the moment Jamie was her only link to Nineveh, and she wasn't sure how much she wanted to confide in him.

'Jamie?'

'Yes?'

'I'll be coming back sometime. I want to have

another go at persuading Gerard to let me see this book of whatever-it's-called. But I'd be coming back for work, not pleasure.'

'Hey – was I really that bad?'

'What I'm trying to say is, if it happens then it happens. OK?'

He smiled. 'Maybe we should try, like, *dating*,' he said in a passable parody of Isobel's American accent.

She found the castle deserted except for Alex, who volunteered the information that Flora had been arrested.

'Good God,' Terry said. 'What on earth for?'

Alex shrugged. 'Under-age sex. Dad's had to go into town to sort it out.' Apparently unconcerned, he wandered back to his computer.

Terry changed out of yesterday's clothes, had a bath and settled down to work. It was after twelve when she heard Magnus's Land Rover pulling up outside. A few minutes later he stormed into the library.

'How's Flora?'

'Never mind Flora,' he said icily. 'Where the hell were you last night?'

'I gave Flora a message. Perhaps she didn't pass it on.'

'Flora told me you'd gone off with a complete stranger you'd picked up at the party. I didn't know whether to phone the police, for Christ's sake.'

'Don't you think you're overreacting? I'm not a child—'

'You're staying in my house. That makes me at least partly responsible for you. And in case you'd forgotten, a young woman about your age was murdered here recently. Don't you think you ought to take some basic precautions before you start screwing all and sundry?'

She flushed. 'I've hardly—'

'And what kind of example do you think you're setting my children?' he continued. 'First of all you tell me you're a dyke. Now it turns out your appetites are slightly more omnivorous. Well, fine. We're not complete Neanderthals up here: your sexuality is your own business, though frankly it would have been more courteous and more thoughtful if you'd just kept it to yourself.' She opened her mouth to protest but he bulldozed on. 'I can live with that, though. What I can't live with is acting like a cheap slag in front of an impressionable teenager like Flora.'

This was too much. 'A slag?' she retorted. 'Your spoilt daughter's the one who's been arrested, not me. All right, I should have made it clearer where I was going and with whom. But in case you've forgotten, you were pissed out of your brain last night. If your precious Flora's a slag you've only got yourself to blame. You're the bad example, Magnus, and a fucking hypocrite to boot.' She stormed out, past a goggle-eyed paying guest, and slammed the door into the kitchen.

Tom was making himself a cup of tea. 'Morning,' he said evenly, though he must have heard the row.

'Morning,' she said dully. Shaken, she sat down. Without asking, he made another mug for her and set it down on the table.

'Thanks.'

'You'll find Magnus a wee bit hungover this morning,' he said diplomatically.

She nodded. 'What happened to Flora? He won't tell me.'

'Och, it's not so very bad. There were a whole lot of police up by the pig farm at first light. Doing some kind of intensive search. They lifted up the roof of one of the piggy huts and found Flora and a young lad curled up in the straw, fast asleep and stark bollock naked. I can't imagine who got the bigger shock.' He chuckled. 'She's a spirited girl, Flora, but awful naughty.'

'How old's the boy?'

'A few years older than her, I think. He'll be in trouble now, of course. And I think Magnus's eyes have been opened too, which between you and me may not be such a terrible thing.'

'I think I just told Magnus his daughter was a spoilt slag.'

'He won't have liked that.'

'He didn't.'

'It's no' surprising she's a little wild. Without a mother and everything.'

'Don't, Tom. You're making me feel guilty. Hungover or not, he had no right to say what he did.'

He muttered something under his breath. His accent was so strong she couldn't catch the words, but it sounded suspiciously like something about Flora not being the only wild one in the house.

She made a sudden decision. 'Tom, would you give me a lift?'

He shot her a look from under his enormous eyebrows. 'You'll be wanting to go to the train station?'

'No. Somewhere else. It's all right, it's only a few minutes' drive. I'll just go and collect my stuff.'

# PART TWO

# EIGHTEEN

For the second time that day Terry walked into the Wiccans' kitchen. It was deserted now except for Zoe, stirring a large saucepan on the stove.

'Hi,' she said, seeing Terry with her suitcases, 'I thought you'd gone.'

'I had. I've come back again.'

'Welcome back then. Could you pass me that jar?'

Terry passed her a jar labelled 'Eye of newt' and watched as she tipped it into the pot. 'And that one?' She pointed. It was labelled 'Puppy dogs' tails'.

'Wiccan humour,' she explained, tipping dried spaghetti out of the second jar. 'The other one's really dried oregano.' She dipped a spoon into the sauce and tasted it. 'Were you looking for Jamie? I think he's out with the other boys, chopping wood.'

'No, it's – look, who do I talk to about joining?'

'Joining?' Zoe laughed. 'You mean, as in becoming a Wiccan?'

'That's right. What's so funny?'

'Nothing. You don't seem the type, that's all.' The sauce made, Zoe came to the table and sat down, fishing a pack of cigarettes out of her pocket. 'Smoke?'

'Thanks. You don't seem the type either, come to that.'

'Oh, I'm new to all this. My last boyfriend was a protester at the Manchester Airport camp. We split up, someone told me about this place. I'm just getting my head together, really.'

'So who should I speak to?'

'Brigid. Gerard's the authority on what you might call theological issues, but Brigid's the one who organizes things. If she likes you she'll put in a good word. Gerard's a bit of an old letch, to be honest, so I don't think you'll have any trouble persuading him – he's perfectly harmless, though he might slobber over you a bit during rituals. Isobel's keeping him occupied in that department, anyway.' She took a drag of her cigarette. 'It's good timing, actually. Since Donna left we've been a woman short.'

'What happened with Donna?' Terry asked curiously. 'There wasn't any trouble here, was there?'

Zoe shook her head. 'Not really. She just got bored. There'd been a bit of tension with Judith, and of course Gerard had made her his playmate of the month, which caused the usual problems with—'

'Nothing to do, Zoe?' It was Brigid, coming in behind them silently. 'Ah. Terry, isn't it? Hello again.'

'Hello.'

'You don't seem to be able to stay away.'

Terry took a deep breath. 'I wanted to ask about joining you. Joining the coven, I mean.'

'Hmm.' Brigid thought for a moment, then called, 'Gerard!'

'What is it?' Gerard came in a few moments later, a cup in his hand.

'Terry has decided she'd like to join us. Doubtless this is entirely unconnected to your decision this morning.'

Gerard stared at her, his brow furrowed.

'You told her that only members of the coven could copy the *Book of Shadows*,' Brigid reminded him. 'She's worked out that if she becomes an initiate, you'll have to let her see it.'

'I admit, that's part of the reason,' Terry said quickly. 'But I—'

'And there are other attractions for her at Nineveh. Jamie Shearn being one of them.'

'Look,' Terry said, 'I admit that I'm partly motivated by curiosity about Catherine McCulloch. But is that such a terrible thing? If I can shed some light on her history, that can only benefit your own understanding of her. And I'll be bound by whatever oath you make me swear not to reveal my sources.'

There was a long silence while Gerard considered. 'That seems fair enough to me,' he said at last. 'My objection earlier was purely based on the word of the *Book*. So long as we adhere to the word, I don't think there can be any problem.'

'You're being naive, Gerard,' Brigid said crisply. 'There's the little matter of her sincerity, for one thing.'

He turned his pale eyes on her. 'Is sincerity a prerequisite for taking part in the Work, my dear?' To Terry's surprise, Brigid seemed to drop her eyes. 'Is it the belief of the coven which makes the rituals work, or is it the power of the rituals which makes us believe?' he continued gently. 'Besides, we can accept her as a postulant without committing ourselves. We'll know when the time comes whether or not she's ready to take the final step.'

'Very well,' Brigid said. 'Terry, you are very welcome here. No, I mean it,' she added, seeing Terry's sceptical expression. 'My objection to your joining us was nothing personal. You must bear in mind that members of the Craft have always had good reason to be wary of strangers. And never more so than at times like these.'

'Thank you,' Terry said.

'Now then. Some practical matters. I take it you'll be sharing a bed with Jamie?'

Terry thought. 'Um – could I possibly have somewhere of my own? Jamie doesn't even know about this yet.'

'In that case, you'd better share Zoe's room. You'll have to work, as we all do. You can chop wood with the boys for now, until we see where you'll be most useful. And you'll need to take instruction in the Craft. I'll ask Isobel whether she's prepared to spend some time with you.'

'I could instruct her if you like,' Zoe offered.

'I don't think that would be very appropriate,' Brigid said bluntly. 'I'll speak to Isobel.'

'Shit,' Zoe said sympathetically when Brigid and Gerard had gone. 'Witchcraft lessons from Isobel. I think she may be trying to put you off.'

'I can handle it. But I hope it's not a problem sharing with me.'

'No, it's fine,' Zoe said. 'To be honest, I'll be glad of the company. It's been a bit spooky, staring at Donna's old bed and thinking about – well, you know.'

Their room was on the floor below Jamie's, and equally bare of furniture. 'Sorry about the mess,' Zoe said, surveying the litter of clothes and cosmetics. 'I'll tidy up now I've got company.'

'Oh, don't worry.' Terry looked round for somewhere to unpack.

'Here,' Zoe said, pulling open a drawer in the only chest of drawers. 'This was where Donna kept her stuff.'

The drawer was full of rubbish. Half-empty Body Shop bottles, sweet wrappers, an empty packet of condoms, a half-full refill pack of Lillets. 'She didn't believe in tidying up after herself, I'm afraid,' Zoe said apologetically. 'Here, dump it all in this.'

Terry scooped the rubbish into the carrier bag Zoe held out for her. There was a piece of paper at the bottom of the drawer, and she unfolded it curiously, but it was only a standard letter of complaint from a bank, warning Ms Donna Fairhead that her account was overdrawn. 'If I have not heard from you in a few days I will assume that you have paid in sufficient funds to clear this unauthorized borrowing . . .' She crumpled it up and put it in the bag with the rest.

'Two thirty-eight p.m.: interview resumed with Andrew Wringe. I am Detective Sergeant Nicola Heron; also present is Detective Superintendent Talbot.' Nicky paused and looked at the young man in front of her, slouched so low across the table that his chin was almost on the formica. Andy looked like he hadn't had much sleep, which was all to the good.

'So, Andy. Getting used to it?'

The teenager lifted his eyes. 'What d'ya mean?'

Nicky gestured at the room around them. 'All this. Rooms without light switches. Trousers without belts. Solitary confinement.'

'Ach.' Andy looked as if he was about to spit contemptuously, but thought better of it. 'Don't give me that crap.'

'It's not crap, Andy. It's indisputable fact. Flora McCulloch is under the age of consent. You had sex with her. That makes you a child molester. You know what they do to child molesters in prison?'

'Don't be daft,' he muttered.

'See, Andy, every single child molester in the system has had the bright idea of claiming that all they did was pull a fifteen-year-old who looked older and was practically begging for it. So, understandably, the bastards who mete out instant justice in our fine prison system tend not to believe that line any more. All that matters is what it says on your file, and *that* will just say under age. You're going to have two years of hell, Andy. Better get used to the idea.'

He was sweating now. She'd seen it so often: the way the bravado crumbled when they realized they were cornered, the eyes literally going from side to side in an instinctive, desperate search for a way out.

'Anyway,' she said, 'let's just park all that on one side, shall we? Tell me about the pig farm.'

'What about it?' he muttered.

'You ever used that place before? One of the pig huts, I mean, not necessarily that exact one.'

'Might have.'

She waited. They needed to feel that it wasn't a question of them helping you; rather, you were reluctantly letting them help themselves. In training they called it 'momentum': making the interviewee feel they were taking you where they wanted to go.

'Yeah,' he corrected himself, pulling his chin off

the table. 'I've used it. Nice and dry, see. There's always a few huts without any pigs in them: you can tell, cos they're the ones without wooden boards on the front.'

'How many times, Andy?'

'Three, maybe four.' He looked sheepish. 'Not with Flora. Others.'

'Use condoms?'

'Yeah.'

'What did you do with them when you'd finished?'

He shrugged. 'Left 'em. The pigs'll eat anything.'

'Ever see anyone else up there?'

'Not really. Saw a woman in one of the pig fields, once. I reckoned she was the farmer. And I saw a van, one time.'

'When was this?'

'A couple of days after Christmas. The day Rangers played Leeds. I was with the barmaid from the Eagle.'

'And this van did what, exactly?'

'It drove around a bit. Then it parked right at the end of the field. Down by the trees.'

'How long for?'

'I don't know. I'd stuck my head back in by then.' He grinned. 'Know what I mean?'

He was getting cocky again. It was time to bring him back down to earth. 'A barmaid, was it? Bit old for a pervert like you.' Nicky waited a beat, then: 'Did the girl see the van?'

He shook his head.

'What colour was it?'

'It was dark, I couldn't see.'

'Number plate?'

'I told you, it was dark.'

'How many people?'

'A few, I think. I heard the doors slamming. That was what made me notice it.'

'But you didn't see them?'

He shook his head again. 'I didn't see anyone.'

Time to wrap up. 'OK. We'll need a written statement, and the names of all the girls you've taken up to the farm. And the nurse will need to see you for a DNA sample. Don't get excited, it's only a mouth swab.'

'What about – the other thing?'

'Flora?'

He nodded.

'You're in luck, Andy. Her dad doesn't want to press charges. Apparently little Flora's been telling him it wasn't your fault. And although we could charge you ourselves, frankly I'm not sure you're worth the paperwork. Three forty-five, interview terminated.'

'Well done,' Talbot murmured as they walked briskly back to the inquiry room.

'Thanks, sir. What do you reckon to this van? Parking at the end of the field would mean it was right next to the death pit. It couldn't have been the farmer – she drives a tractor when she's on the farm, and a sports car on the roads. The bloke who works for her gets there by bike. That only leaves John Hobbes who'd have permission to be on the farm at night, and he's got a four-wheel drive.'

'But if it was someone dumping the body, where was Donna before Christmas? No-one saw her alive after mid-November. If she was already dead, why not leave the body where it was? And if she was alive, where was she hiding, and why?' He reached the coffee-vending machine and punched numbers automatically.

'What about the fact that our friend Andy heard more than one door slamming?'

'It's hardly conclusive. After all, if you were trying to get a body out of a van you'd have to open the back doors, maybe go round to the front again and push from that end.'

'On the other hand, it might mean Donna was imprisoned and killed by a large group of people.'

'Like the Wiccans, you mean?' He sighed. 'It's a possibility, for sure. But it's not enough for a search warrant.'

Zoe lent her some work clothes and Terry spent the afternoon with Jamie and Stephan, cutting up a big pine tree they'd felled in the woods. They took turns with the chainsaw and the axe. Both were hard work, the extra weight of the chainsaw making it nearly as back-aching as chopping by hand. She was soon drenched in sweat, and it was a huge relief when Stephan announced that it was time to stop.

Visibly impressed, Stephan looked at the pile of split logs surrounding her chopping block. 'I think you are a very strong woman.' He reached out his hand to feel her bicep. 'Don't let this one hit you, Jamie,' he joked. Jamie grunted. He still wasn't sure whether having Terry around was going to cramp his style, she realized.

Before they left they planted a tiny sapling, sheathed in a tube of black plastic, as a replacement for the tree they'd sawn up. Back at the farmhouse, where the returning workers were gathered for tea in the kitchen, Stephan continued to sing her praises, the size of her pile of logs growing, like an angler's fish, with each retelling. Most of the Wiccans seemed to accept her without question, only Isobel and Brigid eyeing her warily. The two women, she sensed, were involved in some kind of polite turf war, and were still sizing her up to see whether she would be a useful ally or a potential rival.

During tea they were joined by a taciturn German called Gregor. Towards the end of the meal he announced that the next day he would require some help.

'Excellent,' Brigid said immediately. 'Terry can help you. She needs something useful to do.'

'But no,' Stephan protested, 'we need her on the logs.'

'Does anyone else want to help Gregor?' Brigid demanded. There was silence. Brigid shrugged. 'It'll have to be Terry, then.'

Stephan, slow to pick up on Brigid's hostility to Terry, ploughed on. 'I don't think you'll like so much working with Gregor, Terry. The bees sting you, sometimes a lot.'

Brigid was obviously going to give her all the shittiest jobs. Terry felt like one of those characters in a fairy tale who had to carry out three impossible tasks before finally getting the princess. 'Bees, is it? No problem,' she said, more sunnily than she felt. 'I quite like bees.'

After tea Jamie slipped up to his room, indicating to Terry with the faintest lift of his eyes that she should follow him up. Good, she thought: a chance to talk in private, followed by a long massage for her aching muscles. And not just her muscles either. She was just speculating whether Jamie's oral technique would have improved along with everything else in the intervening years when her reverie was interrupted by Isobel getting up from the table and saying, 'Right, Terry. I understand I'm to instruct you. Shall we get to work?'

An hour later, Terry had learned the position and name of each of her sacral chakras and was being taught how to open them for herself – preparation, or so Isobel claimed, for the influx of new energies which the study of Wicca would engender.

'Draw the energy into your root chakra,' Isobel said, closing her eyes and breathing deeply. 'Picture your butt as a huge tank slowly filling with red liquid—'

'Time to slap on an Always Ultra, then,' Terry muttered.

Isobel's eyes snapped open. 'What?'

'Nothing.'

'Your etheric energy is getting low again, Terry.'

'Sorry.' Terry made an effort to concentrate. 'OK. My, er, butt is a big red tank.'

'Now imagine it rising up your spine to the sacral chakra, like a huge red snake.'

'Got you.'

'What's it doing?' Isobel demanded.

'Er,' Terry tried to think. What was it likely to be doing? Isobel had already told her that the colour of the sacral chakra was orange. 'Changing colour?' she suggested.

'Good. Well done. Now let it spin round and round like a Catherine wheel. Is it getting bigger?'

'It's definitely getting bigger.'

'OK. Now draw it up to the heart chakra. Let the Catherine wheel encircle your heart like a small green pair of fiery hands.'

These chakras seemed to mix an awful lot of metaphors, Terry reflected.

Eventually they reached the throat chakra. 'Can you feel it? Can you feel it in your throat?' Isobel demanded.

'Definitely.'

'Then let it out, Terry. Let it out!'

Terry opened her mouth obediently for the energy to exit. Isobel tutted.

'Let me hear the energy, Terry. Let me hear you sing it.'

Terry gargled a few notes. She had no idea what etheric energy was meant to sound like. She wondered if this whole nonsense was actually an elaborate hoax perpetrated on her in revenge for sleeping with Jamie. She pictured all the Wiccans falling about later: 'What! You never got her to fall for the old singing chakras routine!'

But Isobel seemed completely serious. 'Very good, Terry. Your energy levels are right up now.'

'Aren't they?' said Terry, who wanted nothing more than to fall into bed, preferably on her own.

'That's enough for today.'

'Great.' She started to lever her numb ankles off her thighs.

'Uh-uh. Don't get up just yet. First we have to learn how to close those chakras up again.'

'It's the way she waves her bloody hands around when she's talking,' Terry said. 'It's like watching one of those party political broadcasts on BBC2, where someone's doing sign language for the deaf in the corner.'

Above her Jamie chuckled. She was lying on her front, naked now, while Jamie, straddling her, gave her a massage: something he had turned out to be surprisingly proficient at. The little room was lit by three candles stuck in empty whisky bottles.

'Oh, and by the way,' she said, 'did you know you're sitting on my root chakra? It's actually a big red tank full of liquid energy.'

He shifted his position so that he was squatting further down her thighs, and kneaded her root chakra with his fingers. 'How's that?'

'Terrific.'

He paused, and she heard him plucking one of the candles from its holder.

'And this?' he breathed.

She arched her back, knowing what was coming next, but not knowing exactly where: where on her exposed and fragile skin the first delicate drops of molten wax were going to fall. The anticipation was everything. Every nerve ending in her back tingled, pleading both for the absence of pain and for the exact opposite. She gasped, and a tiny trail of liquid fire brushed across her spine. She closed her eyes and buried her face deeper into the mattress. Behind her she heard the chink as Jamie, reaching onto the floor for his trousers, pulled the belt out of its loops.

'And now,' he said softly, 'for something completely different.'

'What are you doing?'

Iain placed another sheet of tracing paper over the map and picked up his pencil. 'I'm working out the scatter pattern from the death pit.' He pointed to the little plastic bags full of bones on the table. 'Those are what the police found when they did a search of the area.'

Laura made a face. 'Ugh.'

'Don't worry, they're none of them human. Which is the interesting thing, really.'

'Why's that?'

'Because gnawed piglet bones were found dispersed in a relatively wide area. Like this.' He drew a large circle around some crosses on the map. 'Which suggests that the foxes had access to the death pit for quite some time.'

'I'm with you so far.'

'But Donna's body was relatively intact when we found it.'

'Which means it hadn't been there very long.'

'Leaving two mysteries. First, she hadn't been seen since November. Secondly, the body, though intact, was very decomposed.'

'That's simple, then. She was originally buried somewhere else.'

'Yes,' Iain said doubtfully. 'Yes, that's certainly the simple answer.'

'What's the complicated one?'

'Ah. Now that I don't know yet.' He looked up as she placed a glass of wine on the table next to him. 'Thanks,' he muttered, picking up his pencil again.

# NINETEEN

Terry stood very, very still. Three or four fat, furry bees crawled sleepily over her forearm: there was another one on her neck, and what felt like a couple in her hair. Each time one moved she felt the little pipe-cleaner legs prickle against her skin. More buzzed around her; a huge, lazy atom of which she was the frozen centre.

Having lots of bees on you, she discovered, was very different to having just one: not just greater in degree, but a completely different sensation. With one bee you could locate it, watch it and generally make sure that it wasn't about to do you any damage. Having a whole bunch of the brutes meant you couldn't place them: the various crawling feet ceased to belong to separate insects and became one multifaceted, fearsome monster reaching its tendrils around her, smothering her in its soft, wriggling embrace. She shuddered, and took a deep breath. If anything was likely to induce another panic attack, this was.

'Stay calm,' Gregor's voice said from behind her. 'Now I am going to add some more.'

He reached into the hive in front of her and

casually scooped up another fistful. His hands were gloved, but other than that he wore no special protection. Terry had been wearing a hat with a sort of veil hanging from it, until Gregor had decided that it would calm the insects down if they were introduced to the stranger in the flesh, so to speak. In any case, he told her, the protection of the veil was more psychological than real, since the bees were quite capable of crawling under its edges.

'What do I do if I get stung?' she asked out of the corner of her mouth.

'Ah. Yes. That is very important.'

'Why?'

'You must say "ouch" or "yow". Either is permitted. But whatever happens you must not say anything else, such as "Scheiße" or "fuck" or even "ow".'

'Why "ouch" and "yow"?'

He shrugged, standing over her and letting the bees drip from his hands onto her shoulders. 'I don't know. But it is a very old bee-keeper custom. It is believed to help with the pain.'

'Great,' muttered Terry.

He laughed. 'Also, because it is your first time, I have some Wasp-eze in my pocket. If you get stung, scrape the sting out with your nail. Most of the venom comes out after the bee has gone. And you may also try to suck it, like a snakebite.'

'Do you get stung often?'

'No. The bees know me now. They are very clever. Not clever like people are clever, individually, but clever as a group. This is something you will learn about Wicca too, I think. The power of the group mind.'

'And the organization of the hive around the

queen. That's like Wicca too, isn't it? All the rituals revolve around the High Priestess.'

Gregor shrugged. 'Not so like. The queen bee is not really a queen as we would think of a queen. She is more like a slave. She has to do what the men tell her.' He held up a gloved hand on which two or three bees still crawled. 'There. Do you see her? The bigger one is a queen. Except she is not so big now. This one has been starved by the worker bees, to make her light enough to fly away. The hive has got crowded, so it is making a new queen. At the moment the new ones are just larvae, but in a few days the first one will hatch and then she will kill the others by stinging them through the walls of their cells. And the old queen will leave with the swarm.' Carefully he placed the queen back in the hive. 'There is only one queen in a hive, ever. If I put in a queen from one of the other hives they would kill her.'

'Vicious little brutes, aren't they?'

He smiled. 'I do not think they will be vicious to you. Not now they have been properly introduced.' He began to pick the bees off her one by one, flicking them into the air, and she began to breathe normally again. 'See how heavy they are,' he said. 'They can hardly fly. That is because they are all carrying some honey, to start the new hive. They are less likely to sting us while they are like this.'

'Aren't some people allergic?'

'Some, yes. But for most people it is a very good thing to be stung by a bee.'

'Good luck, you mean?'

He shook his head. 'We are not superstitious, Terry, despite being witches. I mean the chemicals in the venom are good for your health. Bee-keepers always live to be very old.'

Gregor was all right, she decided. Apparently resigned to the fact that none of the other Wiccans shared his passion, and that helping him was considered the least pleasant of all the household jobs, with Terry he was neither apologetic nor defensive, methodically getting on with the job in hand.

The Wiccans owned over twenty hives, and Gregor was building up the population even more. That was the purpose of today's expedition. At this time of year the Wiccans were paid a small fee by local fruit farmers to place the hives among crops to pollinate them: subsequently they were moved to the orchards at Nineveh, until it was time to put them out on the moors in autumn. It was one of these that was ready to spin off a colony into a new hive.

'So,' he said at last. 'I think we are ready now.'

Together they manhandled the new hive next to the old one. Then Terry was allowed to put on the gloves and place a handful of insects inside. After a few moments they flew back to the first hive.

'Oh,' Terry said, disappointed, 'it hasn't worked.'

'No, it's fine. Come here and watch.'

She went and stood next to him. 'Just here,' he said, pointing to one of the racks of honeycomb.

A bee was running round and round in a complicated circular pattern.

'This is a bee dance,' he instructed. 'He is telling the others to fly directly left of the sun.'

'You're kidding!'

He shook his head. 'No. It is the language of bees. Watch.'

Suddenly, as if the hive itself had grown a tail, a

stream of bees flowed out of it, threshed from side to side for a moment and then snaked towards the new hive. It was, Terry thought, as inexplicable and as inevitable as a slinky toy cascading from one step onto another. Within moments a river of bees was pouring itself out of their old home and into the new one.

She watched, fascinated. Soon it was over. Like the genie pouring himself into Aladdin's lamp, tens of thousands of insects had crammed inside the new box, and the lids on both hives were simultaneously slammed shut.

'Job done,' Gregor said, carefully brushing a few stragglers from his trousers. 'You did well. Sometimes people get scared.'

'That's it?'

'That's it. Except we take some wax back.'

In the old days, he explained, the job of beekeeper in an abbey or monastery was important not only for the honey it produced but also because the church depended on the wax for light.

'We make our own candles for the rituals. It looks nice and', he shrugged, 'it smells nice too.'

'Can I help make them?'

'Sure.'

Helping Gregor, she decided, was a lot more fun than being instructed by Isobel.

Back at Nineveh they found the kitchen humming with activity. Zoe and Brigid were making cakes, helped by Judith's little boy, Myrvyn, while baby Holly sat imperiously in a high chair, looking like Sir Walter Raleigh in a thick goatee of babyfood.

'How was it?' Zoe asked.

'Terrifying,' Terry confessed; partly because it was

true, and partly because she calculated that if Brigid thought she'd enjoyed it, she'd find her something even worse to do.

As if on cue, Isobel appeared. 'You mustn't be frightened of bee stings, you know,' she said smugly, going to the stove and making herself a pot of herbal tea. 'They're actually very good for you.'

'Yes, Gregor told me.'

'Terry did not get frightened,' Gregor said flatly. 'She was very brave.'

'Whatever. Come along, Terry. I want to be done with you in plenty of time to prepare my energies for the Esbat.'

'Coming, mistress,' Terry muttered behind her back. She'd had visions of quietly searching the farmhouse for the *Book of Shadows* when no-one was looking, but so far she hadn't had a moment to herself. They were having one of their rituals that evening, but she'd already been asked if she'd babysit Judith's children and been given a dozen books on Wicca to read. It looked suspiciously as if someone had decided she needed to be kept busy.

'I thought you'd like to know something about our Esbat tonight,' Isobel said.

They were sitting cross-legged on the floor again. Terry had opened her chakras to Isobel's satisfaction, and the other woman had started to teach her the rudiments of Wicca. They had started with the Wiccan calendar, Isobel explaining how the year was divided into eight great festivals, or Sabbats, with more low-key gatherings or Esbats taking place at each full moon. Isobel had surprised her by being rather a good teacher, both extremely knowledgeable and adept at explaining her knowledge.

Terry, who had done a bit of teaching herself, knew it wasn't an easy combination to achieve.

'The word "Esbat" comes from the old French, and literally means a frolic. In fact, we generally treat the Sabbats as celebrations, and use the Esbats for our magical workings. Tonight, however, it will be a little more frolicsome.'

'Why's that?'

Without uncrossing her legs, Isobel reached out and poured herself some more raspberry-leaf tea from the pot in front of her. 'Tonight we're having an astral mass for our friend Donna. We extinguish the candles to symbolize the passing of life, and then those who wish to, re-enact the Great Rite: celebrating the idea that even amidst death, life is greater.' She sipped her tea, her green eyes holding Terry's. 'You know what the Great Rite is, presumably.'

'Sex magic,' Terry said flatly. 'You don't make it sound very, ah, erotic.'

Isobel tutted. 'You're missing the point, Terry. It's a symbolic union between the God and the Goddess, not a chance to screw someone with the lights out.' She smiled. 'Though that can be an added bonus.'

She means Jamie, Terry realized. She had no doubt that when the candles went out, Isobel would be making a beeline for Terry's lover. Beeline. Funny how bee images were coming into her head today.

She remembered Gregor telling her that the first queen to crawl out of its cell went round killing the other queen larvae with her sting. Isobel, she was beginning to realize, worked on much the same principle.

\* \* \*

'I promise I won't.'

'You'll have to run pretty fast then,' she warned him.

Jamie stroked her wet hair. 'I will instantly perform a magical act which will render me invisible,' he assured her. 'And just in case that doesn't work, I'll hide behind Gerard. He'll be after Isobel himself, and he's a pretty fast mover for his age.'

They were lying in an ancient enamelled bath under the eaves, Terry reclining against his chest. The soapy water made islands of their knees and toes.

'These rituals – they're basically all about sex, aren't they?'

'Not really. Not in the shagging sense of the word.'

'You mean there's another meaning of the word sex?'

'Of course. Sex as in male and female. Gender. It's like a battery – you need a positive and a negative to create energy. Sometimes we celebrate that energy, sometimes we put it to use.'

'Like how?'

'Oh – mundane stuff, usually. Helping someone whose car isn't working properly. Banishing bad feelings. Making sure the earth turns properly, the sun rises every day and the seasons follow each other in their proper order.' He soaped his hands and began to slide them around her breasts.

'Blimey. So when I thought you were getting your leg over, really you were saving the universe?'

'It's like any religion,' he said, ignoring her interruption. 'Ninety-nine per cent rather mundane. Sex is just a tiny part of what we do. Besides, what's the problem? You don't strike me as someone with any major inhibitions.'

'No ... but I think I like sex with people, not with gods. To tell the truth, I'm a little suspicious of this whole Great Mother thing. I think it may just be misogyny under another guise.'

'Mmm,' he murmured, sliding his hand a little lower, in between her thighs. She shifted a little, to allow him access, and closed her eyes, her train of thought broken.

'Anyway ... while I have no doubt that you'll keep your promise not to shag Isobel tonight, I'm going to cast a little magic of my own to make sure.'

'Oh? And which spell would that be?'

'It's called', she said fiercely, 'fucking your brains out.' Lifting herself up a little, she reached between her legs for his cock.


That evening, as she sat with one of Isobel's books in one hand and Holly in the other, there was a knock on the door. She went to open it and found Magnus on the doorstep.

'My god, that was quick,' he said, indicating Holly.

'Very funny. She's one of the Wiccans'. And keep your voice down. They're all in a ritual, and I don't suppose they'd like to be disturbed.'

'Can I come in?'

She shrugged. 'I suppose so.'

'I've come to apologize,' he said, following her into the kitchen.

'Yes, I thought you might have.'

'I was rude and abusive and I said some unforgivable things. I'm sorry.'

'The word "slag" featured somewhere, I seem to remember.'

'As I said, it was unforgivable. I wasn't thinking straight.'

'I suppose you did have Flora on your mind,' she said, softening. 'Or what was left of your mind after all that whisky. How is she?'

'She's fine. She's had the life frightened out of her, of course, but that's probably no bad thing . . . thank you for asking. But Flora—' he hesitated. 'Flora wasn't the only reason I lost my rag.'

'Oh?'

'That night . . . when Flora told me you'd gone off with some bloke. I was . . . worried about you.' He looked down at his feet. 'Somehow you seem to have aroused my protective instincts.' He looked her in the eye again. 'Well, instincts, anyway. The truth is I was jealous.'

'Ah,' she said. This was something she hadn't foreseen. 'Look, Magnus,' she said gently, 'I'm not usually like – the way you saw me when I arrived. Frail and vulnerable, I mean. The real me is a strident, aggressive harpy with a vicious tongue and an even nastier right hook. I'm not so much a lame duck as a slightly bruised pterodactyl. You wouldn't feel protective about me once I'm better, honestly.'

'Come back to Babcock,' he pleaded.

'Magnus, I can't at the moment. I'm sorry.'

'You're still angry with me.'

'It's not that. It's just that . . . well, I'm involved in things here.'

He picked up her book and read the title. '*Witchcraft Today*. I knew it. You are a witch after all.'

'I need to find those missing papers. Nothing makes any sense without them. No papers, no doctorate. It's as simple as that.'

'OK.' He stood for a moment, watching her. 'Just be careful here, won't you?'

'What do you mean?'

'One of them was killed, remember? When all's said and done . . . it is a cult, after all.'

'Magnus!' She laughed. 'I hardly think anyone's going to get upset about me investigating Catherine McCulloch.'

They sat together in the spartan sitting room of her cottage, eating curry washed down with beer.

'Wonderful,' Iain said. 'Compliments to the chef.'

'The chef is probably a computer somewhere,' Laura said. 'It's Mr Sainsbury's finest.'

'Compliments to the shopper, then.'

She had done a run to the supermarket that afternoon, and for once the fridge and cupboards were stocked with food.

'So what made you decide to go all domestic on me?' he asked, stretching himself out on the sofa. 'I was rather enjoying the challenge of cooking in this house, to be honest. It's a bit like one of those survival courses – you know, two weeks seeing whether you can live off the land. I was all set to go and shoot some earthworms.'

'Ha bloody ha . . . I don't know. Perhaps it was guilt. I am taking your money.'

'Not mine. The government's.'

'And also . . . I suppose one feels a bit unfeminine . . . you know, the old cliché. One should be able to provide food for one's man.' Unexpectedly, she blushed. 'Not that you're my man, of course. But you know what I mean.'

'Gareth's got used to it, I suppose.'

She took a deep breath. 'There is no Gareth, actually.'

'Sorry?'

'Gareth doesn't exist. I made him up.'

'Oh. I see.'

Laura sighed. 'When I first came here . . . it was hard enough anyway, trying to get people to take me seriously. Vets, food reps, the people who maintain my vehicles . . . they weren't used to seeing a woman doing it. Some of them came on to me, some of them just patronized me. So I started wearing a ring on my engagement finger. It wasn't even a proper engagement ring, but if anyone asked about that I just gave them the story about not being able to put a diamond up a pig's birth canal. And it worked. I achieved status and sexual untouchability, all in one go.'

'Hmm,' he said, thinking about it. 'I can see why you might . . . but what about later, once you'd established yourself? Why not pretend you'd broken it off?'

'I don't know,' she said, twisting the ring on her finger. 'It seemed . . . easier. I got used to it, I suppose.'

He nodded thoughtfully.

'And I never met anyone worth taking it off for.'

He took the dirty plates through into the little kitchen and started on the washing-up. 'What about coffee?' he called through to her.

'Sure. I'll make it.' She followed him into the kitchen and reached past him to fill the kettle from the tap. For a moment her body seemed to brush against him a fraction longer than was necessary. But it might have been his imagination.

'You don't have to do that.' She indicated the washing-up. 'I usually leave it till the morning.'

'I'm good with a brush. Years of digging out decaying bones have made me the perfect domesticated male.'

226

'He cooks, he washes up . . . is there anything else?'

'No,' he admitted. 'That's probably the extent of my skills.'

He had his hands buried deep in the water, so that when he felt her arm snake round his chest from behind, and her body press against him, he was effectively pinioned, unable to move or react. Lips pressed against his ear, and then her tongue, both thunderous and gentle, slid into the whorls of flesh.

'Sure about that?' she whispered. He turned, and she smiled tentatively. 'Better take this off, I suppose,' she said, tugging at the ring. Then she saw the look in his eyes, and said, 'Oh.'

Perhaps if it had not been her who had made the first move; perhaps if he had come across her sleeping, and reached out his hand to brush hair from her face like loose soil, and she had woken to his touch and smiled at him. Or perhaps if she had been a different kind of person, one not so vibrantly, frighteningly alive. But he couldn't say these things, because they would only have made it worse.

What he did say was, 'I'm sorry. I'm just not very good at all that.'

'Neither am I,' she muttered. She looked at the engagement ring in her hand. 'Looks like I don't need the ring of steel to keep men away, after all.'

'It's not you. It's me. I'm just . . .' He took a deep breath. 'I can't do sex, that's all. I don't know why not. It's like a joke that everyone else gets but I don't. Sorry.'

'Don't be.' She sighed. 'I feel the same, to tell the truth. I just thought I ought to make the effort.'

He laughed. 'Thanks.'

'I didn't mean it like that. You're the first man

in ages I've felt I could even try with.' She went and busied herself with the kettle. 'One sugar, isn't it?'

Somehow they got through the next fifteen minutes. Elaborate courtesy and rational conversation gradually smothered the tiny spark of attraction. But later, as he lay in bed reading an archaeological textbook, he thought he heard the sound of someone crying through the wall.

Terry looked up from *Witchcraft Today*. Holly, propped into a corner of the sofa, was fast asleep. Myrvyn, exhausted at last, lay curled up on one of the chairs, his eyes also closed.

She listened. From what had once been the billiards room, and was now where the rituals were held, came the sound of chanting. That was the one good thing about Wicca: the rituals seemed to take for ever.

Slipping off the chair, she considered her next move. There wouldn't be anything of interest in the communal rooms. Gerard had a study, though: that was the obvious place to start.

She tried the study door. Not locked. She wasn't surprised: Gerard wasn't the paranoid type.

An old desk, a filing cabinet, boxes of paraphernalia scattered around the floor. She opened one and looked inside. It was full of knives – elaborate, ceremonial daggers; some fashioned from deer's antlers, some made from elaborately worked iron. She opened another. It held various kinds of chalice.

Turning her attention to the filing cabinet, she found it locked. She pulled open the top drawer of the desk, and tried the first key she found. It fitted.

She ran her eye along the titles of the files. *Instructions and Guarantees*. She peeked inside and saw the instruction leaflet for a washing machine. *Insurance. Pensions. Tax.* She had a quick look: nothing seemed to be more recent than 1990. *Press Cuttings.* She pulled that one out and flicked through it. Most were clipped from the local newspaper, which obviously used the Wiccans as an annual silly-season photo opportunity. An older cutting caught her eye: a picture of Gerard, very much younger, sporting tie-dyed trousers, a bandsman's jacket and a multicoloured electric guitar. And there in the background, if she wasn't mistaken, was a younger, more curvaceous Brigid, in a quaintly eye-popping Op-art Mary Quant dress, holding a tambourine and smiling innocently. 'New single from The Paper Trees launched on Pirate Radio', was the headline. Terry smiled and moved on.

*House Bills. Receipts.* No ... *Deeds.* That sounded interesting. Some old documents, folded inside a brown envelope, but they were only the title deeds to the house itself, bought in 1973 by John Mcteer from the estate of Mrs Elizabeth Lulworth. *Financial.* She pulled out the whole file and laid it on the table. Hundreds of bank statements, dating back ten years or more. Rudimentary sets of accounts. But nothing for the last few years.

A final piece of paper caught her eye. It was a photocopied receipt for six thousand pounds. Then she saw the name, and whistled. *Received from David Nicolaides, The Old Seminary, Babcock.* When you needed money, there was nothing like going to someone who had plenty to spare.

# TWENTY

Isobel came down to breakfast in a filthy mood, and insisted on grilling Terry on her previous night's reading in front of the other Wiccans.

'In what order do we summon the Lords of the Watchtowers?'

'East, South, West and North,' Terry answered through a mouthful of toast and honey.

'Who are the Elementals and what do we use them for?'

'Elementals are etheric non-physical beings corresponding to air, earth, fire and water. They are visualized as sylphs, salamanders, undines and gnomes. In the sacred circle they are represented by a dish of water, a dish of salt, a candle and scented smoke from incense. We use them to purify the circle and create a psychic vacuum in which all the physical forces of the world are held in perfect balance. The circle is an ancient symbol of wholeness and perfection in which we can exist between the worlds of men and the Mighty Ones.'

Zoe and Jamie led the applause, in which Isobel did not join. She said tartly: 'It also represents the union of opposites, Terry. Astral and physical, ritual and intuitive, question and answer, male and female. Next question. What is the chant for raising power?'

Terry thought for a moment. It had been late when she'd got to this bit, and learning nonsense verse had never been her forte. 'Er . . . Eko, Eko, Azerak; Eko, Eko, Gromelak—'

'Zomelak,' Isobel corrected. 'And what about the Bagahai rune? Have you – I won't say learned it, because you see, Terry, Wicca isn't about learning, it's about relearning what we already know in our deepest hearts but have forgotten with our conscious minds. Have you relearned the Bagahai rune?'

'No,' Terry confessed, avoiding Zoe's eye lest she start to giggle. 'I'm afraid I haven't relearned that yet.'

'She's been too busy,' Jamie said, spreading honey on his toast, 'relearning how to shag.'

Brigid, who had sat quietly through all this so far, murmured, 'I don't think we need to be crude about it, Jamie. This is a communal meal, by which we worship the Goddess.' Judith had turned away from the table without a word and started stacking plates, her baby in her arms.

Isobel's eyes narrowed. 'Your etheric energy is very low, Terry. Perhaps we should go somewhere quiet and meditate.'

'I'm afraid that will have to wait,' Gregor interjected. 'This morning I need my assistant with me.' He smiled at Terry. 'You can meditate while we move hives, yes?'

'Sounds good to me,' she said gratefully.

Alex McCulloch slipped out of the house in the

pre-dawn darkness. In his hand the wooden stock of the rifle felt smooth and muscular, hard as the neck of a horse. Silently, he strode up the path towards the mountain, now no more than a black shape against the inky sky.

In the fields, horses slept standing up. Sheep littered the mountainside like bomb victims, not moving. He gave them a wide berth. On the edge of his horizon a fox lifted its head to watch him, cleared its throat, then jumped delicately away. Alex ignored it. He had never liked shooting foxes. You couldn't eat them, and in any case he admired them: admired the way they killed so efficiently, with just a bite and a shake of the head, so that their prey was dead before it knew it.

On the moor itself he described a large circle, doubling back on the woods. There were streaks of light in the sky behind him, but in amongst the trees it was still black as midnight.

The stag stood on the edge of the wood, nibbling delicately at the leaves of a sapling. Alex breathed exultantly – he could have sworn it was no more than that, but the big head with its three-year spread of antlers swung towards him suspiciously, as if the horns were some kind of radar, aerials that could pick up what no ears could hope to hear. For a few seconds the stag watched the horizon, still chewing; then it finished its mouthful of leaves and turned back to the tree.

On all fours he crept, a few inches at a time, over the rough heather, using the larger bushes as cover. When he was eighty yards away he stopped, and raised his head. It was still there. Knowing that a bird or a sound might give him away at any moment, he pulled the rifle alongside him as quickly as he dared. Through the sights the animal seemed so close he could touch it. His finger slipped the safety catch off. It made no more noise than the click of a ballpoint pen, but he could see a great shudder pass along the animal's body as all its muscles tensed for flight. *Now.* He squeezed the trigger, and simultaneously the deer was flung onto its side, its legs twitching, the explosion catapulting a dozen or so squawking birds out of the trees.

He ran towards the dying animal and knelt down beside it. Blood was pumping from a wound in its neck. It looked at him with terror. Quickly he pulled a hunting knife from its sheath and slit its throat, careful to keep out of the way of the sharp, flailing hooves. Then he stood up and began to pull off his clothes.

Naked, he stood above the animal, holding his knife in one hand. After a moment he crouched down, cupped his hands underneath the wound to catch the blood, and smeared it all over his chest and belly, as far down as his cock, his great shout of triumph making the woods shake for the second time that morning.

They drove on tiny, winding roads in an ancient open-top tractor and trailer. There was only room on the little iron seat for one, so Terry sat on the trailer, facing backwards, with her feet dangling precariously over the edge and her back against an empty hive. Chocolate-brown Highland cattle blinked at her inquisitively over low stone walls; the sun shone on her back, and the engine puttered and spat behind her. She suddenly felt absurdly and gloriously happy. Forget the thesis: I could stay here, she thought; helping Gregor with his honey, screwing Jamie, being accepted by the Wiccans . . . but it was only a pipe dream, and she knew it.

They drove past a small stone farmhouse, high above Babcock. The track they drove on now was too bumpy for her to sit down in the trailer, so she crouched where she could clutch the sides for balance. At last they reached a field full of rows of fruit. Gregor stopped about fifty yards from a white hive, identical to the one they were carrying.

'If we get too close the engine may disturb them,' he explained. 'We will carry the hive from here.'

Together they manhandled the new hive to a spot about ten yards from the old one. Gregor went and peeked inside.

'We're too late,' he said unhappily. 'They have made a swarm already.'

'What does that mean?'

He looked around. 'Some bees have already left the hive to find a new home . . . I'm surprised the farmer did not tell me. Perhaps they are in the trees.'

Together they walked to a small copse on the edge of the field.

'Look up,' he instructed. 'You will hear them, even if you cannot see them.'

They separated. Terry peered through the gloom of the trees. Then she saw it. On a low branch in front of her, an almost spherical object, the size of a basketball. It was partly wrapped around the branch, and partly hanging from it; a buzzing, ticking ball of energy. Bees flopped around it like trails of smoke.

She went and called Gregor.

'Good,' he said, pulling some gloves out of his pocket. 'But this is a little more dangerous than the last time, yes? You must stay close, in case I need you, but out of range of the bees.'

Gingerly he reached into the centre of the ball. The outer layer of insects parted round his arm, then closed up around him.

'Ouch,' he said softly. 'Ouch, ouch, yow.'

He paused.

'This time, we cannot just pick up some insects and put them in the new hive,' he explained. 'These bees already have a new queen and some honeycomb with larvae in it. I have to break off the honeycomb, and take the queen to the empty hive. The other bees will follow the queen. And the queen will come with me because she cannot fly any more. Ouch. Now I am waiting for the bees to get used to me.'

Delicately he groped around in the innards of the sphere. 'I have it now,' he said, almost to himself. 'So.' He pulled away, a jagged piece of comb in his hand, ripping a hole in the side of the swarm. Immediately the bees' hum doubled in volume.

'Now we walk,' he said.

He stepped slowly away from the tree, Terry keeping a safe distance away. Almost at once the remainder of the swarm detached itself from the tree and followed him, leaving a great stalactite of honeycomb hanging from the branch.

'Now we walk faster,' he said. 'I mean very, very fast.'

They hurried through the woods, but it was too late. Bees were clustering around the handful of honeycomb he was carrying. It was like rugby players throwing themselves into a scrum, Terry thought; except that there were tens of thousands of them. Soon Gregor's arms were completely invisible; then his shoulders disappeared. He looked as if he was wearing a cape made entirely of bees.

He tucked his neck down into his collar. 'Tell me which way to go.'

She realized that he was having to close his eyes against the miasma of insects. 'There's a tree in front of you,' she instructed. 'Take one pace to the left. Now straight ahead for a few steps. OK, there's another tree. Not far to go now.'

Eventually, with Terry guiding him, they reached the hive. Gregor placed the honeycomb inside, and within seconds the other bees had followed.

'Were you stung badly?' she asked.

He shrugged. 'A few times.' He looked at her closely. 'And you?'

Only now did she realize that she had been stung several times on her arm. She scraped the stings out with her nail as Gregor had showed her, then sucked the venom out and spat it onto the ground.

'We have done good work today, I think,' he said.

When they got back to the tractor the farmer was waiting for them. 'Good morning, Angus,' Gregor called cheerfully. 'We found a swarm in the trees.'

'I need a word, Gregor,' the farmer said awkwardly. 'You'll have to take the hives away.'

'What? It isn't time, I think—'

'It's the wife. She's been talking to some of the other women. I'm sorry, but she won't hear of them staying.'

'I don't understand.'

'I've nothing against you, you understand,' the farmer said gruffly. 'But witches and magic and all . . . she won't hear of it.'

'But we have always been witches,' Gregor said reasonably. 'And you have had hives here for years.'

'But now the wee lassie's been killed. It's not right, is it?'

Gregor stayed admirably calm. 'No, it is certainly not right. We are all very shocked by her death. But it was not one of us who killed her.'

'And how can ye be sure o' that?' Gregor started to explain but the farmer had already turned on his heel. 'It's no' a debate, Gregor. We don't want your hives and that's final.'

Silently Terry helped Gregor lift both hives onto the trailer.

'He's a good man,' Gregor said at last. 'I did not think he could be so irrational.'

'People get frightened by things they don't understand,' Terry said diplomatically.

'I suppose so.' He sighed. 'I would be very sad if we were not welcome any more, Terry. I was very happy here.'

It was interesting, she thought later as they rode back to Nineveh, that he was already using the past tense.


They grabbed some lunch, and then Isobel grabbed her.

'Time for work, Terry.'

Terry groaned inwardly. Her stings were throbbing, she was tired and she really wasn't sure she could cope with an afternoon of Isobel.

'What's the matter? Etheric energy still low?' Isobel said sweetly. 'Perhaps we should do some exercise first.'

'No,' Terry assured her, 'I'm fine. Let's make a start, shall we?'

She followed her into the sitting room and sank down into the lotus position as usual.

'Uh-uh,' Isobel said. 'Today we're going to make an important step forward, Terry.' She reached up and started to unbutton the neck of her polo shirt. 'Today we're going to go through the different stages of your initiation ceremony. Sky-clad, just as we'll be on the night.' She pulled the shirt over her head. Underneath she was braless, revealing a pair of small, perfectly formed breasts.

Terry glanced at the door.

'If anyone does come in, they won't give you a second glance. To us, being sky-clad is as natural as being clothed,' Isobel continued. 'After a while, you won't be able to imagine how you ever got uptight about it.'

Feeling thoroughly uncomfortable, Terry shed her clothes. At least I was wearing clean knickers, she thought irrelevantly.

Isobel gave Terry's body a contemptuous glance, then stepped out of her tracksuit trousers and sat down gracefully on the floor in the lotus position, motioning for Terry to do likewise. In this position, all Terry's lumps and bumps – and much more besides – were completely on display. Isobel seemed to feel no such qualms.

'When we first shed our clothes, we are like a crab stripped of its shell,' Isobel was saying: 'That is a necessary part of being initiated – conquering our fear, learning to trust those with whom we will soon be forming a single group mind. What you are hearing now, Terry, is the voice of your inner parent, telling you to put your clothes back on, to cover up the shame of Eve. We need to learn to disregard that voice. So much of Wicca will not make sense if we allow ourselves to listen to what the inner parent has to say about it.'

There were voices in the kitchen beyond. 'Oh, Alan,' Isobel called.

Alan appeared at the door. Terry did not look up. 'Yes?'

'I've forgotten the tools. Would you bring them to me?'

'Sure,' he said, slipping away again.

'When you are initiated,' Isobel continued calmly, 'you will be brought to the circle both naked and blindfold. At this point you will be given two passwords. These are secret words which will enable you to identify any other witch, of any tradition.'

Alan returned with a small knife, a sword, a short black stick, a length of knotted cord and a piece of cloth, placing them on the ground in front of Isobel.

'OK,' Isobel said, rising gracefully to her feet, 'let's rehearse it properly. I'll stand in for the High Priest.'

Terry allowed herself to be blindfold with the cloth, and stumbled through the various parts of the ritual as best she could.

'The final part of your initiation is the ordeal,' Isobel was saying. 'It is a common feature of all initiation ceremonies, all over the world, that they involve some trial of purpose.'

Hang on, Terry thought, no one told me about an ordeal.

'In our tradition, the ordeal involves ritual scourging with the rope. The first scourging is of three strokes, the second one seven, the third nine and the fourth and final scourging is twenty-one strokes. After that you will be asked to swear an oath, your blindfold will be removed, and then you'll be a witch.'

240

'Is this, er, scourging a part of all your rituals?' Terry asked.

'No. Just this one. Of course, no-one will think any the less of you for deciding you don't really want to go through with it,' Isobel said happily. 'For some people, the sacrifice is too great. Not everyone has it in them to be a Wiccan.'

Nicky Heron rang the bookshop bell for the third time. At last: someone was coming. She held her warrant card up to the glass door.

'All right, all right,' Russell Kane panted. He was wearing a vast white dressing gown. 'I was in the shower.'

'Can I have a quick word, sir?'

'If you don't mind my being dishabillé.'

'I think I can cope,' Nicky said dryly. She put her case on the counter and opened it. 'Can you take a look at this for us, please?'

Russell took the plastic folder and squinted at it. 'It's a letter, isn't it? Written in the – well, it's hard to be exact, but probably the eighteenth century. What's its provenance?'

'It was found amongst the effects of a murder victim. We were wondering if it could be in any way relevant – if it's particularly valuable, for example.'

'Ooh, no. You pick this sort of thing up at auction for a hundred quid a dozen.' He made a face. 'It's not even clean.'

'That may be a consequence of where we found it.' She started to put the letter away again. 'But you don't think it's worth much?' He shook his head. 'And you couldn't tell me where it came from?' He shook his head again. 'Never mind. As you probably gathered, it's just a routine inquiry.'

Kane waited until she had gone, then scuttled into the back office and reached for the telephone. When the other person answered, he said, 'I just thought you ought to know that the police have been here. With one of the letters.' He listened. 'Absolutely no doubt. Part of a murder inquiry, they said.' He snorted. 'What do you think I told her? I said I wouldn't wipe my arse with it. But it's not just the police. There's some academic wandering round as well, and she won't be fobbed off quite so easily.' He listened again. 'Well, that's up to you, isn't it?'

He replaced the handset and sighed deeply. Above the shop, all was quiet. 'Marky? Turn that shower back on,' he called, waddling up the stairs.

'Gregor,' Terry said, 'tell me about scourging.'

They were out in the old orchard at Nineveh, repositioning the hives they'd brought back that morning.

He shrugged. 'It's part of the ritual. Not a big part, to be honest. Perhaps old John was a bit more interested, you know? I think some of the English used to like that kind of stuff.'

'It's just that I've worked out I'll have to go through a total of forty strokes. It seems . . . rather a lot, that's all.'

He laughed. 'For someone who didn't even notice you had been stung earlier, that's very funny. Our scourging is only symbolic. It isn't meant to hurt.'

'It isn't?' she said, relieved.

'Though I suppose', he added thoughtfully, 'it would depend on who is doing the scourging.'

'Who will it be in my case?'

'In your case, Isobel. She is the coven Maiden.'

'Oh, great,' Terry muttered.

Gregor roared with laughter. 'I think you might have to say "ouch" and "yow", OK?'

'Gregor, will you tell me something?'

'Of course. If I can.'

'Why does no-one want me here?'

He busied himself with the hive. 'What do you mean?'

'It just strikes me as odd. I mean, you were all newcomers once. No-one seems to want me around, and I don't quite know why.'

'Perhaps we're all a little jumpy, because of Donna's death.'

'Yes, but if it was nothing to do with you . . .'

He pointed at one of the hives. 'Will you bring that over here, please?'

'Who do you think killed her?'

'I am going to show you something.' He opened the hive. In his hands were what looked like a tiny pair of bellows. 'This is a smoke machine. Bees are woodland animals, you see, so they fear fire above all.' He worked the bellows, and artificial smoke cascaded over the insects in the hive. They reacted immediately, frantically, crawling over each other in an orgy of busyness. 'When they smell smoke, they start to gather honey, because they want to be ready to abandon the hive at a moment's notice. We use this to distract them, and make them less inclined to sting.' He paused. 'That's a bit like people, isn't it? If you want to distract them, you do it with whatever they fear most.'

'What do you mean, Gregor?' But he didn't elaborate.

'If you really want to know what Donna was like,

why don't you ask your *boyfriend*?' he said, putting a sarcastic emphasis on the last word.

'I already have. He can't tell me anything.'

After work she went upstairs to change. Dog tired, she decided to take a nap as well. She pulled off her overalls and flipped back the duvet.

There was a little lump of beeswax in the bed, about the size of a squash ball. It had been crudely moulded into the shape of a figure, with a smaller ball of wax for its head and four matchsticks pushed into it as rudimentary arms and legs. A tiny fragment of cloth, which Terry recognized as having been cut from one of her own T-shirts, was stuck to its breast. Something silver glinted in the middle of the scrap of cloth. She prised it loose with her fingernails. A pin.

You didn't have to be a Wiccan to know what the purpose of this particular charm was. But whoever had put it there didn't know her very well. It would take a lot more than this to drive her out of Nineveh.

Crushing the wax in her hand, she tossed it into the bag of rubbish.

Iain lowered himself into the death pit and checked his breathing mask. The top layers of decaying pigs had been removed now, their corpses carefully tagged and photographed before being placed in the second pit he'd had dug nearby. If anything, the stench was even worse now than it had been before, the topmost layer having acted as a kind of seal over the older carcasses below. However careful he was, his feet often slipped in the ooze, and more than once he found himself losing his balance and flailing around in the rotting innards of a piglet or an old sow.

There was a huge old boar carcass that he was working on now, black and bloated with decay. The ear tag, although still attached to the ear when he'd first uncovered it, had come away in his gloved hands, so he had photographed it *in situ* before attaching the ropes from the JCB. Worried that the ropes might simply tear the animal's legs off, he had wrapped them right round the body as well, which involved levering the huge dead-weight from side to side with the help of a SOCO Talbot had provided him with. The young scene-of-crime officer's face was green under his mask. Iain wasn't surprised. Even after so much time, the stench of so much death in so small a space was overpowering.

At last the ropes were secure and the SOCO clambered thankfully out of the pit and into the cab of the JCB. Iain stood beside the boar, signalling with his hand to indicate that he should begin to lift. The ropes cut deeply into the black flesh as they tightened, releasing a small torrent of dark-coloured ooze over his gumboots. Then the boar was airborne, its head flopping sideways: a strangely comic gesture.

His eyes were on the pig as it swung in the air, so that it was not until the JCB's cargo was safely delivered that he turned his attention back to the animal corpses at his feet. Where the boar had lain there was now a crater, about five feet long and three feet wide. It had been lying on a heap of dead piglets, their tiny bodies flattened by the dead-weight of all the layers above them. Iain aimed his camera into the crater and took a photograph.

It was through the viewfinder, illuminated with

sudden halogen intensity by the camera flash, that he saw what should have been obvious from the start. There was a piglet in there, its tiny teeth bared in the rictus of death, but there were also other shapes too – the size of piglets – but it took his brain a few moments to catch up with what his eyes were seeing, and he stood frozen in shock, uncomprehending. Gently he reached down and encircled a tiny human leg, a foot with five perfect toes. There was a hand, too, the thumb curled towards the mouth. A baby, he thought numbly. A human baby. And more than one: the leg and the hand belonged to two different miniature corpses, lying entwined in the space between a rotting piglet and the entrails of a prolapsed sow. He heard the SOCO clambering wearily down into the pit behind him, and turned to try to warn him, but he was speaking through the mask and nothing came out. As if in slow motion he saw the other man's eyes widen, and then the mask on his face began to shift and bulge as a dozen thin streams of vomit leaked from the edges and dripped down the man's filthy white overalls.

# TWENTY-ONE

'There are five of them so far,' Talbot said. 'The forensic archaeologist and a team of SOCOs have been working all night by floodlights, but for all we know there may still be more bodies in there. The initial report suggests that they're in varying stages of decomposition. In other words, killed over a period of time. Exactly how long a period, we won't know until the post-mortems.'

'Any connection with Donna Fairhead?' someone asked from the back.

'We don't know,' Talbot admitted. He ran his hand wearily over his face. He too had been up all night, ever since the news had come through. The assembled officers in front of him stared back, grim-faced. It was dawn. The first that most of them had known about the discovery of the infant corpses was twenty minutes earlier, when they'd been beeped to come to an emergency briefing. 'We'll be doing DNA tests, of course, to establish if any of them were hers. But they can't all have been.'

'What about witchcraft, sir?' Nicky said hesi-tantly. 'There does seem to be a possible link there.'

Talbot nodded. 'Exactly.' He raised his voice.

'Listen up, everyone. As you know, we interviewed all the Wiccans about Donna and drew a blank. But now we have to look at another possibility: ritual murder.'

A collective shudder ran through the assembled policemen. 'Just because we don't believe in magic and Satanism, doesn't mean that there aren't some sickos out there who do. One possibility – just a possibility, mind – is that these babies may have been killed as some kind of sacrifice. Conceivably, Donna Fairhead found out and was murdered herself before she could tell anyone.' He banged the table for silence. 'Settle down, will you? Anyway, we've got a warrant now. We're going to take the Wiccans' farmhouse apart. Any occult materials will be brought back here for investigation. Just remember, will you, that we're looking for evidence, not filling hospital beds.'

They were at breakfast when the convoy arrived. The big kitchen was full of noise and chatter. Terry was talking to Gregor about the day's work, and trying to avoid being caught by Isobel. Jamie was making toast on the Aga, while Judith waited with a saucepan of Holly's babyfood for a ring to become free. Myrvyn played under the table with a car.

There was a battering on the door and a shout of 'Police.' Then there were figures coming in from several directions at once, some from the back and some smashing their way through the door. Zoe screamed, and was immediately manhandled away by a WPC. The policemen all seemed to be shouting. Holly started to cry, and Judith swung her in her arms to try to calm her. Then a WPC was trying to grab Holly, and a man in plain clothes was saying

248

that he was a social worker and that the children were coming with him. In the screaming and confusion Gregor calmly got to his feet and punched the social worker, sending him sprawling to the floor. It took three policemen to wrench Gregor's arms behind his back and run him, bent double, out of the room. Judith was prised off her baby, finger by finger. One of the policemen spotted Myrvyn under the table and made a grab for him. Myrvyn scuttled away between adult legs, with the policeman in hot pursuit. Terry found herself shouting 'Don't hurt him,' only to be pushed out of the way herself as the policeman felled Myrvyn with a rugby tackle.

The boy started to cry as he was carried away. When Judith tried to go after him she was pushed back roughly towards the table. Terry got to her feet and, as hard as she possibly could, kicked the policeman responsible on the shins. That's it, she thought, they're bound to arrest me now. Instead, the man looked at her, his arms still wrapped around the struggling boy, and kicked her back, viciously. She felt the heavy boot connect with her ankle and collapsed, howling.

Gradually it became apparent that there was nothing they could do. The Wiccans who had not been in the kitchen were brought to join them. Gerard seemed OK, if a little bewildered. Alan went to the kettle and started making tea for everyone. Christ, he's calm, Terry thought. Only Judith went on screaming, a thin, hysterical wail that went on and on. Brigid was doing her best to calm her. Eventually Judith's screams subsided into helpless, breathless sobs.

A man in plain clothes came in and held up his hand for silence.

'What have you done with the children?' Brigid demanded angrily.

'They've been taken into protective custody.'

'When will they be coming back?'

'When it's considered safe for them to do so.'

'This is ridiculous,' Brigid snapped.

Judith started to scream again. 'My babies,' she wailed.

'They'll be placed with a foster family in the meantime,' Talbot said. 'We're investigating the murder of a number of infants, and we have to be absolutely sure that these children are safe. You'll all be taken to your rooms now and searched.' He had to shout to make himself heard. 'Please go with my officers. We have a warrant to search these premises and we intend to carry it out.'

The search was over in an hour. When the main body of police had gone, the two children, Gregor, Isobel and Jamie were gone too. Isobel had been so verbally abusive to the policewoman who searched her room that eventually, after several warnings, they had arrested her. Jamie had been found to have a large amount of cannabis, and was taken to the station to be charged with possession and intent to supply. He gave Terry a rueful smile as he was bundled away. Brigid and Zoe had taken Judith, still hysterical, upstairs to try to calm her down. The others were told to wait in the kitchen to be interviewed by the detectives, who now took over the other downstairs rooms. No-one spoke much. Anna clung to Stephan, the two of them conversing quietly in Dutch. Alan, still outwardly calm, read a newspaper. Gerard still seemed dazed, sitting on his chair with his eyes closed.

Occasionally Terry saw his lips move, as if he were chanting to himself.

When it was Terry's turn to be interviewed she was taken to the sitting room. The policeman who had come into the kitchen earlier was there, along with a woman who was also in plain clothes. The man introduced himself as Detective Superintendent Talbot, and the woman as Detective Sergeant Heron.

'You weren't here last time we came,' he said abruptly, once she'd given her name. 'How long have you been here, please?'

'About a week,' Terry said. 'Look, this is outrageous—'

'We've got a lot of statements to get through,' he interrupted her. 'It'll be over quicker if you just answer my questions. When exactly did you arrive?'

'Sunday night,' she muttered rebelliously.

'And you're a member of this group?'

It was such a long story. 'I'm an academic,' she said at last. 'I'm studying some of the Wiccans' beliefs.'

'Is there anyone who can vouch for you? For your academic credentials, I mean.'

She gave him her supervisor's phone number. He nodded to the woman officer, who pulled a mobile phone from her pocket and slipped out of the room.

'And what exactly are the Wiccans' beliefs, as you understand them?'

Terry took a breath. 'According to them, they worship a pagan goddess, using the same magical rituals that were used thousands of years ago by the pre-Christians.'

'What about killing babies? Where, if anywhere, does that fit in?'

She shook her head. 'You're thinking of Satanism,

251

which is a completely different thing. Wicca, as I said, is nothing to do with Christianity, although Wiccans do claim that some Christian rituals are a corruption of the original pagan ones. Satanism, on the other hand, is a sort of mirror-image of Christianity – a black host and blood instead of wine, in front of an inverted crucifix, with the Lord's Prayer said backwards, in a church; all that sort of stuff. During the witchcraft trials that took place in the sixteenth and seventeenth centuries the Church claimed that the witches they burnt were really Satan-worshippers, but to be honest there isn't a shred of evidence for that. They had to claim that they were Satanists, rather than heathens, you see, because otherwise they weren't actually evil, only misguided.'

He looked thoughtful and she seized her opportunity. 'These babies you're talking about – how did they die?'

'We won't know that until the post-mortems.'

'But they didn't have their throats cut?'

'It wouldn't appear so.'

'It won't be Satanists, then.'

'How can you be so sure of that?'

She shrugged. 'The whole point of ritual sacrifice is to get the blood. As described in *Tractatus de Confessionibus Maleficorum et Sagarum*, which translates as *A Treatise on Confessions by Witches and Wrongdoers*, written in 1589 by a Jesuit interrogator. He says that the devil demands libations of blood from his followers, but whereas the blood of an infant uncontaminated by the touch of a priest is like the taste of honey to the Devil, the blood of a baptized soul is abhorrent.'

The superintendent held up his hand. 'I

appreciate the history lesson, Miss Williams. But it doesn't really help your friends, does it?'

'Why not?'

'Your point is that witchcraft and Satanism are two entirely separate entities, yes?' Terry nodded. 'And that whoever killed these babies, it wasn't a Satanist in the true sense, because the throats would have been cut?'

'Correct.'

'So that leaves us with the distinct possibility that these babies were killed by non-Satanists, a category which you say *includes* the Wiccans.'

'Your logic is impeccable, Superintendent, but it's hardly likely—'

'Someone killed those infants, Miss Williams. And until I find out who did it, I'm not really interested in historical niceties.'

Her second interview was with the detective sergeant and a man who didn't look like a policeman. His jacket was too trendy, for one thing, and the soft woollen tie was less formal than the policemen's dark blue clip-ons.

'Hello, Terry,' he said carefully. 'My name's David. I work for Social Services. How are you?'

'I'd be a lot better if your lot hadn't come charging in mob-handed, arrested my friends, kidnapped their children, beaten me up and ruined my breakfast,' Terry retorted.

David nodded sympathetically. 'You're obviously feeling quite *angry*, Terry.'

Terry suddenly realized who David reminded her of. If Isobel had been a social worker, this is what she would have sounded like.

'Too bloody right I'm angry.'

'I gather you've not been here very long,' David went on. 'Is that right, Terry?'

She nodded.

'How did you come to join this group?'

'I've already explained all that,' she said, puzzled.

David dropped his voice still further and reached out to touch her arm gently. 'What I'm wondering, Terry, is whether you felt under any *pressure* to be here.'

She laughed. 'What do you mean?'

'Terry, I'm wondering if there were any *techniques* used to try to get you to stay with this group.' He was still nodding and smiling like a puppet, keeping his eyes fixed on hers. 'For example, there's a process that's sometimes called "love bombing". Everyone surrounds you with warmth and affection, until you feel that it's impossible to leave.'

'Warmth and affection?' She laughed, thinking of Brigid's acid disapproval, Isobel's blatant hostility, Judith's wounded looks. 'I haven't been love bombed, honestly,' she assured him. 'Quite the reverse.'

'You see, Terry, we spoke to your supervisor, Jennifer, to check out the details you gave in your interview. She said that you've been *unwell*. Perhaps even feeling a bit *vulnerable*. And she hasn't actually heard from you for weeks.'

'I've been busy,' Terry said wearily. Damn: she should have thought of this.

'And no-one tried – forgive me, Terry – no-one tried to *seduce* you into coming here? It's just that sometimes cults send out their most attractive members as – well, as *bait*, to lure people in.'

She coloured. 'If you mean have I been sleeping

with someone here, the answer's yes. But it wasn't an attempt to try to get me to join, for God's sake. They're not a cult, they're a community. Everyone's free to come and go as they please.'

'I could arrange for *you* to stay somewhere else, if you like.'

'No,' she snapped.

'You did say you were free to come and go as you please, Terry,' he reminded her.

She counted to three. 'Of course I am. I just don't intend to abandon these people now they're being accused of these preposterous crimes, that's all. And please stop using my bloody name, *David*. It makes me sound like a dog.'

She saw the sergeant catch the social worker's eye and nod almost imperceptibly towards the door. 'I'll be off then,' David muttered.

After he'd gone the sergeant studied her for a little while before she spoke. 'Well,' she said cheerfully, 'you don't seem very vulnerable to me. But you can see why we had to be sure.'

Terry nodded sulkily.

'Would you look at something for me, please?' She produced a file and removed something from it. 'I'd value your professional opinion.'

Terry took the transparent plastic sheath and stared at the document inside. 'Where did you get this?' she breathed.

'It was in Donna Fairhead's rucksack. You know who Donna Fairhead was, don't you?'

'Yes, of course. So she *did* steal some letters.'

'Sorry?'

Terry explained about Donna's visit to Sheila Mcteer. 'I always knew there were some more manuscripts around somewhere. I just didn't know where.'

'Is it worth anything?'

'As part of the series it's priceless.' Heron looked surprised. 'Was this the only one?' Terry continued.

'That was the only one we found, yes. But let me just get one thing clear. I was told it wasn't worth much.'

'On its own, it's not that special. But it's part of a sequence. Like having a pair of pots, only more so.' She indicated the paper. 'May I read it?'

'Of course, if you can.'

'It'll take a few minutes – and if you don't mind I'll go and get my laptop, so I'll have a back-up copy.'

A few minutes later she sat back and twisted the screen towards the policewoman. 'Here.'

They read it together, their heads bent over the computer.

My dearest Anne,

I have received your answer. Oh, Anne, how can I ever repay your love and kindness? You are truly the most devoted friend a woman could have.

One word of warning: trust no one, not even my cousin Hamish. I do not believe his intentions are so good as he would have us all believe.

I shall write when it is time – it could be any day now – be ready.

Catherine

'What does it mean?' Nicky asked.

'Not a lot,' Terry admitted. 'Nothing to suggest

why this particular letter was separated from the others, at any rate.'

'And nothing to suggest why it should have been in a dead girl's rucksack, either.' Nicky stood up. 'But if anything occurs to you, will you let me know?'

Dinner that night was a low-key affair. Judith stayed upstairs with Zoe, while the others glumly railed against the police and the brutality with which the operation had been carried out. Even the return of Isobel, halfway through the meal, raised their spirits only momentarily. She had been cautioned and released after questioning, but she brought bad news. The social worker Gregor had thumped was pressing charges. He would appear before a magistrate the following morning, but with no-one to stand bail it was unlikely he would be released. And Jamie was being held overnight, to allow the police to question him again.

'They can't suspect *him*, surely?' Anna said, wide-eyed.

'They're allowed to hold him for eighteen hours before they charge him or release him,' Terry explained. 'My guess is they're just using the drugs charge as a way of keeping him in the cells, so that he'll be that much more amenable when they come to interview him about the dead babies.'

Gerard in particular said little. He suddenly seemed old, Terry thought, the fight gone out of him. The others listened to Brigid and, somewhat surprisingly, Alan, when they wanted leadership.

'There was a similar case in the Orkneys, a few years ago,' Alan was saying. 'Twelve families and the priest accused of ritual abuse. It took years for the accusations to be disproved. And the children were kept away from their parents all that time. If they can believe it of ordinary churchgoing Christians, they can certainly believe it of us.'

'What are you saying?' Zoe asked.

'I think it's probably the end of the coven,' Alan said matter-of-factly, looking round the group. 'Mud sticks. They'll persecute us until we give up and scatter.'

'We must have faith,' Gerard muttered. 'We will ask the Goddess to help us.'

Alan shrugged. 'Yes, there's always the ostrich position, I suppose,' he said dismissively. 'Stick your head in a magic circle and pretend it isn't happening.'

Gerard looked bewildered, but he said nothing. Brigid gazed at Alan thoughtfully.

'There is another possibility,' Terry said. 'If the real murderer's caught, you'll be in the clear again.'

Alan snorted. 'You saw the police today. They're not looking anywhere else. Why should they? They've got a bunch of live witches on the one hand, and five dead babies on the other. The only problem they've got is deciding which one of us, exactly, to pin it on.'

There was a brief silence. They all looked at each other, wondering who it would be.

'That's precisely why you need to do some hard thinking yourselves,' Terry said doggedly. 'The chances are that whoever killed Donna it was someone she knew, which means it's probably someone you all know. I can see why you wouldn't want to tell the police any suspicions you've got, particularly if they're about each other. But if you don't, the coven is probably as doomed as Alan says.'

There was a long silence. To Terry's surprise, it was Isobel who spoke next. 'Terry's right,' she said flatly. 'We've got to be smart if we want to get out of this.'

'It's easy for Terry,' Stephan pointed out. 'She's the only one who isn't a suspect.'

'How so?' Anna asked.

'Because I wasn't here when Donna was killed,' Terry explained.

'Oh. Of course.' Anna said.

'Tell me, Terry,' Brigid asked, 'can *you* help us?'

'Me? How?'

'You've got a trained and analytical brain; you're not a suspect, but neither are you a complete outsider.'

Terry thought for a moment. 'Well – OK. Why don't I talk to each one of you in turn, to see if there's anything the police have missed?'

'Are we going to vote on this?' Alan asked, looking round the table.

'No,' Brigid said crisply, 'we are not. This is a coven, not a democracy, and for once I'm exercising my right as the Priestess to impose my authority. Terry, you're to do whatever you can to establish the innocence of the coven members.'

'Or guilt,' Alan murmured. Brigid ignored him.

'In return we will give you access to the *Book of Shadows* and anything else that relates to Catherine McCulloch.' She held up a hand to still Terry's protests. 'I know that's not why you're doing it, my dear. But it's all we can offer in return.'

The corpses of the five babies had been taken to the Scottish Forensic Facility, a long low building in the grounds of Aberdeen's General Hospital. Under the glare of the fluorescent lights their tiny bodies, blackened by putrefaction, looked more like children's dolls than human beings. Each one had been placed on a separate trolley, and the two pathologists were working their way steadily round the room, cutting them open one by one. Iain watched from the small gallery as they carefully sawed the head of one open with a miniature circular saw. From their comments he gathered that they still had no idea how any of the babies had died. But hopefully the lab reports would tell them more. And as soon as the pathologists had finished with the bodies, it would be his turn.

# TWENTY-TWO

'I'd met Donna's type before,' Brigid said, 'though it took me a while to realize it. There's a certain sort of person who's attracted to Wicca because of the – what shall I call it – the *sexiness* of it. Rituals, mysteries, exoticism, nudity – some people find these things particularly stimulating.'

The two of them were in the sitting room now, drinking tea, Brigid having decided that she would be the first to subject herself to Terry's questions. 'I even wondered whether you yourself might fall into that category,' she continued, 'which was why I was a little wary of accepting you to begin with. But Isobel informs me that, on the contrary, you're rather conventional about such matters.' She shot Terry an amused glance.

'Hmm,' Terry said non-committally. 'Go on.'

'The sensation-seekers I'm talking about are usually men, which is why I didn't see Donna for what she was until she was already part of our community. And a very unsettling influence she was too, for a time.'

'Did you try to do anything about her? Throw her out, I mean?'

'No, I kept my own counsel. As I generally do. And waited for things to sort themselves out, as they generally do. The thrill-seekers never stay long. Once the novelty has worn off, and they've exhausted the various possibilities of the situation, they always move on.'

'As Donna did.'

'So we thought. She'd been talking to some of the others about India – there's quite a long tradition of Wiccans incorporating Indian mysticism into their rituals. So when she announced she was off to Goa, none of us were particularly surprised.'

'This was in November, yes?'

'That's right. Just after Samhain.' Brigid snorted. 'It's one of our most sexually charged rites. She wouldn't have missed that, I can tell you.'

'Did anyone particularly resent Donna? What about Isobel, for example? She can't have liked being upstaged.'

'That's certainly true. I thought they'd made friends to begin with, but in retrospect I suppose they were just sizing each other up. Hostilities broke out about the same time that Donna got together with Jamie.' She sighed. 'But it was Judith I felt sorry for, not Isobel. Isobel can look after herself. Judith was the one who suffered.'

Terry nodded. 'I've seen the way she looks at Jamie. Sometimes it's as if she can hardly bear to be in the same room as him.'

'Oh, she's not stupid. She knows she's got no chance. Even if she lost weight, she wouldn't have the appeal of a Donna or an Isobel.' She smiled faintly. 'Or a Terry.'

'Would she – could she – have done anything stupid? To Donna, I mean?'

'She *did* do something stupid. She tried to get rid of her. Or, at least, she thought she did. About, let's see, a week ago she broke down in one of our rituals and admitted she'd been using magic of her own devising to try to banish Donna from Nineveh. Some stupid little charm or other. When Donna really did leave, she thought it must have worked. So when the body was found, she felt sure she was responsible. She was terribly upset – not least because she was terrified of the Threefold Law taking effect.'

'Any evil that you do by way of witchcraft will return to you three times over?'

Brigid smiled gently. 'I can see you're still sceptical. But look at it from Judith's point of view. As a result of Donna's death, her children have been taken from her.'

'Tell me,' Terry said curiously, 'who else did Donna get involved with? Apart from Jamie, I mean?'

Brigid evaded her eyes. 'I think that's a question you'll have to ask people individually, isn't it?'

'You see – forgive me, Brigid, but I really have to ask this – I've noticed that Gerard seems to be somewhat susceptible in that regard. He and Isobel . . .' She left the rest of the sentence hanging in the air.

Brigid shrugged. 'So?'

'It's just that if Donna and Gerard were ever, how can I put it, sexually involved,' Terry said slowly, 'then it isn't just Judith who could be a suspect. Don't you see? You had far more reason for killing Donna than she did.'

The older woman sighed. 'There's something I need to explain,' she said quietly.

'Yes?'

'I don't believe in it.'

'Don't believe in what?'

'Witchcraft. I think it's a lot of nonsense. I've thought so for years.'

Terry, taken aback, spluttered on her coffee.

'None of the others know, of course,' Brigid continued calmly. 'Or, at least, I've never said anything. Some of them may have their suspicions.'

'Doesn't that make it rather difficult, er . . . ?'

'Being the High Priestess? Not really. I can speak my lines with conviction – more conviction than any of you young girls, come to that. It's all a matter of practice.' She smiled wearily. 'For a while I told myself that I believed it symbolically – you know, the way these modern Christian priests believe in the Resurrection. But I'm afraid even that's not true. The truth is that I simply lost my faith.'

'Why didn't you tell anyone?'

'My whole life has been built around the Craft. In the legal sense, I'm not even married. Leaving the coven would have meant leaving Nineveh, Gerard, everything. At my age, I'm not about to do that.' She shrugged. 'It's more of a problem for Gerard. He prefers a Priestess who believes in what she's doing. So we came to a civilized arrangement. After all, there's no shortage of alternative partners for him.'

'Do you mean magical partners, or sexual ones?'

'I think in Gerard's belief system, the two are synonymous.' She sighed. 'I know what you're thinking. But as Isobel never tires of saying, sexual jealousy doesn't really come into it. Why would I have wanted to harm Donna? There have been many, many Donnas over the years. After all, I know about Isobel, and no-one's tried to kill *her*.'

'I see,' Terry said. Now that she thought about it, it was starting to make sense. No wonder Isobel had been making those remarks about the Wiccans not indulging in sexual jealousy – Terry, wrapped up in her relationship with Jamie, had assumed they were made for her benefit, but in fact they'd been directed at Brigid.

'Thank you,' she said, getting up. 'You've been very helpful. I'd better go and have a word with Judith, now.'

'Of course. I expect she'll be in her room. Do you know,' she said, 'it's been rather cathartic, getting all this off my chest. Gerard's a lovely man, Terry, but he's a fool. A holy fool, you might say. Most of the time he has no idea what's really going on here.'

'How are you, Judith?' Terry said quietly.

The young woman looked at her through reddened eyes.

'I'm so sorry about Holly and Myrvyn,' she continued. 'You must be going through hell.'

Judith buried her head in her hands. 'Holly's still being breastfed,' she said numbly. 'What am I going to do? I should have given her a feed hours ago.' There were two dark patches on the front of Judith's dress where milk was oozing onto the cloth.

'I'm sure they'll look after her,' Terry said awkwardly. 'I know it's not the same, but they'll be very careful with them.'

'Oh, sure. Like they were careful about taking them away. Myrv wets his bed sometimes. What's he going to be like tonight, now he's been taken away from his mummy screaming?'

There was nothing she could say to comfort her. 'I don't know,' Terry said honestly. She waited patiently for a few minutes while Judith cried.

'Thank you for kicking that bastard,' she said at last, drying her eyes on her dress.

'Oh, that.' Terry smiled. 'Least I could do. Gregor's intervention was rather more effective.'

Judith managed a watery smile. 'He was great, wasn't he?' There was another long pause. 'I'm sorry,' she added.

'Take as long as you need.'

'No. Not that. I meant, I'm sorry for, for—'

'It was you who put the charm in my bed, wasn't it?' Terry said gently.

Judith nodded. 'I'm so sorry,' she said again in a small voice. 'I've put you in the most terrible danger.'

Terry shrugged. 'Look, Judith, I'm really not that bothered by—'

'It worked on Donna, didn't it? I know no-one else thinks so but it did.'

'Tell me, Judith, why did you want her gone so badly?' Terry asked.

Judith took a deep breath. 'She was mucking everything up,' she said in a small voice.

'With Jamie? It's all right. Brigid told me.'

'You won't tell him, though, will you?'

'No. Not if you don't want me to.'

'Perhaps if I'd done it the way Donna did . . . you know, just marched in and made it clear what I wanted . . .' She looked at her hands. 'Donna used to tell me when they slept together. What they'd done, how many times, what a good lover he was. That was the sort of person she was – she knew I'd be jealous. And she used to make snide remarks about my appearance. Things like buying a new dress and then asking if I thought she looked fat in it. When of course it was three sizes smaller than anything I could have squeezed into.'

'Did she buy a lot of clothes?' Terry asked curiously.

'Oh yes. Quite a few.'

'Where did the money for those come from? I've seen how poor you all are here.'

Judith nodded. 'When she first arrived she was always moaning about how little cash she had. She even asked me if there was a spell for making herself rich. When I told her not to be so stupid – Wiccans don't do anything for material gain – she said we were obviously using the wrong sort of magic.'

'Were those her exact words? "The wrong sort of magic"?'

'I think so, yes.'

'That's interesting,' Terry said. She stood up. 'Thanks, Judith. I'd better get on and talk to some of the others. Are you sure you'll be all right?'

'Jamie and I,' she said in a small voice, 'I – I don't want you to think I'm being stupid about him. I know he likes me, even if he doesn't . . . you know, fancy me that much. I thought maybe, when he'd got bored of all the others . . .'

Except that when he got bored of all the other Wiccans there was me, Terry thought. And after me, there'll be someone else. Poor Judith. Aloud she said, 'I think, to be honest, that Jamie has a bit of a problem with commitment, Judith.'

'I know. I don't care. I love him just the way he is.'

'He's not worth it,' Terry said. She felt a pang of disloyalty, but even as she said it she knew it was no more than the truth. Pleasant interlude though he had been for her, she had no illusions about her future with Jamie. She sighed. 'I'll send Brigid up, shall I, to keep you company?'

She found Gerard in the large room the coven used for its rituals. The police had left it in chaos, strewing magical paraphernalia all over the floor. He was tidying up, though from the desultory way he did it Terry guessed that he had come here as much to be alone with his thoughts as to repair the damage.

He saw her watching and beckoned her in.

'So. Do *you* think it's the end of the coven?' he said, picking up a pentacle and examining it quizzically.

'I don't know,' Terry said honestly. 'I suppose it depends on the reaction of local people. Whether they make you unwelcome.'

'Unwelcome!' he snorted. 'They've always made us unwelcome. Oh, not so obviously, now, but I remember when we first came here with Old John . . .' He sighed. 'People were less tolerant then. Now they'll be saying they should never have relaxed their guard.' He tossed the pentacle into a box. 'There's been a coven in the Highlands for over two thousand years, you know. I should be so guilty if I were the one to let it be destroyed.'

'Perhaps when this has blown over you'll be able to start again.'

'Perhaps.' He sat down on a stool and motioned for her to sit opposite him. 'If it does blow over. Sometimes I think we made a huge error, coming out of the shadows. Our predecessors understood the importance of secrecy. "Whenever ye have need of any thing, once in the month, and better it be when the moon is full, then ye shall assemble in some secret place and adore the spirit of me, who am Queen of all witches." Ah, well. Perhaps those who come after me will learn from my mistakes.'

'I need to ask you some questions, Gerard.'

'Ask away, then.'

'I need to talk to you about your sex life, first of all,' Terry said. She'd decided that since the Wiccans made a big deal out of how direct they were about sexual matters, she might as well question them about it in the same way.

'Sex. You youngsters think that's what it's all about, do you?'

'From what I've been told, Donna was raped and possibly even tortured,' Terry said evenly. 'I'd say that's an indication that sex is pretty central to this tragedy, wouldn't you?'

'Hmm. I'll answer that in a minute. First let me tell you about my own arrangements. I take it you've spoken to Brigid?'

Terry nodded.

'Wicca is a sexual religion. By which I mean, it's based on the conjunction of male and female, the goddess and the god. Most people misunderstand that – in an age obsessed with the sexual act, they think that means our rituals are one long orgy. In fact Wiccans tend to be rather high-minded, even prudish, about the act itself. On most occasions we enact the Great Rite on a symbolic level only.' His eyes twinkled. 'I know that wasn't quite what Isobel pictured to you in your instruction sessions, my dear, but as you've probably gathered by now, she was trying to rile you just a little. No, what we're concerned with is sexual *energy* – just as a battery generates its electricity from having a positive and a negative, so magic generates its forces from the polarity of male and female. That energy needs to be stored for when it's needed, not dissipated willy-nilly.'

'I'm not sure you're answering my question.'

He held up one hand. 'All in good time. Brigid, you see, is now entering that phase of the Goddess cycle in which she represents the crone, or wise woman. Her female energy is therefore becoming less potent.' He shrugged. 'She also takes less interest in the workings of the rituals than she did.'

'She told me she doesn't believe in them.'

'Exactly, though after much thought I have come to the conclusion that is only as it should be. The wise ancient Goddess no longer concerns herself with the vibrant, charged rituals of the Goddess in her guise as Maiden. Do you follow me?'

'So you did sleep with Donna?' Terry asked, a touch impatiently.

'I take partners other than Brigid for the purposes of the Great Rite. Some of those partners, reasonably enough, demand that we celebrate the Rite for real as well as symbolically. Donna was one of those.'

'Thank you,' Terry said dryly. 'I think I'm clear on that point, at least.'

'Now: you asked whether sex is central to Donna's death. I'd just like to make one suggestion in that regard.'

'Yes?' Terry demanded.

'If you think of Donna primarily as a young and sexually desirable woman, then obviously you're going to think of her death as being motivated by the desire to possess her sexually. But if you think of her primarily as a *witch*,' he paused.

'Go on.'

'Isn't it obvious? You've been studying Catherine McCulloch. You know what she went through before she died.'

'You mean, torture?'

'Exactly.' He sat back and regarded her calmly.

'So what you're saying', Terry said slowly, 'is that Donna was tortured because she was a member of this coven?'

'I am indeed.'

'But why should anyone want to do that?'

He spread his arms. 'For exactly the same reason that Catherine was tortured. To make her give up her secrets. The secrets of the Craft.'

The notion was so absurd that Terry almost laughed out loud. 'You're not seriously suggesting that in the twentieth century anyone would really be that bothered about finding out your secrets,' she scoffed.

'Why not? After all, why are you here yourself?'

She sighed. This sort of circular argument could go on forever. 'Thanks, Gerard,' she said. 'I'll let you know if I learn anything else, OK?'

# TWENTY-THREE

She spoke to Stephan and Anna next, who could tell her very little she didn't already know. It was clear they were already wondering whether they should move on from Nineveh.

The person she really wanted to talk to, though, was Alan. She found him in a room at the top of the house, feeding information into a computer.

'Hi,' she said. 'Can I disturb you?'

'Of course,' he said, not looking up.

For this conversation, she had decided to be deliberately provocative. Of all the Wiccans, Alan was the most unfathomable – sometimes impishly playful, sometimes reserved to the point of sullenness. She had very little idea what really went on inside his head, and she suspected that he would give away little that he didn't want to.

'You didn't like her, did you?'

'Sorry?'

'Donna. You didn't like her.'

He swivelled round to face her, his expression impassive. 'What makes you say that?'

'Because you don't like me either, for exactly the same reason.'

'Which is?'

'That I'm sleeping with Jamie, and you're jealous of him. Oh, I don't mean that you fancy me, particularly. You're just jealous of him in general. Must be quite a problem, always playing second fiddle.'

'Very good, Terry. There's just one problem.'

'Which is?'

'You're quite right that I don't like you, and quite right that it's because I'm jealous. But it isn't Jamie I'm jealous of. It's you.'

'Oh.' Understanding dawned. '*Oh*. Who else knows?'

He shrugged. 'I think Jamie suspects. Zoe probably knows something. Other than that, no-one.'

'Hang on. I've seen you flirting with Isobel.'

'Quite.' He smiled. 'She thinks she turned me down and that I'm heartbroken about it. It was the only way to stop her from suspecting.'

'Why the secrecy? I thought everyone was completely open about sex here.'

He snorted. 'Are you kidding? Oh, they're all perfectly frank about leaping into bed with each other, sure. But you must have had Gerard's famous speech on male-female polarity by now.'

'This very evening.'

'Can you imagine what a gay witch would do to his precious polarities? And if Isobel knew, she'd have gone straight to him to spill the beans. Even before she was sharing his bed, she loved to make mischief.'

A thought crossed Terry's mind. 'As did Donna, I hear.'

He nodded. 'Her too. They're quite alike in many ways, though Donna was a lot shrewder than Isobel.'

'So if Donna found out, and threatened to out you to Gerard . . .'

'I'd have a motive? Come on, Terry. You'll have to come up with something a bit better than that.'

She decided to change tack. 'You look after the finances here, don't you? That was what Isobel said my first morning: "Gregor makes the honey, Alan takes the money". She described you as the resident marketing man.'

Alan scratched his ear. 'Up to a point. Before I dropped out, I was an IT consultant for Bain, in Edinburgh. So I know how to use one of these.' He indicated the computer in front of him. 'But it was Donna who was the real marketing expert.'

'How do you mean?'

'She and I got here at about the same time. Pretty soon it became clear that the finances were on a knife-edge. Donna set to work sorting them out.' He tapped a few buttons. 'Wicca's got quite a big presence on the internet, for example, so she blew the last of the savings on this, and got me to set up a website. We use it to take orders for the honey – holy honey, of course, every jar sealed with a magical blessing. She had the bright idea of e-mailing all the New Age suppliers on the net to see if they'd keep a virtual stock of it – so whenever they get an order, they simply pass it on to us and we dispatch it for them. She was one of those people who have a natural gift for making money. And computers. She picked up stuff in minutes that most people spend weeks getting to grips with.'

'How do you do your banking up here?'

He laughed. 'Banking? To most Wiccans that's a dirty word.'

'Not Donna. I found a letter from her bank in her drawer.'

'That's right – she had an internet account.

Like I said, she really got into it once she started.'

'Is there any way of accessing it?'

'Not without her account number and a password. They're pretty security conscious.'

'Her account number was on the letter. And I think there was a website address too.'

She went and found the letter in the bag of rubbish. Soon they were connected to the bank's home page, and a request for a password flashed onto the screen.

'OK, Detective, what's it going to be?' Alan asked, flexing his fingers over the keyboard.

'Aradia?'

He tapped it in. 'Nope.'

'Wicca.'

'Nope.'

'Cerrunos.'

'Nope. And now it's crashed – you only have three goes before it shuts down. We'll have to try again tomorrow.'

By the time she'd finished with Alan it was after midnight. Terry sighed wearily: that still left Isobel and Zoe. With any luck, she'd be able to keep her conversation with Isobel brief.

She found the American in the kitchen, wearing a dressing gown and with a towel wrapped round her head, drinking camomile tea. Typical, Terry thought. Judith's children might have been put into care, Jamie and Gregor might be spending a night in the cells, but nothing was going to stop Isobel from following her beauty routine. But the thought was an uncharitable one, and she knew it. She'd have liked nothing better than to have sunk into a hot bath herself, and the plumbing at Nineveh was so inadequate that you grabbed the chance of hot water whenever you could.

Terry busied herself making coffee while she tried to think how best to handle this. 'Tell me,' she said at last, 'when Donna went, why did *you* think she was leaving?'

Isobel blew at her tea. 'Honestly?'

'Honestly.'

'I thought she couldn't stand the competition.'

'From you?'

'Sure.' Isobel shrugged. 'I'm being honest. I know it doesn't exactly do me credit.'

'Did you like her?'

'Donna?' Isobel laughed quietly. 'Are you joking? We were competing for the same thing. We didn't have a single conversation that wasn't a cat-fight – oh, we'd be civilized enough on the surface, but every comment she made to me would have some double meaning. And I reckon I gave as good as I got.'

I'm sure you did, Terry thought. If Donna had been anything like as catty as Isobel, she'd love to have seen the two of them together.

'So you didn't pay her to leave, then?' It was, she knew, a daft suggestion, but she was too tired to think of any other way that Isobel could be involved in Donna's death.

'You must be kidding. Why would I need to do that? I'm prettier than she is,' Isobel said simply.

'Was.'

'Sorry?'

'Than she was. She's a piece of rotten meat, now. Who was raped pretty brutally before she died.'

'How can you be sure of that?'

'Sorry?'

'How can you be sure it was rape? Maybe she liked it rough,' Isobel said. She slid her eyes sideways at Terry. 'Some people do, I gather.'

There was a long silence. 'Who the *hell* told you that?' Terry said at last, outraged.

'About Donna? I can't remember—'

'About me. And don't pretend that wasn't what you meant.'

There was a pause. 'Oh heck,' Isobel said. 'See what I mean? I just can't help myself.'

'You don't need to answer, anyway. There are only two people who know what Jamie and I do in bed together, and *I* certainly didn't tell you.'

'Look, Terry, it wasn't what you think.'

'How do you know what I think? For the record, though, I'll tell you what I think,' Terry hissed. 'I don't really care whether he's been sleeping with you behind my back or not. What I do care about is that you've been discussing me while you did it.' She wasn't being entirely rational, she knew, but she was too tired and angry to worry about that.

Isobel looked away. Having said she didn't care, Terry suddenly decided she wanted to know after all. 'Have you or haven't you screwed Jamie since I arrived?' she asked dangerously.

Isobel shrugged. 'Hey, just the once. Oh God, Terry, you mustn't blame Jamie. It was me who—'

With careful deliberation Terry put down her cup of coffee, walked across to Isobel and punched her on the nose. It was a good blow, one that sent Isobel sprawling across the kitchen. Looking down at her, Terry said contemptuously, 'Well, at least we can be sure you didn't kill Donna. You're too much of a wimp.'

'You hit me,' Isobel squeaked, feeling her nose for blood. 'Oh my God. You hit me.'

Terry shrugged. 'Hey. Just the once.'

'Can I come in?'

Zoe, who was reading in bed, looked up and smiled. 'Of course. I wasn't sure if you wanted to talk to me tonight or not.'

'Actually, I was wondering if it would be OK if I slept in here. I don't really fancy Jamie's bed on my own.'

'Of course. It's your room too.'

'Thanks.' Terry cleared some of the debris off the second bed and started to undress. 'Actually, it's not just Jamie's bed on my own I don't fancy. I think it may be Jamie's bed per se.'

'Oh?' Zoe put down her book. 'What's up?'

'Isobel just let slip that he's been shagging her as well as me.'

'Ah. What did you say?'

'Not a lot. I thumped her.'

'What!'

Terry nodded. 'Right on the nose. She couldn't believe it.'

Zoe giggled. 'I wish I'd been there.'

'It was unfair of me, really. After all, she never made any secret of the fact she fancied him. It's Jamie I should be angry with. Her face just happened to be there when I erupted.' She changed into a T-shirt and slipped into bed. 'I should have known something like this was bound to happen. Jamie's not really cut out for monogamy, is he?'

'Will you take him back?' Zoe asked.

Terry thought about it. 'No,' she said at last. 'It was fine while it lasted, but it was probably a mistake. It's like everyone says: never go back. Jamie and I both thought we could reinvent the past.' There was a brief silence. 'How about you?' she said softly. 'Will you take him back when I'm gone?'

'Maybe.'

'Good,' Terry said.

'Why good? I thought you'd disapprove.'

'Anything to stop Isobel getting him.'

They smiled at each other across the room.

'When you shared this bedroom with Donna,' Terry said, following her own train of thought, 'did you talk to her much?'

Zoe shook her head. 'Not really. She used to talk to *me* sometimes. Not specific things. She used to like to pretend she knew more than she did, if you know what I mean. Everything was a big secret or a discovery or a plot. But when you pressed her, she usually didn't know more than anyone else.'

'Can you give me an example?'

Zoe thought for a moment. 'There was one occasion, not long before she left. She'd been out. I was asleep, and she came back late and woke me up. I don't know if she was drunk, but she seemed excited. Like she was burning to tell me something, but she couldn't because it was too important. She kept laughing and saying, "Lord, what fools these mortals be."'

' "Lord, what fools these mortals be"? That's a quote from Shakespeare. *A Midsummer Night's Dream*, if I'm not mistaken.'

'Is it? I took it she was referring to all the non-Wiccans. That's what Gerard sometimes calls them: the mortals.'

'Or to some particular non-Wiccans, perhaps.'

'I suppose so.'

'And that was all she said? "Lord, what fools these mortals be"?'

'The rest was just nonsense – she kept saying the word "Success" over and over. Oh, and quoting the witches from *Macbeth* – "hubble bubble, toil and trouble," that sort of stuff. She'd been a drama student once, you know, but she never stuck anything for more than a few months. Drama, singing, charity work, advertising, you name it, she'd tried it.'

They chatted a little longer, until Zoe yawned and rolled over. But long after the other girl's regular breathing indicated that she had gone to sleep, Terry lay on her back with her eyes wide open, trying to make sense of it all.

# TWENTY-FOUR

The next morning she woke early. Lying there, turning it over in her mind, she realized that she had some more words she could try on Donna's bank account.

When Alan woke up he found her logging onto the bank's website. Just as it had before, a screen popped up, telling her that she now had three chances to enter her password.

'Three wishes,' she murmured, and typed in 'mortals'.

'Damn.'

Alan rolled over and watched her from his bed. 'Any luck?'

'Not yet.' She typed in 'success'. Again the screen stayed blank.

'Try "money",' he suggested. She shrugged, and did as she was bidden. The computer screen flickered, and Donna Fairhead's transaction statement appeared.

'How did you guess that?'

He rolled back over. 'She had a logical mind. Find anything?'

'The balance is zero,' she said. 'But look how

much went through the account. Eight thousand pounds in on November the fourteenth. Two thousand one hundred and eighty out. Then all the rest out by banker's draft on November twenty-second.'

'Just before she left. Getting cash out for her holiday.'

'Over five thousand pounds? That's some holiday. And where is it now?'

'The police did ask us if we'd seen her with any cash. I never realized it might have been so much.'

'Tell you what . . .' She opened a new window and did a search for a travel agent. 'Let's see how much a ticket to India would have cost her. Hmm – stand-by's only about four hundred.'

'How much is business class?'

She looked, and nodded. 'Spot on. Two thousand one hundred and eighty.'

'So she got eight thousand from somewhere, and what she didn't spend on her flight she got out in one lump sum. But I can tell you this for certain, she wasn't making that sort of money dealing in honey.'

'Drugs, then?'

'Eight thousand quid?' He snorted. 'Not unless she offered to come back from India with every orifice crammed to bursting with grade-A heroin. Besides, she'd be a sitting duck for Customs – a hippie in business class, flying in from Goa? She'd have been mad.'

Terry sighed, and shut down the computer. There was something here she still wasn't seeing.

The letters. Somehow, it all came back to the letters. Mcteer had stolen the letters, and God knew what else besides, so that he could start a New Age religion. Magnus wanted the letters transcribed so that he'd have something authentic to base his tourist attraction on. Donna had died with a letter in her rucksack, and five thousand pounds was missing. But something else was missing too: the other two letters she'd signed a receipt to Sheila Mcteer for. And where the hell had five dead babies come from, to end up rotting alongside the pig corpses in the farmer's death pit?

She made a sudden decision. Downstairs, she sought out Gerard.

'I need to see the *Book of Shadows*.'

'What, now?'

'Now.'

He sighed. 'Wait here.'

She waited. After a few minutes he reappeared with a book. She reached out to take it but for a moment he held onto it.

'Look after it, won't you?' he said mildly. 'It's very important to us.'

It was an unprepossessing volume. Not so much bible as scrapbook; a cheap hardbound pad crammed with pieces of paper, photographs, rituals, notes and other fragments, all gathered together in no discernible order. She opened it, and read:

I, John Mcteer, have created this *Book of Shadows* in the image of those books which I believe to have been carried by all true witches – by which I mean, faithful adherents of the Old Religion – as records of their magical workings. It has taken me many years of diligent research, and I should not have come close to my goal, had the Goddess not led me to some papers written by a true witch in the seventeenth century – Catherine McCulloch, who took many of her secrets with her to the stake, but left us these fragments. Guard them preciously, for they are unique, and sacred to the worship of that Great Goddess who is in, above, and beyond all things.

'Oh yeah?' she muttered. She turned the page.

I who am the beauty of the green earth, and the white moon among the stars, and the mystery of the waters and the desire of the heart of man, call unto thy soul. Arise, and come unto me. For I am the soul of nature, who gives life to the universe. From me all things proceed, and unto me all things must return; and before my face, beloved of men, let thine innermost divine self be enfolded into the rapture of the infinite. Let my worship be within the heart that rejoiceth, for behold, all acts of love and pleasure are my rituals and my worship. For behold, I have been with thee from the beginning; and I am that which is attained at the end of desire.

Terry turned the pages impatiently. All this mystical stuff wasn't getting her anywhere. There seemed to be reams of it. 'For mine is the ecstasy of the spirit, and mine also is the joy on earth; for my law is love unto all things. Keep pure your highest ideal: strive ever towards it: let naught stop you or turn you aside.' 'What a load of old bollocks,' she said under her breath. She flicked on a few more pages. 'For mine is the secret door which opens upon the Land of Youth and mine is the cup of the wine of life . . .'

'This is all Mcteer's writing,' she said.

'Of course. We each of us copy out the *Book* in our own hand, according to the instructions John left us.'

'Where are the manuscripts? The originals, I mean, in Catherine's own handwriting?'

'At Old John's own request, they were buried with him when he died.'

'Not all of them,' she said.

There was a long silence. 'You're right,' he said at last. 'There was one document – a sort of diary. We sold it a few years ago, when we were short of money.'

'Who to?' she asked, though she had already guessed the answer.

'You have five corpses of Caucasian infants. Three are male, two female. Milk teeth vary from completely to partially occluded: from this we believe their ages range from five months to about eighteen months. None was genetically related to Donna Fairhead or to each other.'

There was silence in the office adjacent to the autopsy lab as the senior pathologist read out his findings. Talbot blew thoughtfully on his coffee. Iain took notes on a foolscap pad. Nicky Heron, the only other person in the room, stared at the pathologist with a frown of concentration on her face.

'Cause of death was not apparent from autopsy or viral investigation. In other words, it was consistent with a wide range of causes, including asphyxiation, starvation, Sudden Infant Death Syndrome and insulin overdose. However, all the infants display extremely low body weight relative to their age as suggested by dentition. This suggests that, of these possibilities, starvation is the most likely.'

The pathologist paused to survey his audience over his reading glasses. 'In reaching this tentative conclusion we have also been guided by the fact that two of the babies show signs of vertebral deformities, classically associated with infant rickets.'

Talbot stirred. 'Rickets? You'll have to remind me what that is, doctor.'

'Isn't it what my mum used to tell me I'd get if I didn't drink up my milk?' Nicky said.

The pathologist nodded. 'It's a deficiency disease. Your mother was quite right: lack of calcium is one of the chief causes, though it can also be caused by lack of sunlight.'

Talbot leaned forward. 'You mean that if a kid was locked up somewhere dark, he'd get rickets?'

'Eventually, yes. We used to see more of it in Scotland than elsewhere, because the winter months were so much longer and darker here. Free school milk largely wiped it out. It's very rare indeed now.'

'Isn't the really odd thing in this case that you've got it in babies who you'd expect to be still breast feeding, and therefore immune?' Iain suggested. Nicky looked at him enviously. She should have seen that implication herself.

'Absolutely.' The pathologist shrugged. 'We can't explain it, I'm afraid. Perhaps your own investigations can throw some light on it.'

'Anything else?' Talbot asked.

'Measles.'

'Measles?'

'Two of the bodies – the two least decayed – have got traces of the measles virus. We were extremely lucky to get it: another week or so and putrefaction would have eradicated the traces. There's no sign that it killed them, but measles in babies can be an extremely serious condition.'

'Isn't there a vaccine against measles?'

'Yes – there's the MMR, which gives combined protection against measles, mumps and rubella.'

'Maybe we should look at social groups who don't take up the vaccine, sir,' Nicky suggested.'

'Like who?'

'Gypsies, maybe?'

Talbot glanced at the pathologist, who shook his head. 'If they were pure-bred Romanies we'd know from the DNA. They're all dark, as it happens, but we don't see any special significance there.'

'What about non-Romany travellers, then?'

'You mean, as in New Age travellers?' Talbot asked. 'That's an interesting thought.'

The pathologist nodded. 'Well, obviously that's your area, not mine. The only thing I can tell you is that all of these findings, slight though they are, are complicated by the fact that the putrefaction of the bodies seems to have taken a very odd progression. As you probably know, the decay of flesh in any one environment usually follows a fairly consistent pattern, which if you know all the environmental factors such as temperature, soil type and so on, enables you to make a reasonable estimate of time since death.' He stopped and pulled at his ear, frowning. 'What seems to be happening in this instance is that different bodies are decaying in different ways. The most putrefied corpse, for example, is covered in adipocere. You're familiar with that term?'

Heron shook her head. 'You'd better all come

with me, then,' the pathologist said. 'It'll be easier if I show you.'

They followed him into the refrigeration unit. He pulled out one of the sliding drawers, revealing a tiny corpse, the skeleton visible where the bones were shedding soft tissue. Around the cheeks, upper body and thighs, the skin seemed to have melted into a soft, greasy mass. The pathologist pulled on a transparent glove from a dispenser on the wall and touched the corpse's cheek: his finger sank into the substance.

'Adipocere is hydrolysed fat,' he said. 'Happens only in certain burial conditions, and then usually after a couple of years. But now take a look at this fellow.' He slid open a second drawer. This time, the corpse looked much fresher; the hair still present, skin intact and burnished to a leathery brown colour.

'I know it looks more recent,' the pathologist said, 'but actually the insides of this one are just as desiccated as the other chap. Something caused the skin and hair to be preserved. Retention of collagen and keratin – the skin and the hair – isn't uncommon in peaty soils. What's odd is the apparent inconsistency with the other body. And then there's this one.' He slid open a third drawer. Inside was a corpse which, apart from being mottled with patches of black under the skin where static blood had collected, looked as if it had died only a few weeks before. It was criss-crossed with roughly stitched incisions from the autopsy. 'This one looks completely undecayed, doesn't it? But open it up, and the skeleton itself has started to decalcify. And in the case of the two cadavers I haven't shown you, there's no

putrefaction of either the flesh or the bone –
though in one case, that makes no sense at all,
because the flesh has been attacked by snails and
other carnivorous insects.'

'What do you make of it?' Talbot asked.

The pathologist shrugged. 'I simply don't have
enough data to draw any conclusions. If I was an
astronomer I might compare it to the effects of a
black hole, exerting such a strong gravitational
force that it even pulls in time and bends it. I've
certainly seen nothing like it before. Given all the
circumstances, I won't be able to give you a time
since death for any of them, I'm afraid. But your
man here might be able to help you.' He nodded at
Iain.

'What will you do with them that he can't?'
Talbot asked the archaeologist.

'Autopsies focus on a few standard medical tests.
I can be more wide-ranging. With your permission,
I'd like to remove the thigh bone from each of the
corpses and subject it to archaeological dating procedures. They've been developed for longer time
scales than the ones we're dealing with, obviously,
but I think they may be able to tell us something the
forensic tests haven't.'

David Nicolaides opened the door of his modernist
masterpiece himself. His eyes widened slightly when
he saw Terry, though his tone, as ever, was un-
failingly polite.

'Miss Williams. This is an unexpected pleasure.'

'I want a favour.'

He inclined his head graciously. 'Then I had better
do my best to grant it. Those who request favours
of me are rarely so fair of face. Will you join me for

breakfast?' Without waiting for an answer he turned and led the way towards the back of the house.

Taking off her wellies – whatever Magnus had said, the Nicolaides' white carpet was no place for outdoor footwear, and she'd just driven over on Gregor's oily old tractor – she followed him into a long, laboratory-like kitchen.

'Toast and whisky marmalade,' he said, settling himself at one end of the table and motioning for her to sit next to him. 'Breakfast is the one meal the Scots do tolerably well. So long as you disregard their unaccountable enthusiasm for kippers and porridge, of course.'

She poured herself some coffee from a silver pot. 'Do I need to leave some for your wife?'

'She's not here. Some charity lunch in Edinburgh to raise money for Romanian orphans. Now then. Tell me how I can assist you.'

'I want to see Catherine McCulloch's diary.'

'Ah. I was wondering when you would discover that was in my possession.'

'Will you let me read it?'

'Of course. Wait here.'

He went away for a few moments and returned with a slim folder which he laid on the table beside her. She started to reach for it, but he placed his hand on it.

'As you know, I am a businessman. You might find I drive too hard a bargain.'

'What do you mean?' she said; but she could tell from the look on his face that he knew she understood him. She was being sexually propositioned, albeit with enormous tact.

'It could be an entirely civilized transaction. You

will not find me unreasonable.' His eyes twinkled. 'Or greedy.'

Sure of himself, he was playing with her now, enjoying the power he had over her: like a cat, she thought to herself, toying with a mouse before the kill.

'What exactly would be required of me?' she enquired coolly.

He shrugged. 'You give me your services for – shall we say a month?'

She thought about it for a moment. 'Very well,' she said at last.

'You accept?'

'It's the best offer I'm going to get, isn't it? I'd like to finish my coffee, though.'

He shrugged. 'But of course. There's absolutely no need to rush.'

She took a mouthful of the strong dark coffee. 'Tell me,' she said, 'was Donna Fairhead this easy to do business with?'

Nicolaides wrinkled his brow. 'I'm sorry?'

She put down the coffee and got to her feet slowly, keeping the table between him and herself. 'Donna Fairhead. You had a similar arrangement with her, didn't you? For which you paid her over eight thousand pounds.'

'I'm not sure I understand,' he said, smiling politely.

'Oh, come on. You're the only person round here with that sort of cash to throw around.'

'Now I definitely don't understand you.' He was a good actor: had she not known what she did, she would have thought that he was genuinely puzzled.

'Oh, yes you do. Money for sex. A lot of money – more money than most men would be prepared to offer; but then, you have more to give away. What went wrong? Did she threaten to tell your wife? I'm sure killing her wasn't all that distasteful – killing is one of your great passions, after all, that's why you've got this bloody great shooting estate in the first place.'

'Ah,' he said slowly, 'I think I see. Donna Fairhead – she was the witch who died. And now you are accusing me of being involved in her death.'

'Weren't you?'

'Of course not.'

'But the money,' Terry said doggedly. 'She was obsessed with making some money. And she did, somehow. I've seen her bank account.'

'The money for this manuscript, I gave direct to Gerard,' he said impatiently. He must be telling the truth, she realized: she had seen the receipt herself, in Gerard's filing cabinet. 'Permit me to advise you here, Terry, as a businessman, and someone who perhaps understands the mysterious ebb and flow of hard cash rather better than a bookish academic like yourself.'

'Yes?'

'If I sought money,' Nicolaides said, 'I wouldn't go to the richest man I knew. I'd go to someone who was desperate, either to sell or to buy. Such people are rarely the wealthy ones. Wealthy people are cocooned by their wealth, you see: they're unlikely to be so needy.'

'You just tried to pimp *me*,' she retorted.

'I think, perhaps, we have been talking at cross-purposes,' he said gently. 'When I suggested employing your services just now, I'm afraid it was your brain, rather than your body, I was referring to.'

She gaped at him.

'Not that I wouldn't be delighted to sleep with you, were I not married,' he went on smoothly. 'But it's your research abilities I really want. I want you to transcribe this manuscript for me. And to make a study of it for your thesis.'

'Why on earth do *you* want my thesis?'

'Partly because I'm curious to know exactly what I've purchased. And partly to stop you working for Magnus.'

'To spite him?'

Nicolaides tutted. 'That's a very emotional way of looking at it, if you'll excuse my saying so. No: I simply want to prevent him from putting these priceless letters into a stupid museum for gawping tourists to drip their ice creams over.'

'I *see*.' Sweet Jesus, what an idiot she'd made of herself. 'You want it all, don't you – the McCulloch title, the letters, this . . .' She tapped the folder on the table. 'That was why you showed me your library at the party. You were sounding me out even then.' He nodded. 'You must think I'm a complete fool.'

'On the contrary,' he assured her, 'I know you to be an extremely clever young lady. Please don't be embarrassed. Do we have a deal?'

She thought briefly. 'Absolutely not. I couldn't possibly do that.'

'Why on earth not?'

'I'll transcribe this, and I'll give you a copy. But I don't work for Magnus, and I couldn't work for you. It's completely out of the question.'

He laughed. 'Terry, this is priceless. A moment ago you were prepared to sell me your body. But now you won't sell me even the transcriptions of some dusty old letters. How can you be so inconsistent?'

She could not explain, though to her the two actions weren't inconsistent at all. 'I'm just trying to help my friends,' she said lamely.

He looked baffled. 'These people are your friends? Magnus, who you only met a couple of weeks ago? These mad witches, who you've known for an even shorter time? What can you possibly owe any of them?'

Now it was her turn to shrug.

'Your loyalty is admirable, Terry. I just wonder whether your friends will ultimately be as loyal to you.'

She stood up. 'At least I have some friends.' It was a cheap, sixth-form remark, all she could come up with in the circumstances.

'But do you know who they are?' he said, smiling. 'I've offended you, Terry, and for that I apologize. As I said the last time we met, I really would like to help you in any way I can.'

'Only if it means helping yourself.'

He walked her to the door and watched her pull her wellies back on. 'Shall I tell you something, Terry? I think we're more alike than you care to admit.'

Now he was the one making feeble sixth-form remarks, she thought as she swung herself up onto the tractor seat and fired the engine, the precious folder tucked safely away by her side. He raised his hand in salutation, and shouted something she could barely hear over the rattle of the diesel. She wasn't sure, but it sounded very like: 'Goodbye, Terry. What a shame we couldn't go on misunderstanding each other. I imagine it would have been quite an experience.'

# TWENTY-FIVE

*17 May 1697*

Tho' it is hard, sometimes, to follow all the London fashions from Scotland, and though my particular disposition is not to ape the latest foppery from Court, being no slave to dressmakers or my maids as is my lady Trent – or even dear Susannah – I shall nevertheless endeavour to pursue this new custom and make a Diary. I do not have the patience, or perhaps the wit, to devise a code, as Susannah says many in London do, but I cannot think it will be necessary, for who but myself would think to read my journal? I am mistress here.

I am mistress here – it still seems strange to write those words. I had never thought I would: indeed, my Father gave no thought to such a circumstance, having believed that on his death my brother Jamie would inherit. These are strange and violent times. Hamish my cousin believes it was the Whigamores, or Covenanters as they are sometimes called, who have been thrown off their homes and now roam the Highlands like brigands, killing any passers-by for what little they can steal. I cannot think of Father and Jamie without tears, so try not to think of them at all, except when I am sure to be alone, for the servants must not see my frailty. I mourn the Scottish way, in silence. In the meantime there are the farms to run, and tenants to look after. Luckily my father chose good men to help him and, though they are careful to come to me for decisions, they do it in such a way as to tell me what course my father would have chosen. Mr Balwhinnie in particular has let me know, with a pull of his ear and a sideways look, when one of the other tenants is trying to take advantage of my ignorance.

My cousin, however, thinks of nothing but of marrying me off, and the quicker the better. He comes and visits me twice a week, and talks as though Babcock is but a tent in a windy gale, that one more gust could carry away at any time. It is true that estates have been lost before now, plucked from weak owners and given in reward to those who have best supported the King, or Parliament, or the Protector, or whoever is latest in power. He talks at length of the solidity of land, and the stability of the nation. And perhaps he is right. But though I listen politely, a part of me inside says quietly – yes, but I am mistress now, and *I* can decide who I shall marry, and when I do so it shall not just be for the nation but myself. Sometimes I wonder if he is implying that he himself – but no: Hamish is my cousin, though a distant one, and has no land.

He is for England, of course. I do not mean that he wants to live there – he is the kind of Scot of whom they sometimes say the granite of the rocks has seeped into his blood. But he is by nature inclined to the Puritans, and became an administrator for the Protector when that gentleman decided that Scotland should be conquered along with England, lest we harbour English kings. Now Hamish sits in Parliament at Holyrood, and so his Puritan sympathies have been quieted, for neither Puritans nor Catholics may be represented in government. But he talks all the time of a plan to make an Act of Union with England – lest we harbour Scottish Kings, I suppose. I do not care for politics. My kingdom is this estate, my empire Ben Dubh, and I think I should be happy to reign here on my own, unmarried, till I die.

I was wondering, when I started this diary, if I should really have anything to say, or if my reminiscences would all be of the weather and how the wheat is going. Now I find there is so much to write, I hardly know when to stop. But stop I shall. It is nearly lunch, and this afternoon I shall ride with Mr Balwhinnie to Stour, for the market.

### 21 May

Susannah has persuaded me to have a companion. I think I shall. I fear that if I am lonely I may marry after all, for someone to talk to, and give up Babcock and all my independence just for a chance to prate. I mentioned to Hamish when he last visited that I should be engaging someone shortly, and I think he quite approved. I did not tell him why, of course. I imagine he thinks it is a proper, womanly thing to do. Perhaps he thinks a companion will tempt me out of mourning, and go with me into Society, so I shall meet a husband that way. He has even suggested I go dancing, since at a dance one may be introduced to a wider circle of acquaintance: though I almost laughed when he said it, for I could tell by his face that he thinks dances are the devil's playground or some such fancy. Well, we are more alike there than perhaps we care to admit. I have never liked dances either.

### 25 May

I have found a girl who might be suitable as a companion. Her name is Miss de Courcy – a pretty little thing, very quiet, but I think quite clever. Her father came from France, though her mother is a Hedderwick, one of the Hedderwicks of Saltoun, on the other side of Stour. So she speaks French tolerably, and is well read. She likes to walk, too, as do I, and plays the piano. I am having another instrument delivered, from Mister Gausis in Inverness, so we shall play together.

My cousin Hamish has gone a-soldiering, for they say the King's supporters are gathering in the north, and the Western Isles are all in a ferment. I do not mean the King, of course, but rather the old King, who now they call the Pretender. It is a remarkable thing when men may choose, through parliament, which king they prefer to rule them, as the English have chosen William over James. Perhaps one day a woman may even choose her own ruler in the same manner – I mean her husband. A silly, private fancy, which I should not dream of repeating to my cousin!

I shall give Miss de Courcy five shillings and her board. Since I have the money, and she does not, I should prefer to be generous, and so make her like me.

### 2 June

Miss de Courcy makes an immediate impression on us here at Babcock. There is a stillness and a modesty in her bearing that endears her to all – even to old Mrs Westwood, who rules the kitchens with a fearsome temper they have heard of as far as Inverness. Never having had a companion before, I was a little silent to begin with, and since Miss de Courcy – Anne – does not prattle like Susannah or some of my other acquaintance, and was perhaps a little unsure of how to disport herself towards me, we were quiet at first. But then we went walking – I do not mean strolling, as so many women do, around the garden with a parasol and a servant with a dog – I mean we *walked*, along the old sheep path that winds its way up and around Ben Dubh moor to Nineveh, and so on up to Ben Dubh itself, for though it was a sunny day it was cool, and we were not fatigued until we gained the very summit, and rested on a rock. We saw kestrels, and an eagle that took a baby hare, and Anne told me of her family, and I told her of mine, and how Father and Jamie went off one day to Inverness, and were found dead the next week in the valley above that town, their throats and purse strings cut. And I believe I cried, though Miss de Courcy said little, but listened without interruption till I was done. And when we came down it was arm in arm. I think we shall be friends.

## 5 June

The harvest, they say, will be late this year, for the weather continues unseasonably mild and wet. I know I vowed not to write of the weather, but this is important, for the tenants are worried, and some of the labourers have been told there is no work. There seems a restlessness abroad – no-one appears content, and even Mr Balwhinnie, that most dependable of men, is in a sullen mood. Only Anne and I, it seems, are gay. The new piano has been delivered, and when it rains we learn the latest pieces from Vienna.

## 7 June

Today I returned to my bedchamber in the morning for some linen, and found my maid Elizabeth with a curious pamphlet. I asked her quite sharply what it was that she was reading, for the bed was still unmade, and so she showed me. It was a badly wrought thing she had off some pedlar for a penny, a chapbook as they call it, being an account of the trial of some witches in Renfrew near Fort

William last month, when twenty-one were taken and seven condemned to the stake. I did not glance at it long, but saw there were crude drawings of devils and suchlike about their business. I told her, quite sharply, that it was not suitable for her to read such things, and that she should put it in the fire if she did not want to be put out of doors.

My cousin is returned, and says that all over the country it is the same story – unrest, and disorder, and tenants questioning their betters. My Lord of Eglington, in Western Ross, has openly declared for the Pretender, and stands an army of two hundred men – not enough, Hamish says, to be of any consequence, but a danger nevertheless. And everywhere there are rumours that James has landed from France and is hidden among us, with a fabulous fortune to win men to his side. For when the Stuarts fled across the channel they took with them their crown jewels, and now throw them into the game of winning back their kingdom. Hamish looks at me sharply when all this is said, and declares he would not in the usual course of things repeat such nonsense, and certainly not to a gentlewoman, who might become alarmed by it, but that it shows again the importance of my marrying, and Babcock being saved *for the family*. I think I see his intention now, but answered him coolly, 'Why sir, it is already saved for the family, since I have it quite safe, and if I should happen to die unmarried, my cousin Duncan will succeed, and it remain in the family still.' At this he nodded coldly, as if letting the matter drop. But I think Hamish would not be averse to an alliance within the McCullochs, if by it he could gain an estate as well as that influence in parliament that an estate can bring.

*12 June*

I told Anne of my fears regarding Hamish, and she

listened closely, as I knew she would. Then she asked me what I would do. I said I had no mind to marry, but that if I did it would not be to him, for I take his own argument against him, and think that if I have to wed it should be to a landowner the equal of myself, our joint enterprise ensuring a safer inheritance for our children. At this she nodded, and said that it is right to be so practical, for the safety of our kin must come first. And then I asked her if she had any mind to marry, and as I did so I realized that I hoped she would say no. At which she laughed, and said that she had no expectations, and though Mister Balwhinnie had been most attentive to her, she did not wish to give him hope. At which, I confess, I expressed surprise, that he should have been courting her so soon. 'I suppose he wants a wife to help with the farm,' she said with a shrug. I was quite cross, and said I had not been asked. And Anne gave me a strange look, and said that there was nothing to ask, no encouragement having been given. Yet I went to bed with an headache, and had my supper in my chamber.

## 13 June

A Sunday, and so to church. My headache gone, I sat with Anne in the loft and was gracious to the villagers. The sermon was about idolatry, and the need for vigilance. I thought it unsuitable, but said nothing. At the door to the kirk is now a little chest. I asked Anne what it was for and she replied it was a kist, where letters to the Church Court may be placed. I asked why such a thing should be needed. 'Why, so that they who make accusations do not have to give their names, of course,' she replied with a bitter laugh. Something in her manner told me that I should not ask her more. But as we returned – we had taken the carriage, it remaining wet –

she told me that her own mother had recently been accused, by means of a kist, of being a witch, and it was only the goodness of the Minister, who knew the family well, which prevented any charges being brought.

I had noticed during the service that Anne took no part in the prayers – she knelt, and clasped her hands, but did not speak the prayers themselves out loud, as I did. Being in the loft, no-one but myself could have observed this, but I made a joke of it, and said that perhaps Anne should shout out the prayers more loudly, so that people could note her piety. And she looked at me sharply, and answered that she was pious enough, but in her own way. I own I did not know what she meant by this, but felt that I had not behaved altogether well last night, and so did not question her further, and let it pass.

## 25 June

Now the summer has come at last, and everyone is cheerful. We play games on the lawn, and sing in the summerhouse, it being too hot to walk on our beloved mountain. The barley is taken, and the wheat has almost turned, so the farmers are busy, and there is work enough for all the labourers, and they have no more time to gossip.

I cannot imagine what I did before Anne was here, for we are constantly together now, and know each other's inmost thoughts on almost every thing. I have not been writing in this diary these past two weeks, it being almost an effort to confide myself twice over, first to Anne and then again to paper!

We are having a doocot built, out in Hagsin's Field where it meets the hill. This means we shall be able to have fresh poultry all winter, but the noise of the doves will also be pleasant, since we will be able to hear them when we walk. Anne laughs when I say this, and says that it is just like me to be practical first and artistic second. I suppose the kestrels from the moor will kill some of the doves, but that is something that must be borne, for I would not want the kestrels shot. They are so beautiful when they circle over the heather, and even when they take another bird or a mouse there is a terrible beauty about them, an implacable beauty of purpose. I see them from my bedchamber every morning.

*30 June*

Today we went swimming – mostly the rivers run fast and shallow here, but Anne found a pool when we were walking back from Crawford, through the woods. It was so hot, and we were quite alone. Even so I should never have suggested it – perhaps that is the curse of being born so high, that one must always consider what is seemly – and when Anne, with a laugh, caught hold of me and made as if to push me in, and asked why we should not bathe, I felt a strange apprehension, halfway between terror and delight. But Anne was right, we were quite alone: the path, which was some way off, only ever being used on market days, and all the men being occupied in the fields. So we quickly disrobed, and reached out with our feet into the water, which was icy cold. Anne let out a little shriek, and would have stopped, I think, and so I pushed her in, then jumped after. The current was so cold you could not breathe. If you opened your eyes under the water you could see crayfish and trout.

When we returned home my cousin Hamish was waiting attendance on me in the morning room. His mood was poor. He asked me why my hair was wet, and when I did not answer, said it was no matter, as he had important matters to discuss. It turns out he has heard the rumour about Mrs de Courcy, and wants her daughter dismissed from my service immediately. When I told him I already knew for myself that she was thought to be a witch, he seemed quite lost for words, and asked why I had not told him before. I informed him that I did not normally repeat such gossip, especially to a gentleman. Thus did I echo his own words to myself on a previous occasion, at which he flushed. 'There is more to it than her mother,' he said darkly. 'Her father is come from France, and I have heard that he himself be a witch, and was investigated by the Chambre Ardente, the Burning Court, and that is why he fled.'

'So you trust the French courts more than Scottish common sense,' I mocked him. 'Surely, cousin, you are not thinking of following the Stuarts to Versailles?' At this he flushed again, and shortly took his leave. But as he left me he said that I must have a care not to become too independent, or I should find no man at all would want me for a wife, and I should be constrained to marry whomsoever I could, and might be driven to a sorry bargain. I have always thought my cousin Hamish a civil man, if a little eager in his Puritanism, but now I see that his civility may mask a hunger and ambition I must be wary of.

### 4 July

Sunday, and so to church again. I fear there has been some more upset about Anne's mother – she will not come to church with me. I take it she does not want to expose herself to the stares of the villagers, tho' I think she is being too sensitive. I told her so, and were we not such close companions now I believe we should have had cross words, for she will not talk to me about it. Surely, I told her, there are no secrets between us now; but she would not answer me, and looked away.

## 8 July

Something is troubling my darling Anne – something she is not telling me, I feel sure of it. I asked her to bathe with me today and she would not, though it is hotter than ever, and the cool water would be pleasant. So I went alone, and when I came back I found her crying in the music room, but she still will not tell me what is amiss.

## 9 July

I am more than ever convinced that something is not right with Anne. She often absents herself, with excuses that I later find to be untrue, such as saying she needs to speak to one or other of the servants about her room. I have resolved to follow where she goes, and if necessary to confront her with it.

## 11 July

This afternoon, when Anne asked if she might be excused, and made as if to retire to her bedchamber, I followed her. After a little while she went out from the kitchen door, and crossed the lawn in the direction of the village. I was fearful – I know not what I was fearful of. I thought she must be meeting someone. And by the gates she stopped, and looked around, and there a man approached her from the shelter of a bush. And to my very great surprise I saw it to be my cousin Hamish. They spoke in low voices for a while, but I perceived them to be having some disagreement, for Anne shook her head vehemently upon several occasions, and once he took hold of her wrist as if he would have shaken her. I did not stay to see them part, for fear of being apprehended.

I am writing this very late, by a candle in my chamber,

being quite unable to sleep. Later this same day, when Anne and I were playing cards – for I had set myself not to mention what I had observed – she gave a sigh, and asked me whether I should not marry after all. For, she says, it is certainly the place of a woman to do so, and not to set herself up as a sort of petticoat laird. For truly, she says, the only estate a woman should want is the estate of Holy matrimony. At this I confess I threw down my cards and laughed scornfully. 'I swear I had not seen my cousin Hamish in this room, yet here are his words, and his very voice, which I should have found impudent coming from a cousin, and which from a servant are patronage itself.' She flushed, and said that she merely wished to give me good advice. To which I said, 'Then let me give you some in return, my dearest Anne. When you are going to meet your paramour my cousin, do not do so quite so close to the house, lest you be observed.' We glared angrily at each other, and then she rose, and retired without a word for the evening.

But I must cease. Someone is knocking at my chamber door. It will be Anne, I think.

### 13 July

I cannot write – I must not – yet I find I need to make some mark on the page to record what has happened. My life, I think, will never be the same again. Oh Anne, my Anne, how could I ever have doubted you?

### July

I have a decision to make, and must do so alone. A jump into the dark. Where will I land? But there is no point in hesitating on the edge, for in truth I am already falling, before I have so much as taken a step.

*July*

It is done, and done together.

I shall not record dates in this journal again, not wanting to leave any record – let us hope it never comes to that, but it is well to be prudent.

*July*

> Oh lovely and gracious goddess of the night,
> Mistress of the moon, mother of all light,
> I stand in awe and worship thee.
> Come to me now, that we may blessed be.
>
> Blessed be thy feet, which have trodden in the
>     ways of beauty.
> Blessed be thy womb, without which we would
>     not be.
> Blessed be thy breasts, that suckle in sweetness.
> Blessed be thy lips, that shall speak the secret
>     names.
> Blessed be thy eyes, that shall adore and be
>     adored.

*August*

Days and months are no longer important. What matters now is eternity.

I invoke thee and call upon thee, mysterious mother of us all, bringer of all fruitfulness: by seed and root, by bud and stem, by leaf and flower I invoke thee. Voluptuous virgin, bride of the world, descend upon the body of this thy servant . . .

# TWENTY-SIX

She looked up from the computer screen. While she had been transcribing the diary, Gerard had entered the room and was now sitting behind her, waiting patiently for her to finish.

'Well?' Gerard said. 'I take it you have the journal?'

There were too many things going round in her head, too many contradictory clues that would need to settle before she could tease out which ones would lead her to the truth of all this and which were misleading. 'Yes. It's interesting,' was all she would say.

'I read it myself – or, at least, those bits I could make out – when I first met Old John. I was absolutely convinced then, as I still am. Anne was a witch already, when they met – she would have been initiated by her mother. That's why she wouldn't pray in church. Then she told Catherine, who decided to try it for herself. She was initiated into the coven, and started copying down fragments of the rituals, things that made a special impression on her. She wouldn't write down everything in case the diary was found.'

'Hmm,' Terry said. The faintest glimmer of an idea was flitting on the edges of her brain. 'That's one interpretation, anyway.'

Somewhere in the house a telephone rang. Gerard, ignoring it, came and picked up the seventeenth-century manuscript. 'You know what Old John told me? He said that in its way this would turn out to be as important as the Dead Sea Scrolls or one of the Old Testament books of the prophets. It was partly his enthusiasm, of course, that convinced one – he appeared to have what we were all looking for in those days: a system of belief, completely authentic, but also completely new. At the time Brigid and I were followers of Krishnamurti, whose great nostrum was that "Truth is a pathless land". Meeting John – having him explain the rituals – was like finding the course of an old footpath that's been grown over with brambles, but which you know will take you somewhere if you only stick with it long enough. He was a remarkable man. Sometimes I feel I'm not worthy to fill his shoes.'

'It must have been hard to have to sell this to Nicolaides.'

He nodded. 'It was. At the time, we had no choice. But ever since I've felt that we were a little like the Israelites without the Ark of the Covenant. I have prayed and worked to bring it back. And now of course, it *has* come back, if only on loan. Spells always work, if not always in the manner one expects them to.'

'Gerard,' she said carefully, 'don't you ever worry that you're only seeing part of the picture? That you've built all this,' she indicated the walls around them, 'on a few historical fragments?'

'All history is fragments, isn't it? We can never know the past, but we can learn from it.'

'Unless there's more to it than witchcraft,' she murmured, half to herself.

'What do you mean?' But at that moment Brigid pushed open the door and interrupted them.

'Terry, Laura Macpherson just phoned. She's got a problem with the beehive on her farm. I'm sorry to ask you this, but with Gregor not here I don't know who else could do it. Would you go over and see if there's anything you can do?'

'This would be the pig farmer?'

Brigid nodded.

'In that case,' Terry said, picking up the tractor keys again, 'this couldn't have come at a better time. I've got a few questions for Laura Macpherson myself.'

'He wants what?' Talbot stared at his junior in disbelief.

Nicky put her hand over the mouthpiece of the phone and repeated what she'd just said. 'Iain Pullen wants clearance to go and buy some wine, sir. He says it might be expensive.'

'What sort of wine, for God's sake?'

Heron spoke into the phone and turned back to the superintendent. 'He says fine Bordeaux for preference. That's why it might cost a lot. He wants some 1985, 1987, 1990, 1992 and 1995. Apparently they were quite good years.'

'Tell him to piss off,' Talbot snapped. 'I'm in the middle of a multiple murder investigation, and I haven't got time to make jokes about his bloody dinner parties.'

Heron held out the handset. 'I think he's serious,

sir. Perhaps you'd better speak to him yourself.'

Snarling, Talbot grabbed the phone from her. After a while, though, the angry expression on his face died away, and he started to nod thoughtfully.

Following Brigid's directions, Terry steered the little tractor round what seemed like miles of back lanes until she spotted the electric fences and arced huts of the pig farm. A large white tent stood at the end of the field, surrounded by police tapes that fluttered with a whirring sound in the gentle breeze. Perhaps it was the contrast with the pigs' fenced-off enclosures that made Terry feel that the tent was itself the lair of some strange and exotic animal, shut away for its own protection.

A shapeless figure was crouched over a pile of straw in one of the pig fields, flicking at a lighter. The wind snatched the flame away several times before the pile caught fire. Then the figure straightened, and Terry saw that it was a young woman, a blond ponytail protruding from the back of her grimy baseball cap. Terry walked towards her.

'Laura Macpherson? I'm Terry Williams. From Nineveh Farm.' She held out her hand.

The other woman held up her arm, which was covered in what looked like dried blood. 'I'd better not shake hands. Where's Gregor? He usually deals with the bees.'

'He couldn't come.'

'It's a swarm, I'm afraid. Over here.' The farmer led the way across the middle of the pig corrals, stepping over the electric fences with practised ease, until she came to a group of four white hives next to a little copse. She stopped and pointed into the trees. 'They've gone in there.'

311

Terry looked. A round, wriggling, football-sized mass hung from a low branch. She tensed, remembering the fear she had heard in Gregor's voice when the bees had clustered round his eyes. 'Right,' she said briskly. 'I might need your help, if that's all right.'

The girl shrugged. 'Fine, so long as it doesn't take too long. I've got a lot to do before it gets dark.'

She tried to recall what Gregor had told her. 'A swarm happens when a hive gets overcrowded', she said, 'and the old queen leads a delegation off to form a new hive. She can only fly for a few days, because she's been starved, and the other bees will always follow their queen. So if I take the comb that has the queen in, and put her in a new hive, the rest of the swarm will come too.'

'Sounds reasonable enough. Do you have anything to put it in?'

She'd forgotten this essential detail, of course. With Laura's help she located an old crate that would do as the swarm's temporary home.

'And now,' she said, pulling on her gloves and a veiled hat, and stepping up to the mass of bees, 'all I have to do is put my hands in there and break it off.'

Despite the partial protection afforded by the veil, all her muscles were locked solid with terror. Painfully, she extended one arm. The swarm, sensing her approach, hummed and throbbed menacingly.

There was no obvious point of entry. It was as solid as a ball of knitting: a writhing, pulsing mass of insects that offered no way in. Terry pushed gingerly with the tips of her fingers, and felt herself enveloped up to the knuckles. Stings tingled – or was it just her imagination? – through the material of her gloves. It was surprisingly warm, the bees' skins silky-smooth and offering little resistance to the gentle pressure she exerted. 'Thank God for small fists,' she muttered to herself.

A change in the engine note, and she was almost in to the wrist. Her fingers met cartilage, the ribbed secretions of honeycomb. Bees flew in her face, pushing the muslin of the veil into her eyes. Others were settling in the exposed parts of her hair.

For a moment panic welled in her guts. Breathe, she told herself; just breathe. Then the panic passed and she slid effortlessly, frictionlessly in, grasping the ball of honeycomb in her outstretched palm.

'Now,' she said, as much to give herself courage as to inform the watching farmer. She slid her other hand onto the top of the swarm, twisted it gently, and felt the ball rip away from the tree. An angry gear-change from the bees told her that they had realized what was going on. Was it just her imagination, or was her arm being stung to buggery? 'Ouch, yow,' she whispered. Quickly she turned and began to walk towards where the tractor stood with the old crate on the trailer. Squadrons of bees seemed to be dive-bombing her face, battering their tiny fuselages against her eyes and nostrils. The veil, she knew, would be almost useless under the attack of so many insects simultaneously. 'Tell me which way to go,' she shouted, absurdly loud – she had no idea where Laura was now, until the other woman's voice sounded calmly in her ear: 'Go left a bit, and you're there. Careful not to walk into the trailer.' Blindly she felt for the box – feeling Laura's hands guide her – and lowered her double handful of danger into it as gently as she could. When she opened her eyes it was to witness an instant of magic, the genie-into-the-bottle moment when all the bees followed their queen, blindly, into the darkness.

She breathed deeply for a few seconds, feeling the adrenaline ebb from her blood. Laura was tugging at her own overalls with an anxious expression on her face.

'Shit. I think I've got one down – oh hell, it's stung me.' She unzipped the boiler suit, revealing an equally grimy T-shirt, then shucked the arms of the overalls right down and twisted round in an effort to see her own back. 'I think some got in here,' she said in a small voice. 'I'm being stung.'

Two bees flew dizzily out from under the T-shirt. 'Let me,' Terry said quickly, lifting up the back of Laura's shirt and locating the little stings, tiny as eyelashes. She scraped them out with her thumbnail. 'That should help,' she said apologetically. 'You're not allergic or anything, are you?'

'I don't think so. Sorry, I'm being a wimp. You must have been stung all over.'

But in fact she had not been. Terry counted no more than four stings on her forearm and one on her neck – a miraculous escape, it seemed to her. Carefully she extracted the bees' stings from her own skin. 'That was easier than I thought it would be.'

'Is it sometimes harder?'

Terry laughed, relief making her light-headed. 'I wouldn't know. That's the first time I've done it.'

'Well, you impressed the hell out of me.'

Terry looked around her at the pig fields. 'This is pretty impressive, too.'

'Thanks,' the other woman said dryly.

'I didn't mean, impressive for a woman,' she assured her. 'I just meant – well, it's a pretty big operation, isn't it?'

Laura smiled. With a start Terry realized how pretty she was. 'Sorry. I get used to being patronized, I suppose.'

Terry smiled back. 'Don't we all?'

A moment's silence extended itself into two. 'That must be where the bodies were found,' Terry said to break it, shifting her gaze to the white tent.

'Yes. The death pit. It's empty now.'

'Is there anyone still working there?'

Laura shook her head. 'The forensic archaeologist has gone to Inverness. Doing post-mortems on the latest bodies.'

'Oh, of course.'

Another moment's awkwardness. For a moment Terry wondered if the silence between them wasn't erotically charged: then, remembering her terrible faux pas with David Nicolaides, she put the thought out of her mind. The girl was just slightly tongue-tied. Hardly surprising, considering what an antisocial job she did. OK, so Terry was honest enough about her own responses to know that Laura was just the sort of girl she found attractive, but you couldn't go around assuming that everyone you liked the look of reciprocated the feeling.

'Anyway, I'd better get on,' Laura was saying. 'Too much to do, as usual.'

'Sorry, I'll buzz off.'

Laura grinned again. 'With your bees.'

'Oh, yes. Buzz buzz.' I'm talking gibberish, Terry thought: what in God's name has happened to my brain? 'Look,' she said, 'I wanted to talk to you about the murders. The police have locked up some of the Wiccans – including Gregor: that's why he isn't here. Could I see you when you've finished?'

Laura thought for a moment. 'OK. But it'll have to be late. I won't be through until around seven.'

'We could do it over dinner, then,' Terry found herself saying. 'There must be a restaurant in Babcock.'

'There is, if you like Indian.' She was already walking away. 'I was going to get a takeaway anyway, since there's no-one to cook for me now. See you there about eight?'

'Fine.' Terry called. She turned thoughtfully and went back to the tractor. It's just a curry, after all, she told herself. So long as she managed to unmush her brain, there was no reason for Laura to realize that Terry fancied her.

# TWENTY-SEVEN

DW:  So when I press the little buttons, it will start to record everything we say. That's why the light is flashing. So we know it's working.

MW:  [Distorted] Yah yah yah yah.

DW:  But if you shout really loud like that, it may not work so well. It's best if you just talk normally.

MT:  [Distorted] Yah yah yah. Yah yah yah.

PM:  Would you like to look at this toy, Myrvyn?

[Pause on tape]

DW:  Do you know why we want to talk to you, Myrvyn?

MT:  No.

DW:  Sometimes, when people are naughty, we're asked to find out what's happened. We know you haven't been naughty, Myrvyn, but perhaps you know some people who have.

MT:  Holly was naughty.

DW:  Was she?

MT:  She cried at night.

DW:  Was Mummy cross?

MT: Yes. Go to sleep! Go to sleep!

DW: Does Mummy often get cross?

MT: [Unintelligible]

DW: What does Mummy do when she gets cross?

MT: She shouts.

DW: Does she? How about the men that Mummy lives with? Do they get cross sometimes?

MT: Yes.

DW: Do they smack you sometimes?

[Pause]

DW: I bet that hurts, doesn't it?

MT: Ow! Ow! Ow!

DW: Which ones get cross? Can you tell me their names?

[Pause]

DW: Who gets cross, Myrvyn?

MT: Gregor.

DW: Are you frightened of Gregor, Myrvyn?

MT: No.

DW: Why does Gregor get cross with you? What does he get cross about?

MT: When I play jumping on Gregor.

DW: Is that a game Gregor plays with you?

MT: Yes.

DW: Show me how you play it.

[Noises, unintelligible]

DW: Ouch. That's a rough game, isn't it, Myrvyn?

MT: [Laughs]

DW: Who else plays rough games with you?

MT: Jump on Gregor! Jump on Gregor!

PM: Do you like playing jump on Gregor, Myrvyn?

MT: Yes.

PM: Does anyone—

MT: I'm bored. I want to go home with Gregor.

318

PM: When Gregor smacks you, do you cry?

MT: No. I want to go home.

DW: Patricia, I think we should—

[Whispers on tape]

DW: Do you know who Gerard is, Myrvyn?

MT: Yes.

DW: Who is he?

MT: He's the High Priest.

DW: Do you like Gerard?

[Pause]

DW: You're shrugging, Myrvyn. Does that mean you don't like him much?

MT: I s'pose.

DW: Why don't you like him?

MT: He's got a funny face. Like a bottom.

DW: What do you mean, Myrvyn? Why is his face like a bottom?

MT: He's old. So is Granny Brigid. And he's got a funny smell.

DW: What does he smell of?

MT: Poo!

DW: Have you ever seen Gerard without any clothes on, Myrvyn?

MT: Lots of times.

DW: Tell me about it.

MT: When he sits in the garden with his eyes closed.

DW: Does he ever talk to you when he hasn't got any clothes on? What does he say?

MT: Nothing.

DW: Does he say things that frighten you?

MT: Not really.

DW: Does he scare you?

MT: When can I see Mummy?

PM: Mummy's having a rest. Auntie Jane is

319

|     | looking after you at her house for a little while, until Mummy's better. |
| --- | --- |
| MT: | When can I see her? |
| DW: | You were going to tell me what Gerard does that frightens you. |

[Pause]

|     |     |
| --- | --- |
| MT: | He shouts. |
| DW: | What does he shout? |
| MT: | Go away! Go away! |
| DW: | Does he say go away? Or does he say come here? |
| MT: | Sometimes. |
| DW: | It's all right, Myrvyn. It isn't you who's been naughty. |
| MT: | Has Gerard been naughty? |
| DW: | What do you think, Myrvyn? |

[Pause]

|     |     |
| --- | --- |
| MT: | Yes. |
| DW: | Yes what? |
| MT: | Yes he's been naughty. |
| PM: | David, can I have a word? |

[Pause]

|     |     |
| --- | --- |
| PM: | If I give you some paper, Myrvyn, do you think you could draw me a picture of Gerard being naughty? |
| MT: | No. |
| PM: | Why not? |
| MT: | I haven't got any crayons. |
| PM: | I'll give you some crayons. |
| MT: | OK. |

[Pause]

DW [Aside]: I think we're finally making—
END OF TAPE.

DW:   . . . started the tape machine again. Goodness me, Myrvyn, what a wonderful drawing.

MT:   I haven't finished the bombs yet.

DW:   Can you tell me what this is?

MT:   It's an aeroplane. These are the guns and this is a rocket.

DW:   That's lots of rockets, Myrvyn.

[Pause]

DW:   Is Gerard in the picture, Myrvyn?

MT:   No.

DW:   I thought you were going to draw us a picture of Gerard being naughty.

[Pause]

DW:   Tell you what, Myrvyn, let's turn it over and start a new picture.

MT:   No.

DW:   Yes.

PM:   Wouldn't you like to draw a picture of Gerard, Myrvyn? Then you'll be able to go home for some lovely tea.

[Pause]

MT:   Will Mummy be at home?

PM:   I meant home to Auntie Jane's.

MT:   I don't want to go to Auntie Jane's.

DW:   Is that Gerard? He looks very scary.

PM:   What's he done to look so scary?

MT:   Put a spell on someone.

DW:   Is that what he does? Puts spells on people?

MT:   Yes.

DW:   Has he ever put a spell on you?

MT:   Sometimes.

DW:   Tell us about it.

MT: When I had ear ache. He said he could make it better.

DW: Did he make it better?

MT: No.

DW: Has he ever told you a secret?

MT: I don't know.

DW: If he has, you can tell us. We're allowed to know secrets.

MT: Will he go to prison?

DW: Would you like him to go to prison, Myrvyn? Would you feel safer then?

MT: Bad people go to prison.

DW: If he was in prison, would you tell us the secret?

MT: I don't know.

[Pause]

DW: That's a much better picture, Myrvyn. He looks very scary. What's this?

MT: It's a rocket.

DW: What sort of rocket?

MT: It's a missile.

DW: Why's he holding a missile, Myrvyn?

[Pause]

DW: Shall I tell you what I think it looks like? I think it looks a bit like a penis – you know, a willy.

MT: [Laughs]

[Pause]

DW: Is it Gerard's willy, Myrvyn?

MT: Might be.

PM: Well done, Myrvyn.

DW: Has he ever touched you with his willy, Myrvyn? You can tell us if he has.

MT: Might have.

DW: Did it hurt you?

MT: Yes.

DW: Poor Myrvyn. That must have been horrid.

[Pause]

DW: Did other people touch you with their willies too? Is that the secret you weren't supposed to tell anyone?

MT: Yes.

DW: Why don't you draw some of the other people in the picture. Then you can tell me their names, and I'll write them in for you.

[Pause]

DW: What are all those people doing? Are they dancing?

MT: Yes.

DW: Why are they dancing? Are they dancing round you?

MT: Yes.

DW: Show me where you are in the picture.

MT: I'm hungry. Am I having tea here?

DW: You can if you like. Do you like McDonald's?

MT: McDonald's! McDonald's! Can I have a Happy Meal?

DW: If you finish your picture, Patricia will go and get us all a McDonald's.

MT: McDonald's is my favourite.

DW: Let's finish the picture, shall we?

MT: I want to go to McDonald's with Mummy.

PM: Tell you what. Let's finish the picture together.

MT: [Cries]

DW: OK, we may as well leave it there. We've got plenty to be—

END OF TAPE.

DW: Myrvyn, I'm just going to recap on what you've already told us. You said Uncle Gerard and his friends sometimes touch you with their willies. Is that right?

MT: Can't remember.

DW: What can't you remember?

[Pause]

DW: You can't remember what happened or you can't remember what you said?

[Pause]

DW: You see, Myrvyn, it's very important that you tell us the truth now. Do you know the difference between the truth and a lie?

[Pause]

DW: You're nodding, Myrvyn. So you do know what the truth is?

MT: [Inaudible]

DW: Good. And when you told us earlier about Uncle Gerard, were you lying then?

MT: No.

DW: That's OK. No-one's saying you were. We just have to check.

PM: What about baby Holly, Myrvyn. Did they ever touch her like that?

MT: Yes.

DW: Who else was there? Did you recognize anyone else besides Uncle Gerard?

MT: Batman.

DW: Batman? Do you mean someone who looked like Batman?

[Pause]

DW: Myrvyn? Do you mean someone was wearing a big black cloak like Batman?

324

MT: Yes.

DW: Do you know what that person's real name is?

[Pause]

DW: Did he wear a mask so you couldn't see?

MT: I think so.

DW: How about the others?

[Pause]

DW: Auntie Jane tells me that you sometimes wet your bed, Myrvyn.

MT: [Unintelligible]

DW: It's all right, Myrvyn. No-one's cross with you. I was just wondering if you wet your bed because you were frightened of the man who wears a cloak like Batman.

MT: Yes.

DW: How about Mummy's other friends? Were they there when Batman was there?

MT: Yes.

DW: Tell me their names.

MT: Jamie, Gregor, Granny Brigid, Alan, Isobel, Zoe. Stephan and Anna are from Holland which is across the sea. But—

DW: Yes?

MT: I think it's still nearer than France. I think.

DW: Anyone else?

MT: I don't know. Terry.

DW: Terry? Who's he?

MT: Terry babysits us sometimes. She sleeps in Donna's bed but Jamie's too.

DW: If you remember anyone else, Myrvyn, you can always tell Auntie Jane. You've done really well this afternoon.

MT: Can I go back to Mummy now?

DW: Not just yet.

MT:   If you don't let me go back to my mummy
      she'll put a spell on you.
DW:   You mustn't believe that, Myrvyn. It'll only
      frighten you.
MT:   I'm not frightened. She'll turn you into a slug.
DW:   I think that's probably—
END OF TAPE

# TWENTY-EIGHT

The Indian turned out to boast tartan wallpaper and
the ubiquitous stags' heads on its walls. Terry was
relieved to discover that the waiters, at least, had
eschewed kilts and sporrans for the more traditional
turban, though their accents were pure Highlands.

She had resisted the urge to dress up, selecting a
pair of jeans and a shirt from her meagre wardrobe.
Agonizing briefly over make-up – too much might
imply a degree of self-beautification inappropriate
to a date with a woman, too little and she'd end up
looking even more of a dyke – she ended up by com-
promising: a hint of lipstick and some of Zoe's
mascara. When Laura finally appeared, half an hour
later than she'd said she'd be, Terry was glad she
hadn't put on anything more elaborate: Laura was
in a pair of leggings and a baggy sweater that had
seen much better days. She had washed her hair,
though, and it now fell in a soft blond cascade down
to her neck. Terry, whose dark wiry ringlets only
lent themselves to two styles – up or down – felt a
sudden pang of jealousy as well as lust. Try explaining that to a heterosexual, she thought.

'Sorry I'm late,' Laura said breathlessly, squeezing

327

herself opposite Terry. 'I had a couple of litters at the last minute.'

'What does that involve?' Terry asked, and for a few minutes they talked about pigs, until the waiter came to take their order. Laura greeted him like an old friend.

'You must come here a lot,' Terry said when he'd gone to get their wine.

Laura grinned. 'First time in the restaurant, actually. But I live on their takeaways. They're polite enough not to mind when I turn up to collect them in my work clothes. Not like the pub – I get all sorts of strange looks when I go in there.'

No mention of any boyfriend, Terry found herself thinking; then mentally kicked herself for allowing her thoughts to wander down that particular path. She had already noticed that Laura's hands were free of rings. Unable to stop herself, she said, 'You said earlier there was no-one to cook for you tonight.'

'The police archaeologist has been staying with me while he's been excavating the death pit. He turned out to be rather useful in the kitchen.' Something about the way she said it hinted at an untold story, but now wasn't the time to ask.

'And which one of you ladies is going to try the wine?' It was the waiter, his hands busy uncorking the bottle.

'She will,' they both said simultaneously. Then: 'No, you.' They laughed.

'Why don't we both do it?' Terry suggested. The waiter shrugged, and poured a little into each of their glasses.

'I wanted to ask you about the archaeologist, actually,' Terry said when he'd gone. 'Would he talk to me, do you think?'

'I guess so. I mean, I could ask.' Unexpectedly, Laura blushed. 'Actually, it's slightly awkward at the moment. We had a slight . . . misunderstanding.'

'He made a pass?'

'Oh no.' For a moment Laura seemed unsure whether to tell her, then she shrugged and said, 'More the other way round, actually.'

'I see.' Terry felt an irrational sense of disappointment. She hadn't really expected Laura to be gay, but it was still annoying to have her heterosexuality confirmed.

'I made a bit of an idiot of myself. Anyway, you don't want to hear about my disastrous private life.'

'We're in the same boat, as a matter of fact,' Terry said ruefully. She told Laura about her encounter that morning with Nicolaides, eliciting a peal of raucous laughter from the other woman.

'Oh God,' she spluttered, 'I'd love to have seen that.'

'I felt such an idiot.'

Laura reached across the table and squeezed her hand. 'Don't worry.' She laughed. 'Though who am I to talk? I blush every time I think about my own cock-up.'

She's just naturally tactile, Terry thought: that squeeze means nothing. 'Not really a cock-up, though, was it?'

'Sorry?'

'More like a cock-down.' They grinned at each other.

'What would you have done if he *had* been asking you to sleep with him, though? Would you have gone through with it?' Laura asked.

'I don't know,' Terry said. 'I didn't think about it, to be honest. I just said yes and took it from there.

Part of me immediately clicked into thinking about Donna.'

Laura sighed. 'You're so relaxed about sex.'

'*Me?*' said Terry, astonished.

'Wiccans.' Laura blushed. 'I may not get out much, but I do hear some of the gossip.'

'Oh, that. Yes, the Wiccans are all at it like rabbits. But I'm not a Wiccan. I'm only staying with them while I do some research.' She explained about Catherine McCulloch and the letters. 'So I'm just trying to establish whether or not she was really a lesbian, so that I can write my thesis and get the hell out of here,' she concluded.

Laura nodded slowly. There was a brief pause.

'I am, by the way,' Terry said.

'Am what?'

'You're wondering if I'm gay myself. I am. Well, strictly speaking I'm bisexual but', she shrugged, 'that's not a word I tend to use because it sounds so bloody indecisive.'

'Oh. I see.'

There was another, longer pause. 'Don't worry, I don't make passes at straight girls,' Terry said lightly. 'Do you want dessert? I still want to hear about the police investigation.'

Afterwards they strolled back up the High Street towards Laura's little MG. 'Need a lift?' she asked.

Terry shook her head. 'I've got Gregor's tractor.'

'Chilly.'

'I quite like it, actually. It's a bit like driving an open-top car and a lorry all at once.'

Laura laughed. 'We'll make a farmer of you yet.'

She left Laura by the car and went on to where she'd parked the tractor. There were no street lights in Babcock, but there was enough light around for her to see that there was something odd about it. It seemed to have somehow sunk into the ground. Then she realized why. All the tyres had been let down.

'Shit,' she said out loud. It was a long walk back to Nineveh.

Figures rose from behind the tractor where they had been crouching, letting down the last tyre. They must have heard her. 'Bastards,' she shouted indignantly. 'Get away from there, you little toe-rags.' Belatedly, she registered that these were not children or adolescents but four grown men, their outlines bulky as water-butts, and they were not running away but advancing menacingly on her.

'It's one of the bitches,' she heard one of them mutter in broadly accented Scots. 'Fokin' bitches.' No: not *bitches* but *witches*. She froze.

'I'll call the police,' she said, but they kept coming. She caught a glimpse of faces, beards, donkey jackets topped with greasy flat caps, before with a shout they had grabbed her, twisting her round so that she was bent double with her face pressed to the ground. A knee slammed into her stomach like a concrete block, slamming all the air out of her lungs. A hand thrust itself roughly into her clothing, but it was looking for ways to hurt her, not for sex, and she felt herself being held, shaken and flung to the ground again. A boot kicked her in the thigh, and liquid splashed on her face and hair. For a moment she thought it must be beer, but then the acrid reek of paraffin filled her throat. She was still gasping from being winded, and she choked still more on the slimy, greasy muck in her mouth. She glimpsed a canister being vigorously shaken over her and rolled away frantically – the ground was covered with it – only to be sent back again by another blow from a boot. I'm going to die, she thought: they're going to burn me. *Like a witch.* Her brain made the connection suddenly and it was all she could do to hold that one thought in her head while the paraffin and the blows rained down on her. *They're going to burn me like a witch.*

The sky was full of light suddenly and she cringed, waiting for the pain. But the light, she saw, was not a flame but headlights. Somewhere a car horn was blaring. Dimly she became aware that the boots which moments ago had been pounding into her legs and arms were running away now. Then blond hair appeared above her and she heard Laura's voice, hysterical, and felt Laura's hands trying to get her off the ground. She staggered like something newborn, clutching the other girl for support. 'Don't light a cigarette,' she managed to say through lips that had somehow got cut in the fight. 'No matches. Paraffin.'

'Relax, just relax,' Laura was saying.

'Paraffin.' Why couldn't she make her understand?

'Look, I don't smoke anyway.'

Somehow she got herself into Laura's tiny sports car. After a moment she twisted the mirror round to look at herself. The paraffin had matted her hair and her lip was bleeding, but otherwise her face was OK. Nothing seemed to be broken anywhere else, though she was still winded. She coughed, and almost choked on the taste that came up from her lungs.

Laura drove in silence for a few minutes, giving her occasional glances. 'Jesus. Those bastards,' she said at last.

'They must have recognized the tractor,' Terry said when she could speak again.

'Do you need a doctor?'

'I don't think so. There's nothing that needs stitching, anyway.'

'I've got a pretty heavy-duty first aid kit up at the house.'

'What I need most of all', Terry said, 'is a bath. Preferably in Fairy Liquid.'

'No problem.' She looked at Terry anxiously. 'They wouldn't have done it, would they? They wouldn't really have set light to you?'

'Who knows? They were probably going to torch the tractor, and I just happened to come along.' She paused. 'I think I recognized one of them. It was Hector Morrison.'

'*Hector*? But he's my landlord. A pillar of the community. Church warden.'

'All the more reason to hate the Wiccans. And I saw in the churchyard that he had a child who died just after it was born. Someone who's had a tragedy like that wouldn't be very rational about baby killers.'

Laura shook her head. 'Christ.'

'If there's a war, Laura, you must make sure you're not caught up in it. At the end of the day, you probably need people like Hector more than you need the Wiccans.'

Laura pulled up in front of a little cottage and led her into the living room. 'Wait here,' she said, disappearing into the kitchen. A few moments later she came back with a can of lager. 'Drink this. I knew a boy at college who did fire-eating. Apparently lager's the best thing to get rid of the taste.'

'Thanks,' Terry said gratefully, cracking open the

can. 'Any painkillers I could wash down with it?'

'I'll find some Nurofen.'

When the lager was drunk, Terry stood under the shower and tipped a bottle of shampoo into her hair, scrubbing her fingers through it until all traces of the paraffin had gone. Then, wrapped in a dressing gown Laura had lent her, she went back into the other room and collapsed onto the sofa. Laura handed her a glass of whisky.

'I've put your clothes in the wash. They'll be dry in the morning.'

'It's OK to stay the night?'

'Sure. Iain's still away.'

'I can sleep in his bed, then.'

'If you like.' Laura looked away.

It wasn't what she said, but it might have been something in the way she said it, some tiny nuance that inserted itself in the space between the words. Like two satellites, Terry thought, suddenly downloading a million bytes of information in a flash. She let the silence lengthen.

'Are you saying what I think you're saying?' she asked softly.

'I don't know what I'm saying.'

'But your archaeologist. The one you made a pass at . . .'

'Perhaps I just wanted to see if I was normal. Perhaps somehow I knew he wasn't interested – perhaps I deliberately made a pass at the safest person I could have chosen.'

'So what would this be? An experiment?'

Laura looked at her carefully. 'You don't mind?'

'Hardly.'

There was a bruise on Terry's calf, spreading like a huge inky stain through the white skin.

Laura touched it gently. 'Ouch,' she said softly.

'I bruise easily.'

'I'll bear it in mind.'

Terry held her gaze for a long moment, then closed her eyes and let her head fall back onto the arm of the sofa. The other woman's fingers gently continued to circle the bruise, then trailed upwards to find the next, tracing its outline with her fingertips. 'Join the dots,' she said. Gently she lifted the flaps of the dressing gown away from Terry's legs. 'And one just here,' she said, touching the inside of Terry's thigh. 'And here—'

Terry smiled. 'I don't think I remember that one.'

'Oh, it's here all right,' Laura assured her.

Terry sat up, cupping her hand round the back of Laura's head. For a while they stayed like that, looking at each other. 'Nervous?'

Laura nodded, her hair falling into her eyes. 'A little.'

'So which one of us ladies,' Terry said quietly, 'is going to taste the wine?'

'We both will,' the other girl whispered.

Terry nodded, and pressed her bruised lips gently against Laura's.

When she woke it was the middle of the night. There was a cold space beside her, and she reached into it instinctively. Laura wasn't there.

Terry sat up and groped around the unfamiliar table for a light switch. Still no sign of her. Wrapping the dressing gown around her – Laura had left the windows open in the bedroom, and it was a cold night – she went to see where she was.

She found her sitting on the bathroom floor,

naked, slowly rocking backwards and forwards. 'Laura? What's up?'

'I'm fine,' the other girl said, not looking up. 'Go back to bed.'

Terry slid down beside her. 'Hey.'

'It's all right for you, isn't it?' Laura said bitterly.

'What do you mean?'

'In a few weeks you'll have gone back to London. Back in your own world, surrounded by all your gay friends.' Terry tried to say something but Laura interrupted. 'And don't tell me that I could go too. I've got a business to run. Even if I wanted to walk away from it, I'm still paying off my debts.'

Terry said nothing.

'I want children,' Laura said softly. 'I want a farmhouse with chickens and a Labrador and a swing in the garden. I don't want to be gay.'

Terry smiled. 'It was that good, was it?'

'Nothing's that good.'

Terry gently ran her fingers through the other girl's hair, waiting for her to go on.

'And then there's what everyone would say.' She put on a Scottish accent. '"No wonder she's daeing a man's job. She's a bludie lezzie."'

'You don't exactly fit the dyke stereotype.'

'Don't get me wrong, Terry. I haven't had some blinding road-to-Damascus conversion. I'm just saying, even if this could be the real me, I don't want it to be.'

'"You have shewn me that which otherwise would have been hidden from me,"' Terry quoted, '" so that I should not have known my own true self, and led me down that path where once all was dark. Perhaps only women can know such things, for our natures are open to ecstasy as men's are not."'

'Who said that?'

'Another resident of Babcock. A long time ago.'

'Oh. Your witch.' Laura was silent for a moment. 'But there are different sorts of ecstasy, aren't there? When I go round the farm, first thing in the morning, and there's no-one else around – just me and the mountain, and all the pigs just waking up ... I know it sounds corny, but that's a kind of ecstasy too.'

'I understand, really.' Terry stroked her hair again, then let her fingers run on over Laura's face, tracing the shape of her, touching her fingers gently to her tongue, her eyelids, the long slope of her neck. Laura moaned, and Terry leant forward to kiss her.

'So ...'

'Mmm?'

Terry reached across and turned on the bath taps. 'If this is going to be a once-in-a-lifetime experience for you,' she said, 'we might as well make it one you'll never forget.'

# TWENTY-NINE

Iain drew up by the guardhouse and opened his car window. 'I've come to speak to Major Pullen and Major Doyle. They're expecting me,' he told the military policeman on duty.

The soldier stared at the young man's ponytail. 'I'll let them know you're here,' he said curtly, picking up a phone.

Five minutes later Iain was shown into a room in one of the administration blocks. His father, sitting behind the desk, rose to his feet. 'Hello,' he said coolly. 'This is an unexpected pleasure.' He held out his hand, and Iain shook it formally. He nodded at the man next to him. 'This is Major Doyle. Fresh back from Bosnia. If you want to know about war graves, he's your man.'

It was dawn when Terry was woken by the sounds of Laura getting dressed. 'Morning,' she murmured sleepily.

The other girl smiled at her. 'Hi. Don't wake up, it's only six-thirty. I've got to go to the pigs, but you can stay here if you want. You won't find anything to eat, but there's enough milk for coffee.'

'That's OK. I'll come with you,' Terry said, swinging her legs out of bed. She groaned as yesterday's bruises gave a sudden reminder of their presence. 'Oh, Jesus!'

'Can't take the pace, eh?'

'Doesn't look like it,' Terry said, hobbling across the room. 'I don't suppose my clothes are dry, are they?'

'I'll lend you some of mine.'

Terry took the T-shirt and overalls Laura offered her and put them on. 'I feel like a squaddie in these,' she remarked.

'You wait till you get into the pig fields. It's like the Somme all over again. I'll find you some wellies. Tuck the ends of the overalls into the boots, or the mud will work its way up your legs. And put this on.' She handed Terry a baseball cap on which was written 'The Future of Pig Genetics'.

'Very flattering.'

'I get them from the people who supply my sows. Flattering or not, it'll keep the mud out of your eyes.'

They went to the farm in Laura's tractor, an altogether more sophisticated machine than Gregor's ancient Fordson. It had a cab, for one thing, with a tiny ledge for a passenger next to the driver's seat. The dashboard in front of them was full of hydraulic levers. 'Don't touch those,' Laura warned.

'What do they do?'

'God knows.'

At the farm Terry followed Laura round while she checked the farrowing paddocks for litters born during the night. Each sow here had her own hut, a cut-down version of the communal huts in the other fields. Laura peered in each one, careful not to disturb the animals. Occasionally a sow grunted at her curtly.

'Do they recognize you?'

'Of course. They really are as bright as people say. Whatever you do, don't stick your head in. They're used to me, but they'll probably take a large chunk out of your face.'

The fourth sow had given birth to a litter during the night. Terry retreated to a safe distance and watched as Laura crawled on her hands and knees into the hut. When she was completely behind the pig, she started to pummel at it with her hands. Clearly, she was no more than an irritation – the vast bulk of the sow, lying on its side, barely seemed to register the impact of Laura's fists – but after a minute or so it lumbered to its feet and trotted obediently outside.

'When she's not looking, see if you can come in,' Laura called quietly from inside the hut.

Terry waited until the sow had flicked up her tail to urinate, then crawled in. On a bed of straw, wriggling sleepily, were about a dozen very pale piglets.

Laura, cross-legged in the straw, grinned at her. 'Ever play Wendy huts when you were a kid?' She picked up a piglet and handed it to Terry. 'Here.'

Terry took the floppy, blind mass in her arms. It seemed to be all stomach, with tiny legs that scrabbled feebly at her. Its eyes were still closed, and its suede-soft back was streaked with afterbirth. Pushing its snout under her arm, it snuffled at her expectantly.

'Hopes you might be mum,' Laura said. 'Hold it firmly, though, because it won't like this.' She produced a pair of pliers from the pocket of her overalls and, with one deft movement, snipped off the piglet's tail. Instantly it started to scream shrilly.

'Ugh,' Terry said, 'Won't the mother—?'

'Let's hope not.' Reaching into the animal's mouth, Laura clipped its teeth equally quickly, then gave it an injection from a huge veterinary syringe. Then she swopped it for the next one.

'We have to do this,' she explained as she worked. 'If we don't they cause havoc later on, biting each other's tails in the fattening yards. Some people say it's cruel, but I'm afraid it's the price you pay for having cheap bacon in your supermarket.'

At the bottom of the pile were two dead piglets and one that was clearly very ill. Its stomach was concave, and it was breathing lethargically.

'The sow probably sat on these,' Laura said matter-of-factly. Taking the sick and dead piglets with her, she crawled out of the hut.

Terry watched as the sow, barking grumpily, trotted back into her hut and flopped down on the straw again. Immediately the piglets started clambering frantically towards her teats. 'And this goes on all year round?'

'Every day, if we've planned the serving right. Each sow has three litters a year, rain or shine.'

Terry indicated the piglet that had been sat on. 'What about that one? Will you have to rear it by hand?'

''Fraid not.' Laura swung the ailing piglet through the air by its hind legs, whacking its head against the ground. Terry flinched.

'Not my favourite part of the job,' Laura said. 'But even if I had the time to hand rear it, which I don't, it's probably got internal bleeding.'

'So these go in the death pit?'

'That's right.'

They did the rounds of the other farrowing huts. There had been three other litters during the night, and each was checked and clipped. At the end of the field they came to an empty hut, the wooden board which should have kept the pig in overnight lying in the mud.

'Damn,' Laura said emphatically.

'What's happened?'

'Some of them like giving birth outside,' she said, going round the back of the hut. 'Move, you great brute,' she yelled, kicking energetically at a sow that was lumbering reluctantly to its feet. As it got up Terry saw that it had dug a shallow dip for itself against the back wall of the hut. Three newborn piglets squeaked miserably as the sow's teats were pulled from their lips.

'Get that board and hold it in front of your legs,' Laura called. 'Then stand by the hut so she can't get past you.'

Terry did as she was told. The sow, its head down, went to the door of the hut and sniffed inside. With Terry standing alongside it, holding the board, and Laura behind it, it appeared to have nowhere else to go. But the next moment it had placed its snout against the edge of Terry's board, pushed it aside as easily as if it were a cat-flap, and slipped past her legs. She tried to pin it against the side of the hut with her knees, but it was like trying to stop a Chieftain tank.

'Never mind,' Laura said. 'We'll get her in a minute. We'd better find the piglets – they'll have crawled into the wind.'

After a few moments Terry saw a pink blob

motionless in the mud. It appeared to be completely dead.

'Put it under your shirt,' Laura said, 'against your stomach. Sometimes the warmth revives them.'

The piglet's flesh was like ice against her skin. Soon Laura came back with two more, equally lifeless.

'These too?'

Laura nodded, and Terry stuffed them next to the first while Laura checked the rest of the field.

'If there were any more, the foxes must have got them,' she said, returning to Terry. 'How are they doing?'

Right on cue, Terry felt something twitch against her stomach. She pulled up her shirt, and found that one of the piglets was nosing her feebly.

'That's incredible,' she breathed.

Laura beamed. 'Amazing, isn't it? I've seen piglets that have been outside all night come back to life like that.'

They put the live piglet in with one of the other sows to get some milk, and persuaded the reluctant mother back into her hut. Again and again she evaded them, even turning on Laura when she pushed her too hard and snapping at her with her vicious teeth. By the time they were finished it had started to rain, turning the muddy field into a quagmire.

'What next?' Terry asked.

'I think she may have a few more up there,' Laura said. She was limping where the sow had bitten her leg, though she refused to let Terry take a look at it. 'I'd just better stick my hand up her and check.'

'Lucky pig,' Terry muttered under her breath. 'Er – I suppose there's no chance of having a lie-down in one of those nice little huts?'

'No way. There are five hundred animals waiting to be fed, and if we don't do it soon they'll destroy the water troughs. Besides,' she said, giving Terry a stern sideways look, 'I meant what I said last night.'

'OK, OK,' Terry said, putting her hands in the air. 'No more propositions. I promise.'

Talbot and Nicky Heron sat in a darkened laboratory. An ultraviolet light tube flickered on, turning Talbot's shirt a dazzling blue-white.

'This is one of the simplest ways of dating bone,' Pullen instructed them, his teeth and the whites of his eyes moving around the room as if detached from a body. 'Here's one of the babies' thigh bones.' He held up a glowing white cylinder about four inches long. 'I'm putting it under the light, and next to it I'm putting a piece of recent bone I got from the butcher's shop down the road. As you can see, there is a slight difference between the fluorescence each is giving off – about a five per cent difference, in fact, when it's measured.

'We know that bones lose about fifteen per cent of the mineral which causes them to fluoresce over the first fifteen years after death. So I can tell you categorically that all these children were buried sometime in the last fifteen years.' He flicked on a light: Nicky blinked as the room returned to normal. 'Which isn't very surprising, given that the death pit wasn't even there fifteen years ago, but it's a good start. Now then.' He approached a large machine on one side of the laboratory: to Nicky it looked like a larger, and cleaner, version of the machines the people at the tyre depot used to check the balance on her tyres. 'This is an accelerator mass spectrometer. As used in accelerator mass spectrometry, otherwise known as carbon dating.'

'Hang on,' Nicky interjected, 'carbon dating's been discredited for anything more recent than the 1600s. That's why they can't tell if the Turin shroud's a fake or not.'

'That's absolutely right,' Iain said, unruffled. 'But if you already know that what you're dating is less than fifty years old, it can come into its own again. You see, the reason carbon dating isn't reliable for medium-timescale artefacts is that we don't know what the base levels of carbon in the atmosphere were for those centuries. However, what we *do* know is that for various reasons, largely to do with nuclear testing, global industrialization and the destruction of the rainforests, atmospheric carbon levels reached a peak in about 1965 and have been declining steadily ever since. If you've got something which can act as a control to tell you the true carbon levels in any specific year, there's no reason why you shouldn't compare it to the carbon levels in the organic matter you're testing – in this case, human bone – to see if you've got a match. And, as it happens, we do have a control.'

He moved over to the bench on the other side of the room, where half a dozen bottles were lined up next to a series of petri dishes. 'Courtesy of your budget, Superintendent, some very nice Château Lynch-Bages for a range of vintages from 1985 onwards. I went for expensive claret because there was less chance of it being corrupted by chemical additives or poor storage.'

Talbot nodded slowly. 'And do you have a match?'

'We do.' He held up a bottle. 'They died last year.'

'What? All of them?'

345

'All of them.'

'What about the variations in decay?' Nicky asked. 'We assumed—'

'That they'd died over a period of time. It was a reasonable assumption to make, but I'm afraid it isn't correct. I was fooled as well, until these last few days, when I started looking at the exact nature of the death pit.'

Talbot folded his arms. 'Go on.'

Iain paused, arranging his thoughts. 'Normally, as the pathologist said, a body decays in a fairly linear and predictable pattern. In fact, it was something he said that set me thinking. Do you remember – he compared the death pit to a black hole, sucking in time as well as light?

'I first realized something was odd a couple of weeks ago. As I'd expected, the very top layer of pigs was less decomposed than the one beneath it, and the one below that was almost completely putrid. But, after that, the process seemed to go into reverse – the lower I went, the less decay had taken place.

'There were three factors at work here. The first was that the farmer, Laura, had an outbreak of Blue Ear disease about nine months ago. Blue Ear causes abortion storms in pigs – in other words, there were dozens and dozens of dead piglets in the space of a few weeks. And then all the infected animals had to be shot as well.

'The upshot was that a large amount of fresh pig carcasses were put into the pit just after these human babies. Then the second factor was that the death pit is surrounded by an anaerobic, or low-oxygen, environment. It's dug into peat – the same peat in which bodies get preserved for thousands of years. Peat contains a polysaccharide called sphagnum which decalcifies skeletons and tans leather: when I went back to the death pit to check, I found sphagnum in the soil of the walls. I'd guess that it gets washed in with the groundwater run-off from the moor.'

'What's the third factor?' Nicky asked.

'The third factor is that the babies were placed in the pit while they were still alive.'

'You don't know that,' Talbot objected.

'Not for certain. But if we assume that the babies were dropped into the pit alive, and died there of starvation, two things become possible. The first is that they might well have dispersed themselves randomly around the whole area – crawling, or in the case of the younger ones, rolling, until their strength ran out. The other is that they were never exposed, as most corpses are, to the open air.'

He picked up one of the bottles of wine, brought it over to the two police officers and pulled up a chair. 'Here, we might as well drink this now.' He poured some of the wine into three plastic cups. 'It's been open for a day, but it should still be OK. It's a bit like a corpse, you see – air speeds up the process of decay. Stick a cork in there, and you slow down the process so much the wine ends up ageing gracefully instead of rotting. Cheers.'

'Cheers,' Nicky muttered. Despite – or perhaps because of – the subject they were discussing, it was delicious.

'So I went to talk to a friend of my father's,' Iain continued. 'A major in the medical corps. His special expertise is excavating war graves. What he told me confirmed my own observations of the death pit. Graves with a very large number of corpses in them sometimes become anaerobic. In other words, the bacteria responsible for producing decay simply eat up all the available oxygen and die. They can't get more oxygen from the air above, because there's a solid seal of flesh – rotting, bacteria-rich flesh, admittedly, but if it's thick enough, a seal nevertheless, like the rind on a cheese. The corpses in outlying positions will be exposed to decomposition agents through the soil – in the case of our death pit, that meant sporadic and inconsistent levels of sphagnum, depending on how near to the rainwater source the corpse was.'

He swallowed the rest of his wine. 'And that's it, really. The babies were dumped there last year, covered with a mass of pigs, and subsequently decayed at different rates and in different ways. Donna was killed elsewhere during late November: her corpse started to decay in the usual way before she was dumped in the death pit, so her decomposition was only slightly delayed. And by then a fox had burrowed its way into the pit, allowing oxygen access to the top layer of pigs and creating the appearance of normal decomposition.'

'It makes sense,' Nicky agreed. 'But what about the rickets? That didn't develop while the babies were starving in the death pit, presumably?'

'No – rickets is a long-term deficiency. The babies would need to have been malnourished, or shut away in the dark, for all of their lives.' He paused. 'You do realize what this means, don't you?'

'What?'

'As I understand it, your hypothesis is that the babies might have been killed as some kind of Satanic sacrifices. But if they were dropped in the death pit alive, and all together, that theory's a non-starter.'

Since taking Terry back to Nineveh would mean going past John Hobbes' croft, Terry asked if they could call in and speak to the gamekeeper on the way.

'All right. I ought to have a word with him about doing some more shooting, anyway. He hasn't been back since the body was found, and I'm getting trouble with the foxes again.'

'Why do you suppose he hasn't been back?' Terry asked curiously as they set off in Laura's tractor.

'Not a guilty conscience, if that's what you're thinking. Iain told me the police gave him a hard time. He's probably just sulking.'

They found the croft at the end of a half-mile farm track, nestling one of the foothills of Ben Dubh.

'Pretty remote,' Terry commented as they climbed down from the tractor and walked towards the tiny white-painted house.

'There are hundreds of these, dotted round the hills. They used to be farms in their own right, a long time ago. Some of the more isolated crofts don't even have water or electricity. They're mostly deserted now. This, believe it or not, is one of the more luxurious ones.'

A few bantams pecked at the rocky ground, and a cow shook its head at them from a small field behind the croft. Terry's attention, however, was caught by a row of red objects that hung from the low gutter beside the front door, twisting in the breeze. 'Are those what I think they are?'

'Foxes' brushes?' Laura laughed. 'It's not exactly *Elle Decoration* up here, Terry.'

The door was open. Laura knocked and called, 'Hello? John?'

'It may not be *Elle Decoration*, but he could certainly do with a few bowls of pot pourri,' Terry muttered, wrinkling her nose.

'It does smell a bit like he forgot to throw the rest of the fox away,' Laura agreed. She knocked again. 'John? It's Laura.'

Terry suddenly saw something through the window. It was dark in there, and she had to cup her hands against the glass before she could see. 'Shit,' she said urgently. 'I think we'd better go in.'

'What is it?'

'Come on.'

Terry led the way into the house, holding her breath – not because she didn't want to make a noise, but because the stench was even worse inside. She pointed at the wall.

A symbol had been daubed roughly in black paint on the uneven surface. It consisted of a circle with a half-circle intersecting from above. As they looked around them, they saw that there were other symbols on the other walls, all painted in the same hasty style.

'Witchcraft symbols?' Laura guessed.

'Sort of . . . I think we'd better look in the other rooms too.'

Laura pushed open a door that led to the back of the house. 'The kitchen's through here,' she began, then: 'Oh, Jesus.'

'What is it?' Terry looked over her shoulder. There was more black on the walls in here, too, but here it had not been painted in the shape of magic symbols. Here it was as if a tin of black paint had been flung, roughly, at the wall. Even if she had not known it was blood, the stink would have told her. And the man lying on the floor with his head blown away would certainly have confirmed it.

# THIRTY

'Tell me again', the superintendent suggested thoughtfully, 'why you were going to see Mr Hobbes. You'd never met him, had you?'

Terry shook her head. 'Laura wanted to talk to him about shooting some foxes,' she said. 'Apparently he'd been avoiding her since the first body was found.'

'And you were with her because—?'

'She was giving me a lift into Babcock, and Hobbes's croft was on the way,' Terry said patiently. 'I stayed the night with her because of the attack on my vehicle—'

'Which you didn't report to the police?'

She shook her head again. 'There didn't seem any point.'

'And you didn't recognize any of your assailants?'

'I'm hardly likely to, am I? I've only been in Babcock a couple of weeks.' She had decided against mentioning Hector Morrison's name. Unsubstantiated and unprovable allegations would hardly improve her credibility as a witness.

'Fair enough. Though you do seem to have got around a bit in the time you've been here,' the superintendent said genially.

It was three hours later, and Terry was being interviewed by the same policeman she had spoken to after the raid on the Wiccans. The clothes Laura had lent her had been taken away by the police. She was now wearing a curious white paper jumpsuit, which offered little protection from the cold. A WPC sat in the room with them, studiously ignoring the proceedings.

'So this alleged beating: did it leave any marks?' He peered at her. 'For example, it looks as if your lip's been cut.'

'Yes. They were quite vicious. I'm covered in bruises.'

'You'll have to be examined by our FME – our medical officer – so that we can confirm that part of your statement.'

'Why?' she asked, perplexed. 'What on earth has being beaten up last night got to do with finding a body this afternoon?'

'In our experience, people who commit murders often have bruises on their own bodies. There's sometimes been a struggle, you see.' He raised one shaggy eyebrow at her. 'Particularly if the murder was the result of self-defence.'

'That's ludicrous!' she cried, appalled. 'Of course I didn't kill him.'

'Och, I'm not saying for a moment that you did. But you can see why we'd want to eliminate the possibility. The medical officer will be here shortly. She'll do a quick examination, and then you'll be in the clear.'

It suddenly occurred to Terry that the examination might include a test to see whether she'd had sex recently. 'Will Laura be examined too?' she asked.

'I think that would be sensible. In the circum-stances.'

Terry flushed angrily. Laura would be horrified if she had to explain the exact nature of her relation-ship with Terry to the police.

Again the superintendent raised a hoary eyebrow, but he said nothing.

'Very well, then,' she muttered. 'Since I don't seem to have any choice.'

'These symbols you noticed on the walls,' he said, 'did you recognize them?'

'Yes,' she said curtly.

'Would you kindly tell me what they mean?'

'They're occult symbols, as I'm sure you realized. Used in Wiccan rituals, amongst other things.'

He waited.

'But if you're asking whether this murder was anything to do with the Wiccans, the answer's no,' she said impatiently. 'So far as I'm aware, there's no ritual which involves blowing a man's brains out.'

'But what do they mean, exactly? As I recall, you're something of an expert.'

She sighed. 'Do you have some paper?'

He tore a sheet out of his notebook and handed it to her.

Carefully she drew on it the four symbols she'd seen on the walls of the croft.

'This one', she said, tapping the first, 'is simply a pictogram representing the Horned God. It's like a little face with horns, do you see?'

'The Horned God? Would that be the same as Satan?'

'I can see where your mind's going, Superintendent. But the idea of a fertility god with horns on his head is much older than Christianity – there are cave paintings from 2,000 BC in France that show a god of hunting with stag's antlers on his head. In fact, when Michelangelo carved a statue of Moses, he gave him horns to denote his divine status.'

'Let's not bring Michelangelo into it, shall we? Just tell me about the symbols.'

She pointed to the next symbol. 'This is a symbol for the Goddess. It represents two moons, one waxing and one waning, to symbolize her feminine power.'

'And this one?'

'That – I think – is the astrological sign for the planet Saturn. And this one, which is made up of two entwined S-shapes, represents the salute – a kiss – and the scourge, or whip. It's sometimes called the Polarity of Mercy and Severity.'

'How about these?' He showed her a second sheet, on which some other symbols had been drawn.

'They were also found in the house,' he explained. 'Presumably you didn't go into those rooms.'

She pointed to a sign like an italic M with a tail. 'This one's Scorpio. It's the sign of the Lord of the

Underworld, so it usually represents death. This one, a sort of arrow shape, represents the union of the sun and the moon and the power it creates – that's a sexual metaphor: it's generally taken to mean the union of male and female. And this one is a hieroglyph of a sickle. It means "the taker of life".'

'Very good, Miss Williams. You'll be pleased to know that when we faxed these to an expert in occult matters at the University of Edinburgh, he came up with almost exactly the same answers.'

'And did he tell you why they were there?'

'He suggested that it was occult code.' Talbot referred to his notebook. Again one eyebrow twitched upwards. ' "The Goddess and the God, joined together, have used their powers to pass judgement on the agent of Saturn, or Misrule, and thus to kill him." '

She snorted. 'Not a very good code, then, if it can be read so easily.'

Talbot's eyes narrowed. 'What do you mean?'

'Oh, come on,' she said impatiently. 'This murder's about as occult as you are. Someone's looked up a few magical symbols in a book, found some that are vaguely relevant, and decided to throw them at you to muddy the waters. So far as I know, none of the Wiccans even owns a gun.'

'No, but John Hobbes did,' Talbot said. 'Several, in fact. One of which was found beside his body.'

'But why should the Wiccans want to kill him?'

Talbot took back the sheet on which she had drawn the symbols and looked at it carefully for a few moments. 'Now there you've got me, Miss Williams. But for that matter, why should anyone else?' He handed the sheet to the WPC. 'Get that off to the lab, would you?'

Terry looked puzzled.

'We'll just check with a handwriting expert that your drawings aren't an exact match for the ones on the walls,' he said mildly. 'Just to be absolutely sure, eh?'

She had her examination from the medical officer, a brisk automaton who had obviously decided many years ago that there was no point in wasting any sympathy on those she examined. Not so much a bedside manner as a graveside manner, Terry thought grimly as the woman prodded and poked her.

The examination over, she was shown back into Talbot's presence.

'Just a couple more questions,' he said genially. 'The FME tells me that you do indeed have substantial bruising to your legs and arms, which is consistent with being kicked repeatedly.'

'I'm very glad to hear it.'

'She also said that some of your bruises are not consistent with being attacked in this way. She described them as looking remarkably like love bites.'

Terry said nothing.

'In addition,' he continued, 'whilst you said that it was you, and not Miss Macpherson, who was attacked last night, Miss Macpherson also has an almost identical pattern of bruising on her legs and lower body, even down to the love bites.' He paused, and raised not one but two craggy eyebrows. 'Would you like to amend your statement in any way, Miss Williams?'

Terry felt a blush travelling up the back of her neck, and hoped fervently that he wouldn't be able to see it. 'She was attacked by a sow, earlier today. Perhaps she got her bruises then.'

'So she said. A very amorous sow, it must have been.'

Terry shrugged.

Talbot leaned forward. 'If I find there's any part of your statement that doesn't check out,' he said dangerously, 'I'll have you in again so fast your feet won't touch the ground. And we won't be having a cosy chat like this one, either. I don't like the way you keep turning up on my investigation. There's something smelly about you, Miss Williams, and it isn't just the faint odour of pigshit. If I come across you again, I may take the chance to find out what it is.'

'You don't scare me,' Terry said evenly.

'I haven't tried to, Miss Williams. Not yet.'

Eventually the police let her go, still muttering threats and looking suspicious. Terry found Laura waiting for her at the front desk.

'They've kept the car, I'm afraid. Something about matching tyre patterns.'

Terry did some quick thinking. 'I'll phone Magnus.'

She rang Babcock Castle. Magnus, to his credit, didn't ask any questions, promising to come and collect them straight away.

'Are you OK?' she asked softly while they waited.

'Me?' Laura laughed hollowly. 'Oh, sure. I've found a dead friend and all but been accused of killing him myself. I've been stripped naked so that a doctor can poke at me. I've had the third degree

357

from a suspicious policeman and now my car's been impounded. And on top of all that, I still haven't changed the straw in two hundred pig huts, which means I'll be working until midnight.'

'I'll help with the straw.'

'Great. All my problems are over.'

They sat in silence until Magnus came. Terry had asked him to bring some clothes, imagining he'd have the sense to choose some of his own baggy pullovers and maybe some jeans. Instead he brought some of Flora's clothes, which didn't improve Laura's mood when they retired to the Ladies to put them on.

'I look like a tart in this,' she grumbled, pulling a tiny miniskirt down as low as it would go.

'At least you got the skirt,' Terry said. She had squeezed herself into a pair of cut-offs so short and tight she suspected that the superintendent, if he saw her wearing them, would probably arrest her for indecent behaviour. She handed Laura the more respectable of the two tops, a fluorescent mohair sweater, and with a sigh pulled on a midriff-exposing T-shirt with the word 'sexy' written on it in Coca-Cola writing.

'Don't say a word,' she warned Magnus when at last the two of them emerged from the loo. 'You're very close to being stripped and forced to wear this lot yourself.'

'Sorry,' he muttered. 'I thought Flora was about your size.'

Next to her Laura sighed and rolled her eyes.

'Magnus, meet Laura Macpherson. Or do you already know each other?'

'I know the name,' Magnus said. 'You're the pig farmer, aren't you?'

They climbed three abreast into the front of the Land Rover. Magnus managed to keep his eyes mostly on the road, though Terry noticed that whenever he changed gear his gaze strayed down to Laura's bare legs, crammed alongside his own.

'You won't be going back to Nineveh, will you?' he asked Terry. 'After all this, you'll want to keep well away from that lot.'

'Why? "That lot" have been very good to me.'

'Well . . . you know. The finger of suspicion and all that.'

'You'll be telling me next that where there's smoke there's fire.'

'Magnus might have a point,' Laura said. 'The police will really have it in for the Wiccans now. You won't be much help to anyone if you get locked up.'

'You'd be very welcome to come back to Babcock,' he said mildly.

Terry waited for Laura to offer her a bed at the cottage. But the other girl had developed a sudden interest in the fabric of Flora's mohair sweater.

Terry sighed. 'OK. But we'll have to call in at Nineveh and tell them what's been going on.'

She found the Wiccans sitting round the big table in the kitchen, looking even glummer than the last time she had been there. Even her appearance in Flora's clothes failed to raise a smile.

'What's up?' she asked, looking at the long faces.

It was Brigid who answered.

'Jamie and Gregor have been charged and remanded in custody. And now Gerard and Alan have been taken in for questioning.'

'That's odd. We were with the police today and they didn't—'

'Not by the police,' Brigid interrupted. 'By Social Services.'

'Why?'

'We don't know. It seems that, unlike the police, they're not obliged to tell you what they're investigating. We can only assume that it has something to do with Holly and Myrvyn.'

'Judith asked if she could see them yesterday, and she was told it was out of the question,' Anna added. 'And Myrvyn – well, he's at the age where he tends to say what he thinks people want to hear.'

Terry glanced at Judith. She was deathly pale, and looked as if she hadn't slept or eaten for days. She must be going through hell, Terry thought. 'I've got some news as well. A man called John Hobbes has been murdered.'

None of the Wiccans looked particularly shocked by this information. 'There were some occult symbols daubed on the walls of his croft. So the police are going to think it's another Wiccan-related killing.'

'Why? Why should any of us want to murder this – what was his name?' Again it was Anna who had spoken.

'Hobbes. He was the gamekeeper who found the body. Donna's body, I mean. Did none of you know him?'

'I knew him,' Stephan said. 'He was a very quiet man. I don't think he approved of us, but he was always perfectly pleasant. Gregor saw more of him than I did.'

'What were the symbols?' Brigid asked.

Briefly Terry repeated what the superintendent had told her.

'So they think that this man was killed in revenge for finding the body?' Brigid said sceptically. 'It doesn't seem very likely.'

'Besides, the Saturn symbol can mean many other things besides Chaos or Misrule,' Isobel interjected. 'Saturn is also the Lord of Time, for example, as well as the God of sowing and sacrifices.'

Terry shrugged aside these textural niceties. 'My guess is, whoever killed him wanted to make it look as if it was done by one of you for two reasons. Firstly, to divert attention away from himself. And, secondly, to distract the police from the real motive.'

'Which was?'

'If I knew that, I wouldn't be here.'

'So what do we do now?' Brigid asked.

'There's not a lot you can do. You just have to wait and hope that the real killer makes a mistake. In the meantime, you should try to ensure that people don't demonize you. Make sure you're seen out and about – you know, business as usual. Although for safety's sake I'd suggest you do it in groups of at least three.'

# PART THREE

# THIRTY-ONE

"'We give thee hearty thanks, O Lord, for that it hath pleased thee to deliver our brother from the miseries of this sinful world,'" Gavin Fyfe said. Here and there amongst the congregation people nodded grimly, as if acknowledging the truth of the words. Even the minister himself looked suitably depressed, though whether that was because the occasion demanded it or because he was simply frustrated by his inability to inject even a hint of an upbeat message into the proceedings, Terry couldn't tell.

She sat with Laura, Brigid, Zoe, Isobel and Anna in an isolated group on one side of the church. In the week since the discovery of Hobbes's body all the male Wiccans had been taken away, two and three at a time, for questioning. Some of them had even been offered immunity if they helped provide evidence against the others, and it had been hinted to Jamie and Gregor that their charges for possession and assault respectively might be made to disappear if they could help the police with the more important matter of the murders.

' " And though after my skin worms destroy my

body, yet in my flesh shall I see God,"' the minister was saying. Terry flinched. There was a gruesome relish to the old ceremony that seemed strangely out of place in this century of grief counselling and bereavement therapy. But perhaps, she reflected, the Church fathers, with their more brutal attitude, had been nearer the mark after all.

Gavin Fyfe was making his address now, though his obvious lack of knowledge of, and faint disapproval of, his subject was all too evident. The gamekeeper's love of blasting anything with fur or feathers had become 'his deep affinity for our beautiful countryside'; his time in the army had become 'serving his country with devotion'. That he was a loner and a misfit was clear from 'he found in Scotland's mountains the peace that had for so long eluded him'.

The violence of his end, too, was couched in euphemism. 'The inexplicable tragedy of his death, the circumstances of which may never be wholly clear'. That was too much even for this God-fearing congregation. 'Clear enough to them that did it,' a low voice called from the back, thick with anger. One or two others muttered their assent. Gavin Fyfe flushed and ploughed on. Most of those in front of him, though, had twisted round to glare at the Wiccans. Terry buried her nose in her prayer book. 'On the few occasions I spoke to him I was impressed by his straightforward and honest nature'. In other words, she guessed, Hobbes had told the minister to get lost when asked if he was going to come to church.

The minister was scraping the barrel now. 'Nor should we forget his practical help with our local charities, and his diligent sense of civic responsibility . . .' She picked up her prayer book again and started flicking through it. 'A man may not marry his mother,' she read from the 'Table of Affinity and Kindred'; fair enough, but what was the genetic point behind 'A woman may not marry her husband's father'?

As the coffin was carried outside, the congregation got to their feet and shuffled after it. Terry joined them, only to realize that now, in the relative anonymity of the throng, she was being jostled. A sharp, pointed toecap jabbed slyly into the back of her calf. Then a bulky figure in front of her, without looking round, stepped backwards onto her toes, twisting his heel viciously into the bone. She cried out. Figures closed in on her, barging her with their elbows and shoulders. It was all the more frightening because it was happening in total silence. She glanced around, and saw that the other Wiccans were getting the same treatment. Brigid was clutching Zoe for support, while she saw Isobel swivel round and glare at someone who had pushed her from behind, only to buckle at the knees as she was tripped. Terry struggled to keep her own balance, staggering as something hard and thin – an umbrella or a walking stick – was pushed between her legs.

She was being pressed against the table with all the prayer books on it, while the point of the umbrella jabbed her over and over from behind. You could buy a postcard of the church; though the cards, which were black-and-white and rather dog-eared, looked as if there hadn't been a huge run on stocks. 'Please put twenty pence in the box,' she read. The contrast between the honesty box and what was happening to her now was so bizarre it might almost have been funny. 'All profits to the

Fabric Fund.' There were an array of other collecting boxes on the table: the Red Cross, UNICEF, The Romanian Orphanage Trust. Why a Fabric Fund? she found herself wondering. Did they really want to cover the inside of the church with swags of Osborne & Little? The pressure on her back eased a little. Taking her opportunity, she slid the table sideways, creating a space to fall into. Ahead she could see the doorway, and flailed for it, cutting through the throng of people like a swimmer, ignoring the blows that swung surreptitiously out of nowhere into her ribs and thighs.

Then she was outside, and suddenly there was no pressure any more, just a group of people standing around an open grave with such dignified solemnity that she could almost persuade herself she had imagined it. It was raining. The minister lifted his face to the drizzle and proclaimed: ' "Man that is born of a woman hath but a short time to live, and is full of miseries." ' Bloody typical, she thought: they even managed to imply that death was all women's fault.

Terry lifted her arms obediently and allowed herself to be patted down. The prison officer nodded, and she stepped forward.

She was in a small, bare room. At first glance you might have taken it for a cafeteria or a primary-school classroom: tiny formica tables with simple chairs on either side, a few posters on the walls, a soft-drinks machine. It was very hot. Terry sat and waited with the other women and one or two whingeing children. Eventually a door at the far end of the room opened and the prisoners, accompanied by a warder, filed in. The warder locked the door and stood beside it, ostentatiously bored.

'How are you?' she asked.

Jamie nodded. 'I'm OK. It's not so bad. If you're used to coping with Gerard babbling on about the sun and the moon and the etheric energy of the seasons, listening to one's cell mates talking about football and cars for hours on end comes easily.'

'Have you seen the others?'

'A little. They only let us out of our cells for a couple of hours a day. I saw Gregor. He's fine. The other prisoners are terrified of him, of course. Gerard they just think is barking mad.'

'Jamie, I need to ask you some questions.'

'Ah. I thought this might be coming. I heard about your fight with Isobel.'

She shook her head. 'It's not about Isobel. It's about Donna.'

'What do you want to know?'

'She had at least three different partners while she was at Babcock. Gerard, you, and someone outside. Can you tell me what order those went in?'

'So far as I'm aware, I was the first. Then, when she realized Gerard was the boss man, she set her sights on him.'

'And the last?'

He shrugged. 'Someone outside, as you say.'

'Married or unmarried?'

'I can tell you one thing. He was someone quite rich.'

'What makes you say that?'

'I met her once on her way back from Babcock. She'd obviously been seeing someone – she was all dolled up in a little business suit. I made some comment about social climbing and she just laughed and said, "Not climbing, darling. Mountaineering."'

'Why did she leave?'

He shrugged again. 'She was frustrated, too, I think. She was always coming up with mad money-making schemes the others wouldn't listen to. She'd done such a good job organizing the honey business you'd have thought Gerard and Brigid would at least have given her a fair hearing. But they're very anti-materialistic. Anything involving tourists or selling themselves was never going to get past them. So she decided to go travelling.'

Terry lowered her voice. 'Did she ever deal in drugs?'

He shook his head. 'Not that I'm aware of. We didn't have that much, to be honest – there's a little patch of dope plants halfway up the hill, which I assume someone will have had the good sense to destroy by now, but it was only enough for ourselves. Donna liked a smoke, but if she'd been taking it to sell we'd have noticed, wouldn't we?'

She found Magnus in the kitchen at Babcock. The room was filled with the smell of cooking meat, and a huge stockpot bubbled on the Rayburn.

'Magnus,' she said, pulling up a chair, 'it's time you and I had a chat about Donna Fairhead.'

He looked at her neutrally. 'What about her?'

'Why didn't you tell me that you knew her?'

'What do you mean?'

'Come on,' she scoffed. 'It isn't rocket science. She was seeing someone rich in Babcock. There are only two people who possibly fit that description you or David Nicolaides. And Nico – well, let's just say I've established that Nico isn't susceptible.'

He nodded slowly.

'And then there's the museum. It's a brilliant idea, which is how I know it wasn't yours.' He started to protest but she held up her hand. 'So why did it suddenly occur to you last year, and not before? You'd had the Catherine McCulloch papers all your life. What made you suddenly spot their commercial potential?

'Donna Fairhead saw it from the first,' she went on. 'That's why she got those other letters from Mcteer's sister. And then there was the way you described the museum to me – remember? You said that heritage was Scotland's USP. That's marketing jargon, Magnus – second nature to an ex-advertising executive, but hardly obvious language to be tripping off the tongue of the laird of Babcock.'

'OK,' he said defiantly. 'So it's true. It was when I showed all the Wiccans round the house. She got me on my own and said that she thought the Wiccans had some stolen McCulloch papers, and that if I liked she'd try to get them back. I didn't believe her, in fact, but she was a pretty girl, and I wanted to see her again.' He sighed. 'There'd been no-one since Clare left. I hadn't had sex in seven years, for Christ's sake.'

'But you did with Donna.'

'Well, why not?' He shrugged. 'I tried not to let the children know. After all, Donna wasn't much older than they were. It would have been awkward. So we used to go to the doocot. I think Alex may have suspected something, though. He's been a bit, well, a bit *intense* ever since.'

'And the museum?'

'You're quite right – it was her idea. I don't know why it hadn't occurred to me before, to be honest.'

'And not just the idea, was it? She got involved in drawing up the business plans, the cash flow. She loved all that, didn't she? Did she come to the bank meetings with you in a little black suit?'

'Yes.' He looked surprised. 'Yes, she did actually. She really looked the part.'

'So what went wrong?'

He put his hands on the table and stared at them. 'I hadn't realized at first . . . She had other ideas as well.'

'Let me guess. She wanted to be the laird's wife, not just his mistress.'

He nodded. 'When she told me what she was after – I just couldn't believe it. It had never even crossed my mind. She said we were a partnership. The museum, and then marriage. We were in the doocot – it was raining. We'd been making love. She loved sex, I thought that was the point of it for her. But she wanted more. I just said it was impossible – I mean, even if there hadn't been the children to think of, she was, was . . .' He struggled to find the words. 'She had a tattoo, for Christ's sake.'

'There's some you bed and some you wed,' Terry said dryly. 'Then what?'

'We rowed. She had a vicious tongue, when she wanted to use it. Things were said.'

'I can imagine. And then – I don't know – there was some kind of fight, wasn't there? Something happened – well, I've been on the receiving end of your temper myself. How did she die, Magnus? Did she fall, or did you hit her?'

# THIRTY-TWO

'Christ, no!' He looked at her in horror. 'We split up, sure, but I never laid a finger on Donna.' He blinked. 'You surely don't think I'm capable of murdering a woman?'

'As opposed to a stag or a salmon?' Terry sighed. 'I don't know. The trouble with this place is that everyone seems to spend half their time engaged in some sort of nastiness. I don't know who is and who isn't capable of murder any more.'

'It wasn't me, Terry. I swear. We rowed, and I never saw her again. I heard she'd left, and then I heard she'd been killed. That was the extent of my involvement.'

A thought occurred to her. 'So from what you've just told me, you knew the Wiccans had some of your family papers right from the start – even before you asked me to come up here. That was why you wanted a researcher in the first place, wasn't it? It wasn't just the museum. You hoped I'd get your property back for you.'

He shrugged. 'It crossed my mind.'

'More than crossed it – you did your best to make it happen. You hid Mcteer's book until I'd finished transcribing all the letters you had, and then you dangled Mcteer and the Wiccans in front of me like one of Alex's shiny little trout flies. And I took the bait, didn't I?'

'If I didn't tell you everything right at the start,' he protested, 'it was only because I didn't want to over-complicate things before you'd had a chance to settle in. You were having panic attacks, for Christ's sake.'

So she was. It seemed like another age, or something that had happened to another person. ' "Frailty, thy name is woman"?' she murmured. 'Come on, Magnus. You just thought you'd be more likely to get your own way by deviousness.' She thought for a moment. 'So where are they, then?'

'What?'

'The papers Donna retrieved from the Wiccans.'

'Oh, those. Nicolaides has got them. Donna eventually discovered that he'd bought them off the Wiccans when they needed money.' He chuckled. 'Now that we're able to prove they're stolen property, of course, we should be able to get them back.'

She shook her head. 'Not those papers. I've seen those. I meant the letters Donna got from Mcteer's sister.'

'Must have been after we'd split up. She never mentioned any letters to me.'

'That's odd, Donna wasn't the sort of person to let a row stand between her and a deal.'

'Perhaps she got a better offer.'

'Yes, but who from?' She sighed. She suddenly realized she was starving, not having eaten since the Indian restaurant, and the smells from the stockpot were making her mouth water. She lifted the lid and immediately took a step back, nauseated.

'Sorry about that,' Magnus said apologetically. 'Alex finally shot the deer – the same one that attacked you, actually. We always boil the head up to get the meat off before we mount it.'

In the pot, the deer's severed head stared back at her – or would have stared, if one eyeball had not become semi-detached, bouncing and jerking on the end of its nerve like a yo-yo in the boiling currents. Quickly she covered it up again.

'I'll be in touch,' she said.

'So the upshot is, I'm stymied,' she concluded. 'Everything's connected to the letters, somehow, but why should a couple of seventeenth-century letters cause a girl to get killed three hundred years later?'

'Maybe you shouldn't ignore the simple explanation,' Laura said. 'Money. The manuscripts were worth something, after all.'

Terry made a face. 'Not the amount that went through her bank account. And, besides, who'd pay her for them? The only collector round here with that sort of money is Nico, and he wouldn't fork out for an incomplete collection. Magnus couldn't afford it – and if he'd got the letters back, he could have put them with the others, and I would never have been any the wiser.'

They were in Laura's cottage, relaxing. The pigs were shut up for the night, a bottle of wine was open and a log fire smouldered in the grate.

'She seems to have made herself pretty unpopular amongst the Wiccans. Gerard, for example. He might not have liked being thrown over for Magnus. And what if Donna had told him she thought the Wiccans should dress up in their robes and be part of Magnus's theme park? He'd have been furious.'

'I think something like that did happen, actually,' Terry said slowly. 'From what Jamie told me, there was certainly some kind of row over an idea that Gerard and Brigid dismissed as being too commercial. But why kill her? If Gerard and Brigid were against it, the idea would have been a non-starter.'

There was a knock at the door. It swung open, and a tall young man with a ponytail and round glasses stepped in, laden with carrier bags.

'I bring gifts,' he said cheerfully. 'Several bottles of rather fine wine – I'll tell you why in a moment, it's a long story – and since I had the wine and I knew you wouldn't have anything to go with it, I went to Sainsbury's and bought a leg of lamb as well. And mint sauce, rosemary, courgettes, potatoes.' He looked at Terry. 'Hello.'

'Terry, meet Iain,' Laura said.

'Iain.' Terry got to her feet, her hand outstretched. 'Am I glad to meet you.'

Russell Kane flicked on the light beside his bed. The clock told him it was after midnight.

'Marky? Is that you?' he called. Downstairs, in the shop, he heard the sound of someone moving about.

'Pissed again,' Russell muttered under his breath. 'Boys will be boys.' He stood before the mirror and put on his hairpiece and a bathrobe before opening the door to the stairs and stepping down into the darkness. The light switch was at the other end, by the bookshop door. Really, he couldn't understand why Mark hadn't turned it on. Perhaps the silly boy thought he'd be able to creep in without waking

Russell up. 'Thinks he can stumble in here, drunk as a skunk, and have his Saturday night quickie,' Russell said out loud. 'Marky?'

Then something touched him on the shoulder, something that made a spark like a cigarette lighter. But the spark was accompanied by pain, such breathless pain as Russell had never known. It flashed down his left side and grabbed at his heart. As he fell to the floor, his fat body jerking and twitching, Russell saw a halo of sparks.

Had the sparks been a little bit brighter or lasted a little longer, he might also have seen the sign of the Horned God, daubed on the wall in front of him.

'So what are the odds of a normal Scottish child getting rickets?' Terry asked. It was late now, the lamb and most of the wine having been consumed. Over supper Iain had told them everything he'd found out in the last few days, and was now good-humouredly subjecting himself to an intensive grilling from Terry.

'As I understand it, pretty minimal.' He shrugged. 'It's a total mystery.'

'And measles?'

'Virtually nil. Once a child's birth has been registered, you'd have midwives, health visitors, Social Services, doctors, all going on at you to have the vaccine.'

'And there are no babies missing?'

'There's the odd one or two stolen from hospitals and prams left outside shops every year. It causes a huge furore, as you can imagine. It's almost unthinkable that it's all the work of one gang. And for what? Why steal a baby if all you're going to do with it is shut it up in a darkened room, starve it and then dump it on a pig farm?'

'Let's try to be logical about this,' Terry said. 'Let's assume, for the sake of a neat narrative, that Hobbes's death is linked to the babies, and the babies are linked to Donna. We've disregarded the obvious link, which is Nineveh. What's next?'

'Well, if you want to be logical, it's wherever she was before Nineveh,' Laura said sleepily. It was after midnight, she had to be up early to feed the pigs, and unlike the other two she wasn't used to staying up late into the night talking about abstract ideas.

Terry stared at her, open-mouthed. 'Laura, you're a genius.'

'Why?' Laura said, puzzled. 'Where was she before she joined the Wiccans?'

'That's just it,' Terry said. 'We don't know. At no point in all of this has anyone said where Donna came from. I mean, we know what she's done – university, a bit of drama, advertising, charity work – but we don't know where.'

'It's certainly something to consider,' Iain said thoughtfully.

Terry grabbed her keys. 'Come on. Who's coming to Nineveh? Someone there'll know.'

'Hang on,' Laura said, 'I'm not sure you need to go to Nineveh.'

'Why not?'

'Did you just say she worked for a charity?' Terry nodded. 'So did John Hobbes. A couple of years ago the village raised some money to refurbish an orphanage in Romania. He went out there to work on it.'

'Of course,' Terry breathed. 'It was mentioned in

the address at his funeral. I saw the collecting box in the church myself, come to that. What's the betting she met him out there?' She turned to Iain. 'Could those babies have been Romanian?'

He nodded. 'Absolutely. They were all dark-skinned and dark-haired. And it would be completely consistent with the malnutrition and the measles.'

Terry sat at Donna's computer. There was one last thing she had to try.

Everyone who had known Donna had said what a tidy, organized mind she had. And she'd taken to computing like a duck to water. There had to be a good chance that what she wanted was somewhere on here.

She opened up the file manager and scrolled through the folders until she found the word processing program file. Inside were the document folders. She opened one called *Money*. It contained several spreadsheets, labelled in turn *Bees – cash flow*, *Bees – profit and loss*, *Bees – budget versus actual*. She turned to one marked *Maintenance*. Inside was a comprehensive list of repairs done to the house, together with a note of the date, the cost and the contractor.

*Personal*. Her pulse quickened as she opened it. Aha. As she'd hoped: one of the documents was entitled *CV*. So Donna had tried, at least, to get some conventional jobs while she'd been at Nineveh. She scanned it quickly.

1998–9 Management Assistant, Nineveh Farm, Scotland.
1996–8 Aid Worker, Orphanage No. 4,

Bucharest, Romania.
1994–6 Account Manager, Leagas Shafron Davis Chick, Advertising, London.

She closed the file, nodding. *Romania*. They had guessed anyway, but now they had an address.

Another file caught her eye. It was labelled *Correspondence*. An odd word, when you thought about it. Most people would just have written *Letters*, which was shorter and less old-fashioned.

Unless you were referring to old-fashioned letters.

She opened the file. There, on the screen, was a scanned-in facsimile of a manuscript. The familiar crabbed writing of Catherine McCulloch.

# THIRTY-THREE

My dearest Anne,

This is a strange letter to have to write. I shall say it directly: I am with child. I believe I told you that, in addition to so many other torments, I was roughly used by Mr Mann, and also his assistants. I did not wish to tell you how – some remnant of that modesty I once had, but which has now been stripped from me, prevented me from writing any more. That his attentions might have led to this, I never contemplated, being certain I should be dead from the strappado or the flames long before. The absence of my womanly signs I attributed to the pains my body has endured, and the food is so slight here, my belly did not show for many months.

Oddly, I am in good hands. For many of those I am incarcerated with are village midwives, whose skill with herbs and women's ailments led to their being accused of taking the devil's pay. When my condition became known they discussed the matter amongst themselves, and approached me with an idea that they could rid me of the child. This would not have been without its dangers, for by then I was about four months gone; but, as they said, if I die now I shall at least be spared a burning, whilst the child shall be killed with me in any case. For a convicted witch in my condition will either be burnt with the baby inside her or, if the torturers do not wish it known what they have done, they wait until the child is delivered, and then cut its throat at birth, before delivering the mother to the stake. I listened to the women's offer carefully, and thanked them for it, knowing full well how hard it would be for them to get the necessary herbs smuggled in to this jail: but told them that it could not be, since I considered the child's life not mine to give or take away. This decision being made, we put our minds to how best we might save the infant, and whether we could smuggle it out from the confines of these walls. I should have to conceal my condition from the jailers – but that is possible, for the rags I am now clothed in hang loosely on me, and are made of many layers of what were once separate garments. The exodus should be done immediately, when the infant is newborn, and we will need herbs to make it quiet, but these things may be contrived, if we only have somewhere for the child to go. Oh, Anne, I do not know if I can ask this of you – you who have risked so much for me already – but if your husband be willing, would you take my child? Do not write your answer down, but tell the girl who brings you this. She is the daughter of one of the jailers, delivered by one of the women here, fourteen years previously: and since the cord was wrapped around her neck the woman saved the girl's life. If you are willing, it will be her who brings the child to you.

Catherine

My dearest Anne,

I have received your answer. Oh, Anne, how can I ever repay your love and kindness? You are truly the most devoted friend a woman could have.

One word of warning: trust no-one, not even my cousin Hamish. I do not believe his intentions are so good as he would have us all believe.

I shall write when it is time – it could be any day now – be ready.

Catherine

My dearest,

I pray that you get this safely, and also the precious package which accompanies it. He is called Ross, which was my grandfather's name. As I write this he is sleeping on my belly. I have given him a little milk, for the women say new milk is the best, and will make him strong, even though he will only have it for a few hours. Is he not beautiful? Here in this hell of broken and wounded bodies, I had forgotten how perfect the body of a child can be, and how well formed in God's image, so that when I gaze upon it I feel the peace I shall encounter when I gaze upon the face of God himself. Only when he opens his eyes do I feel frightened, for he gazes at me with the eyes of Mr Mann.

The birth itself was terrible – how like Mr Mann that he should still torment me even now. I had not to cry out, less I attract the attentions of the jailers, so the midwives gave me a cloth to bite on. Thus, after many hours, was the child delivered in silence. And the remarkable thing is that when he took his first breath, he made no sound, but merely sighed, as by God's grace he knew to keep his presence a secret.

I have to stop now. The women want to take him presently, while he is still asleep. The girl who will smuggle him out next to her skin is here. Anne, there are so many things I wish to ask of you – and yet I know that you will do them all for him in any case, without my needing to ask. This child should be the heir to Babcock, and walk Ben Dubh as I have walked, yet I shall be content if he never knows his true inheritance, but believes himself the much-loved darling of my own sweet, darling, much-loved Anne.

I shall not write to you again. I should be too fearful, less the interception of our letters lead to the child's discovery. So this is farewell. *Cantate Domino canticum novum, quia mirabilia fecit.* Sing to the Lord a new song: for He has done wonderful things.

Catherine McCulloch, Mistress of Babcock,
14 September, 1698

# THIRTY-FOUR

Two weeks later a dark-haired woman walked up to the door of Orphanage No. 4 in Bucharest and rang the bell.

While she waited for it to be opened she took a step back and studied the building in front of her. Unmistakably an institution, it was built out of brown bricks with ornate wire grilles over the windows. The windows themselves, she noticed, were too high for those outside to see in – or for those inside to see out. From one of them, slightly ajar, came the sound of children playing. Rather to her surprise, she made out the words of an English nursery rhyme. *Hickory dickory dock, the mouse ran up the clock.*

The door opened. A short, neat woman with dark hair and a white coat stood in front of her. '*Da?*' she said interrogatively.

Terry held out her hand. 'Hello. Do you speak English? I'm Mrs Williams. Dr Tarkady is expecting me.'

'I'm Dr Tarkady. Come in.' Her English was good, though strongly accented. Terry followed her down an antiseptic-smelling corridor. Although the dark wooden floor obviously dated from the same period as the building's facade, the walls were painted in bright oranges and greens and were further decorated with cheerful murals of farmyard animals.

Dr Tarkady led the way to a small, crammed office just off the main corridor and motioned for Terry to have a seat. 'So,' she said, settling herself behind a desk. 'Your husband, he is not with you?'

'He's been held up at a meeting,' Terry said. 'Unfortunately his negotiations took longer than he expected, so I decided to come on my own. It's very kind of you to see me at such short notice.'

The doctor lit a cigarette. 'A donation is always welcome, however big or small. Though I think in your case you said . . .'

'That we hope to donate enough to make a real difference,' Terry said. Ignoring a momentary pang of guilt at the deception she was perpetrating, she went on: 'My husband and I have made quite a lot of money out of doing business with your country, and we feel it's time to put something back.'

'Your countrymen have always been very generous,' the doctor murmured. She glanced at her watch. 'Would you like to look round? I can show you where we need most help.'

'That would be ideal,' Terry said, getting to her feet.

They set off down the wooden-floored corridor again. 'We have four hundred children here, between the ages of nought and seven,' the doctor was saying briskly. 'That makes us, though not the largest orphanage in Bucharest, certainly one of the bigger ones.'

'How many orphanages are there?'

'In Bucharest? Twelve. Here, this is the main nursery.' She stopped, and opened the door to a large room like a school assembly hall. It had been divided up with colourful foam cushions, each containing a group of a dozen or so children and a couple of adults.

'You seem to have plenty of toys,' Terry commented, looking at the profusion of play equipment spread across the room.

'Yes. By and large, equipment is less of a problem than people. Even here in Romania, where salaries are low, staff are our largest cost. Now we are bringing in qualified nursery nurses from England and France. As well as working with the children themselves, they also train our Romanian assistants.' She glanced sideways at Terry. 'Some of our donors would rather give us a new playroom, with a plaque on the wall saying who it came from, than pay for an adult to work in it. Which is a shame, yes?'

A little girl of about four came running up to Terry and threw her arms round her legs, babbling in Romanian. 'She wants to be picked up,' Dr Tarkady explained.

'Is that all right?'

'Of course.' For the first time the doctor smiled. 'We may as well make you work while you're with us.'

Terry hoisted the little girl up in her arms. Immediately she began to stroke Terry's face, still jabbering away to herself. 'What's her name?'

Dr Tarkady directed a question to the little girl in Romanian. 'Florentina. She's seven years old.'

'Really? She's so tiny.'

The doctor nodded. 'She would probably have

387

had malnutrition – what used to be called "medical problems". She's catching up now.'

'I don't understand. Surely the fall of communism was years ago?'

'Yes, but it took many years to sort out all the problems we had here. In the first years, we had a lot of people coming out with truckloads of toys and nappies, when what was really required was food and medicine. The international aid effort was most welcome, of course, but it was piecemeal and unco-ordinated. And the economic problems meant that more babies were coming in to the orphanages than ever.'

'Do you remember a group of aid workers from a place called Babcock in Scotland?'

The doctor shook her head. 'I don't think so. But I could ask Daniella. She's one of the few helpers we've still got from that time.' She called to a plump old lady, and spoke to her for a few seconds. '*Da*. She says she remembers a group from Scotland. They helped us put in a kitchen. Before that the children had no hot food.'

The little girl was getting heavy. Terry put her down, and she immediately began to cry. 'I'm sorry,' Terry said in English, 'you're just too heavy. Too heavy, OK?' She knelt down and tried to mime her exhaustion, and the little girl laughed delightedly. When Terry stood up again, Florentina slipped her hand into hers.

'She's a typical example,' Dr Tarkady said, nodding at the girl. 'Laughing, crying, clinging to adult company – these are all signs that she's recovering well. Before the October Revolution, children like this would have simply lain on their beds all day. Without stimulation, they never learn

388

to display their emotions. The first positive sign is that they start to cry. Then they begin to smile, to crawl, to walk, to shout – it's like watching a baby grow up in fast forward. When you have to tell them off for scribbling on the walls, you know the battle's nearly over.'

'Where do you keep the very young babies?' Terry asked.

Dr Tarkady shot her an unfathomable look. 'Upstairs. We'll go there next.'

As they continued on their tour, Florentina's hand still stickily attached to hers, Terry began to realize just how vast a place the orphanage was – a primary school, boarding house, play group and residential home all in one. They passed a kitchen filled with chrome equipment: a hand-painted sign announced that it had been donated by the people of Andover. Then Dr Tarkady led her into a cot-lined room about twenty-feet square, in which three women were feeding a dozen or so babies. One was having its nappy changed on a plastic changing mat. The woman changing it was singing to it in English.

'These used to be dormitories,' the doctor explained. 'We've subdivided them into smaller rooms now, to make working with the babies easier. We try to keep a ratio of one adult to five children, but that's an expensive commitment.'

'So what you'd really like money for is more staff.'

'Exactly. We have – I won't say all the facilities we need, but certainly a good proportion of them. What we need now is a long-term commitment to providing the people to work in them. An endowment which would pay for a nurse's salary in perpetuity, for example.'

'Can we talk in your office?' Terry suggested.

'Of course.' They handed Florentina over to a member of staff. The little girl immediately burst into tears, which just as soon vanished when the helper whispered in her ear. She waved enthusiastically as Terry walked away.

Once they were in the director's office Terry cleared her throat. 'I believe I may have misled you a little, Dr Tarkady.'

'*Da?*' The other woman's eyes regarded her shrewdly as she reached for a packet of Romanian cigarettes.

'I do wish to make a donation, as I said. But I would also like to offer rather more than money.'

'In what way?'

Terry paused. 'My husband and I have not been fortunate enough to have children.'

'You have a medical problem?'

'Yes.' Damn, Terry thought; I'd better not get caught out on this. 'A difficulty with my fallopian tubes,' she said vaguely. 'We have tried to adopt in Britain, but so far we have been unsuccessful.'

The doctor's expression was unreadable. 'Go on.'

'We were wondering if it might be possible, as well as making a generous contribution to your work here, to offer a home to one of the babies. As I said, we are very wealthy people. We would love the child as if it were our own. And it would be a far, far better life than one spent in an institution.'

'I see.' The doctor blew out a stream of foul-smelling smoke.

'Is such a thing possible?' Terry enquired.

There was a pause. 'And how much were you thinking of paying for this baby?'

Terry shrugged. 'I don't know. About ten thousand pounds?'

'You realize such a transaction would be illegal, of course? In both this country and yours? If you were stopped at the border, you might face a prison sentence.'

'We're prepared to take the risks.'

The doctor puffed on her cigarette for a few moments, then stubbed it out in a saucer.

'Let me explain something,' she said quietly. 'For nearly fifteen years, until the revolution in 1989, this country was entirely ruled by one man, Nicolae Ceauşescu. He was kept in power by the combined support of the Russians and the European Economic Community, both of whom it suited to have a neutral buffer zone between East and West. Your own country, I believe, conferred on him the Order of the Garter.'

Her eyes had drifted away from Terry's as she spoke, fixed on a point somewhere over her shoulder. 'Ceauşescu had big ambitions for Romania,' she continued. 'He wanted to turn it into an industrial power. But we were too poor – a nation of peasant farmers. So he decided to embark on a huge social experiment; perhaps the biggest social experiment that has ever been tried.

'First, he confiscated all the smallholdings and turned the land over to huge state-run farms. Then he forced the dispossessed farmers – about half the population of the country – into state-run apartment blocks. Effectively, these were labour camps for the new factories he built. This process was known as "systemization".

'He still needed more cheap labour, though. So he passed a law. He required all women between the ages of twenty and forty-five to have at least five children.' She paused to let the implications sink in. 'Contraception, of course, was banned. Abstinence from sexual activity was banned. Anyone who didn't co-operate was sent to prison.'

'I see—'

The doctor interrupted her. 'Do you? I'm not sure you do, Mrs Williams. Most people were simply too poor to feed five children – the average wage in Romania at the time was less than six hundred pounds a year. But if you couldn't feed them yourself, the state was happy to do it for you. In institutions like this one.' She reached for another cigarette. 'We had a saying. "Three for us, two for the state." In other words, people would keep their first three children, and try to ensure that they had enough to eat. But the price they paid for that was to give up the next two babies to places like Orphanage Number Four.' She glared at Terry. 'This was not the sort of place you see today. The babies were literally left to rot – there were no nappies, and the mattresses soaked up their urine and faeces until, in the worst cases, their skin started to fall off their bones. They had no stimulation, no potty training, no adult contact except for being dragged under a cold shower once a week. They couldn't even play with each other, because no-one had ever taught them how to play. And then, at the age of three, they would be given a five-minute assessment by a government doctor. Those that had by some miracle learnt how to walk and talk were kept in the system. Those that hadn't – the so-called "irrecuperables" – were sent to special institutions. They were called mental hospitals, but in reality they were just human dustbins where the unwanted babies were left to die. This is why, after the revolution, Ceaușescu was convicted of genocide and shot.'

She stopped. Terry, sensing there was more, said nothing.

'In the West,' she said at last, 'you have chosen to call these places orphanages. We are grateful for the West's help, of course. But you must understand the lie you are perpetuating. The children here were never orphans. Their parents are alive, and whenever possible they come and take them away again, back to their own homes where they can be properly looked after. Taking these children back to Britain isn't the answer. What we want is for their real parents to be able to look after them again.'

'I don't know what to say,' Terry admitted. 'I thought—'

'You thought we were a kind of baby department store, where childless couples can shop for the perfect child.'

Terry flushed. 'Not exactly—'

'Do you see why that is so abhorrent to us?' the doctor interrupted. 'In your way – forgive me, Mrs Williams, but I must say this – you are just the same as Ceaușescu. He saw babies as an economic commodity, to be battery-farmed as he wished. In the capitalist countries, you think the same way. You just offer a higher price.'

Terry looked at the floor. 'I'm sorry. I should go.'

'I see about a dozen people like you every year. I send them all away.'

'Where do they go to?'

The doctor shrugged. 'The gypsies? The Mafia? It's none of my business.'

Terry got up. 'I'll see myself out.'

She walked back down the corridor towards the

393

big door, cursing herself. What on earth had she hoped to find here? She felt soiled by the lies she had told.

The little girl who had accompanied her on her tour was skipping up and down the corridor with two friends. ''Bye Florentina,' she called. The girl waved, then turned to her friends and giggled. Terry opened the door and turned round to wave again. Dr Tarkady was standing next to the girl, one hand protectively on her shoulder. Terry closed the door without speaking.

# THIRTY-FIVE

She went back to her hotel, exhausted. It bore the name of a well-known American chain, but any resemblance to a Western hotel stopped at the stationery. The dining room was permanently locked, and the front desk dispensed not only a key, but also a bath plug attached to a large piece of wood and a roll of shiny toilet paper. They also informed her when the hot water was running – even hotels, it transpired, were only allowed hot water every other day, to save power. The electric lights in her room dimmed and brightened according to some immutable tidal pattern Terry was unable to figure out, and the bedlinen smelt suspiciously as if it hadn't been washed since the room was last occupied. All in all, she felt thoroughly depressed.

She tried to phone, but the international line was permanently engaged. Instead, she decided to go for a walk while she worked out what to do next. Buying an English-language guidebook at a street kiosk, she set off on foot. The city had the appearance of a project only half completed. Vast, deserted avenues the width of motorways led to huge triumphal arches, only for the avenue to stop dead on the other side of the arch and turn into a delta of tiny backstreets. Grand government buildings nestled next to tiny scooter shops. The only advertisements on the streets seemed to be for some sort of national lottery, though the occasional shop selling furs or perfume testified to the fact that some people, at least, were obviously making good money. Once or twice she spotted logos she recognized on the outside of shops – Pizza Hut, Barclays Bank, Coca-Cola – though the names themselves had been changed to unfamiliar Romanian spellings.

On every corner street vendors tried to bargain with her. 'Hey lady. You wan' sell dollars?' Telling them she wasn't American only served to prolong these conversations – 'You wan' sell pounds? Deutschmark? Rouble? Hey lady, you wan' buy perfume?' Sometimes, though, the vendors were simply selling their personal belongings – a radio, a wooden photograph frame: these ignored her, knowing that they had nothing to offer a wealthy tourist like her. Eventually she jumped in a taxi, and directed the driver to take her to the presidential palace, having read in the guidebook that it was the main tourist sight in the capital; but when she finally arrived at the enormous wedding-cake monstrosity Ceauşescu had built as his personal residence her revulsion overcame her, and she decided to go back to the hotel instead.

She checked in at the front desk again for her key and bath plug, and was told that some visitors were waiting for her in the lounge.

'Are you sure?' she asked the desk clerk nervously. Apart from the Wiccans and Magnus, no-one else knew she was in Bucharest. For a second she wondered if Dr Tarkady had reported her to the police. But the police, she reasoned, were hardly likely to wait around in a hotel lounge. A knock on the door at five in the morning would be more their style here.

The clerk shrugged. 'In there,' he said, pointing with his pen. 'A man and a woman.'

The vast, dusty lounge was empty apart from Dr Tarkady and a young man, sitting together at one of the low tables, smoking. The doctor looked up as she approached.

'Ah. Miss Williams,' she said, getting to her feet. 'This is Peter Collins. He works with me at Orphanage Number Four.'

Terry had time to notice that she had called her 'Miss' as the young man got to his feet. 'Hi, pleased to meet you,' he said awkwardly.

'You're English?'

'That's right. I'm from Addenbrooke's Hospital in Cambridge.'

'Dr Collins is a paediatrician. He's been coming to us for several years now.'

'I try and do two or three months a year out here,' he explained.

'Well,' she said warily when they had all sat down. 'What can I do for you? Shall I order some tea?'

'I wouldn't waste your time, Miss Williams,' Dr Tarkady said. 'Afternoon tea is one of the social niceties hotels like this one haven't quite caught up with, I'm afraid.' Again Terry noted the *Miss*.

'You know who I am,' she said bluntly.

'We persuaded the desk clerk to show us your passport,' the paediatrician said apologetically.

'I see.'

'You clearly weren't who you said you were,' Dr Tarkady said, puffing on her cigarette. 'So I thought I'd better find out what was really going on.'

Terry sighed. 'Was I that obvious?'

'As I think I told you, I've had a lot of approaches like the one you made today. You stood out like a sore thumb, I'm afraid. For one thing, you're much too young. If the problem had been a fallopian blockage, as you suggested, you wouldn't have come to us at your age. You'd have spent years doing fertility treatment and trying to adopt through the legal channels before your biological clock made you desperate enough to try something like this. And you wouldn't have behaved the way you did, either.'

'Why not?'

The doctor shrugged. 'Like you, real childless women always ask to see the babies. But, unlike you, once they get into the baby nurseries they can't bear to tear themselves away. You can see it in their eyes – a kind of hunger, like an addict eyeing up his next fix. You see them looking at the babies one by one, as if they're already trying to choose. And they never, ever give up as easily as you did. They cry, they increase the size of their bribes, they tell me how terrible it's been for them – anything to get me to bend the rules.' She shrugged again. 'I feel sorry for them, actually. But the answer's always the same.' She looked at Terry. 'Which led me to start wondering what you *are* doing here. So I talked it over with Peter.'

'We thought you might be a journalist,' he said hesitantly. 'In which case, we thought perhaps –

if we offered to co-operate – you might be prepared to put an appeal for funds in your article.'

Terry shook her head. 'I'm sorry. I'm not a journalist.'

The two doctors looked at each other. 'Are you with the police?' Dr Tarkady asked.

'No.'

'In that case, why are you here?'

She sighed. 'It's a long story.'

'*Da?* In Romania we like stories. There's nothing on television, you see.'

'Well,' Terry began. 'I'm actually an academic – a postgraduate student. I was doing some research in a village called Babcock, in Scotland. Unfortunately, there have been some murders there. A woman and a man, most recently. But before that, some babies – quite small babies. No-one seems to know where they came from, or why they were killed. But the man who was murdered came out here once, as part of a group bringing aid to your orphanage. The murdered girl was here too, though probably not with the same group. It just seems too obvious a connection to ignore.'

'What were their names?'

'John Hobbes and Donna Fairhead.'

'I remember the Babcock group,' Peter Collins said slowly. 'They put in a boiler and a kitchen, I think. I don't remember any individuals, though.'

'And what's your interest in this murder, Miss Williams?' Dr Tarkady asked.

'Please, call me Terry. Um – just that some of my friends are suspected by the police of being involved.'

It sounded unlikely even to her, but perhaps in a country where the police were universally feared and despised it made some kind of sense.

Dr Tarkady glanced at Peter. 'Should we help her?'

'One thing I don't quite understand,' he said, addressing himself to Terry. 'These people came out here a few years ago, yes?'

'That's right.'

'Have you established that these babies died at approximately the same time?'

She shook her head. 'No. We know the babies died sometime last year. My theory is that John Hobbes and Donna Fairhead first met when they were working at your orphanage; hatched the plan to sell babies to childless British couples, and then went back to Scotland to find some customers, before Hobbes returned last summer to get the children.'

'Well, he didn't come to me,' Dr Tarkady said decisively. 'I would have remembered a man on his own, trying to buy a child.'

'One of the other orphanages in Bucharest, perhaps?'

'I doubt it. We keep in good contact with each other.'

'Where then? Where would a man with some experience of Romania go to buy a baby on the black market?'

'There are two possibilities,' Dr Tarkady said. 'First, to the gypsies.'

'They would sell him a baby?'

Dr Tarkady snorted. 'For hard currency, they would sell their own grandmothers. They're little better than savages.' Dr Collins winced. Evidently he found this ingrained racism less than pleasant. 'The only problem', Dr Tarkady continued, 'is that they would almost certainly try to double-cross him.

And the child would be very African in appearance.'

'And the other possibility?'

'Somewhere like Toura,' Dr Tarkady said, glancing at the other doctor for confirmation. 'Personally, if I was looking for a baby, I would go to somewhere like Toura.'

'What's Toura?' Terry asked.

There was a brief silence. The two doctors looked at each other, as if unsure how much to tell her.

'Toura', Dr Collins said uncomfortably, 'is, on the face of it, a mental hospital. It's where the so-called "irrecuperables" from Orphanage Number Four are sent, along with those from other orphanages in this area.'

'I know about the irrecuperables,' Terry said. 'Dr Tarkady explained about the test for three-year-olds when I saw her earlier.'

'The thing is', he continued, 'not all orphanages have received the same level of western aid. By and large, effort has gravitated to those that are easiest to reach.'

'Are you saying that there are still places that haven't changed from the pre-revolution days?' Terry asked incredulously.

Dr Tarkady cut in impatiently. 'Is that so surprising? Of course, there has been a debate. Should we try to spread the aid evenly, so that all the children in all the orphanages get just a little, or do we raise standards to an acceptable level in one place, and add more places when more resources are available? In the end you capitalist countries decided for us. You installed bathrooms, heating, laundry facilities, kitchens, all in the big orphanages here in Bucharest. You weren't interested in the little places out in the country. And there still isn't enough

401

money to make a difference in places like Toura.'

'We're talking about fifteen thousand children, spread across the whole of Romania,' Dr Collins said apologetically. 'That's more under-twelve-year-olds than in all of London's primary schools put together. And some of these places are very remote. One simply couldn't afford to staff them on a permanent basis. Any resources that were pumped in would simply disappear into the black market. In some of these areas, the adult population are only just above the starvation level themselves. Sorting out the orphanages, and particularly the homes for irrecuperables, is hardly their top priority.'

'If Hobbes had bought these babies in Toura,' Terry said slowly, 'would there be any evidence to prove it?'

Dr Tarkady nodded. 'Strangely enough, it's one of the few times when an irrecuperable would have some paperwork. Most of them aren't even given names when they're in the system. But to remove them, you'd need several permits and, if you weren't the parents, a formal adoption certificate. Easily available for the right price, of course, but it means there would certainly be records to show what had happened.'

'Right, then. How do I get there?'

'I'll drive you,' Dr Tarkady offered.

'You've already helped me enough already. I'll get a train or something.'

'There are no trains to Toura,' Dr Tarkady said bluntly. 'It's too remote. The only public transport is a bus once a week.'

'I'll wait for that, then.'

The doctor waved away her protestations. 'It's no problem. I'd like to see what conditions are like, anyway. It's been several months since I was last there, and there may be something I can do to help them.'

'Well, if you're sure,' Terry said doubtfully.

'I'm sure. Be prepared for a long drive, though. It's two hundred kilometres, and the roads are slow. If we're to get there and back in a day I'll need to pick you up here at the hotel at six a.m.'

'OK. I'll see you then.'

'And now I must get going,' Dr Tarkady said, gathering up her cigarettes. 'Peter, I'll see you when I get back.'

'A remarkable woman,' Terry said as the doctor made her way out of the hotel.

'Yes,' he agreed. 'I wasn't surprised she offered to drive you there.'

'It's very kind.'

'Maria is motivated by something more potent than kindness.'

'What do you mean?' she asked.

'How old would you say she is?'

Terry shrugged. 'Thirty-eight? Forty?'

'When the revolution happened, she was about the same age you are now. You've probably heard about Ceauşescu's compulsory breeding programme.'

Terry nodded.

'Even professionals like Maria weren't exempt. They were allowed time off to give birth, of course, but otherwise they had to choose between bringing up their children themselves and their medical studies. Maria was lucky: she only had one child. A little girl. She went into an orphanage here in Bucharest. Then she vanished.'

'My God,' Terry said. 'What happened to her?'

403

'Who knows? Perhaps the Securitate – the secret police – took her. Perhaps she was confused with another child and moved by mistake. Or perhaps she was sold. Even in those days, they used to raise hard currency for the state by selling babies to the Americans.'

'Christ.'

He shrugged. 'You can see why she isn't too keen on people who trade in children.'

Terry nodded. 'It was a stupid plan of mine. I just couldn't think of any other way of following the trail.'

Peter got to his feet. 'Are you doing anything tonight?' he asked casually.

'Nothing. I don't know a soul in Bucharest.'

'In that case, would you like to have dinner with me? I could at least show you where some of the less terrible restaurants are.'

'So long as you let me pay, that would be lovely. And I guess we should make it fairly early, if I've got to be up by six.'

'OK then.' He smiled. 'I'll pick you up in an hour or so, shall I?'

# THIRTY-SIX

Dr Tarkady had not been exaggerating when she said that the roads to Toura were poor. For the first twenty miles or so out of Bucharest, they drove on a huge American-style four-lane freeway. Then, gradually, a series of half-finished bridges and bypasses necessitated them leaving the motorway for longer and longer periods. Eventually it became a trunk road, and when they left that, a single-track road with passing places.

'We're heading north now, into the mountains,' Dr Tarkady explained. 'The Carpathian hills. They say that one day this will be a skiing area to rival the Alps, and Romania will make more money from tourism than it ever did from industrialization.'

Terry grunted. The combination of the early hour, a late night and the doctor's chain-smoking was making her a little nauseous. Their car – a tiny, ancient Fiat – groaned alarmingly on every hill. On top of that, the doctor was obviously unused to driving out of town, and overtook other vehicles manically whenever she could.

Her evening with Peter had, rather to her surprise, turned out to be very enjoyable. They had gone to a tiny restaurant in one of the bustling residential areas, and queued for a table along with dozens of shouting Romanians. Together they'd got happily drunk on the local wine. Peter, for all his apparent kindness and approachability, gave the impression of being lonely in Bucharest. She decided that he'd probably become a paediatrician because he found adults rather hard to deal with.

As they drove higher into the mountains she found herself being reminded of the landscape she'd left behind in Scotland. The same dark-green hill-sides, dotted here and there with yellow gorse; the same black-tipped peaks where bare rock poked through a thin covering of grass and heather. What was very different, however, was the impression left on the landscape by its human inhabitants. Instead of huge fields of crops and rolling pastures of sheep, the fields were like something farmed by midgets. Tiny pocket-handkerchief-sized vineyards gave way to goat paddocks the size of suburban lawns. Most of the farming seemed to be done by women, shape-less under layers of clothing, either by hand or with the help of oxen. When she did spot a tractor, it made Gregor's old Fordson Major look positively modern. And passers-by were evidently still enough of a rarity for the farmers to stop and stare at the Fiat as it chugged past.

'This land has all been given back to the peasants,' Dr Tarkady commented. 'So we're back to square one, if you like: a generation behind the rest of Europe.'

They swung off the road onto a dirt track sign-posted Toura. 'Are we nearly there?' Terry asked.

The doctor grunted. 'Another thirty miles or so.'

Progress on this unmade road was painfully slow.

Huge potholes were marked with crossed sticks, and when they got behind a convoy of trucks even Dr Tarkady had to concede that overtaking was now impossible. They drove through a succession of tiny villages, each time sending the local dogs into a frenzy. It was, thought Terry, like something from another century. She got quite a shock when the sign welcoming them to yet another unpronounceable market town announced that it was twinned with Basingstoke.

'Non-identical twins, huh?' Dr Tarkady said.

'Perhaps they were separated at birth.'

'Or perhaps there's an orphanage here.' She glanced sideways. 'Italian villages have frescos, we have orphanages. Perhaps we should sell souvenirs.'

They drove higher and higher into the hills. 'Why did they site a home for irrecuperables up in the mountains?' Terry asked.

The doctor shrugged. 'First, because it's remote. Even under Ceauşescu, who had no reason to care what anyone thought, the government didn't want its secrets too visible. Secondly, because it gets very cold in winter.'

'That's an advantage?'

'From their point of view, yes. It ensured that only the very toughest would survive. It's not as if they had any central heating bills to worry about – in Toura, minus fifteen on the outside means minus fifteen on the inside.'

Terry said nothing.

'I think you should prepare yourself for what you're going to see today,' Dr Tarkady said quietly. 'This is not going to be a pleasant experience. Even as a doctor, I find it hard to distance myself from the suffering I encounter in these places.

'I should also explain that, while orphanages like the one I work in are run by the Ministry of Health, the homes for irrecuperables are the responsibility of the Ministry of Sanitation. Their main job is to look after the country's sewage system: mental homes are just a sideline. Though in a way, the two are connected. The communist regime viewed the irrecuperables as so much human sewage. Although technically Toura is a hospital, not a single person on the staff has any medical training.'

Like a living death pit, Terry thought. She shivered. 'Can't the new government do anything?'

'With what? Don't get me wrong, Terry. The staff who work at Toura are not bad people. Mostly they are local women who need the tiny wages they're paid to supplement what their husbands make from the fields. But there are too many children, and they have too many problems.'

'And there's never been any aid?'

The doctor shrugged. 'Maybe the odd truckload of teddy bears or nappies. We won't see any sign of those today. As soon as the trucks have gone, the staff take what they've delivered home for their own children. And why not? Why should the children in the institution have toys when their own children have none?'

'I see.'

They drove in silence for the next five minutes. Eventually they came to yet another tiny village. In the central square – little more than a dusty space where four roads met – the doctor swung the car left. 'We're almost there,' she announced. 'This is Toura the village. The orphanage is about a mile up the hill.' She pointed. 'There. See it?'

Above them on the hillside was a huge castle.

Magnus would have killed for this, Terry thought: it was exactly as a Scottish castle should be, a forbidding crag of black granite rising straight up from a narrow shelf a little way up the mountain. 'It looks like Dracula's lair,' she commented.

'It would probably have been the property of the local lord, before the communists came. Most of the big houses that weren't sacked were either turned into barracks or mental hospitals.'

They pulled into a courtyard in front of the imposing main door and got out of the car. Terry saw that the little Fiat, which had been bright yellow when they left Bucharest, was now mustard brown from the dust they'd collected along the way. It was eerily quiet.

Dr Tarkady took a large cardboard box out of the boot and led the way to the door. Because her hands were full, Terry rang the bell for her. The place seemed deserted. Then they heard footsteps on the other side of the door. A woman opened it, her suspicious look turning to a wide smile as she recognized the doctor. They conversed animatedly in Romanian for a few minutes before the doctor introduced Terry. The woman nodded and smiled as Dr Tarkady talked to her.

'I've told Helena you are an English aid worker who is shadowing me,' she explained. 'She doesn't speak English, so just ask me if there's anything you want translated.'

The woman led them in to the hall, where Dr Tarkady handed over her box. The other woman placed it on the floor and opened it, cooing over its contents: some medicines, syringes and, more unexpectedly, packets of Smarties and several bright blue tubs of Mr Matey bubble bath.

'What's the bubble bath for?' Terry asked as Helena whisked her treasure away.

'Many of the children are terrified of water. It's because they can only have cold baths. I can't do anything about the lack of a boiler but', she shrugged, 'at least I can make the cold water a bit more fun.'

Terry looked around her. Apart from the institutional smell of floor wax, there was no indication that this was anything but a private residence. Whereas Orphanage No. 4 had been decorated with brightly painted walls and murals, the walls here were painted a uniform drab brown. And while the other orphanage had been full of the noise of children playing, here she couldn't detect a single sound.

'Where are the children?' she wondered.

'Some are just along here.' Dr Tarkady spoke to Helena, who nodded politely. 'Come with me. I'll show you.'

She followed the doctor along the corridor and into a huge room off to one side. Once inside, Terry stopped.

The first thing that hit her was the smell – a potent cocktail of what seemed to her to be cat's-piss and old nappies, heavily overlaid with antiseptic. The room was full of identical white iron cots, each one with high bars around it. At first she thought they had been painted with black spots, until she saw that the spots were where the paint had rubbed away, revealing the rusting iron underneath.

Each cot held a child. Some were asleep, but many were wide awake. They didn't look at her: most stared listlessly up at the ceiling, or played in a desultory way with their own feet. A few were sitting up and clutching the bars of their cots, rattling them: one or two were banging their heads rhythmically against the metal. Other than that, there was no sound. No, that wasn't quite true. Her ears just caught a tiny, irritating squeak, like the chirrup of crickets. It took her a few seconds to work out that it was the sound of grinding teeth.

'Why don't they cry?' she asked Dr Tarkady in a low voice.

'Why should they? Babies only cry because they learn that it brings their mother. If no mother comes, they soon give up the attempt.' She reached down and stroked the dark hair of the child in the nearest cot. It rolled sideways to see what was happening. Terry saw that it had a terrible squint in one eye. The child allowed itself to be stroked, but gave no sign of pleasure.

'They have also forgotten how to laugh,' the doctor explained. 'If they ever learnt, that is.' She picked up the chart from the end of one of the cots. 'This one hasn't even been given a name. It just says "Girl, 4. Irrecuperable. Birth problems." Perhaps there really was a problem from lack of oxygen at birth. More likely there's nothing wrong with her except her upbringing.'

Terry felt blood pounding in her ears. 'I'm sorry,' she muttered, bolting for the door. Crouching down in the corridor, she forced her head between her knees and took deep breaths of air until the feeling had passed.

'Are you OK?' Dr Tarkady had followed her out.

'Sure. I've been getting panic attacks.'

'Perhaps you're a little anaemic. Do you want to go on?'

Terry nodded.

She was led into a room containing two huge cauldrons, being stirred on top of two woefully inadequate gas rings by middle-aged peasant women. 'One is food, one is dirty nappies,' Dr Tarkady said. 'Side by side, because there is only one stove. Hygiene is a problem here,' she added. 'Not least for the staff. Even they get chronic diarrhoea, so you can imagine what it's like for the children.'

Beyond the kitchen was another dormitory, even larger than the first. Cots lined the walls and stood in islands of four or six along the middle of the room. Like cars in a car park, thought Terry: every available inch was being used. To her, the children looked almost identical – all had dark hair and black eyes. She looked into one cot, and almost recoiled from the emaciated monkey-face that peered back at her. Two legs, as thin as broomsticks, poked from beneath the sheet.

' " Ionescu. Medical problems. Walking problems." ' Dr Tarkady translated from the chart. 'He's lucky: at least someone gave him a name.'

Terry moved on to the next cot. Again, the listless eyes regarded her blankly. The head rolled from side to side. She might as well not have been there.

'What's wrong with this one?'

'Birth problems, it says here.'

'Will she get better?'

'Lying here? I doubt it. But yes, she probably could. Many of the children in Orphanage Number Four were as bad as this. The human brain is surprisingly resilient. Without stimulation, it just puts itself into a state of emotional deep-freeze. It doesn't take any high-tech medical equipment to cure

412

children like this. All you have to do is take them out of their cots, play with them, talk to them, react to them. Like sleeping beauties, they slowly come back to life.'

'Why doesn't someone do it, then?'

'There are twelve staff here, and four hundred children. Believe me, they do what they can.'

They walked on, through the silent dormitories. In one room they came across row after row of potties. The children squatting on them swayed lethargically.

'The shower room,' Dr Tarkady announced, opening the door to yet another room. 'Cold water only, of course.' Under the shower were a group of a dozen or so boys. They were older than any of the other children: about fourteen or fifteen. Somehow the presence of sexually mature teenagers in this place seemed almost as bad as anything else she had seen. Unashamed, one gibbered at them like a monkey, while another took his privates in his fist and shook them at the visitors.

'Of course, even if they don't have mental problems when they come, many develop them as they stay here,' Dr Tarkady said dispassionately. 'For them, they will spend their whole life in an institution.'

They were shown a baby ward. 'There are fewer babies here than in my orphanage in Bucharest,' the doctor commented. 'That's because Toura is basically for children who fail the irrecuperable test at three. But an orphanage doctor is at liberty to send a child here at any age, if he wishes. Sometimes it's because they really do have problems. Often it was just because there was overcrowding. Today, of course, the better orphanages would do anything to avoid having to send a child to this place.'

Terry reached down into a cot and offered her finger to a tiny little baby. It couldn't have been more than a few months old. It grasped it and tugged it towards its lips impatiently. Her finger was coated in warm saliva, and then she felt hard, toothless gums close round her as it began to suck greedily. She felt a sudden pang of maternal instinct, a dizzying desire to hug it to her chest, to enfold it in her arms and never let it go.

'Can I pick it up?' she asked.

'Of course.' Dr Tarkady consulted the piece of paper taped to the end of the bed. 'He's a little boy. I'll tell you what, why don't you name him? There's a blank space here waiting to be filled in.'

The baby smelt buttery and warm. 'Tell me some Romanian names,' Terry suggested. 'I don't think I know any.'

'Oh – Bogdon, Michel, Sorin, Ion, Petrut . . .'

'Petrut,' she interrupted. 'Peter. Like Peter Collins.'

Dr Tarkady nodded. 'OK then. Petrut.' She took out a pen and wrote it in. 'Now you should wash your hands,' she instructed.

'Why?'

'Just a precaution. He may be HIV positive.'

After Terry had washed her hands at the room's only tap, they went outside. There was a rudimentary playground, in which thirty or forty older children were hanging around listlessly.

'Poor social skills,' Dr Tarkady commented. A little boy ran past them, playing a game of tag with a friend. Suddenly he stopped, dropped his trousers and urinated onto the ground.

'Poor bladder control as well.' She glanced at

Terry. 'Incredible, isn't it? All the things we take for granted. Like urinating, walking, talking. They all have to be taught to us by someone. Seen enough?' Terry nodded, and they went inside.

'This is the office.' The doctor indicated a door to their left. 'Do you want to see if you can find any trace of your Englishman?'

'If we can, yes.'

Dr Tarkady called for Helena and spoke in Romanian. The other woman smiled and gestured at a large filing cabinet in the corner. 'She says to go ahead and look,' the doctor translated. 'It's best if we do it ourselves. Helena is busy. Do you know what year you want to start with?'

'Not really. Certainly after '95.'

'Let's start in 1996 then.' The doctor pulled open a drawer and began working her way through it. Not reading Romanian, there was nothing Terry could do to help. After a few minutes the doctor paused, lit a cigarette and continued, the cigarette jammed into one corner of her mouth, one eye half-closed against the smoke.

'Here,' she said at last. 'This looks promising.' She pulled a thin sheaf of papers out of the pile. 'Look,' she said, pointing.

She was holding a form covered in tiny print. In one of the spaces someone had typed the words 'Hobbes, Ion' followed by a number.

'That'll be his passport number,' the doctor explained. 'It says here that he adopted five babies. Three boys and two girls. Look, here's his signature.'

'Can I take a copy of this?'

Dr Tarkady went to ask Helena, while Terry examined the papers. There was no doubt about it

415

– despite the misspelling of Hobbes's Christian name, his country of origin was given as Britain. She felt no elation, just a weary relief that now she could get out of this nightmare.

When Dr Tarkady returned she had Helena with her. 'There is no photocopier,' she said apologetically.

'Damn.' Terry thought for a moment. 'Could you ask her if I could possibly borrow the original? I'll send it straight back once I've copied it.'

This prompted a long discussion between the two women. Helena seemed to be objecting, but it was clear that Dr Tarkady wasn't going to give up easily. Eventually, the doctor turned and said curtly, 'She says OK.'

'Please thank her for me.'

This time the conversation was rather shorter.

'And – one last request – could you ask her if she knows of any reason why the babies might not have lived? Could they have had anything wrong with them?'

Again the two women conversed in Romanian. This time, Helena's demeanour seemed to be apologetic, whilst the doctor grew visibly more angry.

'She says she does know a reason,' Dr Tarkady said at last, turning to Terry. 'But it is not a good story.'

'Please, tell me.'

'At around this time Toura somehow got hold of some drugs. There were no doctors here, as I told you, but the women who worked here thought that the drugs would pacify the children.' She shrugged. 'They were misguided, of course. From the sound of it, the drug was probably a measles vaccine. They

416

did not know the correct dosages or how to administer it properly.'

'What happened?'

'Several days after they had been injected with the drugs, the children started to behave strangely. Some got sick, others showed behavioural problems. My guess is that they were brain damaged. It would have been a miracle, really, if they weren't. She thinks the babies your Mr Hobbes took were probably amongst the affected ones.'

'This vaccine – could it have left traces of measles in the body?'

'It's possible. That's what a vaccine is – a controlled dose of the disease. Or in this case, uncontrolled,' Dr Tarkady fumed. 'We should go now.'

Terry thanked Helena profusely in English and followed Dr Tarkady outside. She found the Romanian getting into her car in a foul temper.

'Stupid, stupid,' she muttered under her breath as they set off down the hill.

'I don't understand,' Terry said. 'All the misery you've seen today, and the only time you've got really angry was when Helena told you about those drugs.'

'It's the waste,' Dr Tarkady said tersely.

'Of human lives?'

Dr Tarkady laughed abruptly. 'No, I meant a waste of drugs. At that time I would have killed for a measles vaccine.'

They drove in silence for a few miles. 'You think I'm callous, don't you?' Dr Tarkady asked.

Terry shook her head. 'No. I think you're amazing. It must be very hard to stay professional in places like that.'

Dr Tarkady glanced at her. 'Are you all right?'

'I think so.'

'The first time I went there, I had nightmares for weeks. I wanted to give up being a doctor. It seemed so pointless.' She snorted. 'Our famous Hippocratic oath. What's the use of doing everything you can to keep a child alive, when all you're keeping them alive for is a lifetime in a place like that? Sometimes I think the ones who die are the lucky ones.'

# THIRTY-SEVEN

As her Air Romania plane touched down at Edinburgh, the mostly Romanian passengers burst into a spontaneous round of applause. Terry wasn't sure if it was the smoothness of the landing that was being applauded, or the simple fact that it had happened at all. Certainly she had rarely been on a plane that shook so alarmingly in mid-air. The passenger next to her seemed to spend most of the flight crossing himself and praying. She assumed it was because he was an inexperienced flyer; but again, it might have been the reverse: perhaps he was an extremely experienced flyer who consequently knew a lot more about the risks of flying with that particular airline than she did.

And as the plane turned and taxied towards the terminal, it happened. It was like something giving way in her brain, a barrier suddenly crumbling between two thoughts that had until now been separate. Or it was like that moment when water trapped in an ear suddenly drains away and you can hear clearly again. Her brain, which for so long had been muzzily shuffling and reshuffling the pieces of Catherine's mystery, suddenly regained its ability to see a pattern where others could not.

There was a pay phone in one of the corridors leading to passport control and she stopped to call Laura's number. No-one was in, but the answer machine was switched on.

'Laura? It's Terry. I'm back. Everything was pretty much as we expected. Listen: I want you to get Iain to exhume Mcteer's body. I think I know what happened to Catherine now, and if I'm right the proof's in that grave. I know it sounds like a big number, but Iain must have done this sort of thing hundreds of times. And it isn't like we'll have to dig up a graveyard or anything. Mcteer was buried in the garden at Nineveh. Oh, and make sure Magnus and Nico are there. They'll both want to know what was really going on.' She paused, wondering if she ought to explain more fully, but then the tape beeped to indicate that it was full, giving her no choice but to replace the handset.

# THIRTY-EIGHT

It was raining again, a fine but persistent drizzle that danced in the arc lights Iain had rigged up and shone like sequins in the hair of the onlookers. Of those Wiccans still at liberty, only Brigid had elected to watch the exhumation of their founder's grave. Nico and Magnus were both there, the former sheltering under a huge golf umbrella, the latter standing a little apart, wearing a greasy old cap that dripped relentlessly onto his shoulders. Only Laura, in the cab of the JCB, was dry.

Under Iain's directions a mound of earth was soon piling up on the lawn. 'We need to be careful now,' he shouted in Terry's ear. 'We've gone down about four feet, and although they say he was buried six feet down you can never be absolutely sure. He should be in pretty good condition, though. This soil is almost pure peat. I'd be surprised if he's lost his soft tissue yet.'

'Soft tissue? You make it sound like a packet of Kleenex, not someone's corpse,' she objected.

'Oh, excuse *me*. You're the one who cooked up this highly illegal conspiracy to exhume a body without a licence, remember?'

Terry shrugged. 'It really is the only way. I think I know what happened, but I need proof.'

At a sign from Iain, Laura killed the digger's engine and he clambered into the hole with a spade. There was only room for one, so the others gathered round and watched.

In the car park of the Eagle another group was also getting wet. In their case though, it was alcohol and not coats that was keeping the chill off. There were about a dozen of them, mostly farmers. Torches played on the face of the man standing on the bonnet of the Land Rover as he spoke.

'We have endured this long enough,' Hector Morrison said. ' "He that toucheth pitch shall be defiled thereby. He that welcometh Satan shall know evil himself." You all know what we have to do. Drive the witches from our midst now, and make an end of it.' Here and there heads nodded agreement, but nobody spoke. He levered his bulk back onto the ground, and the men piled into the cars. Still no-one spoke, their faces set grimly as one after another the cars' ignitions fired and they pulled in a convoy out of the car park. As each driver exited he carefully signalled left with his indicator, as if to emphasize that it was their opponents, and not themselves, who were the law-breakers.

After about five minutes Iain hit wood. As he had predicted, the coffin was well preserved, the boards barely softened, but even so he dug round it care-fully before digging two trenches underneath for the ropes.

Terry found herself standing next to Nicolaides.

She looked round: no-one else was listening. 'She offered you a baby, didn't she?' she said quietly.

'Who?'

'Come on, Nico.'

He sighed. 'Yes, she did.'

'Did you give her money?'

He shook his head. 'We promised her money – a lot of money – but only when the child was delivered.'

'One child?'

'Of course.'

'Did she tell you about the others?'

'She implied she had other customers. It didn't seem important.'

'So what happened?'

'Nothing. That was the strange thing. We agreed; she said we should expect a phone call. The next thing we heard, her body had been found up at the pig farm.'

'Why didn't you tell the police?'

He snorted. 'By that time we were trying to get on an adoption register here in Scotland. These people are fascists, Terry. They'll turn you down if you smoke, if you're the wrong ethnic group, if you're too old, too young, too strict, too liberal . . . can you imagine what being investigated for murder would have done for our chances?'

'You had absolutely nothing to do with her death?'

'Nothing. Why would we kill her? She was going to help us.'

'The children were brain damaged,' Terry said. 'Something that wasn't discovered until they were already back in the UK. It crossed my mind that one of her customers might have killed her out of anger.'

'Not us.'

'Can you prove that?'

'No. But neither can you prove that it was.' He glanced at her. 'You know that someone else has died, don't you? Russell Kane, the bookseller. Just before you left for Romania. It was a heart attack, apparently, but there were witchcraft symbols daubed on the wall.'

'The bookseller,' she murmured. 'Yes, I should have thought of that.'

'I'm sorry?'

'It's becoming clearer. I'll explain in a little while, I promise.'

The ropes in place, they moved forward to help lift the coffin onto the grass.

They pulled up on the gravel in front of the house – half a dozen cars that disgorged twice as many figures. Still they were silent, though their silence had an uneasy quality to it now, and one or two glanced at Hector Morrison questioningly. He, however, was already issuing orders in a low voice, touching the person he was speaking to on the arm, making sure they knew exactly what they had to do. One of those he spoke to ran back to the vehicles. The rest of them stood, encircling the house, their silhouettes as ominously still as a ring of standing stones. The runner returned, his arms full of petrol canisters. Hector took one and stepped forward, punching it through the window like a huge plastic knuckleduster. Three other men started to kick down the door, the force of their blows shaking the frame so much the doorbell inside the house began to ring in unison with their feet. Then the door gave way and they were inside. Anna, running downstairs to see what the commotion was, was grabbed, shrieking, and dragged outside by two burly men.

'You'll need this,' Iain instructed, taking a small pot of Vicks Vapour Rub from his pocket and handing it to Terry. 'Put some inside your nostrils. Even if he hasn't decomposed much, the smell will have been confined to the coffin and it may be fairly noxious.'

Carefully he prised the top of the coffin off with the edge of the spade. She leaned forward.

She hadn't known exactly what to expect. As Iain had said it would be, John Mcteer's body was still relatively intact. His lips were drawn back from his teeth in a snarl, and his eyes were blazing at them. It was tempting to ascribe the corpse's expression to its anger at being disturbed, but she knew that it was only the effect of the skin tightening as it dried out.

Lying on Mcteer's chest were a small magical dagger, a chalice and a manuscript. Gingerly she lifted the manuscript away, and saw that, unlike the body, it had already started to decay. Holes and stains peppered the top sheet, but lifting that up, the pages below seemed more or less intact.

Judith heard the feet pounding up the stairs and jumped from her bedroom window, her duvet still wrapped round her to cushion the fall. Isobel, at the top of the house, was not so quick. She woke to find a man crashing into her bedroom. She screamed, and tried to crawl away, but he grabbed her, ripping the T-shirt off her and gazing hungrily at her body before landing his fist squarely into her stomach. She fell to the floor. A boot swung into her breasts, then another into the side of her head. Panting, her assailant regarded her for a few moments, then dragged her by her limp arms into a puddle of petrol. Within moments her blond hair was a greasy, ratty mess as it soaked up the fluid like the wick of a lamp.

Downstairs, Zoe screamed as a chair broke over her.

'Dear God, what's going on?' Nico said. People were running across the lawn – Terry saw Zoe being pursued by a burly lad in his twenties, bringing her down with a tackle that on the rugby field would have brought him a round of applause. Immediately another man, just behind him, leapt on the young woman and punched her in the face.

'It's the villagers,' Magnus said. He picked up a spade and ran to Zoe's side, standing over her with it raised behind him like a baseball bat. Iain and one of the locals were tussling beside the grave: in the JCB cab Laura calmly pulled at the controls, scooped the attacker up and deposited him in the hole.

'Tom?' Magnus said, aghast, as he spotted a face in the mêleé he recognized. 'Tom, what the hell are you playing at?'

'I'm sorry, Magnus. It's nothing personal, you understand? Enough is enough. When they were just killing each other, that was one thing, but when it's bairns an' all . . .' He shook his head. 'We want no more witchcraft, Magnus. And when we've finished here, we'll be away to the castle to rid ourselves of the rest.'

'The rest? What rest?'

'The witch's writings. If it wasn't for them none of

426

this lot would have infested Babcock in the first place. We'll be burning them too, and there's an end of it.' He turned and shouted to the others behind him, 'Come on, lads. Finish what we came here for.'

Someone was crouching by the house striking a cigarette lighter. It didn't seem to want to light: after a second Terry saw that he was holding it upside down. Then a spark caught, and all the ground between the kneeling figure and the house turned blue, a low, liquid shimmer of violet flames, like brandy round a giant Christmas pudding. The effect only lasted for a moment: then the inside of the building suddenly roared, lit from the inside by flame.

'There might be people still in that house,' Terry said frantically. She could see flames leaping like a pack of ravenous animals at the windows. Their attackers stood back, silent now, watching the fire scurry up the curtains and jump from chair to chair. She ran to the door, but one of the villagers pushed her away: not roughly, but in a way that brooked no argument. The men stood there watching for a few minutes, the light from the flames illuminating their faces with a sudden fierce clarity. Then, one by one, without looking at each other, they got back into their cars and drove away.

At the back of the house Terry found Brigid struggling to connect a hosepipe to a tap in the yard. 'Who's missing?' she shouted.

'Isobel. Everyone else got out, but I can't find Isobel,' she said numbly. 'She must be in there some-where, but there's nothing we can do until we get the fire out. All the entrances are alight.'

'Call the fire brigade.'

'We have, but they'll take hours to get here.

Laura's gone to the farm in the JCB to get a water bowser. She'll be back in a minute.'

She found Magnus comforting Judith, and pulled him away. 'We've got to get to the castle before Tom does. Can we take your car?'

'Don't they need us here?'

'They're already doing all they can. What about Flora and Alex? They must be on their own.'

'Christ, you're right.' They ran to the Land Rover and raced out of the drive. Magnus swung immediately left, up the track that led to the moor. 'We'll go round the mountain. It'll be quicker than the roads.'

A short time later they pulled up outside the castle. The front door was open. Magnus jumped down and strode inside, calling: 'Flora? Alex?'

'We're out here.'

They went through the kitchen. Outside, Alex and Flora were standing in front of a smouldering bonfire. In the youth's hands was a shotgun.

'They used petrol, Dad. By the time I found them . . .' He shrugged. 'I chased the bastards out of here, though. A couple of them won't be sitting down for a while.'

'Well done.'

Terry knelt down by the fire. They had mixed Catherine's letters up with newspaper to make them burn more easily. She tried to pull a fragment of manuscript from the flames, but it was too hot. She glimpsed a couple of words: *For my pricking I am charged four pounds and three shillings. I have engaged a lawyer* . . . Above her, in the flames' glassy updraught, a cloud of paper butterflies slowly floated back to earth, their black wings edged with gold. She tugged at another fragment. *I will suffer*

428

*anything, but I cannot admit that I am a witch, tho'
I am very afraid* ... A piece of paper glowed bright,
suddenly, as a glowing ulcer of embers in its middle
caught the wind and spread. *And so she died, a
terrible burning* ... She stood up. The family
watched her, not speaking, as she turned and
walked into the house.

One thing. There was just one thing left to do. As
dawn broke over the mountain, she walked slowly
into Babcock and went up to the door of the church.
It was unlocked. She went into the chancel where
the parish records were kept and lifted the old
volumes down from the shelf. For an hour she
turned the pages, looking for a name.

He came in behind her, surprisingly silent for a
man of his size. In his hand he held one of the record
books.

'Is this what ye're looking for, lassie?' Hector
Morrison asked mildly.

# THIRTY-NINE

In one hand he carried a shotgun, poking it into her back whenever she faltered; in the other the book of records.

'Where are we going?' she asked over her shoulder as they left the road and followed a narrow track.

'Hold your whist, woman. You'll be there soon enough.'

'I understand how it feels,' she began, but something hard and metallic smashed down onto her head. It felt like an iron bar. The barrel of the gun.

'You understand nothing,' he spat at her. 'Nothing.'

She staggered in the muddy ground, and he flung the book at her. 'Here. You carry it, *whore*.'

Silently she picked up the book. They were going uphill now. More than once she stumbled and fell. Hector, though he hissed with impatience behind her, said nothing.

She saw where they were headed now: to the dovecot at the edge of the moor. A moment later Hector confirmed it, muttering, 'The tower. Walk towards the tower.'

Eventually they reached it. She went inside. It was as she had found it before, except that there was a hessian sack in the middle of the dirt floor.

'Open it.'

She pulled out a length of steel chain, some candles and a lighter, a blanket, a bottle of milk and a newspaper.

'Now listen to me,' he said quietly. 'And none of your clever questions. I cannae stay now, but I'll see you tomorrow.' He took a deep breath. 'I'm sorry, but I'm gonnae have tae chain you.'

Wrapping the chain twice around each wrist, he fastened each one with a padlock. To all intents and purposes she was manacled, with just a few inches of loose chain between each cuff. He had to put down the gun to fasten the padlocks, and for a moment she considered making a run for it. He glanced at her face and said, 'Aye, you could run. Do you think you could run faster than a deer? I've had plenty of practice.'

Meekly then she submitted to the chain. When he was done he stepped back. 'You'll do. Now then. If you need the bathroom, you'll have to make do with that.' He indicated the newspaper. 'I'll take it away in the morning.'

'My,' she said caustically, 'you are well organized, aren't you? But then, you should be. You've done this before.'

He ignored her and left, carefully padlocking the door behind him. With the door shut, the only light came from the tiny opening about thirty feet up, originally where the birds had flown in and out. She went to the door, examining it with her fingers. Although the wood was old it was solid, and the surround into which it was set had been recently

431

replaced. For the first time the hopelessness of her situation came home to her. Anxiety and claustrophobia welled up in her guts. She fought it, taking calm breaths, but she desperately needed air, needed to get out of the encircling walls of the tower. As her anxiety turned to panic, she struggled for breath. Tears and snot streamed down her face, and she gulped for air that didn't seem to make it to her lungs. The fear of not being able to breathe was almost as terrifying as the original panic: a fear that fed itself, making each breath harder and harder. She couldn't even scream, could only collapse, shaking, to the ground, letting the tears and the mucus drip down her face onto the floor, until her silent howls became great dry-heaving retches, and she vomited copiously into the dust.

It didn't kill her. That was the first thing she realized when she came to her senses, God knew how long later. She was still alive, and the attack was subsiding. She had outfaced her terror.

It grew dark, and she found a candle and lit it. One of the dove-recesses provided a handy place for the candle to stand. When she placed it there she saw that there was already a little pool of solidified older wax. Once again she had the sensation that she was following in Donna's footsteps.

After that there was nothing to do but wait. She sang songs, she shouted, she read the newspaper by the faint light of the candle and, when that guttered and went out, she cried. For a few hours she slept, wrapped up in the blanket. And then the waiting went on some more, as she watched the faint crack of purple at the top of the tower slowly turn to grey.

The day wore on, and still he didn't come. She drank the milk and blew tunes across the top of the empty bottle. She recited every Shakespeare speech she had ever learned at school: the 'O for a muse of fire' prologue from *Henry the Fifth*; Prospero's soliloquy from act four of *The Tempest*; Cleopatra's great speech to her maids after the death of Antony. When she had done that she moved on to other poets: *The Wasteland*, *The Windhover* and some of her favourite sonnets from Elizabeth Barratt Browning. She was back to Shakespeare again by the time she finally heard the padlock rattling against the door, and light flooded in through the opening, dazzling her.

'I'm sorry it's late. I couldnae get away.'

All the things she had planned, the carefully worded speeches of mingled threat and entreaty, flew straight out of her head. All she felt was a strange wave of relief – relief that she had not been forgotten, that he had come for her, that she was no longer alone.

He refastened the padlock on the inside of the door and tossed her a paper bag. 'There's some food.'

She had to get him talking, she knew. It was the first rule of any hostage situation: establish a rapport with your abductor. Force him to see that you're a person, not just a piece in his game plan.

'What's going to happen to me?' she asked.

He took his time about replying. 'Nothing bad. Nothing really bad.'

'Something bad happened to Donna,' she said. She looked in the bag. Inside was a single loaf of bread.

'Donna tried tae escape.'

'How?'

He gestured upwards. Terry looked. The ledge.

Thirty feet up. If you used the pigeon-holes as toe- and fingerholds, you might conceivably attempt to climb it.

'Sheer madness,' he said, following her gaze. 'Even if she'd made it, there's nae way down on the outside.'

'That explains the wounds on her back,' Terry said. 'She scraped it as she fell.'

'Aye.'

She thought about it, and shivered. 'So. What happens now?'

'First,' he said calmly, 'you write a letter.'

'What sort of letter?'

' "Dear Magnus, I have decided not tae stay and continue my studies. There's nae point now that the letters are destroyed. Thank ye and goodbye." '

'I won't,' she said fiercely. 'I'd be mad, wouldn't I? I'm not writing anything.'

By way of answer he reached into his jacket and took from his inner pocket what looked like a bulbous pen. He unscrewed the cap and came to stand directly in front of her.

'Do ye know what this is?' he asked silkily.

'No.'

'It's a cattle poke. They didn't have these wee fellas in Catherine's day, but I'll wager they'd have appreciated them all right. Here.' He reached out casually as if to place the object in her hand. At the last moment his thumb clicked a button on the side she hadn't seen, and her arm leapt. The pain was something visual, something that boiled purple and yellow behind her eyes. She screamed soundlessly. He clicked his thumb again, and the pain went away. She sank to her knees, howling, holding the wrist, and the next moment he was kneeling behind her, one hand wrapped in her hair, one hand waving the cattle prod in front of her eyes. She could feel the rough tweed of his clothes through her own clothes, the sheer bulk of him pressed against her. She trembled, and he chuckled again.

'Suck it,' he whispered, moving the cattle prod closer to her face. It touched her cheek, and she flinched, waiting for the pain. For the moment, though, it did not come. 'Go on – suck it.'

Slowly he stroked it across her cheek and brought it to rest on her mouth. There was a metal point on it, like a plug, and he insinuated it between her lips. 'Open,' he said, as if to a reluctant child, and chuckled delightedly when she did as she was bidden.

He pushed it to the back of her throat and she gagged. 'Suck it,' he ordered again and she made an attempt to close her lips on the thing. It tasted of bakelite and bike oil. Then – it was like a sledgehammer in the mouth, smashing her head; like some horrible cartoon in which everything in her brain exploded irretrievably – the pain came and folded her in its terrible kiss. She would have done anything, said anything, to escape that pain. Then it was gone, and her numb tongue established that, incredibly, her teeth and palate were still there. She tasted blood where she had bitten herself.

She mumbled something. He had won now, and they both knew it. But the prod, wet with her own mucus, was sliding down her neck to her chest. One hand reached around to gently cup her left breast: the other offered the cattle prod to the nipple.

'No,' she mumbled through burnt and swollen lips. 'Please, I'll—'

'Aye, of course,' he breathed, 'you'll dae anything I tell you.' The tip of the prod touched her breast, and then – like a finger pressing into a balloon – he pushed it deeper, so deep that it hurt, before he tapped his thumb impatiently once more and the current threw her backwards against him, the pain fizzing down her arms and across her chest. She felt her heart catch, and then the thumb was resting alongside the instrument again, and she was trying to regain her breath.

'First,' he said conversationally, 'tell me what you've found out.'

She struggled for words. 'It was about babies,' she managed to say.

'Aye. It was about babies. What about them?'

'Your own child died in childbirth. Whatever it was, it must have been something that meant your wife couldn't have any more. Donna Fairhead and John Hobbes offered to sell you a baby from Romania.'

'You don't know what the poor woman went through,' his voice whispered behind her ear.

'Donna?'

'Donna? No, not that whore. Joan. My wife. The tests and the doctors. The tears every time someone she knew fell pregnant. The pain she suffered.' She felt him shake his head. 'It destroyed her. No laughter. No joy. No . . . relations. Unless I . . .' He paused, and the prod raised up, touched the underside of her chin, pushing it up, pushing her head back with it until her head was back against his shoulder, so far back she could see his eyes. 'Sometimes I had to insist,' he said mildly.

'Why didn't you adopt?'

'Adopt?' He tightened his grip on her hair, as if suddenly reminded of her presence. 'Adopt? Us? Oh, aye. We had an interview with Social Services. After, they told us they didn't think we'd give the child a balanced upbringing. Maybe it was something to do with the fact that we spoke about the Lord and His will. Maybe it was something to do with the way Joan broke down and begged them, literally begged them, to give us a babby. Do you know how that feels, to watch your own wife beg? Knowing the middle-class bastards have absolutely no intention of agreeing?' He tapped the prod lightly against her neck. 'I'm distracting you, lassie. Go on with your tale, won't ye?'

'There was a problem with the Romanian babies – they had brain damage. Someone – I assume it was you – took them off John Hobbes and disposed of them.'

'Aye. John didnae have the guts.' He sighed. 'It's only what ye have to dae to a deformed calf or a lamb. The ewe calls for them for a few hours, then she gets over it.'

'But your wife didn't get over it.'

'Whole days spent crying,' he murmured. 'Refusing tae eat, refusing tae pray. Oh, she said some foul things when the madness took her. Terrible things. Cursing the Lord. Saying He had abandoned her, so she was going tae abandon him.' He tapped the prod again. 'What else?'

She paused, wondering what she could avoid telling him, what omissions she might be able to leave so that others could follow her trail. She paused too long. The cattle prod reached under her armpit, and the pain hit her, making her arm dance like a spastic's. 'What else?' he hissed. She cried for a few moments, and he waited for her to finish, humming with impatience.

'The Romanian babies were only half of the

story,' she said, holding her damaged arm. 'When that scheme failed, Donna turned to some letters written by Catherine McCulloch she'd found at Mcteer's sister's house. She'd been going to sell them to Magnus or Nico, whoever offered the most – I think she tried Kane, the bookseller, as well. But then she transcribed them. She understood the implications very quickly – much quicker than I did, but then, she was a grasping, money-minded bitch herself. I suppose she came and followed the Hughes family tree in the parish records – she knew about the records from her Romanian enterprise: I reckon she'd used them to find out who the childless couples were round here. She found what I was trying to find yesterday: what name the direct descendant of Catherine's baby, the baby she gave up to Anne de Courcy, carries now. And when she found that at some point the de Courcy/Hughes family had become the Morrisons, and that you were in fact the descendant of Catherine's illegitimate child, she realized what it meant. Primogeniture wasn't abolished in Scotland until the mid-eighteenth century.'

'Aye. Under the old law, even a bastard could inherit if it was acknowledged.'

'Which made Catherine's letter, acknowledging her child as her heir, a legal document. And your own child, if you'd had one, would have inherited Babcock.'

'Aye. If I'd had one.'

'I can imagine how that must have felt. If you were desperate for a child before, you'd have been,' she hesitated. 'Deranged' was the word she had in mind, but she substituted something less inflammatory, 'Even more desperate now. But in

Donna you'd met a woman who was motivated both by extreme greed and a hatred of Magnus – she'd made a play for him and been rejected. One of you came up with the idea of her acting as a surrogate mother for you. She was going to conceive, then vanish to India until the baby was born. When she came back she'd hand it over, and you'd confront Magnus with the legal evidence.'

'You're a clever lady,' he admitted. The hand holding the cattle prod came up, in front of her face, and she flinched. What had she said to displease him now? He touched it to her forehead, just between her eyes, and she gasped.

'It's not illegal, of course,' he said mildly. 'Surrogacy is perfectly within the law, so long as the payment is for expenses and not for profit.'

Terry swallowed. 'But something obviously went wrong.'

'Aye,' he said. 'Aye. It was the little whore's fault. She said she couldnae go through with it. Oh, she strung us along for a while – took an advance of three grand, said she was pregnant, took another payment, said she wasn't sure . . . Then one day she told us she'd read her runes or something and they'd told her not tae.'

'She paid you back what she hadn't spent,' Terry said. 'Her bank account was empty when she died.'

'But it wasnae the money,' his voice said quietly in her ear. 'Joan had believed her, you see. She couldn't have stood another disappointment.'

'So you decided to make her go through with it.'

'I offered to drive her to the airport.'

'And brought her here instead.'

'Aye.'

'And forced yourself on her.'

439

'She agreed.'

The cattle prod might have had something to do with that, she thought. 'Once she was . . . impregnated,' Terry said neutrally, 'you were going to do – what? Keep her cooped up in here for nine months? It's hardly an appropriate place for a pregnant woman.'

'There's a croft on the farm,' he growled. 'We'd have looked after her.'

'But then she died.'

'Then she died,' he agreed. 'The stupid bitch thought she could get away from me.' He grabbed the chain between her hands and shook it. 'She wasnae wearing one of these, of course. I don't think ye'll get the urge to go climbing, will ye?'

'And Hobbes?'

'Once they found the babies in the pit, he lost his nerve. Killed himself. Luckily it was me who found him. There was a note. I took it and substituted the witchcraft symbols instead.'

' "I am in blood steep'd in so far," ' she murmured, ' "That to return were as tedious as to go o'er." '

'Talking of returning,' he said, pushing her away from him and getting to his feet, 'I have to be away myself.'

'Are you going to kill me?'

'I havnae killed anyone, lassie. I'm not going tae start now if I can help it.'

It was true, she realized. Donna had been left here until she'd been so desperate she'd literally tried to climb the walls. The babies had been left in the death pit to die of starvation. Kane – the only other person Donna had shown the letters to – had died of a heart attack when attacked with the cattle prod. Hector Morrison was a torturer, but he was also in some strange way a moral coward too.

' "Thou shalt not kill," ' he said, nodding. 'But on the subject of electric batons, the Good Lord was strangely silent.'

'You're going to leave me here to die?'

He smiled at her. 'That all depends on you.'

'What do you mean?' But he would not tell her. He threw a pad of paper and a pen onto the floor.

'Write that letter,' he said. 'I'll see ye when I see ye.' He unlocked the padlock and slid it out of its mount. 'Incidentally, it's a combination lock. So dinnae get any ideas about rushing me for the key.'

# FORTY

She battered on the door, shouting until she was hoarse. When she realized it was useless she collapsed again, sobbing. She sang 'All Along the Watchtower', complete with the guitar solo, and then 'Hey Joe', because Hendrix seemed like a good choice. The circular walls reflected back her words with a faint echo. 'There's no-one to be embarrassed in front of,' she thought, and somehow it seemed as terrifying a way of looking at her captivity as any other.

Night fell. She recalled that Catherine in her letters had talked about being accused of holding a Sabbat in this very dovecot. *The girl Mary Tyler is a simple thing, who says she saw me in the doocot surrounded by spirits, having congress with a devil, and that this devil wore a black cape and his head was crowned with horns. She witnessed that my body was laid out like an altar for the devil to cover, and that she saw him do so, and his body was ten feet tall. And on seeing this she ran away, but I caused a storm to rise up that did pursue her all the way home.* 'Very well then,' she said aloud. 'Let us reconstruct these alleged events for the jury. Since the door is *here*, and Mary Tyler must have been out *there*, and let us assume the candles were roughly where I've put them myself . . .' She stood with her back to the door. 'You see, Your Honour, the girl simply could not have seen right into the centre of the room. The most she would have glimpsed is a shadow on the door. Distorted by candlelight, any person might have appeared ten feet tall. And as for the storm that she caused to rise up, why, show me an evening when there isn't a storm in Babcock.' But the prosecution counsel had leaped to his feet to object, and to her horror she saw that it was Magnus. 'Your Honour, that isn't a storm, it's a very light drizzle.' Drizzle: what a silly word. Wasn't it what you did to cakes? Her mouth watered suddenly and she tore at the bread he had left her ravenously. 'That's supper over, then. I think I might go upstairs to bed.' Upstairs. She looked up at the top of the tower, to where a glimmer of half-light still illuminated the ledge. She shivered. Even without chains, what despair had driven Donna to try to climb up there? She felt another panic attack coming on, and hurriedly switched to hymns. 'Jerusalem'. 'Onward Christian Soldiers'. For some bloody reason she even found herself singing 'Kumbaya', and she *hated* 'Kumbaya'.

She slept fitfully, and then the day started all over again. She had been avoiding the newspaper for as long as she possibly could, but she wasn't going to be able to put it off any longer. Reluctantly, she squatted over it, then wrapped the result up as quickly as possible to minimize the stink. The thought of handing the little parcel to Hector made her burn with shame.

He was a throwback, of course. In his genes the

fanaticism of the torturer who had fathered his line on Catherine McCulloch had resurfaced: first in his religious fundamentalism, then in his murderous obsession. Catherine McCulloch's own brand of mysticism probably hadn't helped the genetic mix either.

He returned some time in the afternoon – she was losing track of time now, not only what hour but also what day and even what century it was. Everything seemed to have coalesced into this interminable present when the door opened and his massive bulk blotted out the sudden explosion of light. He reached down with a grunt of satisfaction and picked up the letter she had written for Magnus. She hadn't written much, but evidently it was enough. Carefully he folded it and placed it in his pocket. Then he took off his jacket.

She watched him. Was he going to rape her? But when he was in his shirtsleeves he stopped, and bent down to take the cattle prod from the inside pocket of the jacket.

She cringed against the wall, blubbing and screaming at the knowledge of what was coming next. He leaned down to wrap his meaty fingers in her hair and pull her to her feet. Then he used the baton on her – first in her ear, and then her armpit, and then in her kidneys and on her forearms. It was far, far worse than any rape she could have ever imagined; and perhaps that was the point of it, because he asked her no questions and seemed to want nothing from her except her screams, and those she gave him willingly, again and again, until the pain each time came and cut them short, exploding the very air in her lungs. For what seemed like forever he used her. The only places he had not touched her with his violence were her genitals, and those she was certain he was simply saving for his grand finale. But eventually he let her go and strode back to his jacket.

'Nae then,' he said calmly. 'Today there is just one question. Make sure you answer it truthfully, though. I'll not be pleased if ye lie tae me, and you wouldnae like to see me when I'm displeased.'

She nodded, exhausted. Anything.

He paused. 'When did ye last have the painters in?' he asked.

'*What?*' Was it some kind of joke he was having at her expense? 'I do my own painting,' she mumbled.

Face darkening, he stood up and flourished the cattle prod. 'Dinnae joke with me,' he hissed. 'Ye ken what I'm asking ye. When was your period?'

'My period?' She tried to think, to get a handle on the timescale. 'Ten days ago,' she said at last.

He nodded. 'Aye.'

Was he worrying about getting her something? 'I'm pretty regular,' she said. 'I usually use pads.'

But he had already turned to go, bending down to gather her little parcel of shit.

It was not until several hours had passed that she understood why he had wanted to know: and why, so far, the electric cattle prod had spared her genitals.

She waited all day. Night fell, and with it a heavy rainstorm that penetrated the slates high above her head and turned the floor of the dovecot into a dripping, soggy mess. It should be possible, she thought, to dig a tunnel: but she had nothing to dig with, and in any case he would be certain to discover it.

He came the next morning, while she was still lying curled up against the only dry patch of wall. She watched as he carefully padlocked the door behind him, and exchanged a small bag of food for her parcel of newspaper.

'You're waiting until I'm fertile, aren't you?' she said quietly.

'Maybe,' he growled.

'It won't work, Hector,' she said wearily. 'You can't keep me here for nine months and hope that I'll stay pregnant against my will.'

'I'll move ye in with the lambs when it's taken,' he said, nodding. 'Ye'll be quite comfortable. And as for keeping ye pregnant, I think nature and good stockmanship will take care of that.'

'You won't be able to use the cattle prod on me when I'm pregnant.'

'Can ye be sure of that, though?' he said. He came and sat on her legs, and showed her what he could do to the soles of her feet, and left while she was still howling with terror and pain.

# FORTY-ONE

As the day wore on she considered a variety of plans, each one crazier than the last. One: his wife's obviously frigid. Make the sex so fantastic he falls in love with you, then suggest he dumps her and that the two of you run off to London together. With a honeymoon in the bridal suite of the local police station, please God. Two: just do it. At least you'd get moved to more comfortable accommodation, where there might be a better chance of escape. Three: or what about making friends with the wife? She might be a fraction less murderously inclined than her husband. The only problem there was that she was certain Hector would be careful to keep the two of them apart.

Perversely, even while she fantasized about getting him arrested, she was longing for him to come back to the dovecot. A craving for the company of your kidnapper was, she knew, a common feature of abductions. It was called Stockholm Syndrome, after the most famous example. Patty Hearst. She'd ended up joining the kidnapper's gang and carrying out an armed robbery: when the gang was caught, far from showing leniency, the judge had sent her to prison. Where, no doubt, she had fallen in love with the warders. Terry giggled out loud. That irony had never occurred to her before, and it seemed so deliciously perfect that she literally started to roar with laughter, lying on the dusty floor and howling until the tears rolled down her cheeks. This must be hysteria, a part of her was warning: but the rest of her was enjoying the joke too much. She laughed and laughed, and then she realized that she couldn't stop. The laughter turned to panic, and she screamed out loud with the sheer bloody frustration of it all.

There were three days to go before the fertile part of her cycle began.

He came that afternoon. She was sitting docilely by then, cross-legged on the floor. As the light rushed in she saw that the chains had turned her fingertips purple.

'I won't do it,' she said.

He threw a bag of food and a plastic bottle of water onto the floor in silence, and collected her parcel of shit.

The next day he brought her a Bible, and made her kneel next to him while he read from it. 'The book of Genesis, chapter thirty, first verse. "And when Rachel saw that she bore Jacob no children, she envied her sister, and said unto Jacob, Give me children, or else I die. And she said, Behold my maid, Bilhah; go in unto her, and she shall bear upon my knees, that I may also have children by her. And she gave him Bilhah her handmaid to wife, and Jacob went in unto her. And Bilhah conceived, and bore Jacob a son. And Rachel said, God hath judged me, and hath heard my voice, and hath given me a son: therefore she called him Dan, or Judging.

' "And God remembered Rachel, and God opened her womb. And she conceived, and bare a son; and said, God hath taken away my reproach. And she called him Joseph." '

'No-one seems to have asked Bilhah how she felt about it,' she muttered.

He took her fingers and closed them round the book. 'Take it, Terry. Read it. We are praying for ye all the time.'

She did try to read, just for something to do, but the tiny print wriggled in front of her eyes like maggots. *Up from the depths I have cried to thee: Lord, Lord, hear my voice.* She tossed the book aside and spent hours staring, blankly, at the patch of sky high above her head.

The door opened, and she had to shut her eyes against the blaze of light. This time he did not even bother to come in, throwing her day's provisions contemptuously at her feet.

Another day passed, and it was the worst so far. Her brain simply began to clog up, to go into slow motion. She could feel her faculties start to become soggy and slack, like muscles that were becoming emaciated from too much time in bed. I'll be like those children, she thought with mounting horror: I'll go into a kind of mental deep-freeze.

She had read that it was the more intelligent prisoners who sometimes suffered the most in solitary confinement, because they were more accustomed to using their minds in the first place. Now she looked at the walls of her cell, and nothing came back. She shouted, and the echo was all that she heard in return. She was empty. A kind of nihilistic lethargy crept over her.

He came in the morning, bearing gifts. A canister of water, some soap and a towel.

'Get yourself cleaned up,' he said, indicating the water. 'I'll be back in half an hour.'

'What does he think it is, a Saturday night date?' she muttered to herself rebelliously as she tried to wash with chained hands and a trickle of water from the can.

When he came back he carefully slid the padlock out of the hasp on the outside of the door and replaced it on the inside, blocking it with his body so that she couldn't see the combination as he locked it. Then he turned to face her.

'Where do you want me?' she asked. For a few moments the balance of power had swung back towards her. It was an illusion, she knew – he still held all the cards – but she enjoyed seeing him discomfited.

'Where ye are is fine.'

She held out her wrists and he unlocked the chain. Ignoring the sudden pain as the blood flowed through pinched flesh, she lifted her dress over her head, then stepped out of her underwear. 'Well?'

'Well what?'

'How do I look?'

'Stop flaunting yesel,' he muttered. 'Get down here.'

She lay where he had indicated.

He took the cattle prod out of his pocket and showed it to her as he shrugged off his jacket. 'Don't get any ideas,' he said curtly. 'And close your eyes.'

'Oh, for God's sake,' she muttered. Instantly, he strode across and flicked her under the chin with the cattle prod, making her scream.

'And I'll thank ye not to profane while we're

about the business of the Lord's creation,' he hissed.

Tears of pain and rage welled from her eyes and he nodded slowly. 'That's better,' he said. 'That's much better.' Raising his arm again, he hit her twice, once on each cheek, first with his open hand and then with the back of it. Her head rolled sideways. This, she understood, was her deserved punishment for insubordination.

'Now. Close your eyes.' This time she did as she was told.

After a moment she felt him refasten the chain around her wrists. Then he got down and straddled her. She could smell the tweed of his trousers, and behind that something more feral. She heard the squeak of a belt, and then his hand was in her hair, grabbing the back of her head, pulling her up so that he could use her mouth. She tried to go slack, but he hissed, 'Do it,' and she dared not disobey. It was a worse humiliation than what was to come, for it demanded more than mere acquiescence: it demanded a parody of involvement and affection and lust. But then he pulled away, and she realized that he had only been using her for lubrication, not pleasure. She felt him separate her legs, swatting them sideways as casually as he had hit her head earlier. His huge knees edged her thighs even wider – painfully wide – and then she heard him spit into his hand, and the handful of saliva was slapped roughly into her crotch.

He forced his way into her. She screamed – the pain and the humiliation turned him on, whatever he said, and he was making no attempt to be anything but brutal. His huge weight crushed the breath out of her. Grunting with exertion, he rocked himself backwards and forwards, getting himself as deep as he could.

451

And as he laboured on top of her, his breath wheezing in her ear, she thought –

*Now –*

And brought her chained hands up to his neck, forcing the chain into his windpipe, locking her fingers behind his head so that she could not be shaken free. He choked, and she levered every last ounce of strength into her wrists, pulling the chain tight against his Adam's apple. He brought up the hand with the electric baton in it, and immediately she forced her wet mouth against his in an obscene parody of a kiss and intertwined her legs behind his own. He rammed the prod into her side, and thumbed the button. Pain exploded in her brain, pain boiled and flashed and scribbled crazy patterns behind her eyelids, but the mouth against hers was open in a roar of agony as the current went through both their bodies. His legs drummed, his body bucked and convulsed, and still she kept on pulling the chain tighter. Then something gave, and there was warm liquid bubbling from his mouth, his eyes bulged from their sockets and – *dear God, no* – his hips shuddered and jerked as his dying body, with one last throw of the dice, involuntarily pumped her full of his seed.

For a long time she lay there, panting, unwilling to disentangle herself from him lest he still be somehow alive. Very gently, she eased the pressure on his neck. A stream of some hot, thick liquid flowed over his lips and down her shoulder. He slid lifelessly out of her, and with a shudder she eased herself out from underneath him.

There was still a little water in the bottle and she douched herself frantically. When it was all gone she went and attacked the body, hammering it with her feet and then her fists until she had no energy left. Eventually exhaustion stopped her, and she began to consider her options.

In his pockets she found keys to the padlocks on her wrists, but nothing to indicate what the combination of the padlock on the door might be. Rubbing her hands to get some life back into them, she reluctantly accepted that there was only one way out. She was going to have to climb.

She could wait, but the patch of daylight from the ledge provided little enough illumination anyway, and the longer she left it the more likely it was that she would have to finish the climb in darkness. She ate the last of her food and went to the wall.

The first pigeon-hole was too high for her to get a foothold. 'Damn,' she said out loud. She looked round: there had to be something.

There was. The body. She got her hands under the shoulders and pulled him across to the wall. It was not easy: he had been vast when alive, and his dead weight was as solid as a horse. Eventually, though, she succeeded. Propping him against the wall, she used one shoulder as a step, and jumped. Her fingers scrabbled for a purchase in the dusty recess, and a few ancient feathers floated out. But she was up, onto the first layer of pigeon-holes.

*This killed Donna*, she thought, and for a moment her body froze, unable to go on. *But it's the only way out*. Carefully she placed her feet in the next toehold. Dust and the residue of some long-gone nest made it slippery, and she scuffed her toes in it to make her grip better. *Take it slowly*.

She was fifteen feet above the ground now, high

enough for the drop to look threatening. *To return were as tedious as to go o'er.* Step by step she hauled her aching body higher. *Thattagirl.* There had been a cliff once, in Cornwall: her brother had dared her that she couldn't get up it. She had, and he, though older, hadn't been brave enough to follow her. That was when she knew that, whatever he said, being a girl made no difference. *Another twelve feet.* Poor Matt: he'd never recovered. She had always been a tomboy, though as she got older her competitiveness had been channelled into more cerebral challenges. *Seven feet.* Below her the corpse was tiny, a Guy Fawkes propped against the wall. I will not die here next to him, she thought, and with that the ledge was there, a rectangle of sky six feet wide and two feet high. She hoisted herself over it as if she was wriggling over the side of a boat, and then she was out, breathing cool clean Highland air for the first time in days. It was just getting dark: in the distance she could see the lights in the castle's uncurtained windows. There was the room she had slept in, the four-poster bed just visible in one corner. Though she couldn't see it, there was Catherine's portrait, staring out at the mountain and the tower. And there, praise God, was Magnus, crossing the gravelled drive to his parked Land Rover, Flora next to him. 'Magnus,' she shouted: 'Magnus, help me.' Again and again she screamed. From the angles of their heads it looked as if they were arguing about something. What time Flora had to be in by, whether she could drink in the pub. 'Magnus,' she screamed again, and a gust of cold wind carried her words high over the fields. The ant-figures turned, and she waved her arms frantically. And then they got into the Land Rover.

Hadn't they seen her? But the Land Rover was turning, driving not over the gravel towards the road but directly over the lawn, charging through the field, a spray of mud flinging up behind it like the wake of a ship.

# FORTY-TWO

Terry stood naked and blindfold, her wrists and ankles tied, only the faint breeze on her skin and the warmth of the sun on her back telling her that she was outside. For a moment, all was silent. Then, somewhere near her, the baby cried once.

A whip flicked lightly across her back. She flinched, but the unseen hand was wielding it with restraint, and it barely stung. Again and again it touched her, until she felt her skin glow warm.

'Thou hast bravely passed our test. Art thou now ready to swear that thou shall always be true to the Art?' a voice asked gravely.

'I am,' she replied in a clear voice.

'Then say after me this solemn oath: I, Terry, in the presence of the Mighty Ones, do of my own free will and accord most solemnly swear that I will ever keep secret and never reveal the mysteries of the Art, except be it to a proper person and in a proper place. And this I swear by my hopes of a future life, mindful that my measure hath been taken, and may my weapons turn against me if I break this solemn vow.'

Carefully she repeated the words. An oiled finger

touched her just above her groin, and this time she could not help but recoil. For a moment the memory of her ordeal in the dovecot was all too strong, but the finger had moved on, gently touching her breasts before reaching down towards her stomach again.

'I consecrate thee with oil, I anoint thee with wine, I consecrate thee with my lips.' She felt Gerard's mouth brushing against hers, before he finished, 'I welcome thee to our coven, priestess and witch.'

There was a smattering of applause as the blindfold and cords were removed. She blinked as her eyes got used to the sunlight.

They had made the Great Circle on the lawn at Nineveh, where the trees hid them from public view and the sun shone directly on them from above. The Wiccans had been lucky: the combination of Laura's water bowser and the rain that had been falling that night had prevented the fire from wrecking the entire house. What was left was covered in scaffolding, the rebuilding works having been covered by the insurance Donna had made them take out. Only Isobel, dead in the fire, was not there to welcome Terry into the Coven. Jamie, Brigid, Zoe, Gregor – holding little Holly as if he would never let her go – Anna and Stephan, Alan . . . Behind Terry, outside the circle, were tables laden with cakes, a bowl of punch and trays of glasses. On Terry's left Laura, also naked, caught her eye and smiled. Beyond her Magnus, looking extremely self-conscious without his clothes, clapped nervously.

'Friends and witches,' Gerard called, 'we are met in this circle to welcome new witches, but also to ask the blessing of the mighty God and the gentle

457

Goddess on Holly, the daughter of Judith, so that she may grow in beauty and strength, in joy and wisdom. There are many paths, and each must find her own; therefore, we do not seek to bind Holly to any one belief while she is still too young to choose. Rather do we ask the Goddess and the God, to whom all paths must lead, to bless, protect and prepare her through the years of her childhood; so that when at last she is truly grown, she shall know without doubt or fear which path is hers and so shall tread it gladly.

'Judith, Mother of Holly, bring her forth that she may be blessed.'

Judith took Holly from Gregor's arms and handed her to Gerard.

'Are there three in the circle who will stand with me, as goddess-parents to Holly?'

'I will join with you,' Terry said, recalling her lines. A moment later, she heard Laura and Magnus echo her words.

'Do you promise to be a friend to her, to aid and guide her as she shall require, to watch her and love her, till by the grace of Aradia and Cerrunos she shall be ready to choose her path?'

'I do so promise,' they all said.

Gerard held the little girl aloft, towards the sun. 'The Goddess and the God have blessed her,' he called. 'The Lords of the Watchtowers have acknowledged her; we her friends have welcomed her; therefore, O Circle of Stars, shine in peace on Holly.'

'So mote it be,' the whole coven chanted, and then Judith rushed forward to reclaim her baby, who by now was bawling lustily. 'Then let us feast,' Gerard cried over the hubbub.

Terry drank some of the punch obligingly, but she was still nauseous from the effects of the morning-after pill she'd taken to rid her of the consequences of Morrison's final cadaveric spasm, and she quickly put her glass back on one of the tables. Despite the return of the children and the need to celebrate Holly's Wiccaning, Isobel's death had cast a sombre shadow over the proceedings. As soon as she decently could she went into the house and found her clothes. Magnus, who had clearly been dying to do the same but was terrified of giving offence, immediately followed.

'We should go,' she murmured to him.

'OK. Shall we say our goodbyes?'

She looked around her. Some of the Wiccans were already starting to dance their quaint spiral dance, while even Jamie and Alan seemed to be urgently addressing themselves to the business of getting seriously drunk and seriously stoned. 'No,' she said, 'let's not break up the party. Let's just go.'

As she turned away only Laura, deep in conversation with Zoe, gave her a slight wave. A look passed between them. Terry lifted her own hand in reply, then walked quickly towards the gate.

They had walked to Nineveh that afternoon, taking the short cut around the mountain, and as they panted back uphill there was little conversation. Only when they reached the top of the path did she stop and turn, looking back at the little farmhouse with the dancing figures in its garden.

'That was interesting,' Magnus said behind her.

She laughed. 'Don't lie. You hated every moment of it.'

'Not quite every moment. There were . . . compensations.'

'Dirty old goat,' she said. Then: 'I saw the way you looked at Laura, Magnus. You're not only an old goat, you're a fickle one to boot.'

'Old is certainly right,' he agreed, sitting down on a rock. 'Mind if we have a rest?'

She shrugged, and sat next to him.

'Actually, I was wondering about Laura,' he said at last. 'Did you ever – I mean, it occurred to me that she might be—'

She shook her head. 'Nothing ever happened,' she said firmly. 'More's the pity. Look after her, will you? I like her a lot.'

'I'll try,' he promised. He plucked a stem of grass and began to chew it thoughtfully.

'I do owe you one explanation,' she said. 'About Catherine. I need to tell you what her letters were really about.'

'So you know?'

'More or less. Here, you'd better have this. It's technically your property, in any case.'

As she passed him the envelope he said, 'What is it?'

'It contains the manuscript we took from Mcteer's coffin. The last testament of Hamish McCulloch.'

'Hamish? What did he have to do with it all?'

'Quite a lot as it happens. Take a look sometime – I've included a transcript. You have to read between the lines to some extent – Hamish doesn't seem to have had a monopoly on the truth, any more than the other participants in this little drama. But it certainly tells his side of the story.'

He put the envelope away carefully. 'And this is what gave you the explanation?'

'Yes. But I guessed before then.'

'How?'

'Oh, a whole bunch of things . . . When I was on a plane, coming back from Romania, the man next to me crossed himself before we landed. And it occurred to me, why would someone who until recently lived in a communist country cross himself?'

'That's easy,' he replied promptly. 'Everyone knows that the communists didn't eradicate Catholicism. They simply drove it underground.' He glanced sideways at her. 'A bit like what the Wiccans claim happened to the Craft. Is that what you mean?'

'Sort of . . . then there was the scene in the tower. Remember? One of Catherine's accusers said she'd seen her having congress across an altar with a ten-foot devil, a devil dressed in black with horns on his head. Well, when I was in the tower myself I did a sort of reconstruction. The girl couldn't really have seen that much, because the door opens inwards: she'd only have seen a shadow, which explains the ten-feet-high bit.

'But then I went on thinking. If Catherine was in there with someone, what was she doing? Not making passionate lesbian love, that's for sure. I don't think they'd discovered refinements like black leather in the seventeenth century. So who else wore black in those days? And who had a hat that might have thrown a horned shadow?'

Magnus shrugged. 'Who?'

'And then there was Hector, with his dreadful insistence on justifying himself from the Bible . . . he even left me a Bible to read, while I was shut up, and it started me thinking about Catherine again.' She took a deep breath. 'It was all in the letters, you see. When I went back to the letters, and stopped trying to think of her as either a lesbian, or a witch, or even a woman, it was all so blindingly obvious.'

'What was?'

'The problem is, you see, that we're all as bad as the witch-burners in our way – we look at the evidence through our own set of values, instead of letting it speak for itself.'

'Right now I'm looking at it through a complete fog,' he confessed. 'What are you trying to say?'

'"*Esurientes implevit bonis, et divites dimisit inanes.*" "He hath given good things to the hungry, but the rich He hath sent empty away," ' she murmured. 'All the biblical quotations in the letters – they were in *Latin*, Magnus. Do you see? They didn't come from the dour, nasty little bibles you had in your local Presbyterian church. They were from the original, Roman bible – the Vulgate. Catherine and Anne were Catholics. That was their secret.'

'But the letters – the erotic language—'

She laughed. 'Erotic? *You have shewn me that which otherwise would have been hidden from me, so that I should not have known my own true self, and led me down that path where once all was dark. Perhaps only women can know such things, for our natures are open to ecstasy as men's are not . . . O sweet and terrible were the cries of thy passion, yet I cried with thee, for my passion was as thine . . .* That was something someone else said to me, though I chose to ignore it: there are many kinds of ecstasy, not just the sexual kind.' She was silent for a moment, remembering her night with Laura. 'For some people sex is the only ecstasy they know, of course. But for others it can be a job, or a place – somewhere like this.' She indicated the mountains,

462

the view, the clouds scudding overhead. 'For Catherine it was a religious thing. Ecstasy, passion – she meant passion in its original sense, the passion of the Cross, and the original ecstasy, the ecstasy of the saints. She and Anne were close – perhaps they even loved each other – but they weren't lovers.

'The scene in the tower – it really was an altar. But the man in black was a Catholic priest, who was being kept hidden somewhere on the estate – probably in one of the same remote crofts Hector was going to hide me in. The horns Mary Tyler saw were the silhouette of his priest's hat. And, of course, that was the reason that Catherine told Anne that it was unthinkable that she should abort the baby. Her new faith was always against that particular practice.' She plucked a little crozier of fern from the ground beside her and uncurled it with a fingernail. 'It would have been the heir of Babcock, you know,' she murmured.

'Who? Catherine's child?'

'No – well, yes, of course, but that wasn't who I meant. I meant mine and Hector's child, if there'd been one. Legally speaking, it would have had some kind of claim to your estate.'

'Was that why you—'

'Took a morning-after pill? No, that had nothing to do with it, though I must admit I wouldn't have wished that particular genetic inheritance on any child. No: Catherine carried her torturer's baby, and in much the same circumstances I chose to get rid of mine. We're very different, you see, Catherine and me. For a time in the tower I thought we were sort of becoming the same person, but of course that was nonsense.' She sighed. For all her certainty that termination had been the right decision, she felt a sense of loss. Perhaps this is grief, she thought. Or perhaps she had simply heard the distant ticking of a different clock, one she had so far in her life been able to ignore, both in her career and her sexual choices.

'And the Wiccans? What about their rituals?' Magnus was asking. 'Where did they come from?'

She shrugged. 'Some of them incorporate hymns that Catherine wrote, glorifying the Virgin Mary. The Wiccans assume they're poems to the Goddess, of course. As for the rest – well, I've been through their *Book of Shadows* carefully, and I'm afraid it's just a hotchpotch of bits and pieces, culled from various sources. There are some snatches of medieval poetry, quite a few borrowings from Yeats, even the odd bit of Kipling. The overall structure was clearly invented by Mcteer himself, who then passed it off as Catherine's own work. When he found Hamish McCulloch's testament, he realized how wrong he'd been. But he chose to have the evidence buried with him rather than admit his mistake to his followers.'

'Wow.' He thought for a moment. 'Will you publish?'

She shook her head. 'How can I? It would totally destroy everything they believe in. What right have I to take away their faith?' She shot him an amused glance. 'Besides, I've sworn to protect their Craft now, remember? As have you.'

'How could you do that,' he protested, 'knowing it's all a fake?'

'As religions go,' she said slowly, 'I don't mind Wicca. By and large, it seems to agree that people are ultimately more important than gods, which is pretty much where I come out too.'

He was silent for a moment. 'What about your thesis, though? Can you still write that up?'

She shrugged. 'Now that most of the letters have been destroyed, the transcripts are unverifiable. And that's it as far as my academic career's concerned, unfortunately. I'm out of time. No letters, no thesis; no thesis, no doctorate; no doctorate, no grant.' She smiled ruefully. 'It won't make any difference to your museum, of course, but for me – well, let's just say I'd better start looking for a job.'

He took her hand, and for a few moments they sat there, basking in the sunshine. Above them a hawk, gliding in vast circles on the warm currents of air, inspected them suspiciously, decided that they were not food, and passed on.

'Come on,' she said at last, getting to her feet. 'I've got a train to catch.'

# EPILOGUE

In this, the autumn of the Year of Our Lord 1715, I, Hamish Edward McCulloch, MP, presently of Westminster in the city of London, formerly of Edinburgh, intend to set down what I know to be the true circumstances of the trial and burning of my cousin, Catherine McCulloch, all those years ago. I write these words for three reasons: first, that I may make my peace with God, for I am in my seventy-fourth year, and shall by His Grace not be long for this world. Second, that for reasons which shall become apparent I do not wish to dictate this testament to my secretary, and my eyesight, even with lenses, will not allow me to use a pen much longer. And my third reason for writing is that one day you, my future heirs, may chance to hear something of my involvement in this desperate matter, and I would not wish to be judged without first giving my version of the tale.

Before you come to a verdict, then, you will need to recall what dangerous forces were at work in those chaotic years I write of. The Lord Protector, Cromwell, seized power in Scotland in 1651, when I was still a child, and as I grew older I found myself increasingly drawn to his Puritan persuasion. When Charles II was restored to the throne, and all that I believed in consigned to oblivion with a casual wave of a royal hand, I vowed to work ceaselessly for the return, if not of a parliamentary protectorate, then of a constitutional monarchy, answerable to parliament. Nor was I alone in this. In both Kingdoms – for Scotland was once again separated from England – unrest against the Stuarts continued. At this time I moderated my religious beliefs somewhat, joining a Presbyterian congregation; and, believing that in due course Parliament should and would become the most potent force in the land, I became a member of what was then the Scottish Assembly in Edinburgh. I discovered I had some aptitude for administration, being by nature disinclined to sentimentality, mirth and all the other distractions which cloud the mind and colour the judgement of most young men. Suffice to say that I prospered along with my party, and was one of those who voted to recognize William of Orange as the constitutional King of Scotland.

The battle was not yet won, however. The Stuarts, though exiled, were still a force to be reckoned with, and nowhere more so than in Scotland. The great families of the Highlands and the Western Isles, never having been answerable in the past to any king or rule of law, saw no reason why they should answer now to Parliament. Religious rivalries increased – not least because the Stuarts, desperate to curry favour with the populace, had allowed every man to worship as he pleased, as if the faith of the nation could be ordained by plebiscite. By the grace of God we avoided the extremes of religious debauchery that plagued Southern Europe, but it was by no means a foregone conclusion that we did so, and the ecclesiastic courts were kept busy weeding out all manner of cranks. That they burnt many innocent women as well, as I have heard it said, is true, but what is also undeniable is that these courts had a vital part to play in maintaining public order and the rule of law.

In the years after the Glorious Revolution we of the parliamentary party were kept busy searching out Jacobite plots, of which there were many. Rumours abounded that the Stuart crown jewels, which the English had somehow allowed James to retain when he fled into exile, were now somewhere in Scotland and would be used to pay off a huge army of French and German mercenaries, who would shortly be arriving to sack all our cities and take dreadful revenge on the Jacobites' enemies. Several times James got as far as landing on our shores – but each time, the incipient rebellion snuffed, he had to take himself away again, his tail between his legs. In fact, it was not until this very year of 1715 that his son, a Pretender also called James, landed with enough support to raise an army – only to let his faction be split in two, one to be defeated by my Lord Campbell and the Argyll regiment in Scotland, and one by the English at Preston. Now the Earl of Derwentwater and Viscount Kenmure are to be executed for high treason: five others who helped them still await the King's mercy.

I mention all this only to be absolutely sure that it can be understood how things stood at the turn of the century, and how carefully matters hung in the balance. When Duncan McCulloch and his son Jamie were killed by cut-throats in 1697, it was not only my natural inclination to see propriety observed which prompted me to advise my cousin Catherine to marry, and secure Babcock's future, as quickly as possible.

Yet Catherine proved herself a reluctant bride. At first I attributed this to a seemly desire to mourn for her father and brother: subsequently I may even have believed she was waiting for me to declare myself. I soon realized, however, that far from desiring the protection, guidance and discipline a husband would provide, she was actively relishing, and therefore prolonging, her so-called independence. She engaged a companion, an empty-headed local girl, and though by great good fortune the estate continued to run itself with no major mishaps it was clearly not a situation which could be allowed to continue. I took it upon myself to find her a husband from a suitably well-born Presbyterian family as soon as possible.

And then I discovered that the companion was a Papist.

For some time Louis of France had been expelling his own Protestants, or Huguenots, and our shores were consequently flooded with religious fellow-travellers. It was a relatively simple matter for the Catholics to insinuate their own men amongst them, and by the time we were onto de Courcy he had been in Scotland long enough to raise two daughters, one of whom was the girl Catherine had engaged. On discovering this information, a dreadful possibility presented itself to me. If de Courcy's daughter, far from being empty-headed or innocent, was actually under orders from Rome, it could only be with the objective of converting my cousin to the Papist faith, so that she might be married to one of the other rebel families in Scotland, thus adding all Babcock's land and influence to the Romans' side.

I immediately asked my cousin to dismiss the girl, without of course telling her the true reason – I think I used the mother's reputation as an excuse. To my amazement, she defied me. Through an intermediary I then arranged to meet the girl and offered her money to leave my cousin's employment immediately. Again I found myself defied. I increased my offer until the sums I was offering were frankly unreasonable, and still she would not accept. Having failed to resolve the matter by peaceful means, I realized that something less pleasant would now be required of me.

At this point an accusation of witchcraft was made against my cousin by a young girl, Mary Tyler. She said that she had seen Catherine in the doocot, while a devil in black fed her from his hand and suchlike. I immediately realized what this nonsense meant. Catherine had been given the Catholic rites by one of the rogue priests who still scurried round the country, despite our best efforts, concealed in haycarts and other hidey-holes. Straight away I went to my cousin and demanded to know whether my suspicions were justified. They were, and all my entreaties could not convince her of the folly of her ways.

Things were now desperate. As soon as my cousin's apostasy became public knowledge, Babcock, whether she wished it or not, would become aligned with those very interests I was pledged to destroy. And whether she married or not, when the rebellion was over and its leaders crushed, all Catholics with land and position would be crushed with it, their wealth and influence removed for ever.

I had been alerted to the charge of witchcraft against Catherine by my contacts in the judiciary, who expected me to use my influence to have it dropped. Instead, I used that influence, and my money, to ensure the opposite. Lest you think me unduly harsh, I should say that since the outcome of the trial was a foregone conclusion I did try to get her spared the worst of the tortures, but by then the matter had taken on a momentum of its own.

I will readily confess that as I watched the executioner get up on the stack of pitch barrels and firewood that was to form her pyre, and wrap his strangling rope around the long, fair neck I had once hoped to caress myself as a husband, I felt an uncharacteristic weakness, and if it had

470

been in my power to do so, I believe I would have stopped her execution, no matter where my duty lay. But of course I could not do so, and so my cousin died.

I knew of course that she had been writing to her companion – during the early period of her captivity I had her removed from the common jail to an apartment in the barracks, the better to have her letters scrutinized. It only remained, therefore, to get the correspondence back, and all traces of the business would be in my hands.

Some months after my cousin's death I went to the farm where Anne, now married to a prosperous gentleman farmer by the name of Hughes, resided. She had clearly lost no time in cementing the ties which bound him to her. When I was shown into her presence I found her playing with a baby, a fat and noisy creature whose constant screaming, I will own, caused me some discomposure, and I was glad that, as soon as the lady of the house perceived who her visitor was, the servant was told to remove the child, the better to allow us to converse.

In truth, it was not only the noise of the child which disconcerted me, for I had always found Anne de Courcy's manner towards me, despite an outward affectation of modesty, somewhat contemptuous. She did not offer me refreshment, but picked up a piece of lace from the table, and pretended to work on it while we spoke.

'So, sir, have you come to gloat?' she said at last. I confess that I was so irritated at the sentiment, that I neglected to be censorious of the direct and haughty manner in which it was expressed.

'Gloat?' I said. 'I would not waste my time with such an occupation. If I have foiled your plans, and the designs of those who command you, I have merely performed a painful but necessary duty.'

'What plans?' she asked, affecting puzzlement.

'Come, we are alone. I know what you and your

471

friends were after, and I may assure you that, although my influence might have been invisible to you, I have been working diligently to thwart your purpose.'

She still affected to be bemused, only murmuring, 'So Catherine was right,' under her breath. I heard her, though, and my anger was raised.

'My cousin was misguided in many things, madam, and the blame for that must lie with those who sought to influence her,' I said.

At this her eyes flashed, though she spoke mildly. 'Your cousin was the purest, best,' she paused, as if searching for the word, 'most *good* person I ever knew. I had no plans for her, nor would I have been able to exert any greater influence over her than that exerted by her own conscience, by which alone she was always guided.'

'Come,' I scoffed. 'Your father has confirmed the substance of what I say.'

At this her expression and her tune changed sharply, as I had thought it might. 'My father? What of him?' she cried.

'He was arrested yesterday, and is even now being questioned,' I informed her.

'Questioned? You mean tortured. An old man who has harmed no-one. What manner of person would contemplate such a thing?'

'One who was pleased, as I said, to have his suspicions confirmed,' I retorted.

'Under torture? Your own cousin confessed to being a witch, which you know to be a lie, and yet you still believe my father when he lies to you?'

I own that I felt a little uneasy at this, as I knew full well that torture is a powerful lens, one that can distort as well as magnify. 'In any case, it is not relevant,' I said, 'since I am offering to release your father immediately. Give me that which Catherine passed to you from prison, and he is a free man.'

472

She glanced at the door, then at me, her face ashen. 'You know, then?'

'Of course.' At that she buried her face in her hands and sobbed. 'Come, come,' I said impatiently. 'The letters are worthless. I simply wish to ensure that no evidence of her conversion survives in your hands.'

She raised her head and looked at me. 'The letters?'

'The letters. Now.' Even making allowance for the limited faculties of her sex, her powers of reason seemed to have entirely deserted her.

'Then I will get them,' she said, turning to a drawer in the settle behind her. 'And if you wish, we shall burn them now, in the fire.' She made as if to throw them in the flames, but I stopped her.

'I will destroy them at my leisure,' I said curtly, taking the papers from her grasp. Once I had them, my business with her was concluded, and I left at once.

Why did I not then burn the letters, as I had suggested? I certainly believed it to be my intention. Yet I have an abhorrence of disorder – the result, you may say, of a lifetime spent dealing with administrative matters – and I consequently find it hard to destroy any record. Or was it simply that I found it hard to consign my cousin for a second time to the flames? For many years I could not bring myself to destroy the letters – nor yet to read them. Several times I began the attempt, only to be overcome by an unaccountable and unwarranted sensation of what might be termed regret.

And so it was that several decades passed before I came to look over the piles of manuscript in my possession. They were incomplete – even in the moment she had gathered them from the settle, Anne de Courcy must have contrived to remove some without my noticing. But there were enough to make it plain how the woman had tricked me for a second time.

As with the first, it would have been a simple matter to undo her work. Despite my years, I am still a man of influence in Scotland: one word from me, and Catherine's bastard and all his family would find themselves at the bottom of a loch with their throats cut. And yet I have done nothing. These old hands are spotted with enough blood already, and I know that Anne de Courcy would not be fool enough to tell the boy his parentage. I shall leave a note in my will, saying that all my papers are to be given to the library at Babcock. This testament, and the letters, I shall conceal amongst them, for future generations to make of what they will.

Anne de Courcy called my cousin Catherine a *good* person – that is the phrase that has haunted me, that haunts me still, down all the years of my prosperity and success. Sometimes I wonder how history will speak of those like myself, those who did not do what we knew to be good, but who did what we thought to be right. And sometimes, thinking, I grow cold and shiver, even on the mildest of days, for my blood has grown old and thin. And as my servant puts a taper to the kindling in the grate, it seems to burn with a strange green flame, and I smell again the stench of flesh consumed by hellfire, and hear again the muffled bells that call us to a burning.

Hamish McCulloch
17 October 1715


THE END

# THE POISON TREE
## by Tony Strong

'A début to die for' Marcel Berlins, *The Times*

In the wake of a failed marriage and a misguided love affair, feisty academic Terry Williams moves to Oxford to resume her abandoned doctorate in detective fiction. But her new home, a terraced house on quiet Osney Island, was previously the scene of a savage sexual murder, and Terry soon finds the past returning to invade the present with horrific consequences.

A traumatized stray cat which eats its own babies, a famous neighbour involved in a hushed-up sexual scandal, and the discovery of a series of pornographic letters all serve to involve Terry in a mystery more brutal and more elusive than any tackled by the fictional detectives she studies. And still a killer walks the streets of Oxford, protected by the night, empowered by violence, determined to exact a bloody revenge for a crime of passion.

'Ingenious' *Daily Telegraph*

A Bantam Paperback

0 553 50542 4

## SINS OF OMISSION
### by Gemma O'Connor

'Full of the tensions of oppressed emotions...a welcome twist on the genre' *Sunday Times*

Two women, Grace Hartfield in London, Bid Lacey in Dublin, and one man – the wealthy head of a Dutch development company. No apparent connection between them, yet their lives are destroyed by one searing incident, resolutely buried.

Bid, younger and more trusting, is caught up in this web of secrecy and half truths which leads to three violent deaths. Or is it four?

A Bantam Paperback

0 553 81263 7

## FALLS THE SHADOW
### by Gemma O'Connor

'A gripping tale of moral rottenness and manipulated innocence in which the reader becomes increasingly entangled' *Irish Independent*

Buller Reynolds was murdered on 31 May 1941, the night central Dublin was bombed. Fifty years on, elderly Lily Sweetman – child witness of that long ago murder – is killed. A hit-and-run accident? Lily's daughter doesn't think so. There are too many similarities to that ancient crime.

But now Nell has stepped into mortal danger...

A Bantam Paperback

0 553 81262 9

# GARNETHILL
## by Denise Mina

*Winner of the John Creasey Award for Best First Crime Novel*

'Funny, raw, compassionate, often brutal...romps its way to a satisfying conclusion' *Independent*

Maureen O'Donnell wasn't born lucky. A psychiatric patient and survivor of sexual abuse, she's stuck in a dead-end job and a secretive relationship with Douglas, a shady therapist. Her few comforts are making up stories to tell her psychiatrist, the company of friends, and the sweet balm of whisky. She is about to end her affair with Douglas when she wakes up one morning to find him in her living room with his throat slit.

Viewed in turn by the police as a suspect and as an uncooperative, unstable witness, Maureen is even suspected by her alcoholic mother and self-serving sisters of being involved. Worse than that, the police won't tell her anything about Douglas's death.

Panic-stricken and feeling betrayed by friends and family, Maureen begins to doubt her own version of events. She retraces Douglas's desperate last days and picks up a horrifying trail of rape, deception...and suppressed scandal at a local psychiatric hospital where she had been an inmate. But the patients won't talk and the staff are afraid, and when a second brutalized corpse is discovered, Maureen realizes that unless she gets to the killer first, her life is in danger.

'Mina, a feisty new crime-writing voice, carves a taut, human whodunnit into Glasgow's impassive face' *Scotland on Sunday*

A Bantam Paperback

0 553 50694 3

# A SELECTED LIST OF FINE NOVELS
# AVAILABLE FROM BANTAM BOOKS

| | | | |
|---|---|---|---|
| 50329 4 | DANGER ZONES | Sally Beauman | £5.99 |
| 50630 7 | DARK ANGEL | Sally Beauman | £6.99 |
| 50631 5 | DESTINY | Sally Beauman | £6.99 |
| 40727 9 | LOVERS AND LIARS | Sally Beauman | £5.99 |
| 50326 X | SEXTET | Sally Beauman | £5.99 |
| 50540 8 | KILLING FLOOR | Lee Child | £5.99 |
| 50541 6 | DIE TRYING | Lee Child | £5.99 |
| 81185 1 | TRIPWIRE | Lee Child | £5.99 |
| 50475 4 | THE MONKEY HOUSE | John Fullerton | £5.99 |
| 17510 6 | A GREAT DELIVERANCE | Elizabeth George | £5.99 |
| 40168 8 | A SUITABLE VENGEANCE | Elizabeth George | £5.99 |
| 40237 4 | FOR THE SAKE OF ELENA | Elizabeth George | £5.99 |
| 40846 1 | IN THE PRESENCE OF THE ENEMY | Elizabeth George | £5.99 |
| 40238 2 | MISSING JOSEPH | Elizabeth George | £5.99 |
| 17511 4 | PAYMENT IN BLOOD | Elizabeth George | £5.99 |
| 40845 3 | PLAYING FOR THE ASHES | Elizabeth George | £5.99 |
| 40167 X | WELL-SCHOOLED IN MURDER | Elizabeth George | £5.99 |
| 50694 3 | GARNETHILL | Denise Mina | £5.99 |
| 50385 5 | A DRINK BEFORE THE WAR | Dennis Lehane | £5.99 |
| 50584 X | DARKNESS, TAKE MY HAND | Dennis Lehane | £5.99 |
| 81220 3 | GONE, BABY, GONE | Dennis Lehane | £5.99 |
| 50585 8 | SACRED | Dennis Lehane | £5.99 |
| 50586 6 | FAREWELL TO THE FLESH | Gemma O'Connor | £5.99 |
| 50587 4 | TIME TO REMEMBER | Gemma O'Connor | £5.99 |
| 81263 7 | SINS OF OMISSION | Gemma O'Connor | £5.99 |
| 81262 9 | FALLS THE SHADOW | Gemma O'Connor | £5.99 |
| 50542 4 | THE POISON TREE | Tony Strong | £5.99 |